Trick of the Light

"Rob Thurman's new series has all the great elements I've come to expect from this writer: an engaging protagonist, fast-paced adventure, a touch of sensuality, and a surprise twist that'll make you blink."
—#1 *New York Times* bestselling author Charlaine Harris

THE KORSAK BROTHERS NOVELS

Basilisk

"Thurman has created another fast-paced and engaging tale in this volume.... Fans of great thriller fiction will enjoy *Basilisk* and the previous novel *Chimera* quite a bit." —SFRevu

"*Basilisk* is full of excitement, pathos, humor, and dread.... Buy it. You won't be sorry. It is one heck of a ride!"
—Bookshelf Bombshells

Chimera

"Thurman delivers a fast-paced thriller with plenty of twists and turns.... The characters are terrific—Stefan's wiseass attitude will especially resonate with the many Cal Leandros fans out there—and the pace never lets up, once the two leads are together.... Thurman shows a flair for handling SF/near-future action." —SFRevu

"A touching story on the nature of family, trust, and love lies hidden in this action thriller.... Thurman weaves personal discovery seamlessly into the fast-paced action, making it easy to cheer for these overgrown, dangerous boys." —*Publishers Weekly*

Nevermore

A Cal Leandros Novel

Rob Thurman

A ROC BOOK

ROC
Published by New American Library,
an imprint of Penguin Random House LLC
375 Hudson Street, New York, New York 10014

This book is an original publication of New American Library.

First Printing, December 2015

For more information about Penguin Random House, visit penguin.com.

ISBN 978-0-451-47340-0

Printed in the United States of America
10 9 8 7 6 5 4 3 2 1

Penguin
Random
House

For G.L. and R.—see you on the flipside.

ACKNOWLEDGMENTS

All my thanks to but the smallest amount of those who held down a hand to lift me up when I needed it most—and then told me to stop my bitching and kicked my ass promptly into gear: Jeanne C. Stein; Di Pharoah Francis; Barb Hendee; Farzana Karim; Marcia Howard—there is nothing she can't do and very little she hasn't *already* done; Christopher Lynch; Zach Adams; Sadie Ballesteros Romine; Theresa Bane; Glenn Bane; Nix Rodriguez; Rhiannon Miller; Matthew Boronson (a research god); then the goddess among women, Flora Demuth, and her partner in crime, Winston Demuth; Drew Bittner; Betsy Dornbusch xoxoxo; and J. C. Ferguson, who says he has been saving himself for me since college—he is a man among . . . well . . . he's a man! Also, thanks to Nicole Paone, Liza Tobias Hebert, Rachel Eckstein, Desiree Adams, Joni Carrigen, Patrick Hadrian, Tracy Wood, Jamie "Cat Hat" Arnold—the very first fan for whom I signed a book—and Kate Baird.

This only is denied to God: the power to undo the past.
> —attributed to Agathon (448 BC–400 BC) by Aristotle (384 BC–382 BC), *The Nicomachean Ethics with English Translation* by H. Rackham (1926)

I never claimed to be God, just a helluva lot more motivated.
> —Caliban Leandros

Prologue

People die.

All the time. Everyone knows that, right? The world is dangerous. Existence is precarious, the footing beneath you shaky. Your first breath isn't a guarantee and if you get that, your next breath is the same. Touch and go. Life doesn't come with a warranty. It's something to be snatched, clawed for, and held in the tightest of grips. Life cuts you no slack, doesn't care if you're around or not, but death ... death can't wait to drag you to his party. And once he does ... you know that old song is as true as they come, "It's hard to leave if you can't find the door."

People die ... but they usually don't die over something so meaningless. Me? I was the exception to that. I was the trigger. At least thirty people died all thanks to my one seemingly harmless mistake, one trivial, overlooked chore.

I forgot the pizzas.

Insane, right? That the world should end because I forgot several boxes of cheese, pepperoni, and grease. They weren't even the best pizzas in town. But that didn't matter. I'd brought down Heaven, lifted up Hell, and set the world on fire, all thanks to one slip of the memory.

How's that for the worst fuckup of all time?

One casual everyday event like forgetting my phone and running back a block to our place for it. That meant a five-minute shift in my routine, just enough to sidetrack my brain to revert to my normal schedule. I unconsciously skipped over the irregular task of the pizza pickup I'd been stuck with at the last minute, and that was it ... the world ended. Not with a whimper or a thousand radioactive mushroom clouds. No, it ended because I was an idiot.

It ended because I'd forgotten I'd lost a coin toss.

The only reason I didn't end with it as well was just dumb luck. I'd remembered at the last second fifteen feet inside the bar, cursed, and left, annoyed and impatient enough to use the "emergency door" to get them. I should've been there when it all ended, but, again, dumb luck.

No. Not true.

It wasn't dumb luck. It was bad luck. Worse luck. The darkest of goddamn fucking fortune.

Hell, wasn't that the story of my life?

There was a certain grungy bar, cramped, but popular among a certain crowd, that I'd been standing in less than three seconds ago when I remembered the pizzas. The name of the bar didn't matter. That I worked there most nights didn't make a difference either. What did matter was that the building where it squatted on the first floor slinging alcohol right and left was hit by an eye searing blast of light. It was as bright as it was incomprehensible. It was barely dusk. What could be that bright? I'd seen the flash from the corner of my eye as I stood at the pizza truck parked at the other end of the block. I turned to see what it was, not where it was. I should've known the where was what mattered, but I didn't have a flicker of suspicion that it was the bar, my bar. The one full of people, my people. It was one of those things you can't think. You can't know, as once you do you can't unknow it. That part of your brain shuts down. If it didn't all of your brain would stop ... stop thinking, stop feeling, stop everything, and chances were good it'd never start again.

It was too late for all that now. I had turned. When I

did, I wished I'd been smart enough to not turn, and when I had, then to not look, to live in blissful ignorance a few seconds more. But I wasn't that smart, never had been. I didn't register that it was an explosion, one that temporarily deafened me. In that silence I had turned. I had seen. I had seen it all.

It was as if the sun had plunged from where it hung bloodred and low to crash down on top of the city.

It was all it could be. The sun had fallen from the sky, I thought numbly as the money drifted from one hand as the pizzas slipped off the balancing palm of the other to tumble through superheated air to the street. The sun had fallen and we were all on fire—not the city alone, but everything. It was early evening with thin stripes of twilight purple clouds, and we should've stood in shadows, but we didn't. It was bright as day on the street and we were on fire.

The entire world *was on fire.*

I fucking prayed the way atheists like me do when the sky falls and their world is ripped away. I prayed that it was a lie. But I got what prayers gave you when you need their help the most. A kick in the gut and a spiteful laugh in your face as it was granted.

Because the world wasn't *on fire.*

It would've been better if it were.

No, the world didn't burn, I knew, only a small piece of it.

That I'd had the thought at all—the whole world burning to a cinder—had been shock and despair tearing my brain to shreds—not for thinking that it was true, but because I knew it wasn't. The world gone with a fiery snap of some child-eating pagan god's fingers, all of us . . . to the very last of us, dying with the earth, I could take that. I could take it with a, yes, sir, may I have another. But being left behind, a survivor who had no fucking desire to survive? That was the true nightmare. That I couldn't take.

I stared at the inferno that raged; it already had consumed the first floor front of the building. Gobbled up where I'd worked and drunk for years and had just stood heartbeats ago. I hoped with everything in my tarnished soul that its appetite would spread to at least the city if not to everything flammable on the planet. I hoped that it would roll over me like a wildfire and take me along with the rest of what it had already stolen.

It didn't happen. What you want the most hardly ever does. What you need the most never does.

Instead, it concentrated on my handful of the world, small as it was, with more inescapable flame than could remotely be needed for one small bar. The fire had grown before I could take a single breath. It was a breath I didn't want to take, knowing that the Auphe in me, compared to the human, would sharpen every scent a hundred times over. I didn't care if I took another breath again, for that reason and a thousand others, but your body overrides your wishes, no matter how desperate. Lungs rebelling, I gasped, pulling in that unwanted breath. I smelled ammonia, nitrate, other chemicals I didn't bother with. . . .

And flesh. They smelled different, the roasting scent of several Wolves from the lesser number of peri, and both distinct from the crowd of vampires. Every group similar but not the same as the other, but soon to end as identical charred fumes. Above them all, I caught the smell of two others. Not a group—just two. The two that mattered most.

Until now one had smelled of grass, fallen leaves, loamy earth, and musk. The other of sweat and weapon oil for cleaning every type of blade at the end of sparring, of goat milk soap and unbleached cotton from the shower that followed, of the clean bite of a chill wind only truly found on the top of a mountain where the air grew thin.

One puck.

One human.

Neither would give off their born scent again, the way they once had. Not in reality, and not in my memories that would be as blackened as the mound of rubble that would act as the tomb that covered them when the fire eventually died.

Not that I would be around to see their makeshift grave in the aftermath and not that I would have memories of any kind.

The smallest sliver of a second later there came a second explosion, a massive fireball ten, twelve stories high erupted, though the building itself was only four stories tall. It came close to incinerating anything left of the brick and metal of the bar and the bodies inside. The backwash of incredible heat and a concussive wave threw me flat, knocking the air from my lungs before I was able to vomit at the stench that had crawled inside me to stay.

An infinity of fire: Hell couldn't have claimed it all.

I sat up slowly and painfully to the sight of what the second one had birthed, a Jacob's ladder of fire that stretched up to touch the sky, maybe Heaven itself. It made the first look like an amateur attempt at a Boy Scout campfire. It burned with the rage, flame, and heat of a hundred phoenixes. Yet when it finally would burn down, hours maybe days—ashes to ashes—no new phoenix would rise from it. Nothing would. The reaper owned this place now and everyone who'd been in it. One swipe of a scythe hotter than the sun had taken it all.

Now I am become Death.

Something that had been said in history a time or two.

Now I am become Death, the destroyer of worlds.

I didn't think about who had done it—who was Death. I already knew the answer to that.

I didn't think about how it had been done.

I didn't think why. I knew the why was a who. And I was still here as the fuckers had missed.

I didn't think anything but the bottom line of it all.

I didn't care.

Who, why, how, none of that mattered now.

My own personal Armageddon had arrived.

As the heat seared my skin, I sprawled on the asphalt with—unbelievably enough as forcefully as I'd been thrown back—the pizza boxes that had landed with me, one beside me, the other against my leg, almost in my fucking lap. A mocking jeer from the powers that be. "Your life is over, but dinner's on us!" My eyes were half-blinded by the fire, not that I cared to better see details of the apocalypse meant for me personally . . . but had missed.

It hadn't been able to steal my life, but as a trade, it had taken and destroyed my reason for living it.

As much as I hated to give them the satisfaction, they'd won. I didn't have to be at their ground zero in a failed aim at wiping me from existence. One block away was close enough to know that your heart could beat and your lungs could fill with oxygen, but it didn't make you less dead.

Wasn't that a trick?

I slid my hand inside my jacket. I touched the only comfort left: the leather holster that cradled my way out. The metal of the trigger, the hard plastic of the grip, and the grimly comfortable weight of my escape.

Sliding my Desert Eagle out, I placed the muzzle under my chin. My finger captured the trigger tight without any thought from me.

It didn't need any. It was automatic. I didn't have to think as I'd already thought about this too many times before. The end had come, no surprise. I'd been waiting on it for a good part of my life. But I hadn't thought it would be like this, unbearable as the lone survivor on a burnt and bloody battlefield. Dying was easy. Being alone, the last standing, having seen the others fall, it snatched away the relief and turned a mercy killing into a grim surrender.

Fuck it, surrender, retreat, despite being coward enough to not only think I'd go first, but to hope for it, I'd been prepared for years, waiting for the feel of the metal, the resistance on the pull of seven pounds of trigger pressure.

Seven pounds was my ticket out of this hell.

And it was hell, more of one than I'd ever end up in.

All because I forgot the goddamn pizzas.

But I'd forgotten something else too. The pizza guy. And he had something to say.

First, he said my name. I barely heard it with what small amount of hearing had returned. Whether what came next would have my finger sliding off the trigger, I didn't know. I doubted it.

Then he said a second name.

One that made me question, finger still on the trigger, yeah, but . . .

It made me . . . not hope. Hope was too hard, too distant. It didn't do that. Yet . . .

It did make me think. It made me consider the metal muzzle under my jaw as a sealed letter dropped into my lap, smelling of anchovies. With that second name said aloud and with me climbing out of the muffling quicksand of borderline catatonia, another form of escape that I hadn't bothered to fight, things changed. I began truly thinking instead of letting the smothering shock pull me deeper. I stopped my body and mind from reacting mechanically as both had from the first moment of the explosion. I did it solely because I could guess what that letter might say considering who had written it.

Tricks and truths . . .

It wasn't over until it was over and in this one unique case, maybe . . . maybe not necessarily then either.

Once, three or four years ago, I'd said something profound as hell—also wrong as shit—but it had sounded good and I thought it true at the time. I had said that what had been made couldn't be unmade.

What had been done couldn't be undone.

I'd been wrong.

I was going to do all that and more now. Undo this all. If I had to unravel reality itself at its seams, as a result, that's what I would do.

Why the hell not?

If there were consequences, if there was a cost? So what?

I'd already fucking paid it.

1

I believe the future is the past again, entered only
through another gate.
— Arthur Wing Pinero, 1894

History.

They say that those who don't learn from history are
doomed to repeat it.

They also say history teaches by example. History is
written by the victors. God himself can't change the past,
but historians can. And a thousand more sayings about
it. But the last one was the one I was holding on to with
both hands. God can't change it, but historians could.
They could write, erase, delete, and write a brand-new
version.

They say a lot — hell, yeah, they do. But who cared?

History was, for the most part, boring.

Not like fire. Fire was anything but boring. The starkly
chemical tainted smoke, now more of a taste than a smell,
still coated my tongue and throat thickly enough to make
me want to puke. The stink of burnt blood, sizzled to
nothing in seconds. The heat of the flames had been intense enough that I'd been dully surprised my face wasn't

seared to a blackened mask, despite feeling normal when I rubbed a hand roughly over it.

Then there was the image of it all locked inside my brain and tattooed behind my eyelids whenever I blinked, an afterimage of everything I saw: the explosive eruption of fire and fury that streamed upward with a raging hunger that made it seem possible for it to set Heaven itself on fire, devour God himself if he had existed. And the sound . . . shit, the sound, or the lack of it. The explosion, the roar of not flames, but of not one but *two* unstoppable infernos, yet not a single scream or shout. Not a sign that anyone had been alive in a building before it had become what Hell longed to be. No sign of it, life, but there had been.

Before.

There had been brothers, friends, others. They hadn't been alive, though, not after that. They'd died with the initial flash of light—there was nothing to hear from them. The Reaper had stolen their voices. They couldn't scream, couldn't say my name as they had since the day of my birth. They couldn't. . . .

Shit. I couldn't do this. I couldn't function with this memory, only a half hour old and yet at the same time one that came from an event that wouldn't happen for eight more years. I took that moment and pushed it away, buried it, as I couldn't do the job, couldn't do what I needed to if I had to see it in my head every minute of the day. I couldn't *fucking* breathe if I had to carry that weight on my shoulders.

Forget that was where half of it belonged.

And there was no goddamn hope of having the strength to carry that.

Ignoring the mental accusation, I took in the situation at hand and the alley I stood in. Both were grimy and ugly. One, the alley, was expected and two, the situation, wasn't precisely unexpected.

In this alley, in fact, this circumstance had been a routine risk in the day.

If nothing else, it could be a needed distraction. But with my luck, which was no luck, it would be nothing but an inconvenience. I found out which when I sidestepped, with little effort, the shard of metal rusty and crusted with old blood swung at my face or throat, his aim wasn't good enough to make an estimate, by a stinking, filthy waste of humanity. He'd leaped out of a bed of alley trash, his tainted harsh exhalation the hiss of a snake thanks to several missing teeth. He wore a stench of living on the street that was one step from decomposition and eyes muddy brown swimming in wide pools of deep piss-yellow.

Inconvenience it was.

Putting a boot in his lower back as he passed me unable to stop in time, I helped him continue his headlong rush attempt by sending him the rest of the way across the alley to slam into the opposite wall. As inconvenience was more likely to piss me off than distract me. But I'd smelled what was on the knife. I couldn't let that go. I'd have to make do because this was what I had.

There was the sound of crushing cartilage and the scent of blood when he hit the brick. Someone had bought themselves a broken nose. Those were a bitch. It would be several seconds before he could see through the tears of pain to attack again. I folded my arms to wait. Inconvenience and then some. If not for what coated that damned knife . . .

I'd originally planned coming here eight years in my past to stop an assassination, my own assassination, by the Vigil. Pretentious asshole name aside, they had played a big part in history as well. They'd been human, but they hadn't interfered with the *paien* world often, didn't care if a boggle made a meal of a human. It was the circle of life, in their opinion—no more, no less, and their group had been around thousands of years, long enough to see the truth of that. Humans, thanks to a population of billions, were on top of the food chain as a species, but not individually. If it came down to a war, humans would win with their bigger weapons. Unimaginable monsters worse than anything you dreamed could live in your closet at night, even they couldn't walk away from ground zero of a nuke blast. Yeah, humans would win, but, first, the *paien* would make them damn sorry they played. Second, when it came to nukes, and it would have to come to them to end up on top, collateral damage to your own population will be a bitch.

The Vigil had one rule: stay hidden. Humans do not need to know mythology books are actually wildly incorrect, but with a grain of truth, history books. Do not show yourself in a manner that humanity might find out werewolves, vampires, lamia, revenants, ghouls, hundreds of other "bogeymen" existed. Let humans live in the ignorant bliss that fairy tales were just that. That fairies weren't real, spit acid in your face, and sucked off the melted flesh. Eating was a necessary sin of survival, of course, and some *paien* are predators. They have certain nutritional requirements. Merely don't be seen doing it unless it's by who you're currently consuming.

Slipups were understandable, but make certain they're at night and only at night and by no more than two or three people who will easily convince themselves it was a trick of the light. Admittedly, the *paien* were here first. It's a big world and they wanted to share it. But the average human, masses of them, wouldn't understand, the Vigil had said. They'd panic, and it'll happen as it has always happened when one civilization discovers another. War. We don't want to be pushed into that corner. If a *paien* follows the rule, we won't have to put that *paien* down. We don't *want* to put you down. We—

Aaand here he came again, interrupting my train of thought. With his nose bent to the side, blood gushing from it, I'd thought he'd have learned. Nope. This attack was crazed wild motion like the first. He was fast, I'd give him that, but fast is useless when your ambition wildly exceeds your ability to aim and your victim can . . . hell . . . practically Sunday fucking stroll out of your target area. With this attack he managed to hit the opposite wall himself, no assistance called for.

This was a chore and a half. I had to face it. I wasn't getting an iota of distraction here. It was down to business on his next try.

Back to the Vigil until then.

One rule. It seemed simple. It wasn't.

I broke that fucking rule like it had *never* been broken.

But I'd had a good reason, and I'd do it again.

The Vigil hadn't seen it that way and turned out to be aggressively armed with weapons, stolen *paien* artifacts, biology labs, and assassins than they'd been remotely upfront about when it came to the subject. For all the sharing and fucking caring they spouted, they had the type of Cold War arsenal they hadn't hinted at wanting or needing. Pity it wasn't as effective as they'd planned.

In the end, when it came to the world, humans would win. When it came to a throw down in NYC, the Vigil was wiped out except for my guess of two or three members: one a custom-made assassin with a stolen time traveling artifact.

They couldn't fix their wholesale destruction in the present, but they *could* send their hypocritically fabricated, mutated hope, Project Lazarus, back. They could kill me, the younger me, before the Vigil had known of Caliban Leandros, before I'd known of them, before I could break that rule. Then they'd be reborn. They never would've died.

Aside from the assassin, the remaining one or two members would've been all that had been left of the last cell. And every cell had one of their goddamn psychics the Vigil had loved for their spying. They would've briefed the cell, before we'd wiped them out, that a *paien* friend of mine, with contacts and spies better than psychics on his payroll, had already discovered what the Vigil had stolen years ago. The psychic would've told the cell we knew what we'd need to stop Lazarus when he used the artifact. They had known we already had a twin to their stolen one.

That was the two pieces of information my friend's contacts hadn't found out, that the Vigil was aware we were equally equipped to their assassin and that any of the Vigil survived aside from that assassin. The Vigil had been closer to being Nazis than the shepherds they painted themselves, but they were loyal—fanatically loyal. The single or few left made one last ditch effort against us. A truck packed with ANFO—overkill, not that they'd cared. The ammonia and nitrate reek I'd smelled was the un-mistakable sign of a tool popular when the monsters were human and homegrown. The one or two Vigil who'd survived—it had probably been two, to gather all the com-ponents necessary, pack them in barrels, load the truck as that shit sounded heavy—had planned to keep me from using my own borrowed artifact to following Lazarus when he used his. They had tried to catch me at the bar.

By driving their bomb on wheels into it.

Funny, wasn't it? All that work and I was the only one they hadn't caught.

Funny.

But if they could undo what had been done, so could I. I'd still stop the assassination of an eighteen-year-old me. That goal would stay the same, but I had to do so goddamn much more now. I had to also fix a world, *my* world. It was a small part of the whole, but all I wanted or needed. The rest of the world—I didn't give a shit about, not anymore. If I couldn't remake mine, if I failed, what was left could burn for all I cared. Hell, I'd start the fire myself.

Anyone have a match?

Or maybe a lighter.

"You have a lighter I could borrow, shithead?" I drawled, tired of waiting for the third attempt. Shit, he'd been playing possum. He might have a brain cell left that the drugs hadn't eaten. Coming off the wall, quicker than before, the jagged steel was now whipping at my throat. The hand that held it was white knuckled with tension where it wasn't encrusted with dirt, and it slashed with vicious force, but no skill. Too easy. I didn't have to waste any effort on a fight this pathetic.

That was the trouble with what lurked in dirty, ugly alleys. Dirty, ugly assholes who will cut your throat for a dollar. Drugs aren't easy to come by when you have no money. I might have money. If nothing else my jacket would go for ten.

I didn't let my mind fixate about how this was holding me up. I needed to go, but I also needed to crush a poisonous scorpion under my heel. Dripping venom from its stinger, it hid in the trash and the dark. Deadly to anyone who wandered off the path, the single safe place as all fairy tales tell you. It wouldn't take long and required little effort, handling the scorpion, I had to think of that, think of anything that wouldn't have me throwing him to the side and running to save the people I knew, not strangers.

It would take minutes, less, to save those strangers and those minutes were nothing compared to the time I'd need to change everything back. I could spare it. Nik would want me to.

Shit. Shit. Okay, then, big brother. For you.

I scavenged in my thoughts for anything else to concentrate on besides abandoning wandering sheep to this murderer. As inefficient as this dick was at cutting throats, I had the time. What had I been dwelling on—during my first step into the alley? Before the burnt and bloody thoughts. The boring side of history, that's what it had been. Dull, boring, cruel and unusual punishment. Ask any kid in school.

The generation of Saturday morning cartoons had it so much easier, the middle-aged bastards.

The shot heard 'round the world . . .

Was the beginning of the revolution. . . .

Take your rifle, take your gun. . . .

Knives hadn't made that list. I didn't know why. They were as good in the right situation. Good, well-made ones at least.

Mine was very good.

That's what I thought as I changed mental paths with a quick and savage satisfaction. I grabbed a handful of greasy hair as I evaded the man's lunge at me. It was as unexpectedly fast, if as unskilled as his knife-work. Desperate and fast go hand in hand sometimes. I yanked my attacker's head back, and did what he'd tried to do to me, only more efficiently. I cut his throat with one slice, blood

erupting to paint the dirty brick wall of the alley with
vivid crimson. It was almost twilight here as it had been
almost twilight there—eight years in the future.

When you're killing someone, whether it's self-defense
as they tried to kill you first or you're a jackass who tries
to kill for the hope of five bucks in your wallet, twilight is
a good time for it. Alleys are a good place. Anyone would
be less likely to be seen. It was probably why this one had
chosen it.

I'd slid behind him before using my knife as that was
some small piece of history, for once, worth remembering.
I'd learned it long ago and it remained useful. Stand in
front of someone when you cut their throat and the force
of the crimson carotid spray will cover you from face to
chest. As much as you wipe, you never get it all off either,
not until you hit the shower. It makes for a cannibal-
fresh-from-an-all-you-can-eat-buffet look.

And it makes catching a taxi impossible.

The man—no, not the man, not some guy—the *shithead* was what he was. And he proved that further by
collapsing onto the asphalt and continuing to breathe. Not
too well as he was doing it through a few pints of blood.
It was pointless, but it didn't stop him from making the
effort. Some people, the assholes like him, refused to
make your life any easier by just dying already.

I could've helped him along.

But considering what I knew he'd done—bad.

That I knew what he was—a human monster.

Nah.

Let him suffer. Slow and painful was what he deserved.
At least he hadn't turned while falling and hit me with
that hosing down of blood I'd been so careful to avoid. It
didn't change my opinion on history, though, that one useful cut from behind, dodge the blood, if you plan on catching a cab later little fact picked up along the way.

I'd always thought history was boring. I thought that
the books were too thick, and whoever once gave a shit
about memorizing all the tedious dates of this war or
that ancient plague or some long dead philosopher who

made logic so illogical you wished he'd died sooner?
Dull as dirt, plain and simple.

Or so I'd believed.

But look at me now. According to one of those sayings about history, in this place, I was a historian. I could
do what God couldn't.

I could change the future by *rewriting* the past.

I hoped.

Fuck, I hoped.

Giving the twitching body lying facedown at my feet
an encouraging nudge, some might say kick in the ribs
with my combat boot, I snapped, "Move your ass, you
son of a bitch. You're already aimed in Hell's direction.
Slide your metro card and go already."

A thin wet whine managed to work its way from his
throat as the body, ninety-nine percent dead makes you a
body in my book, struggled toward me with one shaking
hand clawing at the asphalt and the other hanging on to
that knife as if he'd superglued it to his homicidal hand.
He was still coming after me. If he were at a funeral home,
they've have embalmed him already and, yet, here came
the knife weakly slashing at my ankle. Was it six feet away
from his maximum reach? Details. Nothing but details.
Motherfucker. I wanted him to suffer for what he'd done,
but I was suffering too. The stench was only getting worse
and he was getting more homicidal the less blood he had
in him. How was that possible?

Sheer willpower to be the most annoying dick he
could conceivably be?

Fingers kept scratching in the trash of the alley floor
as the choking became louder and stubbornly continued.
I exhaled, miles past pissed now. Asshole didn't begin to
cover this one. I squatted to capture glazed eyes, once
muddy, now dark as grave dirt. But there was a flicker in
them, hate, vicious and brutal. It was fading, but I didn't
know if it was fading fast enough. "You're a monster," I
said, matter-of-factly. "Punishing monsters like you is a
hobby of mine.

"But I'm on a tight schedule. Half a minute and I'll

finish what you started. And I'll make it hurt. You think
this is bad? Drowning in your own blood, agonizing breath
by agonizing breath?" I smiled the special, nasty one I'd
learned the two long years spent in my own monster hell.
Fourteen years old and I'd been dragged there by the
thing that bred my mother like she was a show pony, if
show ponies accepted cash for services. The monsters
there, the Auphe, had taught me death was a *game* and life
was too dull to tolerate without the razor edge possibility
of losing it at any second.

"This . . . this is *nothing*." I didn't sound anything but
unrepentant as that's what I was, no more, no less.

Sometimes I was a monster too.

Sometimes I was a lion.

It depended on my mood and my mood now was not
fucking good.

"This is flowers and fucking sunshine compared to
what I can do to you. I'll make thirty seconds feel like
thirty years. See if that motivates you to get your murdering ass in gear. Oh, and pray if you want. Won't work,
but it's fun to watch." I slapped his patchy bearded cheek
lightly. "Good talk. You've got fifty seconds left."

Standing back up, I kept count under my breath.
Monsters and murderers both, true, but no one knew
how to motivate like an Auphe. And they'd taught me,
whether I'd wanted to know or not. I'd managed to bury
most of the memories of those two years. Some resur-
faced now and again and a few I'd never forgotten at all.
This one refused to go. I hadn't made up my mind on
whether that was for the best or not.

It *was* convenient. As long as you kept it a bluff. So far
I had.

I was pretty certain.

Did my best, what else could anyone want from me?

I avoided the puddle of dark red edging toward my
boots. Evidence was bad. Revealing. Avoid it whenever
possible. It was part of being on constant guard—Nik's
number one lesson when I'd been a kid when it came to
Auphe and humans—*Be on guard, Cal. Always. Don't let
the monsters come up from behind, don't let people see*

how different you can be. See them, but don't let them see you. You're a lion, little brother, remember? Watching from the tall grass. Invisible.

I'd listened to Niko my whole life. And being on guard was a behavior I hadn't outgrown. Never be seen by those you might not escape and be on guard against those who didn't already know what I was. Being dissected by the government is not a healthy career goal. I'd listened, but sometimes no matter what choice you make, it's wrong. There isn't a right one and you are fucked—no escaping it. Being on guard hadn't changed the truth that during one desperate, otherwise hopeless moment when I'd had to make a decision to break Niko and the Vigil's rule.

To come out of the grass.

A lion in the light of the day.

One in the shocked sight of an entire herd of dazed and staggering human sheep.

There was no taking that back, leaving the tall, tall grass.

And here we fucking were.

No. Here I was.

Alone.

Until I made things right, and I would. No matter who had to die, no matter what I had to do. I'd already torn apart time itself to walk years into the past. I didn't know the consequences of that and I didn't care. Those were considerations that could kiss my ass at their very best, that's how little I gave a shit.

Weepy consciences are for people who have the luxury or the biological wiring.

Right now, I had neither.

There was the scraping of metal against the asphalt as the dick's knife hand spasmed, dirt rimmed nails clawing the ground. Too bad it wasn't dirt under him. He could dig his own grave. A wheezing explosive cough sprayed red on the alley floor and the random trash that littered it. Christ. The asshole absolutely refused to die. He wouldn't let go of it, his life or his knife.

Okay. Enough. This was over. Time for a countdown.

"Fifteen seconds. Ticktock," I reminded. "Ever wondered what it would be like to be skinned alive? It's time consuming as hell, don't get me wrong, but don't worry. I don't have to actually do it to make you fucking feel like I *am*."

I'd appeared out of thin-fucking-air, eight years rewinding in the absence of an instant, blinded momentarily by a blaze of the purest of white light. If OSHA had been around a millennia ago there would've been warning labels about bright lights/possible loss of vision everywhere in the time travel artifact industry. It had faded slower than my sight returned—I saw my own ink black shadow projected against the wall. I must've looked like an angel wanting to do some smiting. Wasn't that ironic? You'd think that would make an impression on the bastard who tried to slit my throat. It didn't. A fiery sword added to the mix wouldn't have made a difference. He was crazy enough it didn't get a blink from him as he had instantly lunged out of his makeshift bed and tried to bury that piece of shit blade of his in my throat.

The knife . . .

The knife told his story in excruciating detail of who had died by the blood-dried streaks on the metal. There was the scent of the heavier dose of iron that sped through the veins and arteries of men, the naturally wild honey fragrance of women, and, worse, the fresh bright tang of new life—kids. He killed fucking kids. I'd have finished him immediately when he was slow to haul ass to Hell if it hadn't been for the kids. For that I had no problem in letting him pay. Making certain he paid and paid and then paid some more.

I could still smell that new life, innocent children snatched and slaughtered, their lives snuffed out as I stood over him. He was a bastard of a monster who simply happened to be born completely human. That wasn't new to me. I'd stopped being surprised at how the human ones outnumbered the supernatural kind long ago.

I was about to give him a ten-second countdown when the smothered gurgling at my feet became a convulsive seizure. It was quick to start, slow to end, and fierce as I could've wanted between. And then there was one last gasp—an exhalation soaked in blood. One breath finished. I waited for the next to begin. It never did.

"Ten seconds left, asshole," I muttered. "You got off easy."

The entire thing, attack and a kid killer too stubborn to die, had taken three minutes at most—quicker than the majority of his victims took to die at his incompetent hand I'd bet. Minutes in reality until his last breath, but that didn't stop me from hoping it had been an eternity for him. Either way, it didn't change my thought of an impatient, "Finally."

Now *he* was history.

And I had work to do.

Absently, I slid my knife, a favorite KA-BAR in matte black, back inside my jacket after I finished cleaning it with one last automatic wipe-down with the Greek take-out menu I'd snagged off the asphalt. Yeah, definitely, enough of dwelling on the how, the why, the what of why I was here. Now came the important part. It was time to rewrite what should never have been written.

I had to get moving.

I patted the body down for his cell phone. Everyone had a phone, junkies and murdering monsters too. Slipping it in my jacket pocket, I then stepped over the slumped form of what had been a snarling, filth spitting, rusty blade wielding addict. He'd wanted money for drugs. I could smell the chemical imbalance cascading out his pores the same as I'd smelled the blood of all his victims on his knife, and he'd been desperate. Too bad for him he had been in an equally desperately wrong place at a far more desperately wrong time.

Then I walked out of an alley I had once known well. Twilight didn't mean anything. It could've been afternoon or morning. That particular slice of space between two older buildings was forever a place of gloom and shadows. It didn't make a difference what time of day it was, in that place it was always night. It was why I chose it to take the eight-year step into the past . . . that and its location. I wouldn't be seen. It was a good guess that's why the son of a bitch who'd tried to stab me had picked it as well.

Bad luck for him was the thought of less than a second, and then I forgot.

Forgot about the asshole.

Forgot his dead body.

Hell, forgot he'd ever existed.

Scanning the surrounding area, I recognized the landmarks of a hole in the ground from eight years past. It was six blocks away from where I needed to be, and I started walking. The cars, I dodged. The people I less than politely elbowed out of my path in the routine New York way. The noise, the stench, none of it was that different despite the eight years difference. I inhaled the scent of Chinese kebab from a nearby street vendor I'd been to at least fifty times. I'd lived for that shit when I'd lived in this area. But things were different now and not because I'd moved.

I immediately felt a fist of nausea that twisted my stomach, stretched up to claw at my throat, and filled my mouth with bile at the odor of the roasted meat. It happened too fast to move, much less run for a garbage can. Bending over, I vomited on the sidewalk.

Straightening, I wiped my mouth on my jacket sleeve. Hygiene wasn't high on my list of concerns right now. I ignored the bitching of the people milling around or lined up at the food carts. Instead I stepped over my pool of sick and stopped at the corner. I could've kept moving. I didn't have far to go to my destination as planned days ago. But plans had changed. And while I hadn't eaten today, food could wait . . . if I managed to be hungry again. I had my doubts.

As for meat, I had no plans of eating any ever again.

It was time to get moving. I damn sure wasn't waiting on a miracle.

Miracles never happened. That's why they had been and always would be the most painful and ugly of words. That's why you did it yourself. There was no one else. I didn't need a miracle. Miracles never failed to let you down. Miracles were for shit, plans changed and failed in the worst of ways, but there was me. I was for shit myself, no denying, but, unlike the lie of hope for the hopeless, I wouldn't fail in this.

I stepped off the curb at the red light, which for taxis means go five mph slower and caught an off-duty—sorry, not happening—cab by refusing to move as I stood in front of it. I added a polite slamming of my fist on the hood of the car when it tried to push me out of the way. Polite enough whatever cursing the driver spat. I had a new plan, a different and more important destination, and unexpected problems to solve. After that I'd be back here to put the ragged remnants of the old plan into motion. I'd be a few hours at the most. I had the time.

I had the time.

That should've, would've been funny barely hours ago. It wasn't now.

2

When I returned two hours later, my driver was a happier man with the fare and a two-hundred-dollar tip to keep him from calling the cops when I needed him to wait for me a time or two. I had gotten out to take care of one precaution before moving on to the next. I'd debated punching him in the face at his nonstop bitching and slowing down long enough to roll him onto the sidewalk, but while maybe one or two New Yorkers would call the police, neither would remember the cab number. But when the driver woke up, he'd remember and for once in my life I could not afford cops anywhere near what I was doing. Money worked as well as a punch, if not as satisfying.

Back where I'd begun, on the same damn curb even, I started walking. It was full dark at seven thirty, October edging into November. The sun disappeared sooner and the monsters came out early. It didn't make a difference, light or dark. It was safer to walk the remaining three blocks than have anyone, cabdriver included, knowing where I was going. When I arrived at my onetime original destination, it was as humble as I remembered. There was the cracked concrete stairs that collected a hundred stains, vomit, blood, other bodily fluids you didn't want to know about—every color different and a brutal blend spelling out the dregs of NYC life. Rip it out, hang it in a gallery and someone would pay you ten thousand dollars for it.

Down the stairwell to the basement, there were several piles of trash that were home to rats big enough to eat a Chihuahua in a swallow, no chewing required. I heard the rustle and squeal of them as I waded through the stinking bags. The rats hadn't bothered me before and they didn't now. They were New York's real citizens, not the people— if you went by head count. I ignored the rustle under the garbage and the slink from pile to pile. Standing on the bottom stair, I blinked dubiously at the door from the bottom stair before snorting despite myself and shaking my head.

I hadn't remembered this little detail.

This bar had no name.

It had originally, long before I'd known about the place. There had been a neon sign spelling out Talley's once upon a time. Some of the wire and glass was still on the door, but I didn't know what color the sign had been as it'd been long shattered before I came along. Never fixed, it was the invisible label of one of the many nameless pushers of alcohol in the city. It was the perfect place for a kid three years shy of being legal to work in a bar to fork over a fake ID, one out of ten or so, all with different names. They were names just like Talley—his was gone, the kid's weren't real. Same thing in the end—nameless.

This no-name bar was what that kid had needed. It had been one of the best options to get the privilege of working under the table for poverty wages as he slung beer and mopped up vomit. Not a great job, a shitty job in fact, but better than nothing at all.

There were a helluva lot better things than nothing at all, but there were worse too.

That I was here was proof of that.

I zipped my jacket a third of the way up to keep the metal of knives and other weapons muffled from scent and sound. The jacket was beat-up black leather worn enough to be cracked and shot with creases of gray. Plan-

ning for this, I'd gotten it this morning from the Salvation
Army. It was comfortable and the brutal weathered look
fit the neighborhood. More important, it didn't smell of
home or family and it had cost only fifteen bucks. It also
gave me room where I needed it. Automatically, I shifted
my shoulders to adjust my holster, double-sided with a
gun under each arm. It was habit, no more. I couldn't
shoot who was waiting inside. I could do barely more than
give him a hangnail, which was going to be a trick as he
might not feel the same about me.

He was a cranky son of a bitch. I knew that better
than anyone.

And with every right to be one, my brother would've
told me with disappointed reproval if he was here.

But he wasn't.

Closing my eyes for a second, I settled into a crucial
frame of mind. Then, stepping down over the trash, I
took the two steps necessary, if that, to put my hand on
the door. I hesitated, then pulled my shit together with
every ounce of determination I had within me and every
ounce I didn't, but would lie to myself that I did. As my
best friend often said, fake it until you make it. He also
said, if that doesn't work, stab them in the eye and steal
their wallet. Since this one was hands off, I'd have to go
with his first piece of advice.

"Hurry up, asshole. I got places to be." The rumble and
growl of warped vocal cords came from behind me. Wasn't
that the way to be on top of things? I could forgive missing the smell. Wolves were all over the city, living their
crooked lives. I caught their natural cologne of wet-dog at
least a few times every day. Having one sneak up on me
without trying, that was pathetic. What was more pathetic
was he'd done it while I was brooding. Worrying whether
I had the skill to make it past our natural suspicion and
get me to believe myself.

Yeah, odds were my life was over. I had to remake
and undo the worst of nightmares and while I had an
opportunity, a second chance when I didn't have faith in
second chances. I'd used all mine up. That made this a
bad day, fuck did it, but focusing to the point that I wasn't

aware of what was around me, that would have me dead before I could begin to save anyone else.

I turned around to face the Wolf who was two steps up. He was wearing a longer leather jacket over a hooded sweatshirt. And need the sweatshirt he damn well did. The hood was pulled up and forward to hide as much of his face as possible. Shadowed face or not, I'd come across more than my share of this kind of Wolf and knew what I'd see, more or less. With an under bite of fangs too large to close his mouth over, inhumanly pale amber eyes, and a fine coat of brown fur climbing up from beneath the shirt to cover his neck not quite to his chin, he was one of the Wolves that would never pass as human.

I saw something else: an inch and a half of metal showing below the bottom of his jacket. There were nicks and a ragged look to what was one of the worst sawed-off shotguns I'd had the misfortune to see. If that was the best he could do, I had no reservations that my younger self could handle it. Hell, I could've handled it when I was thirteen, much less eighteen. But it would be a complication to what was going to be complicated enough. I didn't have the patience for this kind of shit. Not today.

"You're goddamn kidding me with this," I growled, harsh toward the back of the throat. My ex was a Wolf. She'd taught me how to throw a measure of lupine threat in any growls or snarls I might want to hand out. It wasn't speaking his native tongue, but it let him know I was familiar with it in a manner that meant I'd picked it up by running with Wolves.

And Wolves did not run with just anyone.

"I know Wolves who could do more damage with one fang and half a claw than that piece of shit sawed-off will do. But you're not that kind of Wolf. Can't run with the real ones. An omega who's licked the boots of every other Wolf in the Kin, so weak you need a gun." I lifted my upper lip in a display of scorn. "The weapon of a sheep." Wolves did love throwing the word sheep around. If you were human, you were sheep, prey. I ratcheted up my growl. It was shading into something else, less and less Wolf. "But I shouldn't be an ass. I like guns too. What do you think of mine?" I spread my jacket open to let him see the Desert Eagle and the Sig Sauer in my holster and the eight knives that practically covered the lining.

"No comment?" I took a step nearer to him. "Then how about this?" I stopped growling, but my voice wasn't any more human now than the growl had been. I spoke the language of broken shards, crushed metal, avalanche shattered rock. "I smell you, *dog*. Why don't you do the same and take a whiff of me?"

He did, his already wide nostrils flaring. All his fangs were showing now, but that was the type of instinct that was a lie, a bluff. The sharp tang of urine filled the air as the crotch of his faded jeans darkened. That was another instinct, but one that told the truth. He didn't know me, but he thought he did. He knew what had made me, and while we weren't identical, our scent was to most.

"My kind doesn't play well with yours. You're boring. You're too easy. It's over too soon. You taste like crap, like you live on rats. And coughing up hairballs for days is an absolute fucking bitch." I took another step. "But you are still standing here boring me. *Annoying* me. I guess I can make an exception." I moved to take another step and he fell, all Wolf grace lost. He did crawl up the stairs with impressive speed to disappear, leaving only the stench of piss behind.

That taken care of, I rezipped my jacket partially as it had been before and headed for the door. No more over-thinking. No more waiting.

It was showtime.

Pushing the door open, I walked in while rubbing my palm on my jeans. I was liberal with my disgust. "Jesus, that is the most goddamn disgusting sticky door I've touched in my life. You can get 409 by the gallons you know. Or soap. Soap works. Steal it from the bathroom."

I'd forgotten that too, the filth. Inside the place it was dim, if you wanted to be generous with the word. Too cheap for lightbulbs could be one excuse. Another could be that the gloom conveniently concealed the very worst of the grime, the Talleywhacker's sharp business sense hard at work.

It didn't surprise me he didn't recognize my voice. Whoever does in similar situations?

I walked across to the bar and picked a stool directly across from the bartender and plopped down, casual as they came. I grinned, trying for friendly, but I'd lost the ability for the genuine article around when I was five or so—unless I slapped on my best imitation. And I could imitate the fucking hell out of the real deal normally, but not to him. He, if anyone, would know the falseness of it immediately. Not that he was looking. His back had been to the door when I came in, but that didn't mean he hadn't been aware and alert—he had once been a lion, too, before the Auphe had taken us, and habits lingered. Were they skillful as they had been? No. They did linger and that was something.

I had seen him glance up at a dingy fragment of mirror duct taped high up on the wall. That was Talley's idea of security, letting you watch your back, get a look at who came in the door if you were busy washing glasses, see if they already had a weapon out to rob the place. I didn't miss Talley at all, the cheap, sleazy bastard. The kid had finished checking my cloudy, fly-specked reflection, not seen a shotgun in sight—which was nearly all the visual accuracy the DIY security system was good for—and silently finished up drying the glass in his hands while dismissing me without a second look.

He was a rude little asshole.

Made me kind of proud.

He was also careless as hell.

Made me rather embarrassed.

Most of all, it made me think how easy it would be to put a bullet in the back of his head. Sloppy and young as he was, he wouldn't see it coming. He'd drop instantly, a painless death. I would disappear, as I wouldn't have existed those eight years from eighteen to twenty-six. The Vigil wouldn't have crossed my path and never would have created Lazarus to end what never had begun. Everyone who had died in the bar would live. Goodfellow would live. Niko . . . Niko would not. He'd use a different method, but the result would be the same as my finger pulling the trigger while surrounded by fire and death.

When one went, the other followed. Always. In every life we'd lived.

No committing a suicide bizarre enough to make Guinness, then. I released the grip of my gun and slid my hand silently back out of my jacket. He still didn't notice that or what a wide-open target he'd made of himself. Maybe that wasn't fair. I'd come a long way in eight years, walked a long, more than human, path.

"So, hey, Junior, what's on tap?" I asked, letting go of the failure of the buddy-buddy tone. I did keep the grin, but this one was a neutral and narrow baring of teeth. I was genuinely distracted with my own view of the mirror. He'd given my reflection a quick and disinterested look for blatantly visible weapons, hadn't seen any, and then ignored me.

Sloppy. Considering how many weapons I did have—not just in hand for but a moment, but more than enough in my jacket, and one still lingering with the faint smell of blood—very sloppy. I went with moderately humiliated instead of merely embarrassed. I hadn't gone with the same quick glimpse in the mirror that he had. I'd scrutinized his likeness when he'd looked up at the dirty silvered glass. Having only the short length of assessment he'd spent on his visual weapons check, I was lucky I'd learned in my business that facing down misbehaving *paien* mean each second counts. Use that second or two to examine every detail as closely as possible.

We weren't twins.

I hadn't expected us to be. I'd known that eight years can make a difference, sometimes big, sometimes small. It depends on how you age. Do you look younger than you are? Older? Do you look almost precisely the same but with more scars? I didn't know. I hadn't thought about it before. Why would I have? Rewatching old sci-fi movies I'd seen as a kid to be braced and ready for *time travel* wasn't something that had crossed my mind as being prepared for potentially dangerous situations that could jump out at you.

Until it did.

Leaving fuckup number three hundred and ten behind, I was now thinking, with morbid curiosity, what a person's reaction would be to seeing themselves sitting on a stool three feet across the bar from them.

What would I have done in his place, what if I'd seen what he was going to see? I had a good guess and it was—the thought was cut off as he finally turned around, ready to tell me what was on tap. It would be watered-down piss if I remembered right, but that hardly mattered as I found out about this particular person's response to facing themselves. This copy of me . . . no, not a copy.

This was me.

A particular puck had been right days ago when giving me the usual hard time. I hadn't been bad-looking, barely legal baby face and all.

How the hell had I not gotten laid sooner?

He, the kid, had frozen, still and unblinking but that didn't last long. The eyes that had fixed on me narrowed to slits. The mouth that had gone fractionally slack with surprise, tightened to a hard line, then bared teeth in a snarl, and the baby face disappeared beneath the cold menace of a predator. He didn't know. He really didn't know. He had no idea that I was him, and he was me.

What he thought I was could only be someone else—*something* else he hadn't imagined existed—until he wrongly guessed he was facing it. And there had been someone else—several, in fact, but only one that was functional. Cal and I, when we were one instead of two, we'd been blind and conceited to think we were the single half-breed born of the Auphe. I'd learned differently, and Cal was assuming differently now. And he was shocked as hell. I knew that, as I had been surprised myself when I'd met my genetic "cousin." I shouldn't have been. I'd known a long time I was an Auphe experiment, made with a purpose. No good experiment has only one subject. I should've known better.

This younger me thought I was that kind of family, linked by DNA only, not the family you'd ever claim. It was a reasonable guess, as technically it could've been true.

"Don't get your panties in a bunch, kid," I drawled. "I'm not what you think." And I also didn't have much time to convince him of that, as my prediction minutes ago of what he'd do when he saw me for the first time was on the money. There went the hand reaching under the bar for either a weapon or a cell phone.

Which would I have reached for eight years ago?

Both.

Drumming all ten fingers on the bar, I leaned back and tried not to smirk, but it was hard to hold back. It was no less than he deserved. I'd screwed with everyone I knew my whole life, delivered sarcasm and snark to anyone who crossed my path, family and friends more than most. You torture the ones you love, else how would they know you gave a shit about them? That was my code through and through. This was the opportunity to fuck with myself and I couldn't pass that up for anything.

I knew I had it coming.

But as I thought that, I thought something else. Did I sincerely deserve it? I'd forgotten this was also the me who was barely two and a half years back from being kidnapped by the Auphe. They'd snatched him/me through the explosion of glass that had been a trailer window and told me they were taking us home. My brother, trapped in a burning trailer, couldn't stop them, and Sophia, giving them the entertainment they suddenly couldn't get enough of, lit up like a torch and burned to death in the frame of the door.

We'd seen it, the two Cals that then had been one, before we were pulled through a hole in the world, a rip in the air itself to a place outside this reality, a place that would put Hell to shame. Two or so years later I'd torn open my own ragged doorway that I'd instantly forgot how to make and crawled through it back home, back to my brother. Two years, but not. My brother had guessed that for me, now taller by several inches and hair longer by at least a foot, that it had been approximately two years. For him it had been not quite two days. Time ran different in Auphe-Land, where it's all-you-can-eat so long as you can catch it, and the screaming is free!

When I'd returned, I'd spent my time alternating between acting as predatory and feral as the monsters who'd taken me or too terrified to crawl out from under the bed while clutching a knife twenty-four seven. I had reason for both behaviors, as in the beginning I'd remembered the years with the Auphe. Tried not to—what had been done to me, worse yet, the things I'd been forced to do. Tried to bury it, tried to wipe it clean.

Like I'd ever thought I'd be clean again.

But when I'd slowly realized the feral side, vicious side of me made my brother fear for me more than the horror that kept me shaking and hiding under beds in the safe dark under sagging box springs, inhaling the must of cheap motel carpet, I'd shed the savage side of me little by little for him. My brother needed me back, needed me sane, needed me to be more human to blend in as now we were on the run from the Auphe, the monsters. He needed, for him as much as for me, to keep me safe—this time.

I'd suffered, but my brother had suffered too—fear I was gone forever, guilt that I could smell on him. Guilt that he hadn't been able to stop them from taking me. Guilt that he *hadn't* kept me safe. Guilt that he couldn't get me back. Guilt that I'd never talk again instead of growling, clawing, or screaming, much less wear shoes or recognize a fork. Guilt that I might never stop trying to stab strangers. And then the worse guilt of all: that what for him had been close to two days in this world had been two years for me in their world. Taken at fourteen and returned approximately at sixteen, all in less than two days.

That type of thing tends to fuck up everyone in the vicinity.

I'd told myself it wasn't any different from a Halloween costume, pretending to be something you weren't for one night a year, except my costume was a human one and I wore mine and pretended every minute of every hour of every day, all three hundred and sixty-five of them for several years. I'd worn that human suit so thoroughly that I'd brainwashed myself into believing that I was something I was not.

Human.

Human with bad, bad genes, but human.

Tame.

Until fourteen I hadn't thought I was an Auphe. I knew I had part of them in me, but that didn't make me one of them. It made me only something new. I had no problem with knowing that I was as far from being human as I was from being an Auphe. Niko had told me I was a lion. Lions weren't human, lions were hunters, but there was nothing wrong with being a lion. Nature made us how we were meant to be.

If that meant taking a bite out of a kid's ear in a competitive game of dodgeball, so what? If the gym teacher told me to play to win, then I played to win and screw the rules. Lions don't have rules. That was who and what I was.

And I'd *liked* it.

But what is "like" compared to "love"? And I loved my brother. He'd protected me my entire life until the monsters snatched me. I couldn't bitch that it had been my turn to do the same to help him in any way I could. I stopped trying to eat people in the McDonald's bathroom. I learned about shoes and forks and words, English ones at least, again. I was what my brother needed me to be if we were going to outrun the Auphe who hadn't let my escape go lightly. No regrets.

I was lion no more.

The tall grass I'd lived in hadn't been my home any longer.

Besides, in the end it had made no difference. Eventually I'd learned to enjoy my life again, to take pride in who I truly was inside. It took years, but I'd rediscovered a self-esteem sketched in blood and violence, had remembered how to laugh my ass off while scaring the shit out of customers, clients, and targets. I tore off my human suit in strips and handfuls and went back into the grass. I remembered how to be a lion.

This Cal, though, still thought he was a layer of human holding down the other half, a monster made of mayhem and murder. He believed he was a bad guy, *the* bad guy, the monster Sophia had always labeled me and, worse, he was kind of a little emo bitch, too.

I'd brainwashed myself a little too well.

Sitting in front of this baby Cal I was a lion again.

And lions are not little emo bitches. Mind made up, I had no problem teaching my younger self that, whether I should or not. If I changed the years to come or I didn't.

A lion had to have some fun.

"I only asked for a beer," I pointed out with a mocking innocence that did nothing to cover up the potential for violence painted in black and red violent strokes that rode along my voice.

"Hell, card me if you want. No need to pull out the . . ." Crap, what had I stored under the bar when I was eighteen? I concentrated. Hmmm. Oh, yeah. Baseball bat, yep. The one Cal whipped out and didn't call his shot, but swung for the wall all the same. I leaned back rapidly enough to be missed having my skull crushed by an inch, then wrapped my hands above his grip around the scarred wood and then tore it from his hold. Letting it fall to the floor, I sucked at a drop of blood on my thumb. "You're a rude son of a bitch. I told you I'm not who you think I am."

"If you're not what I think you are," he snarled, "then you wouldn't know what the fuck that is."

"Yeah, we're wrong there. We were wrong a lot these days." I didn't expect to convince him. I was biding my time, basically, waiting for the one that I could convince. Not that I was biding without the expectation that Cal would settle for one attempt at homicide. I could check off the bat. What else did I keep under . . . ? Christ, a thirty-eight.

"A thirty-eight?" I grimaced at that particular memory. His eyes widened at the mention of it, quickly enough most would've missed it before they narrowed again. He didn't know how I was aware of the gun and he wasn't going to ask.

"The baseball bat I can semirespect"—especially when it was wrapped with barbed wire, which was how I'd received the drop of blood while grabbing it—"but a thirty-eight?" I said with a large dose of disgust. "What the hell had I—damn it—what the hell are you thinking with a thirty-eight? You can't even kill a cockroach with that. You've got better shit at home by miles and you're letting your life here depend on a gun too lame and small for Bodyguard Barbie to carry? I'm embarrassed for you, Cal."

With the words and knowledge I shouldn't have hanging in the air, and the name I shouldn't have known, he twitched and his hands froze under the scarred wood of the counter. He was pale in the indistinct light—but we were pale in any light, and he stared. His black hair was pulled back into a ponytail, the same color and style as mine if a few inches shorter. He wore a black T-shirt and a bar apron. I wore a black T-shirt as well. I unzipped the jacket as the time for hiding weapons was over, but my shirt wasn't a plain black like his. It said, (more or less), in steel gray letters COME WITH ME IF YOU WANT TO LIVE.

Clichéd? Sure. But I respected the classics and I couldn't resist the sarcasm. I couldn't resist sarcasm at any time when it came down to it. I ate it sprinkled like parmesan on my spaghetti and substituted it for Tabasco sauce on my tacos. Plus it had been free.

Cal's face, now that I could see it clearly instead of as a grubby reflection, was mine, if a little fuller—not close to baby fat, but that didn't mean I couldn't wait to lie and tell him so. He did lack my scars—too many to list in my brain just now. There were a few that made a difference, that made *me* different from this younger version of me. The ones not hidden by my clothes. The ones he could see and doubt even more when the truth came out. There was the one that stretched from my temple to an inch or so above my right eyebrow and the ones that circled both my wrists several times that looked as if playing with razor wire was my favorite hobby. Although the scar around my left wrist was concealed by braided metal. I adjusted the thick band of twisted black and red that started around my wrist and wrapped its way like a tangle of poisonous vines to just below my elbow.

"Thirty-eight or not, I don't need a gun to kill you, asshole," he said flatly. "I could kill you with the ink pen by the cash register, a dirty glass, or a used napkin folded in the shape of a motherfucking swan. And don't think I wouldn't have enough time to do some origami, shove it down your goddamn throat and watch you choke on it before you could move."

Heh, good one.

Of course, good one or not, he was still a liar as we'd been since we'd learned to string together more than three words as a baby. He had the thirty-eight, no origami, halfway up, the muzzle over the counter and the grip still below. But with the muzzle pointed at me, I didn't give a damn where the grip was. He was a stubborn asshole, I thought as I slid to the side as if the air were oiled, seized my barstool, pivoted to slam it into his hand holding the gun. As the gun skitted across the bar and flew several feet across the room, I considered such success should be rewarded. Slamming was working well for me and I repeated the action, this time with Cal himself and not simply a gun.

I threw myself on top of the bar—a lion perched on a rock ledge—rested on my stomach, folded my arms, and peered both over them and the edge of the counter. Cal was on his ass, tangled in the remnants of the stool, and glaring up at me with an unbelievably young, eighteen-year-old smooth-skinned face as icy and empty as any you'd see on death row. He wasn't as emo as I remembered . . . or maybe I'd been the only one to know it then, keeping it inside. He was afraid, though—of what he thought I was. Terrified as I would've been back then in his practically preteen combat boots, but he didn't let me see it.

Real lions or those that had forgotten they ever were, it didn't matter: We always made fear our bitch.

"I warned you about the thirty-eight." I grinned then advised, "You should've gone with the origami."

"Give me the fucking napkin and I will fucking happily prove your ass right," he snapped, throwing off pieces of the stool. He might have a bruise or two, but I'd pulled that punch as much as I could. I didn't want to wake up in the future missing an eye or an ear.

"Damn, I had fucking attitude out the ass even in di-

apers, didn't I?" It was a compliment whether he recognized it or not. I freed one hand, plucked up a crumpled
napkin and tossed it down to him. He hurled back a
metal leg with all the force he had. I pulled my head
back, waited, then risked another look. This time I kept
my arms unfolded and tapped the fingers of both hands
idly close to the edge. "You're one cranky dick, considering you started this. And I'd rather have a dinosaur than
a swan with the napkin, but, whatever, it's your weapon
of choice."

I didn't give him a chance to respond—it would've
been annoying anyway—instead looking around. "Where's
Meredith? She's chronically late, but damn it gets old."
The bar's only waitress . . . when she felt like showing up.
"Is she here or out getting her third boob job?" I asked,
not bothering to fake a laugh. She ended up dead and
mutilated by the Auphe thanks to me . . . or us. Laughs,
fake as they would be, weren't wanted regarding this. But
Cal didn't know about Merry's end yet. "Doesn't it piss
you the hell off that you never get a single tip the nights
she works? I've seen guys stare at a chick's tits, but I've
never . . ."

"Seen a woman stare at her own twice as much," he finished, almost free of the rubble I'd buried him in. He was
abruptly calmer now, oddly so, to what I'd have counted as
beyond the strange and eerie at his age. Getting his ass
kicked by what he knew, absolutely had complete faith
was a monster. Hell, considering that, he was practically
relaxed.

And that . . . that was a giveaway.

I knew what that attitude meant.

His lips curved, sharp and lethal, and that softer-edged
face became as hard as the one I wore. All the uncertainty
and fear inside him was gone. He had reached for more
than a baseball bat and a gun under the bar from earlier.
He'd gone for what was a hundred times more deadly
than a thirty-eight. A phone with an emergency code. The
jagged-glass smile widened. It was an expression I recognized well.

I know something you don't know.

Unfortunately I did know. I had some serious talking to do ahead of me to get out of what was to come, but I'd expected that. I groaned in annoyance and moved my right hand, fingers still tapping, a fraction enough that the point of the switchblade went between my fingers instead of through the back of my hand. Cal's own hand had appeared from beneath the bar along with the rest of him as he stood, swaying scarcely any. The knife throw had been damn fast, impressive in a kid his age, but damn fast wasn't good enough anymore.

"I'd forgotten about that too," I mused. "Took it off a drunk hooker whose boyfriend was her pimp slash cop of all things. The *To Protect and Perv* engraved on it was classic."

It wasn't the most lethal choice he'd latched onto below the counter, that I knew for a fact, but I liked it. I had fond memories of it. I might keep it.

Then came the fact.

I'd already admitted to myself that I hadn't thought in the past on how a near twin would react to seeing himself. In the end, I didn't need to think about it. He would see what I would've seen—a twisted genetic mirror, a relative in the worst possible sense. It was all either of us could comprehend. I knew how he would respond. I knew what he would do. We were the same—how could we act otherwise?

I knew what both of us would do: We'd call in our brother. It was what I'd been waiting on—someone who had brain cells and logic to drive them. We were going to need a huge amount of that logic now.

"Whatever you are, whoever you are, move away from him and you're dead."

It was his voice, frigid ice that was echoed in the cold metal of the katana blade resting against the nape of my neck. It was my brother's voice and it hurt to hear it. Hurt like fucking hell, but at the same time it brought me back to life. Confusing as shit, but both were true. I'd been all but dead from the moment I'd appeared in that alley. Nothing had seemed real, not the people, the buildings, the city . . . not me.

Until now.

It was absolutely Niko, all of it. The voice, the katana, the fact that he didn't say "step back from him *or* you're dead." No, there was no choice there. It was "step back from him and you are still dead."

"That kind of honesty isn't the best incentive, Nik. For future reference." I sat up slowly, the edge of the katana's blade against my skin every millimeter I moved, then turned my head carefully enough to not incite immediate decapitation to look at him over my shoulder. I let him see my face, my eyes the same color as his, Cal's, our mother's eyes. I let him see because I knew who could. Cal probably didn't have the capability to overcome the distrust that was more a part of him than the humor or the monster genes. But Niko was smart. Niko could see the truth . . . hopefully.

I almost choked on my next words. At the last second, though, I managed to confess as casually as I decidedly did not feel. Apart from my effort at casual, I said the words exactly as I felt them. Warm and true.

"Hey, big brother. I've missed you."

3

"And please don't cut off my head."

That hasty addition wasn't due to an unrealistic fear. The casual let's-all-be-calm attempt had been for a reason. Niko was not a fan of the unexpected, especially not around his little brother. It made him twitchy, although he was a statue on the outside. It hit him internally, where he thought no one could see. No one did, except for me.

Seeing him turned out to be worse than hearing him had been.

I wouldn't have thought it possible. I grinned anyway, one of my rare authentic ones. I couldn't help it. I hurt, God, I hurt, but ... it was Nik. It was Nik and he was right fucking here. It was my big brother who'd kicked my ass in sparring just yesterday without half trying, and yet now, like my younger self, he was a baby. Tall, muscular but flexibly so and one of the best in the world with any kind of sword. A deadly lethal MMA freaking baby.

All right, not a baby, but there's a big difference between twenty-eight and twenty, especially in the lives we led. Rode hard and put up wet should've been stamped across our ass.

"Always your brother's keeper. I've told you about that. That I can take care of myself," I said ruefully. "Unfortunately that hasn't proven true." No, it had not. "But now you're here, it's a party." The pressure of the blade increased, unimpressed with me, my words, my everything. My brother was not and had never been or would be an easy man to impress—that was a fact.

"I did ask about not taking my head already. You wouldn't do that to me, your little brother, would you, Niko *Pali-busno* Leandros? It's the only one I have and you're always telling me even one brain isn't enough to keep me alive. What would I do without one at all?" I didn't deny the truth of it. I had done some sincerely stupid shit in my life.

"Then there's the fact that I've come one hell of a long way, eight years to be exact, to see you and ... shit ... myself," I added.

I studied him harder than I had Cal. At this point Nik was in every way more intelligent, imaginative, and reasonable than Cal ... and me, Cal eight years later. We weren't ever going to be as smart as Niko. He was also a better fighter than eighteen-year-old Cal, although that Cal was innately cunning. He was also genetically gifted or cursed in his juvenile opinion, but it worked or would in the future and that's what counted. Cal, though, could wait.

Niko couldn't.

And this *was* Niko, twenty or twenty-eight, I needed him on my side; I needed him invested. He was my best hope. Cal ... the younger me ... he was good with a gun, but he didn't have our more lethal fighting abilities yet. The kind you can't buy but are born with, and the ones you can't use until Auphe puberty hits you like a sledgehammer. They were the same skills I didn't want to use in front of the two of them if I could avoid it. They weren't ready to see what I could do, no one else needed to know, and then there was the prospect of driving Cal into a flashback ending in a foaming psychotic split.

I could say from experience that a theme park waiting to happen, they were *not*.

For now I was waiting to see if Niko was the same as I recalled. I hadn't bothered to guess. Big brothers are always giants in our memories. And at eighteen I had worshipped my big brother ... in the same way I had at five ... and at twenty-six. What had he been like though, not seen through the haze of that little brother reverence? What was the reality of him now when Cal was eighteen, he was twenty, and everyone in the world was assumed to be against us?

As most of them had been.

"You're saying you're Cal?" he questioned slowly, but I wasn't fooled. After twenty-six years I recognized suspicion and surprise on my brother's face when I saw it. He had a hundred masks to hide his emotions, but none of them worked on me. "You look almost identical, save for the scars"—Nik was more observant on that than the younger me as some things never did change—"but you could be a relative and you know the kind of relative I'm speaking of." Not the human kind ... not the all human kind at least. "Then again, you know my name." And that wasn't possible was what swam unsaid under those words.

"Yeah, yeah. Eight years changes you some, okay? I'll invest in a skin care regimen in the future if it makes you happy. And, yes, I'm Cal. An improved, faster, sleeker, undeniably extra ass-kicking future version, but I'm Cal." I didn't pay attention to Junior's offended rant at that. I stayed focused on Niko. As for knowing his name ... "Little Billy-goat. That's your middle name, because you were stubborn; from day one Sophia said you were probably the only baby who potty trained himself in three days from birth."

Swiveling back to Cal, I made no further move to vault down from the countertop. Neither did I react to the edge of the blade of Niko's sword following me. "And Caliban *Beng-rup* Leandros. The monster. The devil of silver." Caliban for half-breed monster and *Beng-rup* for silver devil. "That describes an A—a Grendel"—because neither of them would know the word "Auphe" as they hadn't met ... hadn't met the one who'd told them yet—"all over, doesn't it? Sophia had a knack for being a hateful, hurtful but one damn well-read bitch."

I laid down the final proof with a familiar and affectionate exasperation I couldn't have stopped if I'd tried. Nik was careful in all our years. I was used to it. "Could anyone else know what I know and as a bonus be this annoying and obnoxious?"

He considered that for a moment as a very fair point, but gave a small negative shake of his head. "Killing you would be easier and safer than believing you," he said as matter-of-fact as calling in a take-out order. Great. Nik would kill anyone to save his brother. I had never guessed it'd be me. That was serious irony there. I was about to gate my neck to a safer location—the hell with Cal's possible psychosis. It wasn't as if I could save them both if my own brother killed me first. But just before I did, Niko exhaled and let the katana fall down to his side. "Unfortunately, I do believe you. I know what could be my brother when I see him . . . and hear him and his tactless tongue." How about that? Obnoxious and annoying finally paid off for me.

"Time travel." He didn't ask it, he said it—as if it were not simply the only option, but so obvious that he pitied those who didn't know that. He was freaking smart as they came. That would never change with his age. "Hmmm. Interesting. However—" His voice sharpened.

"Say that word again, call him monster again, and I will go with the easy route. I'll take your head and make a new future, not yours, for my brother and me. As no matter what you say, you are *not* him. You are not my brother. You could be, you might be, but right now you are only the possibility of one." I'd forgotten about how touchy Niko came to that word when it was applied to the brother he had now. Fiercely, rabidly, intensely touchy.

"Okay. I'll be good." That made him twist the katana's grip in his hand, more skeptically prepared than before. "Not good, that would be suspicious. I'll be as good as I've ever been. How's that? I'll do my best to not kill me over the M word. Better?" I pulled the switchblade out of the scarred wood, retracting the blade, tossed it back to Cal, and slid off the counter back down to the floor.

"Heads up though," I added. "I become used to that word down the road. You will too. You won't like it, but you'll get over it. You might want to try sooner rather than later on that, if you can, or you'll be beating the living shit out of assholes right and left twenty-four seven."

Niko *was* as I remembered him. Tough, willing to take out a threat to his brother without a second or first thought. He had no rose-colored glasses involving any-one except me . . . his version of me at least. Tough as hell when it came to anyone else, one protective son of a bitch when it came to his little brother.

He did look younger to me than I'd have thought. I didn't know if he would have to anyone else. His face, too, was a tiny bit fuller, his build a shade less leanly muscular and iron-hard. In my imagination, Niko was ageless. In reality he was human. Mortal. Born with an expiration date. The Auphe lived a long, long time unless another Auphe had killed them for shits and giggles. I didn't know about me, if I'd eventually age or not.

I didn't know and I didn't want to know.

Shaking off the thought, I concentrated on the rest. The long dark blond braid was there, the dark clothes and long coat, the forbidding expression now fading that said he'd fight to the death if you gave him a reason. He was Nik in all the more important ways. And he was here, right here . . . *real* . . . and that was something I couldn't . . . didn't . . . *fuck*. I dropped back onto the stool next to the one I destroyed, propped my elbows up, and let my head fall into my hands.

I had time for other issues but not time for a psychotic breakdown of my own. Accepting this Niko was correct was the better road to take, sanity-wise. I wasn't his brother, simply the potential of one.

Cal, full of empathy as usual—because if Niko went into a box labeled NOT MY BROTHER then Cal went in one labeled NOT ME. It was the only way to survive mentally. "Me? How can he be me? You don't believe this bullshit, do you, Nik?" Cal demanded, flicking the lever on the switchblade I'd just returned, and made an effort at stabbing my hand again. This being the hand that was holding up my head. At my count, this was the third or fourth attempt at profound bodily harm and I was done with it.

I had the switchblade out of his grip before he was able to trim a single strand of my hair. I'd done it with a trick, a twist, and a lift that Goodfellow had taught me, combined with a speed that had made it virtually invisible. I twirled it with one hand, fast enough that it was a continuous circle of silver; that was one Niko had trained me to do himself and had me practice endlessly. It showed Cal how slow he'd been in his currently second try at using it.

"Look at that. Nice, huh?" I said, admiring my moves. If I didn't, who would? "Listen to your brother when he says practice makes perfect. He's irritating as he never shuts up about it, but he's right. I've damned sure improved from the fetus-years." Cal growled. I wondered if I growled that often and had gotten used to it enough to not notice.

"As for believing me"—I shrugged and shifted the blade to my other hand without pausing its whipping rotation—"what would you rather believe? That I am you eight years from the future or there is another half-Grendel running around. Or maybe twenty of them. Maybe a thousand." There was a piece of the coming days he wasn't going to be happy about, but he didn't need to hear it. Deserved to hear it, but we had plans to make and no time to waste on revenge. Justifiable as it was.

"Besides"—I watched the silver of the blade and ignored the flicker of imaginary flames reflecting in it—"the only way I would look so much like you and have the eyes of you, Niko, and Sophia would be if Sophia whored herself to another Grendel years before Niko was born. And if she had, I don't think she'd have repeated the experience with you . . . us. She hated us more than she loved money and that is saying something."

I could see that one hit home, but he went on to another subject as he, like me at his age, didn't want to think about the monstermonstermonster. "Give me that back, you thieving son of a bitch. It's my favorite switchblade, you asshole, and you don't get to keep it," he growled, going back under the bar, for . . . what was left? Nothing that I remembered. That had been— Ah shit, the shotgun. Rusty, older than not only Cal but Sophia too, and bought off a guy missing three teeth. Not sawed-off, but smaller, for a thirteen-year-old ready to slaughter his first wild turkey. It worked though. We'd tested it.

"Don't be a baby," I advised. "Naughty toys aren't for little boys. You tried to stab me in the head, you dick. If I see a fucking molecule of that shotgun show up in your hand, I'm taking your cute little knife here and I'm cutting off your trigger finger. And as I know us and guns and what we can use to pull a trigger, that's ten fingers and ten toes. I'm here to save your life, so stop acting like the fucking Grendel you wish you weren't."

He flushed to a murderous red, a color I didn't know existed under my pale skin, but I let it go and went on, not caring Niko had moved close enough to take us both down if he had to. "I know we slept with a knife under our mattress since we were six," I announced flatly. "I also know we slept with a T-shirt under our pillow. It was one we stole out of Niko's laundry when we were too old to sleep with him anymore. We slept with it because we could smell him on it. He might have only been a bed or a mattress away in the same room, but we slept with that shirt for years. We slept with it when we were fourteen and he went to college.

"Not convinced yet?" I alternated the knife again and practiced spinning it in the opposite direction. "I could tell the story of the first time we jacked off and which of Niko's mythology books turned to the page of a mermaid with naked boobs was collateral damage."

"No. No stories," he denied instantly, knowing the price he'd pay if Niko found out which of his favorite books that had been. "No mermaid b— No, I believe you. You're me . . . only old."

Twenty-six was old? I had been such a punk. Still was, but it was less fun on the other side.

"Glad you're caught up, Mini Me." I slapped the knife down on the bar to be instantly snatched back by him. "Take back your poodle-sticker, no way it could take out a pig, and try not to stab me again. I get annoyed easily. You, of anyone else in the whole goddamn freaking world, should know that." Know thyself, after all.

"We've established who you are, but why are you here? How are you here?" Niko would be the one with the smart questions.

"I'd like to hear why first," Cal added. "Because right now you're my own personal number one hell."

I ran a finger across my T-shirt, underlining the message for the second time. "I told you. I'm you, Tiny Tim, from eight years in the future. You've seen the movie. Get a fucking clue. You're Sarah Connor, someone's out to terminate you, and I'm here to save your ass."

Reaching for the petrified pretzels, I made no move to eat them, but I spun their bowl lazily in circles. "According to some information retrieved by G—" My hand jerked, knocking over the bowl, spilling pretzels far and wide. I stopped before the name escaped, tasting salt from a viciously bitten tongue. Goodfellow—shit, I hadn't meant to think his name. Niko's younger reflection was in my face, no escaping that, but Goodfellow I'd hoped to keep a blank as long as I could. It was my only option in trying to hold back part of the flood that threatened to drown me in a guilt and grief I couldn't show anyone.

"Faster, sleeker, and improved, my ass," Cal snorted. Niko remained silent, but from the lowering of his eyebrows and the faint dip between them that would one day become a hard-earned permanent line, he suspected something other than poor coordination had been the cause.

"According to a friend's contacts," I started over, with caution and care on each word, "the assassin is called Lazarus. He's genetically altered. Pumped full of a mixed bag of monster blood. Fuck knows what he can do with that." I shook my head. I couldn't begin to guess and didn't particularly want to.

"He was named for the Lazarus Project as it's about

raising the dead. Bringing an entire organization of corpses back. Resurrection. Is the title a little too fucking cute or what? I haven't decided," I commented with derision and spite heavy on my tongue. Flipping over the bowl, I started filling it back up with pretzels. There was nothing on the bar that was any more toxic than what had been living on the pretzels for months. "Lazarus is arriving late tonight or tomorrow. He was sent to kill Cal by the Vigil. They *were*—loving the past tense on that—a human organization that considered it their fucking calling to keep humans from finding out about the nonhumans. They'd thought, and probably correctly, that if the world found out the bogeyman was real, it would be all-out war."

Bowl filled, I pushed it away. "Humans aren't known for being open-minded about those who are different. And sharing the planet? They'd sooner nuke the entire thing to a cinder first. Niko, I know you remember the Cold War when there was one plan that topped the list on both sides and both sides were proud to have it. Mutually assured destruction. Everyone dies, but they die satisfied that no one else won either. If your country wasn't even involved? They'd take you as well. Why waste all that hard work and leave what's left to the peace-loving slackers? If we lose, the entire world loses. That's humans for you."

He didn't deny it, and Cal's face didn't show any more surprise than mine had when I'd found that out. Humans. What wouldn't they do if they could fabricate a shred of justification?

"Is the information reliable? How did your friend's contacts obtain it?" Niko questioned.

"Stole it."

If stole meant gained by imaginative questioning methods that gave every member of Amnesty International a simultaneous nosebleed of unknown origin that had the CDC in a panic. The two of them didn't need to know that though. We stole to survive as kids. I'd stolen a motorcycle with a side order of blackmail when I was four years old. It was nothing new. Interrogation, to put a very polite name on actions that in no way deserved that name, different story. They—Niko more so than Cal—would've had a problem with it, and Nik suspected. *How* the hell had we been so young?

"Our lives never changed, did they?" he asked. He didn't want to know, but he had to ask. Big brothers, taking one for the team.

But he was wrong there. Could not be more wrong.

I could've been worse if we'd taken one wrong turn.

So much damn worse.

Our lives had changed. The difference was that it was a choice now. We'd always been warriors, soldiers, fighters, we always would be. Hell, we were paid to do it. It was our job, the perfect one for the adrenaline junkies a life of running would turn us into. Once the bogeymen chased us, now we chased them. It wasn't as bad as he thought. Except for occasional cluster fucks like Lazarus, I couldn't see doing anything else.

"That's not true. They changed or it could be we changed. I *like* our lives. We both do. It's not the perfect picket fences, golden retrievers, and PTA meetings. You didn't expect that on a postcard from our future, did you?" I came close to laughing at the thought. "That isn't us. It never was and it never will be. We're Rom and I'm a little more than that. Could you imagine a life where you didn't have a sword in your hand? It's as much a part of you as the hand that holds it. Would you rather move to Jersey, mow your grass, and keep the pH in your pool at the perfect level?"

Niko blanched. It was subtle, but I caught it. "I wouldn't want those things if I could have them. A Stepford life, no thanks." I went with the bottom line. "You saved me, my life, and my sanity, Cyrano," I reassured. "You always do. Give yourself credit I'm not wearing a jacket that ties in the back and, hell, I'm *alive*. Twenty-six and twenty-eight, did you really think we'd ever live that long?"

"I—"

"No, you damn well did not." I answered for him. I

knew my Nik, this Niko, and I knew neither would've wanted to tell the truth there.

And that was without knowing the hundreds of other species of monsters that roamed the earth. Thanks to the Vigil freak, Nik was going to get that cherry popped a little sooner, but only by a few months. This was when we'd been in New York a mere few weeks. It hadn't taken long for the city to open our eyes to the fact we didn't live in a single horror movie. We lived in *all* of them.

"But here I fucking am. We did good." We had, too . . . up until Niko had been murdered, but that was a truth I didn't want to and couldn't tell. "Pat yourself on the back. You dragged us through some unholy, absolutely terrifying shit. You saved us. You saved me."

"This is Hallmark as goddamn hell and all, but could we get back to the part where someone wants to kill me? And *why*?" The angry mask of Cal's face tightened further. Sharing me with Niko, with his brother, was not number one on his Christmas list. "Methuselah the assassin? That ring a bell? Someone from the future? 'Come with me if you want to live' like the movie? You're telling me the older I get the less taste I have? And I am *not* Sarah Connor."

Big brother or not, Niko couldn't keep a straight face at bitching of that epic proportion. It was a quickly smothered laugh, but it was there.

"Jehoshaphat. *Jehoshaphat* the assassin. Keep up." I lied, as I invariably do, with a clear conscience. "And this is the most tasteful T-shirt I own, Junior, so prepare. And we've had monsters follow us our whole lives; you find a little time travel hard to believe?" I reached forward and flicked his forehead. "But you're right about you and Sarah Connor. There isn't a gym in the world that could give you her muscles."

The switchblade came out again, and I promptly repossessed it to return to my jacket.

"You don't look like you could take on any kind of Terminator, no matter how good you are with a knife. And don't call me Junior, asshole." Cal glared resentfully at me, then passed his palm down over his face and let his shoulders slouch, suddenly too tired to be eighteen. Realizing if he couldn't take himself—that would be me, with several weapons—what were his chances with a genetically altered super-assassin? Reading my T-shirt one more time in a clear hope that the message had changed, he grimaced. "Come with me then? Like right now?"

"Thanks for the vote of confidence on my own terminating skills." I checked the cheap watch I'd bought off a street vendor as the stolen cell phone was either telling the time in New Zealand or had a glitch somewhere.

"As for right now, nah." I leaned back on the stool, suddenly exhausted in every part of me. "Not this second anyway. The Vigil didn't know your home address as Niko was smart enough to fake all our IDs, names, addresses, ages, pictures. That means Lazarus doesn't know, but he does know the address of the bar. He knows you work here as this is where we first ran into the Vigil, so this is the last shift you can pull until we get things straightened out." By killing the Vigil bastard.

"For today though, yeah, we've got some time. As long as we're back to your place before midnight or later, we should be good," I assured. "The information was no sooner than three a.m. but a few hours either way to be on the safe side."

Tomorrow was when we'd have to begin watching for the shit to start going down. "Since you have a problem with Junior," I added, "call me Caliban and I'll call you pretty much whatever I feel like. It'll be simpler in keeping things straight. And I know if I call you Caliban, Niko will punch me in the face."

I couldn't let myself forget that these were the bad old days when I wore my human suit and held on to enormous angst, enough to haul around in a tractor trailer, about being part monster. And Caliban equaled monster thanks to Shakespeare and our mother's constant use of it—Caliban the monster and Caliban the demon. Cal didn't care, not enough to count, but Niko cared enormously. Call his brother that and he'd either gut you, decapitate you, or both.

"Oh, and one more thing, Tiny Tim," I remarked.

"Cal," he gritted as I heard his jaw begin to grind in frustration. "If you're Caliban, I'm Cal. Use that, because if you use Junior or Mini Me or anything else again, I'll rip out your eyeballs and use them as cocktail olives, got it?"

"Fuck if I hadn't been a goddamn adorable baby psychopath. 'Eyes as cocktail olives.' Cute as hell with the nasty temper and baby face. If I didn't think you'd bite my hand off at the wrist, I'd be tempted to give you a pacifier." I settled for pinching his cheek grandma-style. That, too, had him trying to bite off my hand. I wasn't surprised.

"Now, Niko, Cujo," I said, "back to the one more thing I wanted to tell you."

I had the switchblade out yet again, it was developing into a twitch. I started carving shallowly into the surface of the bar. *Laz.*

"We've got the who. How about we finally get to the why someone wants to kill me bad enough to freaking time travel? What the hell did I . . . oh. Not me. You." The question became sharper, grew teeth enough to try to eat me alive as Cal snapped out the accusation while planting a finger forcefully in my chest. "What did *you* do? And stop with the graffiti. I don't get paid enough to have my under-the-table grubby cash *docked* or I'd already have tore the hell out of this stupid bar myself."

Beat.

Huh. I was smarter than I remembered when it came to blaming me. But not smart enough to realize naturally I was going to ignore him ordering me to do . . . mmm . . . anything. Niko should've put me in day care rather than letting me run wild at eighteen. I had not been ready to play with the big kids. "Aw, you want to do it yourself. You've hit the 'me do!' stage. What an independent little shit you'll be." He hissed silently—completely without words or sound, but the air between us vibrated unnaturally—holy shit, that was an accomplishment for anyone to inflict on either of us. I freely admitted it.

You. I kept digging the point of the blade into wood.

"What did I do?" I contemplated. "Why is the more pertinent question, but, all right. We'll go with yours: What did I do?

"I broke a rule. I broke the *fucking* hell out of it." I bared my teeth with dark cheer, as predators do. "No one in over a thousand years has broken these assholes' rule anywhere close to how I did."

Here.

"I told you how the Vigil wanted to keep humans in the dark about nonhumans. They said they didn't want war. They wanted to share the planet, buddies, pals, Best Fucking Friends Forever, kindergarten all over again. Not for *us*." I grinned lazily and without any guilt, entirely guilt-free. "Not when we were biting the normal kids to see if they tasted like hot dogs. Better than the kosher beef kind." Which they had. Even at five years old I wasn't into false flattery. So I'd told them. I'd thought they'd be happy. You have pretty hair, you have a cool lunchbox, you taste like the really expensive hot dogs. I was wrong. They were not happy.

No one was happy.

"But you get my point." I would've forgotten the hot dog incident except for my Nik; he wouldn't let me. The first few times it'd been just as funny to me as to anyone listening. I wished once in a while after the tenth or twelfth time he told it, his eyes gleaming with retribution for the therapy sessions he had to take me to during his lunch period, that he'd let it go.

Instead, *he* let go and fell out of this life. It wasn't the same, was it? Letting it go compared to letting yourself go.

Not. The. Goddamn. Same.

Stole. I dug the knife in deeper with careless force, the wood splintering.

"The Vigil had one rule. Do not be seen in the light of day as the most oblivious humans will notice. Stay hidden. But they were not my god and One Commandment or Ten, I didn't have to bow down to them and their one shitty precious *rule*." Pride. Spite. Venom. Hatehatehate. "If I had to break it, I would. And I did. I just wish they'd had nine more to break."

It was the truth. I'd not only broken their rule, I'd shattered it. I'd opened a gate, ripping and tearing a wound in the fabric of reality that was more than obvious as it circled in midair flashing in the colors and shades of a bruise. There wasn't a human alive blind enough not to see that. I had done it in the light of day, fading light—but day all the same. I also did it in front of an abandoned church in the sight of the people passing by on the sidewalk. I'd then walked through it and disappeared.

Your.

With that, I had announced to the ignorant and naive: Here there be monsters. The nightmare with bloody claws living under your bed is real. The fanged creature in your closet that called your name in a hungry whisper existed outside horror stories. I showed a crowd of humans they were not alone. I hadn't meant to, but I hadn't meant not to either. I had one thought and one goal and hiding from sheep wasn't it. I basically just didn't have it in me to care by then.

Target.

People in the city didn't notice much, too busy minding their own business, but that was something, average New Yorker or not, none of them could miss seeing. The Vigil, forgiving of nighttime slipups, were less forgiving of the ones that took place under the sun. They weren't at all forgiving of the ones that took place in front of twenty or more people. Not a one of them had missed that magic show. I should've tossed out cards, gotten little kid birthday gigs.

When I broke a rule, I didn't fuck around.

Stole.

"Why?" Cal challenged. "Why screw up by breaking a rule like that if you knew they'd want you, now me, dead over it?"

Your.

I could've said rules weren't meant for lions, but that hadn't been the reason. I let my eyes drift to a shadowy corner, deciding what to tell now and what to wait until later to reveal. There'd be more questions I couldn't answer, but this one I could. Diverting my attention back to the younger me, I took in our differences. Physically we weren't quite identical. Neither were we mentally, too many years of bad, bad experiences between us, but in this one thing, we were, without a doubt, the same. I turned half of my attention back to the switchblade and half to Cal.

Moral mirror images.

Toy.

Our native tongue had always been practicality—with all its different dialects of lying, stealing, violence. Arson and blackmail before the age of eight as antibiotics were hard to come by when you had no money, no insurance, no identity, and no parent who gave enough of a shit to take your brother to the doctor. Whatever it took to help Nik and us survive childhood, we'd done without thought.

What *I* had done several years from now was something he'd understand without any explanation required. "I broke it to save Niko's life."

He stared into the eyes of a remorseless reflection, searching for the truth or searching for himself. He must have found both as he let his finger fall and folded his arms as a good chunk of aggression melted away. "Okay. Good reason. I have no problem with that. You were—"

"Practical?" I finished before he could. He wasn't a lion anymore, but he remembered, at least this once. I could see it.

One corner of his mouth crooked upward. It was the closest thing to a smile you'd get out of me at that age. "Practical," he confirmed.

"The funny part is—funny, incredibly goddamn motherfucking *funny*." I was tense with a rage I could barely control. After a few breaths to calm down, I started again. "The funny part is that I did it in front of around thirty people and not one of them believed it. They all thought it was a publicity stunt for some sci-fi or superhero movie. No one found out the big, bad monster secret, but the Vigil didn't take chances. If I broke their rule once, I could again. They didn't care about the reason—about Nik, I was stamped rabid and scheduled to be put down. For nothing. Which means the Vigil, they all died for nothing, with no one to blame but themselves. They were *not* practical."

YOU. I went back to the knife.

Not care about Nik? No Cal would find that acceptable and every Cal would make you pay for thinking it. "No, they weren't practical," Cal agreed grimly. "And if they're all dead, they deserve to be."

"I'm glad you two agree, although I wish you, Caliban, would be somewhat less of a homicidal influence on Cal. We'll discuss that later as I have a few questions as well. Important ones to which I want answers," Niko said, and his orders, whether he was younger or not, I would tend to listen to.

"How did this organization send an assassin back in time? How did you come back after him? For that matter why didn't they kill you in your own time?" Niko demanded, his habitual patience fading fast, evident by a jaw tight enough to grind molars to nothing. "And how many nonhumans are we speaking of that require an entire organization with access to science fiction such as time travel—" He closed his eyes. "Buddha, no. Tell me it's not magic. I believe in too many unbelievable concepts as it is. I do not want any part of magic."

I could've yanked his chain, his rational and logical chain that had been yanked since the day of my birth, but I didn't. "No. There's no magic. The *Kyntalash* is an artifact, but a technological one. We'll get to that later, but not in here." I tilted my head toward the dead-drunk patron who was still blowing bubbles in his vomit, but I was less trustworthy now than I'd been at eighteen as impossible as that seemed.

"Very well and don't think I'll forget. To repeat, then, why didn't they kill you in your own time? And how many nonhumans are we speaking of that require an entire organization with access to technological artifacts capable of time travel when we only know of three?" At their ages, that was true. Vamps, Wolves, and Grendels. And with the exception of two Wolves, one a healer and no part of the Wolf mafia, they weren't on speaking terms with any of them.

LOSE.

I laughed and if it sounded like the rasping bark of a feral junkyard dog, it was on the money. "They tried to kill me. They tried their gold-star, A-plus best. They tried enough times I lost goddamn count. But they never pulled it off. Meaning that now killing Cal is their only hope. In my time—hell, in this or any time—killing this me won't repair the damage to the Vigil and we did an absolute shitload of damage." If nothing else could make me smile, that did. Blackly satisfied, but a smile.

MOTHER.

"Resurrection, I said. Remember? Raising the Vigil's dead because we wiped out every single one of those fascist fucking assholes except Lazarus. What they started, we finished. Lazarus could kill me a hundred times and they'd be just as dead and decomposing. Humans would win against nonhumans worldwide. But in this city we *owned* those bitches."

Even Cal took a step back at the bile in that last line. Niko looked at me as he hadn't before, not once, not even when I had wholly deserved it. His expression was the cautious, alert one you gave something dangerous . . . poisonous.

"Did we talk three minutes ago about humans being the only species capable of coming up with mutually assured destruction? I know you don't want to hear the word, but this isn't aimed at Cal. It's for your kind, Niko. Not you, but your species. Some humans can be monsters worse than any others. Sophia, don't tell me you think she wasn't one. Being a monster was what she was born to do, and she was the best of the best." I snorted, "Army Strong."

FUCKER. I finished my love letter to Lazarus with a last twist of the blade.

Cal was getting it, I could see it in the sharper glint of his eyes—like glass that, if you had it coming, would cut you—human or not. But Niko . . . always ruthless when he had to be, always noble when there was an opportunity to be. He'd come around some day. Mine had. I cleared my throat and rubbed at tired eyes.

"I'll tell the tiny down and dirty details that no one but your ravenous brain cares about as soon as we're someplace safer," I promised. "Outside. No one will hear us with everyone squabbling and squawking while they go out to eat or have coffee, the weird human shit. We'll leave in a few minutes. Midnight will be here in a few hours or our people might've screwed up and Lazarus will show up sooner. Our flux capacitors didn't exactly come with down to the second instructions." And I was almost done with my scratched and slashed graffiti.

Done with the knife, I used my hand to gesture at the unconscious regular whose name I'd once known better than my own. "And I don't trust the unconscious not to listen in and neither should either of you. You'd be amazed how many people can fake unconsciousness next to a puddle of their own vomit if they're paid enough."

Satisfied, I looked over my message to Lazarus, the lab rat Vigil Frankenstein monster of a freak. *Laz Beat You Here Stole Your Target Stole Your Toy YOU LOSE MOTHERFUCKER.* Carving graffiti didn't make for great punctuation, but I was satisfied.

"Now," I said, "I told Cal too damn long ago"—curious, they were so damn curious—"that I had one more thing to tell him." Rapping the wood of the counter under my fist, I gave Cal the words that would determine the future. That would decide whether we, no games involved, lived or died.

If my world lived or died.

I tossed him a ten I'd had folded up in my hand to land on the bar and skitter toward him and gave him my hopefully perfectly human grin. Spreading my jacket, I gave him one last look at my T-shirt and hopefully his and our lifesaving motto written on it.

"Give me a real beer," I said.

"And then come with me if you want your ass to live."

4

After the beer, drinkable this time, Cal closed the bar early by about eight hours, leaving the unconscious patron inside with a casual shrug, and we went back to their apartment. Theirs, not what had once been mine. I had to separate it. Cal was not me, not yet. Niko was not my Niko, same reason—that and Cal would only get more pissed and possessive if he had to share. His behavior didn't bother me. I could handle his asshole ways as they were after all my asshole ways.

Or I could be wrong and we'd kill each other, annoying each other to the point of homicide. Asshole always looked better on me than anyone else—even if that anyone else *had* been me once. And my younger self, less patient with undeniably less self-control, would without question feel the same.

That didn't bother me either. It'd make a good distraction if our irritation did get physical. I needed one of any kind to take my mind off what did bother me. That was the fact I might go insane thinking this Nik was my Nik. This Niko had been mine but he wasn't the brother I had left behind. Eight years of memories gone. This Nik . . . no, this *Niko* knew me, but only part of me. I needed the brother who knew all of me, all of what I might do, all of what I was. But he wasn't here. So I took that step back, put distance between us, and didn't show a single sign of how being gutted would be less painful.

"Time travel," Niko said, keeping his voice down enough to be as cautious as I'd asked him to be. Although, unless you were unlucky enough to pass the wrong person—a human one as the Vigil were alive now almost a decade before their massacre. I had no idea if Lazarus would involve them or not. I was leaning toward not considering how it had gone for them the first and only time they'd screwed with me.

"No," I assured him. "Ancient technology from a few thousand, ten thousand, I don't know, a long time ago. Meet the *Kyntalash*."

I pulled up the sleeve of my jacket to show an arm brace of a black-and-red metal, a composition I didn't recognize, couldn't guess at if my life depended on it. Several strips looped my wrist and then braided upward to end in a band two inches below my elbow. The pattern had no logic to it I could see and less than a minute of looking it over would trigger the beginning of a headache. The longer I'd studied it the worse the headache became until it was a full-blown postconcussion migraine. To keep that company, following the intertwined path of the weaving made your stomach rebel and gifted you with the kind of dizziness you should have only when falling down drunk, and drained you until you were exhausted enough to want to keel over for a ten-hour nap. It drained you less when you didn't see it, but it definitely fed on you. If you wore it, you were its battery. Whether you looked at it for a second or ten minutes, your brain was telling you nonstop that it was not for you. Whoever made it, their minds were nothing similar to ours. Didn't function the same. They had lived in the same world as other *paien* and humans, but they hadn't lived in the same reality.

I didn't look at it anymore.

"Hike up your diaper, Tiny Tim." That was for Cal who was far less interested in Niko and my discussion and was zeroing in on a kebab stand. I didn't remember it, but eighteen had been an all-about-kebabs and seared-meat year for me. I barely held the gagging back by saying sharply, "This is time travel one oh one. Your life, guess what, fucking depends on it. So listen up."

He scowled but moved back over to our side, took one glance at the *Kyntalash* and gagged himself. "What the hell is that?" Jerking his gaze away instantly, he swallowed and then said flatly, "That is wrong. That is alien and unnaturally wrong, so phantasmagoric in its wrongness that it has to be Satan's pinkie ring."

"Tell me about it and since I have to wear it until this is over and I can go home, you can invest some of your attention in the group effort of keeping your ass alive." I switched my attention to Niko. "Sorry, I know your—have to say it—suspiciously strong fixation on obtaining knowledge, but keep looking at it and it'll either melt your brain or make you wish that it had." I tugged my sleeve back down, hiding the brace from sight.

"There was technology thousands of years ago that can to this day accomplish time travel." He was only repeating what I'd told him, but that was Niko. He didn't want to know how. He wanted to know how, who, why, be given a copy of the schematics, understand the principles on which it worked, and could he make one himself? It didn't matter to him that he was already rubbing his forehead with a *Kyntalash*-induced headache after barely a minute and a half in study of it.

Niko was a need-to-know type in that anything he didn't already know, he needed to with an impatient, frustrated hunger. I'd once made the mistake of labeling it as OCD. He'd told me I only wished it were OCD as they made pills for that, but they didn't make anything for his appetite for the curious and unknown. I'd grumbled and kept following him around a dusty old bookstore run by a Druid who might've been human once, but wasn't any longer. He was every bit as dusty and old as his books, but with the smell of fresh goat's blood and mistletoe on his breath with fingernails that I knew were wood, grown from his flesh, not fake. I didn't like him, but he wasn't killing humans. That actually meant less to me than the fact he was killing goats. The majority of people I could take or leave. I didn't mind goats. I'd never been provoked or pissed off by a goat. I did try not to chew on that fact as I'd continued carrying at least ten books for Nik. Heavy books.

The road could lead to regrets. Niko's regrets. While I wouldn't have any on the issue, Niko would pass his on to me somehow. He was inventive.

Two days later, which was one day longer than I thought I'd hold out, I'd killed the Druid. I'd gone for the goats, but I'd lucked out. There'd been a sci-fi convention in town that had a fair pick of virgins and the temptation had been too much. The Druid had probably pissed tree sap in his big-boy panties with glee. He'd decided worshipping trees and Mother Earth wasn't getting him anywhere and moved up from goats to human sacrifice. He was right. It did get him something more tangible.

A bullet in his brain.

Then, being absolutely justified—a perk I had not expected—in shooting the asshole and burning down his creepy store, I'd "borrowed" Niko's car to drop off a pimply fifteen-year-old at one of the hotels. I'd found him in the Druid's basement, tied to an altar. The kid had a trident, a short blond wig, and was dressed in fish-scaled swim trunks and green boots. If that wasn't the same as writing virgin across your narrow hairless chest in bright red marker, I didn't know what was. I'd yelled after him as he bolted screaming out of the car to get laid or hide in his bedroom until puberty passed if he didn't want to die really, really young.

Considerate, caring, and a giver of knowledge, what else could anyone want from me?

After that, I'd driven the three panicked but unharmed goats in the backseat upstate to a rescue farm. They were spares, I'd guessed, in case human offerings didn't work out or became slim pickings once the convention packed up. Nik had bitched forever about the farm smell and had huffed, unimpressed, before he'd bought me a supersized Snickers when I'd complained about my unnoted heroism in saving Aquageek.

A good memory, but not one I needed now. With the heel of my hand, I rubbed at painfully dry eyes. They didn't ache any less from the flash burn of the second explosion.

"Yep." I dropped my hand before I tried to scrape off my corneas. "Technology same as time-travel tech in most of the movies, but less moving parts. In theory anyway. Do not ask me anything about physics and how it works. It just does." I gave a shot at walking faster, but it didn't happen. I was too damn tired. "It was the Namaru who made the *Kyntalash*," I continued on, not that any of us much cared except for Niko.

"Thousand of years ago, give or take, there was a race that built all sorts of technological crap people took as magic." Nope, no magic. Just a caveman seeing his first TV. "The Namaru. They're long dead, long enough that humans don't remember them to be able to write up a myth or two. They lived in lava fields, active ones, can you believe that?" I pictured giant jellyfish made of living fire for some reason—floating and burning with hundreds of tentacles to use to build. "They created some serious *skata*"—as that unnamable friend would've said—"including this stone box thing, a mold, that could create any weapon. It created Thor's Mjollnir, so they say, although probably by mistake.

"Thor's such an annoying dudebro—alcoholic frat asshole," I sniped, going accidentally, but catastrophically regardless, off subject. "He was more likely asking for a mug of ale or mead or whatever alcoholic idiot Norse gods drink, but it couldn't understand his drunken babbling. So, hammer instead."

"Norse gods are real?" Niko questioned.

Ah, damn.

Time travel was forgotten as utterly as if I'd been trying to sell him fake Rolexes from an alley entrance. He was incredulous, excited, and pupils blown wide with anticipation, all for his one true academic love: mythology and all its pantheons of gods. Hey, pantheon, big word for me—exciting as hell. It made for a nice distraction from the feel of the brittle shell that had been forming and thickening around me every hour since I'd run from the fire.

I leaned away from him a few inches. He didn't smell like arousal, I'd been twenty-four years old before I could pick up on that scent, but he smelled a shade too interested for it to be a mere hobby.

"Nik, you don't smell like this sort of thing is a sexual fetish for you, but it's close enough to make me extremely uncomfortable. When I get home"—if I did and my Niko was there, had never died—"I'm giving your lady friend a book on mythological role play in the bedroom because obviously you're not walking away with your needs completely satisfied." The only person whose face twisted into a more horrified mask than Niko's was Cal's. TMI about your brother's sex life; I related on too many levels.

"Let's forget the sex," I said hastily, vaulting over a wiener dog on a pink-and-black skull-and-crossbones leash. It snapped, snarled, foamed at the mouth, and tried to maul my ankle. Big dogs were terrified of me and my own monstrous—sorry, Niko—scent; little gerbil-dogs thought that made me an intriguing challenge.

"Norse gods. Yeah, unfortunately, they are real. Or two of them are. I don't want to know about the rest." After experiencing only two, I had no desire at all to know if there were more. "We met them at our friend's party slash optional orgy." One of Niko's shoulders shifted minutely, his version of a full body shudder of disgust and terror. "No lie. You'd avoided them for years, but this one you couldn't miss. That's how much you wanted to see some gods, thanks to your hard-on for any and all mythology."

The gods had been a onetime, insignificant part of our life. Three hours of a party, that was it. Real, but, who cared? I didn't think there was any harm in telling this part of the future as it had no effect on our lives that I could tell. The harm would be to me. I couldn't tell the story and block out thoughts of Robin. There was no escaping the pain that would come with them and the memory. But I was going to bring him back and I shouldn't be the coward that refused to give him his due. Until I had him home, did what Project Resurrection planned but did it better, the least of what he deserved was to be forgotten, buried, pushed aside all to save me from a despair that came hand in hand with having a family, small as it was.

It didn't matter telling Niko not to go despite that us being there had nearly given Ragnarok an early kick start. To see a genuine Norse god out of mythology books he'd read since he could read at all? Niko at any age would go. Nothing and no one would be able to stop him. Nothing I could do or say. It wouldn't faze him if I told him he would lose both balls in a catastrophic accident with the bidet. Of course Goodfellow, being the snob he was, would sooner hold it and never take another shit again if he had to do it in something as common and ordinary as a toilet.

That goddamn bidet.

To the few people I didn't begrudge oxygen, there were two or so who knew I grew up thinking the poverty line was something to shoot for but probably an impossible goal. I know it wouldn't have surprised them that I hadn't heard of or seen a bidet. My first time was in Robin's penthouse. I'd thought the knobs, dials, all that extra crap was a puck with too much money who'd put a sound system in his toilet. The rich are crazy. Pucks are crazy. A rich puck? Sound system in the toilet seemed right up his alley.

How wrong I was. I'd found that out seconds later when I thought I was the victim of a wet and ruthlessly forceful invading alien parasite that was using the worst orifice possible as its chosen entrance.

Jeans pooled around my combat boots, I had shot the bidet. Emptied an entire clip into it. To this day I have no regrets and no remorse whatsoever. Remorse free. Would shoot it again someday just on principle. It deserved it, particularly considering I'd had no desire to watch any repeat of the *Alien* movies for three years after that and had to listen to back door references from a demonically entertained Goodfellow for months. Okay, there was a regret after all. I should've shot the bidet *and* Robin.

But the Niko here and now wouldn't want to hear that story, not that I wanted to tell it. It was bad enough that he'd find out in a few years on his own. I'd have to leave about half or more of it out, but why not? As much Vigil crap as I had sent his and Cal's way, he deserved to hear some real mythology.

"A Norse gods story, then. Okay. Why not?"

5

I shoved one hand deeper in my jacket pocket and kept the other ready if I needed to grab a weapon. "At least I can tell you about the two I know for a fact exist—proof positive thanks to G . . . to our friend's party, the one that put me off any kind of party for the rest of my life." I yanked the ponytail holder from my hair with my free hand and let it fall. I dropped my chin enough to let the smoke-tainted, sweat-dried mess of it partially cover my face—ink-colored grass for a lion to disappear behind and conceal the pain of remembering Robin. I couldn't tell the story without him exploding out in vivid colors with his smug sarcasm and mocking arrogance; I wouldn't be able to hide him away any longer.

I wouldn't have this story to tell if it hadn't been for him and his black belt in persuasion. It hadn't ended well, that particular gathering of booze, more booze, and optional orgy. It had been enough to give anyone a new-found distrust of gods, alcohol, and believing a puck when it wasn't a life or death situation.

Beyond the rest of that, thanks to Thor, I was now a brand-new if not a sympathetic puker, then a profoundly sympathetic gagger.

The asshole.

"Like I said, Thor's an alcohol-soaked idiot. He also bleaches his hair and is covered with a bucketful of spray-on tan. Orange. The guy's a god and he can't do better than looking like a giant Cheeto. Pathetic. I'd say he's a dick, but I don't think he has enough brain cells to be a dick." I curled my lip in relived disgust as I recalled the heap of his body. Facedown—his most common position we came to discover as the party progressed—he was in a pile of vomit and blocking the door to Robin's condo.

"If he tried to kill you, he'd only pull it off by tripping and falling on you. Making the huge assumption the asshole was ever upright long enough, a minute or so out of the day, to fall on anything. But if he did, you'd smother under all that mass of muscle gone to flab. I guess Odin cut off his supply of godly steroids." I looked up at a flock of crows, blackbirds, I couldn't tell. They were shadowy sketches flying overhead between my line of sight and the lit up windows. Their cries were as harsh as metal against metal. They reminded me of who came next in the story.

"And then there was the other one . . . you don't want to fuck with that one," I warned. I had, that went without saying, but he'd started it and for once that was the truth. As a rule, if you weren't me, a mix of overconfidence and attitude to spare, you didn't want to cross him.

No, you did not.

Loki, *God* of Chaos and Mischief—and use the proper title, I was informed, when speaking to a god the likes of him. He did add that it should be unquestionably evident that there were no gods the likes of him—I felt the floor shake slightly as he said that and he was the epicenter.

"Loud and clear, no gods like you. I got it." Blah blah blah. My hand was hovering in midair anyway, so I used it to give him a thumbs-up on his MVG, Most Valuable God, status. Number one fan. BFF. Getting on to more important issues. "Congrats. Now could I just get past—"

"You could show the proper groveling respect especially when you are nothing but a disgusting puddle of goat semen same as all Auphe." The explosion of verbal abuse interrupted me midsentence as he continued talking over me with a detached tone, unhurried pace, and disciplined words formed for the same purpose as bullets, to wound or kill.

"*You.*" He said it as if it were the highest insult conceivable, the others cotton-candy, sticky-sweet next to it. "You are also a pile of squirming maggots that feed on feces and rotting flesh, an intestinal parasite alive solely due to the same essence of life you steal and siphon from the soft innards of others. Worthy of nothing was my kind, save the most agonizing of deaths his limitless imagination could weave."

The guy was wordy.

Detailed, too.

As I'd been reaching past him—plenty of room, didn't crowd him or anything—to tap a server with a tray of the best gourmet sliced sausage on the face of the earth, I thought that was one helluva overreaction. And not to mention—no, let's mention it—my hand was getting tired as it hung in the air, dodging back and forth to get to the tray while he blocked me each time. Seemingly without moving. Impressive—if you weren't as hungry as I was. In that case, it was irritating as hell and nothing more.

"Okay then, soft innards. I'll keep that in mind. I sound like a pretty nasty guy. Thanks for the enlightenment. I'm a better person for it. Owe it all to you," I said with as an insincere and wickedly angled slide of my lips to show all my teeth as I could manage . . . and then a few more. "Now, moving on. Loco, you are wiener blocking me in the worst way."

"I am *Loki, God* of Ch—"

I tuned him out. Use his proper title, he insisted? I didn't know the guy by sight. How would I know his name or his title? Robin might party with gods on the regular, but I didn't, and that meant I didn't know him from Adam—yeah, I knew that was a Sleipnir of a different color, but the point held true. This guy could've had his own Facebook page—did they still have those? If they did, his face could've been plastered over every inch of it, and it wouldn't have mattered. I wasn't a thirteen-year-old girl. I wasn't into social media crap. And if he was, I was humiliated for him.

Relationship status: Turned myself into a mare and snap! Bred by Hot Stallion

Location: Straw-filled stall shared with goat. I specifically said no roommates

Update: Bundle o' interspecies mutant joy on the way!

That was not for me.

I had a life to live and lives to take.

When it came down to it, how the hell did he expect me to know he, the *god* Loki in case anyone missed the multiple "gods" he was throwing around, was real? Half of human documented mythology were lies and the other half a confused snarl of mostly untrue gossip. Robin had said two gods were coming to this thing. I didn't bother to ask or care which two they were. Niko would've, there was no conceivable reality in which he hadn't, and likely had to resist with everything in him to keep from carving their names in Norse runes a hundred times or so into our walls with his katana. Mythology was his one true love, not mine.

I was there for two entirely different reasons: the food and to hopefully satisfy my dick before it started demanding flowers and dinner before letting me jack it in the shower or my bed or the couch . . . or in Niko's car as I waited in a parking lot in Jersey while he hauled baskets of heavy-duty dual-function garbage/body disposal bags. It'd been over a month since I'd gotten any and neither of us, my dick or me, were too damn happy about that.

In complete innocence, it did happen—occasionally, I was there for the free food and to, if lucky, get laid. That was what I had in mind, nothing else. Did either of those call for the wrath of a god—a Norse god especially who considered eating and screwing a holy sacrament? Did it make any of this my fault? Deserving of some incredibly long-winded and disgustingly descriptive name calling?

Nope.

As far as I'd known or cared before this cluster fuck had started, he was a random guy, with an unblinking serial killer stare as cold as arctic ice and a face void of ex-

pression as a blue ribbon prize-winning embalmed corpse.
A potentially random tightly controlled sociopath who
kept his industrial-sized freezer stocked with well-seasoned,
Donner approval stamped, jerky covered skeletons *or* a
plausibly random tightly controlled homicidally insane
psychotic freak who was one *"thirteen items in a twelve
items lane"* killing spree waiting to happen . . . but, bottom
line, just a random guy. That he had the oxygen-sucking,
light-devouring black-hole aura of someone who used
blood-covered ice picks in his dental hygiene regime was
not my problem. I didn't care. I cared about only one thing.

He had happened to be in the vicinity of my targeted
sausage, that's all.

If I'd known he was a god, and I didn't, until he
opened his mouth, as it wasn't stamped on his forehead,
I'd have guessed Native American or Mayan from the
waist-length black hair and the copper tint to his skin,
not Norse. I'd always assumed Norse gods would be pale
and pasty, bearded, and wearing leather and lice-infested
mangy fur. His introduction clarified that misconception
for me. It could've clarified it considerably faster, but
with the threats and insults and repeated reminders
making certain I didn't forget the god part, I was halfway
to Alzheimer's and no memory to speak of before he
wound it all up with another repetition of his résumé.

"Right. *Loxley*." I snapped the fingers of my free
hand. "I'm not good with names. Remembering them.
Caring about which one goes with which person . . . or
god. I'm not good at giving a shit in general. Sorry." I
wasn't sorry and the disinterest in my voice showed that
clearly. "I had no idea who you were. I'm not on Twitter,
Tweeter. Whatever that shit is. But keep working at it.
I'm sure someone will eventually, no idea, 'buddy you'?
'Stalk you'?" I shrugged. "Yeah, I'm not up on the terms
of preteen communication. Good for you that you have
the free time and no fear of being put on a cyber watch
list for possible sexual predators."

With a thoughtfulness so mocking that I was surprised
Scout and Boo Radley weren't around to applaud, I

tapped his chest, covered by a deep red shirt and a casual black suit jacket, to advise, "You know what would've been a good idea? In the area of more recognition, less furry Norse panties in a twist? A name tag. You should've worn a name tag."

"I wore mine." I spread my leather jacket to show a black T-shirt with reddish-orange, pepperoni-colored letters that spelled out: IF YOUR DEATH DOESN'T ARRIVE IN 20 SECONDS OR LESS, LAST RITES ARE FREE! "See?" I let the jacket fall back. "Problem solved."

As for the rest of it . . .

It wasn't the first time being part Auphe had gotten insults and threats aimed my way, hardly. But the "use my title, worthless peon scum. You are the lowest of the low among the repulsively slimy, gooey classification of parasites and much more deserving of being crushed beneath my boot" attitude, that I didn't hear too often. And when I did it was because we were already trying to kill either a rabid psycho trickster, an ex-angel serial killer, a resurrected cannibal who'd once eaten thousands, or a Black Death–causing antihealer back and ready to destroy every living creature worldwide. I expected snotty narcissistic raving from them. What was a good fight without some trash talking?

But this?

When all I'd wanted was a slice of herb-and-cheese bread with a piece of sausage on it?

Yeah, that attitude was not making for a good mood—and the fact the sausage was getting farther away because of this shit-fest was making it worse. I managed to snatch a handful of the little suckers before the server escaped and popped them in my mouth. Better. It didn't erase my temper, but it didn't increase it either.

"What a pity Goodfellow didn't have slices of soft-skinned infant and brie instead of pork for you," Loki said, silky and smooth. His expression remained as empty as if he didn't consider revealing his repulsed and possibly violent emotion warranted the effort on his part. *I* wasn't worth the effort. Killing me was on the table, yes, with a garnish of high probability. Reacting to me other than that? Allowing me that minute amount of satisfaction that I affected him or his emotions? No, he wasn't the type to give away the smallest of glimpses inside his head. "The local hospital maternity ward must be running low on births. How your palate must be suffering."

The baby-eating thing, that was what pushed him over the edge of the usual verbal abuse. I didn't like it. I didn't like it because it was true. An Auphe would've eaten a baby if it was feeling too lazy for a genuine hunt. While I wasn't an Auphe now, there'd been times I had been. During the two years I'd spent at their summer home, in the several episodes in which I'd have a flashback where I was finally home but would forget that I was—forget which of the two was actually home. Fighting through the nearly thousand days that had been the vacation of my fucking life. Both the living it and the time after that it took me to recover after my escape from that hell.

That didn't mean I had done *any* kind of shit that he was saying, but the sins of the father bullshit wasn't as bullshit as I wanted it to be. I hadn't done . . . babies. I hadn't done that, but I'd lost enough control during Tumulus and after Tumulus both, enough to forget who I was for a while, long enough to do other things. Bad ones. I didn't want to hear that insult and think, no, I had never done babies. All that meant was that if I'd had less human in me or no brother to hold me back, there was a good chance I would've done what a pureblooded Auphe would do.

Anything.

I'd heard it only twice before to my face and the two who'd said it would never say it again. For that matter, they'd never say anything again. The dead usually don't. That was what made me decide that five or ten bullets in his dick might improve the asshole manners of Loki, God of Fucking up a Decent Party and All Around Asshole. I remember your name now, you son of a bitch. Those bullets in your *sausage*, that would be a done deal, as soon as I finished my mouthful of sausage and cheese.

No lie, it was the best spiced, herb-infused pork product shipped from a German monastery full of men of God. Each with but two fingers left to them as they prepared the sausage by the old-fashioned method, using hand-cranked grinders that liked fingers as well as meat. You had to suffer for your God and for your sausage. It went without saying, I was showing their creation the respect it was well worth by waiting a few seconds before I called him the shithead he was ... and then shot him in the dick. I rarely if ever make idle threats, that it was a mental one didn't make a difference. He was a dick and giving him a permanent reminder of that dick or lack of it status would be a goddamn public service.

I had kept chewing as I pulled out my Glock and aimed it at his crotch. One more swallow, maybe two and I was good to go. He'd ignored the gun as he'd started his list of favorite deaths to toss at me. There was the Blood Eagle—I had to look that one up later, and, holy shit, nasty way to die, but then he dismissed it as but child's play. Toddler fights ended up in worse damage. My kind deserved much more advanced punishment. Perhaps bringing my intestines to enraged life, gifting them with teeth and a voracious appetite and sitting back with a fine honeyed wine while observing how long it took for them to eat the remainder of my internal organs would be a fine start. There was no magic in the world, all *paien* knew that, but he was a *god* in addition to being a trickster and a liar. Who knew what the bastard could do?

His face hadn't changed despite the list getting more wildly disturbing. And I knew disturbing like nobody's business. As unsettling as the list was, that *void* that hovered within him was worse. For a god of chaos, he was bizarrely still, inside and out. It was the kind of stillness I associated with the long dead and far longer buried. Although now, with the longer and more freakishly weird the death o' the day menu became, his eyes had begun to change.

They had become more black if possible. Black as the sky at the end of all days when the stars had died and life of any kind and anywhere was long gone. Nothing was left—nothing except waiting for the tsunami to come rolling out of the darkness, one that would unravel the order of death itself. An abyss would not take its place. That was too much. There would be only null. Nonexistence of any kind.

And that tsunami of shadows that would bring it would be named Loki.

He would wipe away the universe as easily as a child's hand would wipe away the white moisture from a foggy winter window.

But . . . it wasn't the end of days yet.

How did I know?

Robin would have thrown a much bigger party if it was the end of all ends.

Whether Loki could turn my intestines into his pets hadn't been number one on my list of things to know when Niko tutored me in mythology as a kid, but from what I saw in his eyes it was number two with a strong lean toward "fuck me, yes, he can." If I could kill the bastard with a gate, now *that* was need to know: number one with a bullet.

I finally had swallowed my last sausage bite, tasty in the face of death, and suggested, "Fish fetus?"

I'd kept the gun pointed at his Viking jewels as I did so. I knew it wouldn't kill a god, this god at least. It might not severely injure him, but I could hope at least that it would hurt. I had used my other hand to offer him a crusty speck of bread covered with caviar that had been forced by another server onto my ridiculously small plate that could handle only one crumb of food at a time—rich people, so annoying. The sausage server hadn't returned and salty fish eggs were not my thing, which made them a perfect peace offering. I was defining peace as a "distraction while I gate your molecules into a hundred different places at once."

In any case I didn't want it and this bloodthirsty, Auphe-prejudiced, somewhat scary as hell nut job was from or ruled over at some point the great white north where the human part of the population ate the testicles of a seal if they were lucky enough to catch one. Fish eggs should be his thing.

It was as close to social as I could fake ... before I'd given him a grin as cold as the ice that I assumed had birthed him. "Or does that glacier stuck up your conceited ass screw with your bowel habits?"

Then, as I'd internally promised myself, I slapped his true name on him by adding, "Shithead." I'd also simultaneous pulled the trigger of my Glock and opened one hundred gates inside of Loki, god of Chaos, Mischief, and Speciest Fuckers, to every place I had ever been in my life or had ever seen with my own eyes—including the sun, the moon, Mars, Venus, and Auphe homeland/hell, Tumulus. Let his atoms rest with their radioactive ones. As a Rom who'd also been on the run from monsters as well as the authorities twenty-five years out of twenty-six years of his life, that was almost too many places to count. The sun and the moon had been a challenging bonus.

I had taken him apart. I'd sent piece after piece through each gate simultaneously. Every last part of him. The biggest fragment anyone would find of him would require a microscope to see, if things went as I hoped.

Things, unsurprisingly, did not go as I hoped.

Goodfellow had appeared out of nowhere. He was paler under the green tinted olive skin than I'd ever seen him. "*Din jävla* idiot ... you ... he ... *dritt, dritt, dritt.*" He dropped down to sit on the massive coffee table of quartz marble.

He had dropped his face into his hands, muttering, "The Unmaker of the World." That'd be me.

"And the Destroyer of All Worlds," he groaned. I could travel to only two worlds, making that not me.

"Are we keeping count of worlds we can each fuck up?" I'd already holstered my gun. From the manner that Robin's eyes had raised upward in disbelief (I didn't know if Zeus or Mount Olympus was that high, but I'd go with it) regarding my idiocy before he had let his head fall forward, bullets were useless anyway.

"If we are keeping count, that's not fair," I complained. "If I'd known we were keeping score, I could've tried harder." I didn't mean it. Not now. There were times in the past, however, that I would've meant it and sincerely. But I was better about that these days ... when it came to targeting entire worlds, if not singular abrasive individuals who pissed me off.

Goodfellow had ignored me and kept on with his monologue of despair. Robin did love his drama. "And I invite you both to the same party." His fingers were now tightly enmeshed in his curly brown hair and he appeared on the verge of yanking out a few handfuls. "How could I possibly conceive that was anything other than a trigger for the apocalypse, an RSVP to Armageddon?"

"Not a good idea?" I'd asked. Did he think Loki, god or not, could come back after being separated at what approached the molecular level?

"No. It was not a 'good idea,'" Loki had said, voice as barren of life as the Dead Sea, his teeth bared the same as an attacking wolf. Out of nowhere he was there. There was nothing similar to the curdled gray/purple/black light show of my gates when I traveled from here to wherever. He had been gone and then he was simply there.

He had then held out one hand in a fist, opened it, and let six crushed bullets cascade in a gleaming pile to the floor below. That answered that question.

"Bullets might not work on your dick, but it doesn't change the fact that you *are* a dick," I'd pointed out.

Standing close in a third point to the triangle of me standing and Robin, who on hearing that, was no longer sitting on the table, but had fallen onto his back, groaning. It wasn't a melodramatic groan, as usual either. This was a true "how long ago was it that I updated my will" groan. Across the room I'd seen a distracted, who to be fair could be distracted by only one thing, Niko crouched down talking to the other god Thor. He was facedown, situation status quo, and couldn't be too great at conversation right then, but Nik was trying. My brother had one of his highest level of disappointment expressions in place, but I knew he was thinking how often would he ever meet another god. He wasn't giving up that easily, although with his eyebrows in a sharp V and lips curled down in a severe curve when he wasn't speaking, it was taking obvious effort on his part. That had been fine. If the curtain was going down with Loki, and I had every expectation that it was, I'd rather Nik be disappointed over there than in the line of fire over here.

"Besides, the motherfucker started it," I had added. I'd been on the edge of death enough times in my life to know that you'll live or you won't. Praying won't help. Begging won't help, although I never had and never would. You faced your fate and rolled the dice. And on the chance you did die, you made sure you annoyed the hell out of them on your way out. I folded my arms and let remnants of the Auphe left in me flood my eyes an unblinking crimson. Loki had tsunamis to wipe out the world in his eyes. I had the blood of *all* the world in mine.

It had been a bare flicker that registered on his blank face, but it was there. I'd caught him off guard. The great Loki whose tongue told a million lies, or so said the books, and I'd caught him off guard with a simple playground taunt. I knew it and he knew it. His lip had curled on one side fractionally, almost invisible and almost amused, possibly? He could've thought, despite my previous sarcasm mixed with my usual total lack of respect, that I would revert to the threats of an Auphe, every word made of cutting glass and bloody death.

The Auphe, as a rule, hadn't bothered to verbally torment their prey before eating them. Why would they? Would you bother to threaten your steak or hamburger? But on the rare occasion they'd made an exception, they had been terrifyingly eloquent. Terrifying as threat and promise was the same word and concept in their language. Every word had been the truth, and the truth had also been mentally fragmenting and hideously shocking enough to be a horror inconceivable. Those fractured glass and twisted metal words burrowing into their victim's brain . . . If you'd had a choice, being eaten alive in silence would've been less agonizing.

No Auphe would have told Loki he had a glacier stuck up his conceited ass, you could put fifty on *that*.

The god's lips had lowered over the predatory gleam of teeth to press to an invisible seam except for a flash of silver lines, scars, they came and went so quickly I'd thought I'd imagined them. "Did you actually say that I, Loki, God of—"

"Chaos and Mischief. Yeah, yeah. We've all got it memorized by now. All bow down. You should add 'and Bigoted Dickery' to that, but with the whole trickster, god of lies thing, truth in advertising is probably not a big deal to you."

I narrowed my eyes as I accused, "And you did fucking start this whole cluster fuck. I hadn't done a goddamn thing"—for once—"didn't say word one and you're in my face telling me exactly how you were going to kill me. Intestines with teeth? That is twisted and more than sick enough for me to take your ass apart molecule by molecule. And, guess what. I'll do it again. And again. I can keep that up a long, long time. Every time you put yourself back together and pop your psycho, horror show, mind fuck, piece of shit self back here, I'll take you apart again. I repeat, every . . . fucking . . . time," I'd growled. "We'll just have to see who gets tired first."

Wolf against Lion.

Goodfellow had abruptly sat up, smoothed his hair and stood in time to take in the black of Loki's eyes suddenly spreading to ebon veins curling in an elaborate pattern, nearly Celtic if the Celt who tattooed it had been on serious acid, on his face, on his neck, and hands. I'd wondered how a god of chaos was so self-contained, calm, and composed despite his completely opposite words. Now I saw. As I had the tall grass between me and the world, Loki had something else. The Wall of Loki, and it had come crashing down. Behind it was more than chaos—there was an insatiable hunger for havoc, pandemonium, destruction, unending devastation.

I had felt it in me, electricity flying through my veins instead of blood, because, for a moment . . . a long moment, I wanted that too.

We both had barriers, nearly unbreachable ones, Loki

and I, and wasn't that a good thing? For the world at large?

"No." The puck had denied it all with a tone that had made the entire penthouse vibrate, which made Loki's mild shaking of the floor beneath the two of us appear pretty damn tame. Goodfellow's wasn't like that, not like an earthquake, nothing moved, but it could be felt in your bones—the thunder of an overhead killer storm spawning twenty multifunneled F-5 tornados, which are never known for their mercy.

It made it clear that something wicked didn't this way come—something wicked was already *here*. I sometimes forgot. Robin wasn't a god, but he was the second trickster born and over a million years old. He'd mellowed and changed since then, but he'd hinted that at one time he would've considered genocide too easy, too boring, a waste of his time. No, not a god—he predated gods.

A god I'd take on. Goodfellow, even if he hadn't been my friend . . . even as *my* friend, no fucking way.

"Both of you will be quiet." He speared me with a quick assessment. I raised my hands in surrender and then put them behind me, linking my fingers, all without a word. A first in my lifetime.

He gave a nod of approval and turned to Loki, planting a finger in his chest the same as I'd done, but with what looked like considerably more force. "You made a vow to me about your behavior at this party. You were bored with that long con you're running in Vegas, nice disguise by the way if a little over the top—remember: Less is more. You should've gone with an alabaster pale tourist in white socks and sandals. Switch to a new one every week as to not arouse suspicion. Then . . . never mind. It's your con. If you want to be a Native American Fabio, that's your business. I'll bet you have a sports car and date strippers constructed in a silicone factory. Ah, youth. Babies. You do so love to show off," he snorted and then frowned. "Now. Where was I? Ah, Loki, *you* wanted to show Thor how to 'drink and whore in a manner befitting gods, not rutting hogs drunk from fallen fermented orchard apples.'"

"That is the worst told of any lie, one without a seed of truth, you bastard of a puck," Loki refuted instantly. "You blackmailed me. You said you would tell Thor I was the one who cut off Sif's hair, 'the golden treasure of his heart.'" I could hear the quotation marks around the golden bit. "Amusing as it was"—a smile appeared, a razor blade scattered path of the wildly immoral showing that there were tricks in him in addition to the chaos and destruction—"making it permanent was a mistake. Now she wears that flea-ridden horsehair wig, and whenever Thor hears her name, the idiot weeps—no, he sobs uncontrollably like a child. Her hair was the only reason he married her, their 'matched gilded locks.'"

I'd seen the roots on Thor when I stepped over his unconscious body to get into Robin's penthouse. All my life, when my hair was too long, I handed the scissors to Nik and told him to whack off about four inches; I'd been to a barber only once—a *barber*, not a nine-hundred-dollar-a-cut salon like Goodfellow—but that didn't mean I couldn't identify a truly shitty Clorox DIY job. Gods were freaks, every last one of them.

"*You* threatened me with that. Do you know what would happen if you dropped the hammer of that revelation on his boulder dense head? It would double the drunken weeping and wailing, and then he'd run home to Daddy Odin, who as my concerned father, would arrange yet another intervention—number six hundred and two." The grin unholy enough to stop your heart slid away, and he spat, "The senile old shit who can't remember he is *not* my father, but my blood brother and that due only to a blackout drunken state celebrating some battle or another. A regret I am bound to for eternity or until I kill the bastard," he said, the words barely escaping the tight, grimly flattened lips. "I should've known better to drink around Odin who, senile or not, was a trickster before I was born. But there was no other choice for me when it came to entertainment as I hadn't yet glimpsed puberty and wasn't old enough to be with a woman."

"How old do you have to be if it's a horse?" Ah shit.

I winced. "Fuck. Completely my fault. It slipped out, autonomic reflex: heart, breathing, sarcasm. Sorry, Robin." And I was sorry when it came to Robin. Loki, on the other hand or hoof, could suck it.

Goodfellow waved me off, frowning as he tapped his chin silently. Loki looked less forgiving with the temperature around us falling dramatically enough that frost began to form on my best dress Goodwill combat boots. I wasn't taking the blame on that one.

"Hey, asshole," I snapped, wriggling cold toes. "When you lie down with stallions, you get up with foals. That was your pervy mistake, not mine."

I'd used up my one free pass to be a dick, and Robin slapped the back of my head as Niko often did, but Nik did it lightly. Goodfellow wasn't about lightly. He was about education in one easy lesson. "Ow, what the hell?" I ran my palm over his target, feeling for a bump. Instead I felt a trace of wetness. Yanking my hand back, I glowered at the two small smears of red. "I'm bleeding, you goat humping—"

Shutting me up with one hand covering my face from forehead to chin and one shoving what felt like a napkin in my hand as I was now half-blind, he advised, "Ponder that lesson. Only the first is free. Loki, behave or I'll whip out one of your IOUs and use you to cool my refrigerator for the next ten years while forcing you to live in the salad crisper for that decade. And I know you would never show me a disrespect so reprehensible as to refuse such a luxuriously decadent housing offer of a host as gracious as I. Finally, from this second on, the both of you will shut up and let me think."

Which he did, dropping his hand from my face, giving me the gift of vision again. He paced, sat back on the table, staring sightlessly into the distance, stood, and paced some more. "Confusing," he muttered. "That does sound typical to my repertoire, but I do not remember that at all. And I never forget the more entertaining blackmail I commit. Nor would I forget to not invite the two of you to the same hemisphere, certainly not the same party. There's entertainment and then there is insanity. Why do I remember Loki asking me in an amusing and humiliating"—he slowed—"manner that he would never employ?" He centered on me. "Why would I insist Niko bring you? You walking into a room where you are bound to cross paths with Loki is the same as you being the Sixth Seal in Revelations—a cataclysmic earthshaking event. The Wrath of God poured upon the dying earth."

"If I ever grow feelings some day, you are going to make me cry. You know that, right?" I drawled, crumping up the napkin with its two small drops of blood. I was ignored—as usual when Robin was on a roll.

"I don't remember it happening that way, not with Loki begging to compete against Thor, not thinking ahead to drug you and ship you to some tiny village in Kazakhstan until the party was over, for the safety of all humanity and *paien*-kind. I wouldn't have done any of that while in my right mind, but I did. Why do something so entirely and unnecessarily dangerous for no discernible reason that— Oh."

He stopped and stayed unmoving with a sudden bizarrely bright glitter to his gaze, identical to the light reflecting from a lens of a microscope or telescope. It could've been a sign of a sight beyond the rest of us. If you believed in signs. I didn't. I didn't care if Loki begged or Robin blackmailed. I didn't know, and I didn't want to know. I ran out of fucks the moment Nik said I was going to Goodfellow's party if he had to tie me up and toss me through the door announcing me as a stripper who wore his bondage gear instead of carrying it.

One thing I did know that while we stood here that someone out in the party was eating the last of the sausage appetizers and that was torture. Sheer fucking torture.

Goodfellow blinked once and the unnatural shine was gone. "Ah ... I see it now. I see all the ways and all the paths, the why and wherefore. That was one I didn't see coming. Nor did I see it going." He shook his head. "That is going to be extraordinarily ..." He laughed. "No, that *was* extraordinarily fascinating."

He briskly clapped his hands together once as he turned

to Loki. "What is done is done, however it is done. Here's a hint. It was done by me, therefore it was done brilliantly. Now, back to reality as we know it. Loki, I do know I had you sign a vow of no killing inside my penthouse. And you *did* sign it, with the blood of you and Fenrir, making it legally binding among your pantheon. Not that it matters. A simple nod from you would've been binding to me."

"I did not break it." The swirls had disappeared from the god's skin and he had sounded much more calm, less violent, not as interested in animating my guts to eat me from the inside out. With a smooth face and that long hair twisted into a black braid, he stood motionless to the point of not breathing but with his body tense enough that he was coiled for action. If he'd had a goatee he would've vaguely reminded me of Nik's evil and opposite-colored twin.

"To whom do you think you are speaking, Lie-smith? Tell me, can you be a lie-smith without a semibelievable lie ready on your tongue? I don't think you can." Robin sighed as if lamenting the unadulterated quantity of naiveté present in this existence that would have a trickster attempt to deceive *the* Trickster. Pivoting to his right, he lifted an entire bottle of wine from a server's tray with a thief's touch. Unnoticed and unseen by the waiter. He didn't have to. It was his wine, but he said once you're at your peak and lose your touch, you'll never reach the top again.

Facing Loki again, he took a swallow straight from the bottle. Robin was richer than fucking God, but he'd lived a hundred thousand years before bottles were created. "Yes, I annoy you with my constant rampaging virility" — he passed the bottle to the Norse god who took a long drink after a resigned groan — "and my love of reminding all about it, sending you pictures of it with my phone now that humans eventually invented something worthwhile, irritating with my never-ending tales of adventure and war, and causing you rampant envy over the franchise of whorehouses I owned in early Rome. And it is a bright moment in a boring morning when I turn on the TV and discover you're furious enough with me for sleeping with your ex-wife and your daughter in a very kinky three-some, enough so that you're tearing down an entire mountain in one impossibly large avalanche." He took the bottle back for another swallow. "That made up for the lightly underdone crepes I had for that breakfast. That cook has to go—out the door or to Salome and Spartacus as a cat toy. But, back on track, do keep that up, the bitching and destruction. But . . .

"Do *not* lie to *this* liar."

The voice was inhuman. I couldn't scrape up anything in my brain to compare it against. It simply wasn't human, inhuman, animalistic. It came from a place that was not here, where gods above other gods above other gods played dice for the fate of the universe.

Robin was my height, a few inches under six feet, but I'd have sworn then he stood above us, a towering idol hungry for sacrifice. "You forget that I am the Trickster Second, born of Hob the Trickster First. You are a god with the power of chaos linking your existence into a tangible mass. You were born of chaos, you *are* living chaos, but you were not born a trickster. Trickery was not in you. You chose it. You wrestled with it, seized it, and finally humbled yourself and invited it into you."

Taking one last swallow of the wine, a drop of crimson smudged his lower lip. He ran a finger over it, studied the dark scarlet streak, and then placed his finger to the middle joint in his mouth to suck his skin clean. It wasn't sexual in any way, shape, or form, and Goodfellow is *always* sexual in any way, shape, or form. He could pass out drunk in a ditch wearing a clown costume and spooning a lipstick, fake eyelash wearing donkey and the son of a bitch would somehow, someway make it into *Playgirl* magazine as the Sexiest Man of the Decade centerfold with that precise picture in it.

That this wasn't aimed at being sex incarnate was freaky as fuck. That it was the opposite—a god above Loki's list of them—a god who craved sacrifice, blood, and lives was bizarrely atypical, too, I admit, but, knowing Goodfellow, the sex thing was actually more so.

"I won't deny you're an excellent trickster, little wolf,

little snake, slippery fish," Robin said, lazy and unsettling the shit out of me, with the boredom I hadn't seen in him before. Naturally I'd seen him bored, normally bored the same as everyone can get, and I knew beneath his happy-go-orgy-it-up mask he wore, he had to be unbelievably bored at times as long as he'd lived. This, though, to not simply know it, but to see it. To witness what his life had been and the parts that lingered still when he was one of those among the first on the world—with nothing yet to do and no one yet any fun to trick.

And hundreds of thousands of years to wait for any of that.

How the hell he'd survived that, I didn't know. I wouldn't have.

Robin placed the empty bottle on the marble table. "You're one of the best, of the *self-made* tricksters. You do your best to forget that, don't you? But you, Silver-tongue, Sky-traveler, Lie-smith, were not birthed among our kind. And if you had been, it would make no difference. You still would not be *me*." He didn't say it with a vicious bite. He said it as an undisputed truth is said, plain and simple, and that made it worse. "Trickery is fickle." He placed a firm finger in Loki's chest. "Oh so very fickle. It's your guest now. It lives within you as it finds you interesting, but it is not an innate part of you. More than merely that, as it is not part of you, not born within you, I can take it away."

Holy shit. He could do that? I had then started thinking seriously of buying Robin a new bidet to replace the one I had shot . . . and maybe send an "I'm sorry. Please don't rip my ability to piss out of me" Strip-o-gram.

"You would not." Would not—not *could* not. That was the problem with being a liar. You couldn't lie to yourself, Loki included.

"Hob is gone. I am First now. You would never have the desire to lie, steal, manipulate, con, or trick again. You'd still have chaos, which is its own kind of party, but once you've been a trickster, you have little desire to live as anything else. You know that. Don't be an impossibly stubborn bastard. Let this go. I did it. It was essential.

Believe that I would not have put Caliban and you face-to-face if it weren't. No trick would be worth that." Goodfellow exhaled and instantly he was himself again, smirking and losing the heavily laden presence that demanded you throw your firstborn at his wrathful feet. "Look how long you hated me and now we coexist in blissful irritation and ire. If you survive me, you can survive Cal."

He had removed his finger from Loki's chest and patted it lightly. "Cal threw the first punch, but I know that was only because he was taught his entire life that self-defense has no timeline. If you fight fair, an oxymoron if ever there was one, if you wait for your turn, then you won't survive. And I've no doubt it was self-defense with your temper and hatred of the Auphe reaching such heights that you'd risk breaking a blood oath to kill one." He snatched another bottle of passing wine and emptied at least half before using it to point me out.

"I know as well you're not blind enough to think he is a true Auphe. His father was one and his mother human. He is half of one and half the other, but neither at the same time. He is something old and something new and something unlike anything on this earth." He flashed me a grin at the often repeated in-joke. "And he fears no gods, past, present, and future." There was an odd emphasis on that last sentence. "Do you, Caliban?"

He didn't give me a chance to answer although I thought having tried to kill Loki was a good enough answer. "He is more a victim of the Auphe than anyone else in history. He also destroyed the entire race ... with a little assistance, but at the end of it all, with or without help, he was the only one who could end them. And he did," he said with an awe none of us had lost to this day. We had defeated the Auphe Nation. "He *ended* them all."

He waved both hands, but didn't lose a single drop of his precious wine. "Loki, send Caliban a fruit basket for destroying those you hated most outside your own family. Now, go. Mingle. I invited an incredibly sexy *kitsune* with you in mind. She just earned her ninth tail, ascending to goddess status. A trickster god and goddess? Think of *that* sex. They'll feel it all the way over in Japan. I've four bedrooms. Feel free to destroy them all."

Loki hadn't moved right away, instead looking at me, then *through* me. I felt it, a touch of crop-killing frost that radiated doubt ... but a little curiosity too. "The Auphe, you killed them, to the last? And know as the god of lies, it's a given I will know if you do not tell the truth."

It had been as Robin had said ... I had killed them all, but not alone. It had taken his and Niko's help, but as I'd died twice to do it, it was truth enough right now. "I did. Like any beaten lab created mutt, I bit the hand that made me. However much you hated them, I hated them more. My only regret is they didn't suffer a thousand times over, but they did suffer." I had grinned at the memories. It was a grin too Auphe to be human, too human to be Auphe.

"So does that happy thought of my Auphe genocide melt the glacier up your ass?" I added with a curled mockery of a smile.

Loki's high-class, superior accent had vanished to be replaced with one more appropriate for whatever con Robin mentioned that he was working in Vegas. It was deeper and a shade more touched with sandpaper. He suddenly smelled of the desert and crappy buffets too as he scowled at me, then transferred it to Goodfellow before trying for a bargain. "Let me kill him. The bastard has no sense of self-preservation. I'd be doing Darwin's work. He's a suicidal obnoxious shit. I'll snatch the spear from Odin's feeble, filthy, syphilitic hand and make you king. You're conceited enough to think you're one as it is. I'll make it true. I'll give you Valhalla as a vacation home and all the Valkyries your horny, groping self can handle. Just let me kill the son of a bitch."

Robin's smile was as sly as they all were. "Like I could not have all that if I wanted without your help. Yes, roll your eyes. Very befitting a god. One last thing. It's the entire reason you're here, both of you." He seized one hand from both of us and slammed them together. "Clasp, grasp, shake, pick a time period. You are here to meet each other. Caliban, the Unmaker of the World and Reaper of the

Firstborn, now he has become Death, destroyer of the Auphe, greet Loki, the Destroyer of All Worlds, the Alpha and Omega that is Ragnarok, now he has become Death, the destroyer of existence in its infinite forms. You've met. You will respect each other and remember, Loki, qualities you admire in Caliban, such as Auphe genocide and biologically inventive ways of killing, and, you, Caliban, with your enjoyment of widespread chaos and destruction the same as a toddler enjoys fingerpainting every square inch of freshly painted white walls. No one is better at chaos and destruction than Loki. You are now comrades-in-arms. This is not optional. If you forget this, I'll make certain you have no arms left to be comrades with anyone. They are decent arms. I could get a good price for them."

His grip on our hands that was holding them together was . . . yeah . . . painful as hell.

Squeezing tighter, for emphasis no doubt, he then let us go, took his phone out of his suit jacket, and snapped a picture of Loki and me basically holding hands as neither of us could decide between the clasp, grasp, or shake. Or unbend our fingers yet as Goodfellow had done his best to break them.

"*Skata*, could you be more adorable? Caliban with his shocked expression and nearly drooling air of catatonia. Loki with an absolutely blank expression as empty of thought that I've only previously seen its equal on Thor—and is that the trace of a tear? No? Watery eyes? I didn't know gods had allergies. This will be my Saturnalia card this year. Check your e-mail. The two of you are cute as fluffy brain-dead puppies. But don't forget. Fight again and I sell your arms on the black market."

He'd then turned Loki and pushed him into motion in the opposite direction, muttering, "And we're mingling. No killing. Mingling. Let's find you that fox-spirit before Thor stumbles over her, gropes her tails, and puts her off gods forever, never mind she is one now."

That had been the end of the party mostly, except for Thor puking on my shoes, gallons and gallons of it, too projectile to escape, and that was one time I did not exaggerate. Gods' stomachs, unlike tanker trucks, had no limits. I did have limits though and that had been one. I'd decided then and there that gods were above my pay grade and I didn't want to see one again as long as I lived.

The end except for one small, tiny issue.

Niko had crossed paths with Loki and it was a trashy talk show special of twin brothers separated at birth. They'd met when the *kitsune* couldn't be found and ended up confiscating Goodfellow's huge spread of coffee table, cleaning it to an immaculate empty space with a casually intimidating sweep of Nik's katana. Sitting on the couch, they'd put their heads together in deep discussion while pointing at various points on the marble. Every time one of them did, a small spot of glowing color lit up ... red, blue, green, purple ... too many to count. I hadn't been interested. I'd played this game with Niko before. My brother was having a good time, and it was my turn to find the same.

Going to clean my boots of whatever had been in Thor, internal organs included I didn't doubt, I'd found the *kitsune* drying off her fox tails in one of the bedroom master baths—despite being a Japanese trickster spirit, she hadn't had any idea about the bidet obsession either. And Goodfellow had been right: Sex with a trickster spirit turned goddess was ... *damn*. What she could do with those tails ... If I was capable of getting it up in the next *year* I'd be surprised.

Later, Robin had come up to me as I sat on the floor in a corner with an entire sliced sausage platter resting on my legs and my gun beside me to shoot anyone who was suicidal enough to try for a single sliver of one. He was paler than usual. "What's up?" There was concern in my voice and the way I curved my arm protectively around my food platter, just not concern for him.

He'd crouched beside me and answered, "Your brother"—paused to massage his temples as if that aneurysm had finally burst—"your *brother* has strategized with Loki and come up with a battle plan that will allow Loki to be the victor at *Ragnarok*." He lowered his voice to a whisper, looking around us with rapid glances to make sure he wasn't overheard. "And it will *work*."

I tried to laugh and ended up choking on the appetizer or five I had in my mouth. After I'd managed to get it all down, I coughed, finally saying, "When I was a kid, Nik found some stupid 'take over the known world' board game at the Salvation Army from, shit, decades before we were born. He made me play it with him a thousand times. 'To sharpen my strategy and tactics.' I was in the fourth grade for Christ's sake." I dove for another piece of sausage. "But I'm twenty-six now and he still has that mold-covered piece of crap in our closet. He breaks it out every month. I've never won a single game in my life, not exactly a challenge for anyone much less Niko, but it's his drug of choice."

I had leaned backward, tilting my head back to rest my head against the wall. Looking up the necessary few inches for the perfect angle to see Robin's expression. I had known it would be a good one and it was. "Niko was Achilles, Alexander the Great, Arturus, Hannibal, and more. You know. You were there. He didn't ride along with history, he *made* it."

I smirked. "And you invited him to this party. You let him know Loki was a guest. Loki who starts the battle of Ragnarok, so infamous that *I've* heard of it and we all know I can't be bothered to read up on or remember shit. Then you turned your back on them for a second and didn't expect this?"

I flicked his forehead, unable not to gloat some after the years of smug conceit I'd endured, laid on thick and deep the way only a puck could. "Not as smart as you imagine, are you? You were the one who told us the stories about the good old days. Of who we were, what we did. Of how Nik had a hobby of taking over the world. Repeatedly. Loki has a hobby of ending it . . . mostly. Put the two of them together and naturally they'd figure out how to have both the battle *and* keep the world in one piece to rule it. Some trickster you are."

Laughing, I mocked, "Sac up. Loki's your friend, acquaintance, a person he knows—in the sense that he doesn't hate you with everything in him and hasn't killed you yet. I'm sure when 'the Twilight of the Gods' comes, he'll let you hang out, eat, drink, and won't remember at all you threatened to strip him of his trickster status, talent, and *arms*, not swords or daggers, his physical fucking arms." I yawned and reached for more sausage before advising. "Just stay away from the stables. I hear bad things happen there when you can't resist a horny stallion."

I'd gone home later with a black eye that hurt like hell. Goodfellow could throw a punch. My ordinarily stoic brother—he'd been closer to a kid at Christmas than he'd ever been in his entire life. I slung an arm over his shoulder and he elbowed me in the ribs, big brother to little brother, when I'd said Loki would have to crown him queen for his contribution to the planned coup. He'd elbowed me a second time for talking trash about his new favorite god, and then kept on spinning out the plans for Ragnarok, his words tumbling over one another. This was my brother who thought one word was babbling as the minimal raise of an eyebrow was communication enough. He'd said it was something he hadn't believed at first. Norse gods or any god, but with Loki . . . *the* Loki—with Ragnarok, he was a true believer. Converted. It was an experience he swore he wouldn't forget.

He didn't have to worry about that. Forgetting . . .

As two weeks later he was dead.

6

"How much of that story did you leave out?" Niko questioned.

Long story, a memory both only weeks behind me and yet a long time to come. I'd stopped walking, caught in the flash of the heat of that fire, the knowledge that crumbling ash was all that was left of my brother. I closed my eyes, took several deep breaths and gave myself a fiercely hard inner shake to refocus on *when* I was right now. To concentrate on what I had to do to stop an inferno....

Eight years before it happened.

This Niko, not mine—no, he was waiting for an answer. And this Cal ... if Loki thought I'd been an obnoxious, suicidal little shit at twenty-six, what would he think of this version of me eight years younger? I'd be willing to go a round of rock, paper, scissors on which of us held him down and which of us beat the shit out of him. Tapping one hand with first and middle finger spread in a V on top of a round fist must've had an air of cagy enthusiasm around it as Cal was currently watching me with fixed and frozen suspicion.

I put my hands back in my pockets. "Jesus. Give me a second."

I'd left out the gating—they couldn't know that before it happened to this Cal. That could screw up everything in a hundred different ways. I hadn't said Goodfellow's name or that he was a puck and trickster, no mention of killing all the Auphe, of my eyes turning red, or reincarnation. Holy hell, definitely not the reincarnation. *I* was boggled about that at least once a week despite it being six months after that revelation. I'd text Nik a few times when he was teaching history or at the dojo—few, several, every week when the revelation blew up in my brain on no particular schedule. We developed a shorthand. I'd text him: schizophrenic?? He'd text back: Not today. Try again tomorrow. It worked for us.

Counting them up in my head, I was certain that I'd managed to keep the important parts, buried and silent. "How much did I leave out? About three-fourths? To keep the future safe, leaving out seventy-five . . . eighty, ninety-five percent at most isn't unreasonable. And trust me, if you knew what I know, you'd prefer my math." I wanted to shrug, but I was stiff and aching from being thrown against the asphalt in the explosion. It had been hours ago, for me, only hours . . . it was close to unfathomable. I was tired too, exhausted enough to have to concentrate to keep from stumbling once I started walking again. The *Kyntalash* was treating me like a D battery when I was thinking I was a AAA at best.

"Sounds like all one big lie to me. You—and I don't give a shit about your 'superior-practice-makes-perfect' knife skills—you took on Loki, god of Chaos, with what? A gun and some lame trash talk?" Cal scoffed, not impressed and equally not convinced.

Had I looked that perpetually pissy all the time? Did I still? I snapped a quick picture of him with my phone and then of myself while still walking. Flipping back and forth between them, I muttered a few Greek curse words picked up from Robin under my breath and then deleted the shots. That was a truth that didn't need documenting for anyone to find. And it was badass, not pissy, I assured myself silently.

Bad. Ass.

"It was prime trash talk and I shot a god in the dick six times. Not to mention the fish eggs. You can weaponize that crap." Without gating, surviving Loki long enough for Goodfellow to intercede was part of the ninety percent ... ninety-five ... whatever ... that the CIA would label redacted. Need to know and no one needs to know who doesn't already.

Junior dismissed the entire thing with an identical lack of interest in gods that I had. "How about something more important than parties and fucking finger food? Like, I don't know, how are we going to find this bastard who's trying to kill me? Isn't that what you're supposed to be here for? The keeping me alive thing?" he snapped. "Although I have to say if killing me erases you from the future, I have all the sympathy in the world for whoever it is because you are one massive asshole."

Again with "asshole." He was getting monotonous as hell with that. I was going to work on expanding my profanity and vulgarities, if I survived. This was what people or *paien* heard from me two seconds before I made them *dead* people or *dead paien*? I was embarrassed for myself. It was humiliating that I didn't do better, try harder. I took my insults almost more seriously than my executions.

I had been going to tell him stay away from gods. Every bad thing you've heard about them is true. But he wouldn't. Niko would, for now, always be too caught up in the wide wild world of mythology and Cal would be at his side as I had been. No need to try to change that. We'd survived my brother's curiosity, and, for putting up with me, he'd more than earned his hobby/avocation.

Nik, my Nik, who hadn't stopped being an endlessly questioning bastard from the day he'd read his very first word. Hadn't stopped and wouldn't have if not for me. I tore the memory to confetti for more than one reason and let the pieces drift away.

Instead of that advice, I flipped off toddler me and

moved on. "Everyone tries to kill us sooner or later. We're not a popular guy. I'll get to the specifics of who this particular time when we're off the street. I'm tired, my head is killing me, the *Kyntalash* is draining what energy I had left and every single word you say is a finger poking a hole in my brain, turning it into Swiss cheese. Now shut up for five fucking whole minutes and let this kick in." I shook an empty bottle of Tylenol I took from my pocket. "Unless you want me to tell you every detail about Nik's future sex life. I do his laundry—"

"His sex life?" Cal smirked. "Wait. Here's something I *want* to hear. You do his laundry. Every time? I don't do his laundry except as a birthday present and you're Mr. Badass from a fabric softener future. Pathetic."

"Hell, yeah, I do. He cooks, when I don't order in. He still spars with me when I say I've gotten as good as it gets. Let's let this go. He tells me I'm wrong and I am. I get better all the time, which keeps me alive. He keeps the rest of the place clean. He does it all and he's my big brother. My lazy ass owes him everything. So, yeah, I do the laundry . . . but not because of that."

I shot a confused Niko an amused glance. "I do it because one time after years and years of me living happily in my pigsty, Nik lost it. He was coming down the hall, looked at my room same as a thousand times before, but this time, for no reason, nothing new or changed, he lost his fucking mind. No monster in the world could break him, but my room did. By the time I heard him from outside where I was dumping the trash and ran back in, he was cursing me in languages I don't think *exist*. He'd sprayed lighter fluid on the mess in my room, which, bad luck for me, is *everything* in my room and had just thrown in a match."

Fortunately, a year before he'd made me keep my weapons and ammo out in the sparring area since if I needed it in an emergency situation, in my room I'd never find it.

"Buying a new mattress, cleaning out the Salvation Army to replace my clothes, sneakers, combat boots, but couldn't do anything about the one hundred and fifty issues of classic porn gone forever. Once was enough. Now I do his laundry and he doesn't burn down my room—as long as I keep the door shut so he can't see it." Then I concluded Cal's lesson in shutting up with a threat as nasty and god-awful as I currently felt. "I wash his sheets. He's the boy toy of a very wealthy woman with, from what I can tell, an incredibly demanding sex drive. I'm a scratch-and-sniff story at your disposal."

I leaned toward him and growled. "Now . . . shut . . . up."

"You—" I'd never been one for shutting up and I'd forgotten how much worse I'd been at eighteen.

"Fine." I shrugged. "Your fucking funeral. Your big brother who raised you all your life, your perfect brother you don't only love but *worship* like a god deep down inside though you don't let it slip. So you're dying to know how a diet of carrot and wheatgrass juice makes his jizz smell on the sheets—"

"Shutupshutupshutupshutupshut—"

But I could be taught at that age, it seemed, if the method was traumatic enough, I thought, as satisfied as I could manage, considering why I was here. A hand covered both of our mouths from where Niko had slid up behind us. "I think we should all be quiet until we are home or I may set both of you, not your rooms, no, but the two of *you* on fire. I have a growing headache of my own." Smart man, he didn't begin to trust us on silence. He kept our mouths covered until we were in sight of their building.

Cal was speaking before Niko had a chance to wipe the saliva from his hand on his younger brother's jackets. "Thanks, you dick." He raised a hand as if to shove me.

I grinned and taunted in a good mom's singsong introduction, "Once upon a time . . ."

That apparently made him think I might finish that story if pushed and instead of going with physical violence, he bit off, "You've just ruined any hope of my having a sex life ever," Cal complained. "After that, I don't want to touch my own dick and I will never let anyone else within fifty feet of it. Let the assassin kill me. I have no reason to live."

"Get over it, King of Emo. Sooner or later you'll get laid, stop buying pornographic comic books, and cancel your monthly delivery of vats of zit cream, you whiny virgin." I went on in picture-perfect innocence to give him a tip. "And by the way, jacking off with gun oil not only ups your psycho sex-killer quotient, but it gives you a rash that is embarrassing as hell to explain to the nurse at the free clinic."

"I do *not*—" I raised my eyebrows. He could lie to anyone, including Niko though that was uncommon and more uncommon that we pulled it off, but he couldn't lie to me about my own unfortunate and embarrassing past. He switched tactics, proving we did have an ounce of self-preservation.

No matter what my new BFF Norse god had said about Cals in general.

The apartment Niko and Cal lived in now and I'd lived in years ago was within walking—running, to be more accurate—distance of Talley's, which had almost saved my life once. You've got to love the "almost" there, but I said nothing aloud. That nightmarish experience was at least a year yet to come and if we changed anything about that at all, all worlds would die, not just mine.

Several blocks from the bar, lights were strobing on police cars. They were parked in front of the alley I'd stepped out of from the future into the past, the dark into the light. Nik and JV Cal gave it an uninterested look with Cal grumbling, "Shitty neighborhood," and both kept moving. And it was. There could be any reason why the alley would have cops swarming, but there was a tickle at the base of my brain. I didn't . . . not for a moment or two, then . . .

Oh yeah.

That incompetent crackhead junkie asshole, who hadn't cared I'd been thrown back eight years through a blaze of light as strange and bright as a solar flare. He either didn't give a shit or, craving a fix so badly he didn't realize reality had twisted itself enough to dump me practically in his lap. A man with priorities, he ignored what should've looked like magic to him or an impossible manipulation of physics to anyone smarter—he'd merely jumped from his bed in a pile of garbage and tried to slit my throat. Priorities in plenty, skill, however, that he lacked five ways to fucking Sunday.

"Bad neighborhoods do make for great training grounds," I replied carelessly. "And the dead guy murdered people. Murdered kids. Killed them for drugs. No loss."

"How do you know that?" Cal questioned, his suspicion making a return in the twitch of his fingers toward the weapons concealed in his own leather jacket.

I shrugged and tapped my nose with a mocking curl of my lips. "You've got one skill"—that would change—"Wee Willy Wonka. Use it."

He took a deep breath and I saw the moment the co-agulation of hours-long death, the drugs released through every pore of the chemical-soaked body, the blood not of the addict alone, but the older blood on his knife and clothes. Blood of other people. The men, women, and children—too many to count. "That's why I couldn't smell the Grendel in you in the bar," he said, it hitting him suddenly. "Because you smell like me."

Then he tacked on with resentment in every tense line of his body. "And the Wonka shit is worse than Junior. I will kill you in your sleep, I swear to fucking God. I'll shove Nik's feather pillow so far down your throat that if you survive, you'll shit an entire flock of live geese the next day."

I nodded. Expecting a threat and not bothered by it, approving if forced to admit it—it wasn't "asshole" and that was an improvement. But . . . holy shit, I'd always been a dick, hadn't I? Made me want to give myself a proud pat on the back. "Like we ever had feather pillows," I dismissed, avoiding a crack in the sidewalk wide and deep enough to swallow me whole. "Everything in Niko's room, once we started making more money a few years from now by . . . ah . . . an occupation you'll find out . . . everything Niko owned was . . . is hypoallergenic.

If they sold surgically sterile pillows at our local store, he'd have had those."

Good threat though. If I survived this, I was ripping off that one and several others for the future. It wasn't stealing. Can't steal from yourself, right?

"And, yeah, it's the same reason you didn't recognize my voice," I affirmed. "No one recognizes their own voice." I could see my old apartment/converted warehouse one block down. It was the same and nothing like I remembered. Memories are strange like that.

But it didn't make me forget Cal. The goose insult had been a good one, worthy of swiping, but despite that, he was going to pay for it. What could I say? I held grudges against nearly everyone, myself included.

Equal opportunity son of a bitch, that was me.

I went on to add, offhand as I could get without caring a damn how fake it came off, "Not recognizing my smell I get. I do. But why you didn't notice I was armed, heavily and noticeably to all but the blind, I put down to you being a lazy, cocky little shit. Cockier than you have any reason to be."

"And you're not?" His glares were becoming frequent enough I feared for our future eyesight.

"I'm not cocky. I'm legitimately that good, but no changing the subject." I pointed up at nothing in particular, but if we'd been standing in the bar, it was where that fragment of mirror would be. "It doesn't matter if you look up at Talley's security mirror and don't see a gun already out. I'm carrying four guns, I won't count the knives, and you didn't catch scent of the metal on any of them. I could've put two bullets in the back of your head before you could drop the glass you were cleaning. A double tap special that Talleywhacker would've named a drink after to up the bar's business.

"What comes through the door doesn't need white hair and red eyes or to smell like a werewolf to be dangerous," I moved on, tone reasonable. I wasn't saying anything that wasn't true. Cal thought he was dangerous, but he'd never met what he would become. And there were things out there more lethal than me at eighteen or twenty-six, whether he knew about them or not. I'd been stupid at his age to think differently. Thinking life wasn't that hard to lose unless it was an Auphe coming through the door was his assumption, one that could've gotten us killed. I could've gotten him killed. That wasn't a lie. I was older, more skilled, and could've killed him quicker than a snap of the fingers.

That we'd survived our first years in New York had been ninety-five percent skill. Easy was the farthest description from what the reality had been. The other five percent had been pure luck. I knew it was a part of our survival, as I knew Nik and I shouldn't have lived through what we had—with the help of a trickster or not. The last thing I needed was my younger self believing that simply staying alive would be a walk in the park with monsters throwing rose petals at his fucking feet. He had to earn his future in order to *have* a future, and that meant fighting off death around every corner.

I flashed in front of Niko to pull one of Cal's guns, our favorite Desert Eagle, out of his jacket before either of the two could move. I flipped the trigger guard around my finger gunslinger style in a way that would have had my Nik slapping the back of my head and spraining my trigger finger fiercely enough to need a splint. As our lives became more dangerous, he'd become more and more imaginative with reminders that stupidity and showing off were death sentences.

Keeping it close enough to blend in to the black of my shirt and my own jacket, I flipped it again, forward, backward, forward again. Then grip first, I handed it back to Cal, his jaw tightened in a mixture of anger and reluctant vigilant caution. Except for his brother, it'd been two years since anyone had disarmed him. Lips tight and silent . . . for once, he holstered it in a subtle, close to invisible move that avoided the attention of the crowd milling at a fast pace around us.

"Aside from the assassin, there are plenty of other things out there that can kill you, Junior. And, unlike me, they will be happy as fucking hell to do it."

I gave him a Cheshire-crazed grin. Everyone knew that cat was crazy as hell and ate Alice before she ever made it out of Wonderland. Down to the bones and cracking them to suck out the marrow.

As fortune would have it, that lesson was about to be proven in minutes.

7

He had his gun back, but Cal was struggling, caught between the obvious desire to break my nose or come up with an excuse to wipe the expression of unholy biblical wrath from Niko's face. Niko hadn't been pleased at all by what I'd spilled about Cal's slacking, suicidally sloppy ways. Cal made the best decision and went with the greater threat. "Nik, I . . ." He grimaced as he obviously scrambled for an excuse. I'd have felt bad for him if I hadn't been the one to throw him in the alligator pit to begin with. "The bar's mirror is crappy as hell. I'm lucky to tell if it's a human being or the Loch Ness goddamn Monster in that thing. Security measure, my ass."

"You're telling me that you couldn't spend three dollars on a new mirror to save your life? Is that what I'm to understand?" Nik's voice was smooth, the slippery silk I knew from the many times I'd screwed up with what he cared about most—his little brother's life. My life.

"Didn't smell the gun oil either," I added in the true giving spirit for which I was known. Completely constructive criticism, not a small revenge for my douche bag younger self's shitty attitude and lack of appreciation that I'd traveled eight damn years to save his life. That it was my life as well . . . not the point.

"You shithe—"

Niko rode over the top of him without pause. "Cal, why am I training you to survive if—"

I ignored them both. There was something else to concentrate on. The door to the apartment building was broken as I recalled. I pushed it aside, the metallic screech more of a scream, and stepped inside. The building itself was a helluva lot more dilapidated and filthy. It wasn't surprising I hadn't wasted brain cells remembering that. Up until about two more years, dilapidated and filthy was the standard curbside-appeal description of every place we'd ever lived, from childhood on. It didn't matter. Nik had always done his best to keep the inside of where we lived as clean as humanly possible. I could live with dirt and despair that leaked out of the hallway beyond the door. I'd survived worse. I'd survived this same building in fact. I could live in it again for a few days if I had to.

What I didn't want to live with was the lamia and her *rusalka* roommate one flight up—you could have your blood drained or you could be drowned in a half-inch puddle of NYC dank gathered on the floor, choose carefully. There was also a wendigo in the basement and the *yee naaldlooshii* four floors up. I rubbed a hand roughly across my face, but I knew it didn't wipe away the disappointment that I aimed at both Cal and Niko, interrupting their squabbling. "I don't remember us being this stupid, but the both of you are plenty damn naive, that's for damn sure."

It wasn't fair of me, not really. At eighteen I'd had the scenting abilities of an Auphe, partially—I didn't hit Auphe full-on puberty until nineteen and despite that it had taken a few more years to get the full package. It also didn't help that at eighteen I knew only Auphe/Grendels, Wolves, and vampires by scent. I hadn't run into any lamias, *rusalka*s, the rest—that I knew of—to store in my memory. I hadn't known they existed, much less lived in my building. Yeah, the building smelled funky, but most buildings in New York I had business in weren't anywhere close to swimming in perfume. We should've recognized a general nonhuman taint to the air, true, but . . . it was over and done. For me anyway, but I'd managed to screw that up for him. I let the irritation melt away. He was a kid and I'd been a kid, neither of us with the information we'd needed at the time.

"Lamia, *rusalka*, wendigo." I pointed the general location of the less-than-humans out for them without leaving the stairs I'd hit after covering the few feet of hall and kept heading up them flight by flight to the apartment I'd once lived in. "And best of all, a *yee naaldlooshii*. Normally I'd say leave them alone as they didn't notice us before, not at eighteen. Your blood, Cal, can still pass for human to anyone without a nose that'd put a bloodhound to shame, like a Wolf." However, the older I'd become the sharper my own Auphe signature became—in my blood, skin, every part of me—to *paien* who depended on their own scenting skills to hunt.

Auphe late puberty—it had been a bitch. "But I can't. They'll know I'm here, if they don't already. You can threaten or kill them later." *Rusalka* were usually reasonable enough, particularly if you treated them to fresh fish once a month. "It's your choice on those three. But we don't have the time for minnows when we have a shark to catch."

"*Yee naaldlooshii*, 'he who goes on all fours,' they are real? Lamia, *rusalka*, and wendigos are real?" Niko already had a hand on his katana to draw it from its sheath strapped to his back and hidden under his long leather coat.

God, how had we ever survived to even this age?

"Niko, if Norse gods are real, what in the whole fucking wide world wouldn't be?" Me. The voice of reason. It was so wrong. "And you're getting a little repetitive."

"What's a *yee naaldlooshii*?" Cal demanded. He mutilated the pronunciation as much as I had the first time we'd encountered one. And the second time. After the fourth one, I'd gotten the hang of it.

"A *yee naaldlooshii* became the legend of a skin-walker, but the legend is off. Way the fuck off. They're three or four monsters for the price of one. The very least of the problems with them is that they have excellent vision and a better sense of smell. It probably caught my scent when we were still a block away."

"I'm guessing they don't like Grendels," Cal said without much surprise, a little winded, but not much. Niko's exercise program at work.

"Ninety-nine percent of *paien* don't like Grendels," I said, the wicked smirk in my words if not on my face. "But seventy-five percent are scared shitless of them. We've had a lot of fun with the shitless part, I promise."

"And the *yee naaldlooshii*?" Niko, forever the voice of reason.

"You can't have it all, Cyrano." The nickname was out before I could stop it, but I pretended not to notice the slip and kept moving.

The three of us rushed up the last several flights of stairs until we hit the seventh and top apartment of the converted warehouse. Cal was pulling out four keys to the apartment door. He didn't need them. It was open, the slightest crack, but enough to let us know. We could back off and let it come to us, but there was less room to fight in the hall than the place we'd gotten cheap for its size. Unfinished except for unreliable plumbing, the size, and the huge round window that nearly covered one entire wall had the lack of anything else that made apartments livable more than worth it.

In a year we'd find out how much of a mistake that window was.

But for me that was over and done. I was better off surviving the waiting skin-walker. "It's inside," I said, unnecessarily, not bothering to lower my voice. There was no point. He heard me probably before I'd entered the building. I knew he could hear me breathing through a half-open door. We all moved through the doorway, one at a time, fast and agile enough that to a human it would've appeared all three of us entered at one time — but cautious enough to have a hope of avoiding anything waiting just inside. The kids were somewhat impressive there, but what was more impressive was they didn't look shaken that the *yee naaldlooshii* was already there waiting for us, not out of breath, acting bored we'd taken so long. They were fast. I always forgot how unbelievably quick, but I'd seen them before. This Cal and Niko hadn't . . . or hadn't known what it was or viewed it in action.

He was the landlord. Another thing I'd forgotten. You didn't tend to remember random people in the city. You saw too many humans and humans . . . hated to break the news, they weren't a threat, except for the Vigil. If you weren't a threat, you weren't worth paying attention to. This one though, he should've been an exception, memorable if we'd been lucky enough for him to be nothing but human. I hadn't known he was a skin-walker then, but he was one helluva big guy. Huge. A massive figure, practically a tank covered with flesh, dark reddish bronze skin, and perfectly white, square teeth a little too large to be normal. I could've written them off as oversize dentures. I honestly didn't remember, had never suspected a thing. Hell, I'd even brought the guy leftover half-full pony kegs of beer from the bar to knock a few bucks off our rent.

If we didn't have a good chance of dying at the claws, fangs, and venom of the skin-walker, I would've taken the time to knee my younger self in the balls for being so oblivious. But then I'd have to let him do the same to me. At this particular age, he and I had been one in the same—I couldn't blame him without blaming myself. And the dying, claws, fangs, and venom, it did put a cramp in all that. Too bad as he and I both undeniably deserved it.

The skin-walker was about six-eight, six-nine, looked around forty-five in human years but with the wide physique and thick musculature of a man fifteen years younger. Not that guessing in human years did any good. He could be a thousand years old for all I knew. He had two shoulder-length iron gray braids, glittering dark eyes, and a deeply sun scarred face as creased and furrowed as a dry river bed. Dangling a loop of nearly sixty keys from his right hand, including the keys to this apartment—he was the landlord after all—he grunted, taking one more whiff of the air in my direction from where we had spread out, and then exhaled it with a snort steeped in disgust.

"I did not know, not on the younger one." His voice was desert sand blowing storm-hard over barren rock. Harshly unforgiving. "He is an impure mutt. Half predator, half prey, but an unripe thing, too, not yet grown. Not yet the hungry tooth, nor the eager claw. Not yet the eager taste for death, and blood. It confused, his smell too weak, too different." The dark eyes that were slowly reshaping to inhuman narrow ovals were fixed on me. "Not like this one."

That wasn't strictly true. Cal had been all those things once, in Tumulus when he'd run with the Auphe, but that was mentally. To the Auphe he'd been far from adult, five years at least. As they lived thousands of years, he was lucky it wasn't five hundred. But here was one positive thing about completely forgetting two years in that hell, about faking being human so well that you believed it. You made a skin-walker believe it too. Cal and I, we'd acted human at eighteen. Surly and grim, but human enough to fool ourselves and a skin-walker. Around people, we moved like a human, not too fast, not like the strike of a snake. We didn't bare our teeth in a threat to tear and bite. We smiled, not goddamn often, but if we had to. We didn't stab the hand of Meredith, the chick who worked at the bar with us, when she stole french fries from my take-out container. Our human suit was near perfect, couldn't even see the zipper. How we behaved around the Wolves and vamps was a different story, but with humans or who we thought were human, we pulled it off without fail.

Until now. I'd come backward in time in all my glory, late Auphe puberty come and gone. I was an adult, more or less, and while I wasn't an Auphe *or* a human, I had enough of the one ingredient strong enough for a *yee naaldlooshii* to think he knew what I was. In the end he wouldn't have cared if I had a single drop of Auphe blood in me. Skin-walkers are all about an excuse, any excuse, the judgmental psychopaths. That gave me the same thing . . . an excuse to kick his multitude of asses.

If only skin-walkers weren't such tricky bastards. If I was in top form, he'd still be a chore with the weapons I was limiting myself to. And I was tired, bruised, emotionally un-fucking-sound as they came and I didn't want to play. Not now. Top form was way out of reach.

Too bad for me.

Bare feet, dressed in loose, faded sweats, good for fighting, the *yee naaldlooshii* slithered, too broad-shouldered in build to be so lithe in movement as he was, past Cal and Niko with the speed of a rattlesnake. He used that speed to slam and lock the door behind us.

He turned then to face us again before Cal and Niko had made it more than halfway around, Cal pulling out a Glock and a Desert Eagle as he moved. The skin-walker was fast as hell, I gave him that, but I'd learned and progressed considerably since my first *yee naaldlooshii* and so was just as quick. He hissed, and not the human version of the sound, when he saw I wasn't like Niko and Cal. I was ready and facing him. The second membrane on his eyes flickered, unsettled, as I stared him in the face with challenge and exhaustion. Anger was too much trouble. "You sure we couldn't do this another time? I've got more important jackasses to deal with than a walking, talking zoo right now."

Uncertainty disappeared in the face of my smart mouth. I wasn't surprised. It had that effect often enough my tongue had been nicknamed Deathwish by Goodfellow when we'd gone on jobs. At least it gave Niko and Cal time to get in position with sword and guns drawn. Measuring me with scorn and disgust, the skin-walker mixed the high-whine buzz of a chilling rattle in dry grass with the sound of scales sliding over rock and dirt. "The younger is but a fetus. He needs to die, even if he knows not why, but I have time for that." The eyes of a pit viper focused on me. "But you—on you, I smell it. I see it. I hear it. I taste it." His tongue, forked, darted out to taste the air. He spat on the floor. "There is no mercy for you. You are Auphe. The first to walk this earth. The first to kill but not for food. The first to murder, not for sustenance, but for perverse pleasure alone."

"First of the perverse. Yeah, yeah. Like I haven't heard that more times than I could count," I responded, too familiar with the words to be offended anymore. "Give me time and I'll put it on a T-shirt."

Of the first, yes, but I hadn't been there millions of years ago. My ancestors, partially my genetics, but not me. I wasn't responsible for what they did. I wasn't Auphe as long and as ruthlessly as they'd tried to shape me into their image, mentally and physically. Not human, no, but not Auphe either—that assumption got annoying after a while. I was something altogether different.

Not that it mattered. Skin-walkers proclaim far and wide and proudly about their fierce sense of guardianship of who they considered their people. You found skin-walkers in many cultures, not solely Native American ones. That meant "their people" isn't necessarily a tribe, they could have come from across the ocean or up through South America and left those particular people behind hundreds of years ago. That didn't stop them from choosing new people wherever they settled. It had nothing to do with a skin-walker's pride or duty—they needed those people, any people. They weren't protecting their chosen ones.

They were defending their refrigerator.

If you had a skin-walker watching over you that meant you were part of their herd. A roaming pantry of goodies. There was enough for frequent if not daily fresh meals depending on where the walker set up shop and the people, a group of some sort to make it easier to keep an eye on if they clustered. They had enough in every case I'd seen to share with other walkers, but they wouldn't. They'd sooner fight to the death. It was one of those "I can eat you, but no one else can" romantic relationships. This skin-walker cared less that he thought I was Auphe and more that he thought I'd steal his living breathing snacks "grazing" on this block or five blocks. Only he knew.

"Auphe?" Cal asked. "What's an Auphe?"

Everything was going sideways. Fine. I'd tell them now instead of Goodfellow a year later. Shakespeare himself said it: What's in a name? "Grendels. *Paien* call Grendels Auphe. It's their real name."

Niko didn't have any interest in names currently. With his katana between him and the skin-walker, he slid sideways to get close enough to kick me sharply in the shin to get my attention. "He's nearly seven feet tall and broad as a barn, but not enough to hide a bear. A mountain lion?"

I laughed. I couldn't stop myself. "Remember ten seconds ago when I said the legend was way the fuck off?" I had crossed my wrists and tucked my hands inside of my jacket but hadn't pulled the guns out of their holsters yet. I wanted at least one surprise on our side to equal the two minimum the skin-walker was going to throw at us. He thought I was Auphe enough to fight their way, a thousand teeth and bladelike talons. He thought wrong. I wasn't equipped like that any longer. And the other good stuff, I couldn't show Nik and Cal. They would lose their shit, their minds, and any hope of taking this bastard down. "A mountain lion most likely, a bear is a long shot at best, but whatever it is, that will be only the first layer."

"First?" Nik said sharply. These were the days when we'd first begun to learn mythology books were ninety-nine point nine percent bullshit and gleefully wrong gossip spread by the supernatural, the *paien*, themselves. Why would they tell humans the truth, any truth, about them?

"First, yeah. You take it, Niko. What do you want, Mini Me? The rabid and fanged or the poisonous multitudes?"

Cal made a face, so goddamn young, at the last word: multitudes. I didn't blame him. It was more work, and no Cal, in any time period, liked work. "Rabid and fanged."

"I thought so," I complained, but not seriously or surprised. I'd have made the same choice.

That's when the landlord shed his human skin. It was

as if it was diseased and peeling away, but not like you'd think. Not human skin and flesh with a raw red meat beneath. It was more like a cocoon, with a milky fluid that coated bloodless gray-white pulpy tissue that had hidden under the human disguise. It bubbled, flowed, and hissed as it poured to the floor. It stank of all things venomous and poisonous. To the skin-walker, however, it was useless to him in this fight. It peeled away, wet and vile, taking his clothes, ravaged face, and thick hair with it. Out of it sprang, as predicted, a mountain lion— hallelujah it wasn't the bear. That was an all night's work if a bear was the outer layer, as then the next would be a mountain lion then . . . so on and so on.

Not that a mountain lion was five dollars, park your car, and done. The skin-walker kind were closer to skel- etons than anything else—if twice the size of a true mountain lion's dried carcass with bones twice as thick. You could hear weathered and molting fur-covered bones snap against one another as it moved. Every step sounded like a hundred breaking bones, but it didn't show any pain. Its eyes were a solid milky white as if it had stared at the desert sun for a year and a day, never blinking, but it wasn't blind. I had a years-old scar on my hip for assuming that.

It crouched and leaped over our heads before Cal could fire. I didn't bother. If he had killed it, and he wouldn't, it took more than bullets for the mountain lion, then its dead body would have still done the same as it was doing now. It was vomiting up, one after the other, six coyotes—if coyotes were demonic with glowing red eyes, legs three times as long, and twice as many teeth, four times as long, as any you'd see on a real one in the wild or urban-wild. They, too, were a framework of cov- ered bone with every movement a cracking sound that made you wince with the echo of the snapping of your own broken bones if you had ever had any. I did. We all did. It wasn't anything you wanted to hear again.

The coyotes in turn howled, a rasping death rattle wail nothing like a live, real coyote's song, and then they humped their backs, lowered their heads, and retched forth snakes and spiders. Three devoted to snakes, the other three to spiders. The snakes were rattlers drawn by a schizophrenic, wildly enthusiastic homicidal mental patient—dark gray on dirty black, three or four times the normal size, and with fangs half the length of my forearm, made of cloudy quartz veined in bloodred poison pulsing eagerly to be injected into flesh, and that was okay. It was. Toxin with a mind of its own. Snakes, giant poisonous zombie-style snakes. That they didn't slither sinuously, but moved as rapidly in a zigzag motion of sharp angles that was wholly unnatural, that wasn't new. No problem. I'd dealt with them before.

But then there were the spiders.

They were tarantulas, five, six times . . . yeah, forget that. It was better that I didn't estimate how much larger than normal they were. A good thing if I didn't dwell on the rivers of venom dripping from their pincers onto the floor as soon as they hit it, or how the floor was melting as if acid had been poured on it. I'd been on one job a few years ago in which I was attacked by four or five German Shepherd–sized spiders whose bite would either erase your memories or paralyze you until you died of asphyxiation . . . and that was only day one. By the time it was all over, there'd been so many of the damn hairy, giant monsters from the depths of the darkest parts of your subconscious that I lost count, killed enough to be voted exterminator of the century, and didn't want to see another one again. That was thanks to the amnesia. I went from "who am I?" and not checking under the bed for the bogeyman to "the world is full of evil, carnivorous monsters that used the bogeyman to floss their fangs and you kill them because the pay is better than the McDonald's drive-through wage." To add insult to injury, one of the spiders had also burst through a bathroom window while I was taking a piss and was armed with nothing but a maple-syrup covered fork.

I didn't like spiders.

The coyotes bared their teeth and gave an encore of their strangled and starved cackle of a howl again, the same as if the dying could howl to show us how hungry, ecstatic, and eager they were to drag us with them into the endless dark. Their red eyes bled tears of viscous black, thick as tar, a mocking mourning of our fate.

They shook their oversize rattles—each one the size of a newborn baby's skull—opened their mouths impossibly, flickered triple-forked tongues that should've been accompanied by a hissing enough to fill the apartment, but, unlike with the coyotes, we heard nothing. The rattles despite their whipping shake and the hissing, both, should've filled the air—but it didn't. With each *yee naaldlooshii* I fought, the snakes were as silent as if they carried a death shroud of choking, airless vacuum around them. For all their motion and aggressive threats, the worst was they gave nothing but the hush of the grave. And their eyes, the polished white of bone as their scales were the gray and black of decomposing flesh, showed how the quiet of the dead and buried was worse and more hopeless than any warning sound, hiss, howl, or the sizzle of venom.

It was creepy as fuck the first time I fought a skin-walker. And it stayed creepy as fuck with each one that followed.

There was worse than creepy though. There was dull. I'd been there and seen it all before, but, much as I hated to admit it, skin-walkers were never dull. Better than Netflix and unlimited satellite, no lie.

"What the hell?" Cal wasn't as enthused as he headed for higher ground, settling on top of the couch's back. "I've *never* seen anything like this on the Nature Channel," he said, sounding as betrayed as was possible at the fact. "Those lying motherfuckers."

The skin-walker was now going to see that he thought I was Auphe, but I was going to fight as a human. There was no reason to not shrug off my jacket for easy and quick access to my weapons, all of them. If I didn't have everything that counted in my life, the real one eight years out of reach, resting as a crushing weight on my shoulders, I would've laughed at Cal's outrage. A real laugh. None of the fakes I'd handed out since I arrived.

"Just wait a few years until an eighty pound spider tries to kill you in a bathroom and your only weapon is a fork. Now that buried the Nature Channel. I couldn't piss for an entire day after that." I paused and glanced toward the kitchen sink. It wouldn't do to leave anal-retentive Niko out of the fun. "Not in the bathroom anyway." I couldn't give away what was their future, but that was small and random enough not to be predicted or to matter if it was. And it was worth it to see the expression of distaste mixed with a touch of panic cross Cal's face.

"I hate you," he sniped. "I hate you so much."

He fired again at the coyotes. His silencer wasn't that great, less effective than a plastic soda bottle, which I'd used before in a pinch. It wasn't his fault, hadn't been mine either. At eighteen we hadn't had the money or the materials to make better ones. Or the contacts from which to buy them. Not that it made a difference. In this neighborhood, you could fire an AR-15 converted to full-auto, and no one would call the cops. If anything, they might ask to borrow it like people borrowed a cup of sugar in ye olden days.

"Quit your bitching and I'll get you enough of these scaly suckers to make you a pair of snakeskin boots," I promised.

"I don't think—wait." He had tilted his head and was scrutinizing one closely from head to tail. The gray-and-black pattern was shaped more in ovals like a chain of skulls than a true rattlesnake's linked diamonds. Skin-walkers were vain bastards. They had picked a theme, death, and stuck with it. "Zombie snake boots. That could be badass and scare the living— *Damn it!* Bad dogs!" He shot one of the coyotes in the face. That he hit it that easily was because it was in *his* face before he noticed.

Niko, who hadn't waited for the coyotes to produce more if smaller nightmares, had gone straight through them to take on the mountain lion. He'd impaled its mangy hide numerous times with no effect and had switched to slashing long, deep cuts in its stomach and chest. It was the same tactic he'd tried our first time with one . . . our other first time now. Or did it count as second thanks to this one? Did I care? No.

"Nik." I ducked one spider that ended up sailing over

my head, and dodged another two coming from my right, neck and hip height, pincers raining poison as they came. I allowed myself one atavistic shudder and then my head was back in the game. "Niko," I repeated, loud enough to be heard over the snarling and snapping of coyote jaws. "You can't disembowel it. Its intestines, organs, everything inside is petrified. Cut off its head."

That was easier said than done. You would think by its appearance that you'd stumbled over a mountain lion who'd starved to death a month ago and had been mummified by dry air and the hot sun. By the way it maneuvered, you'd think something else instead. Such as it was a lion in its prime and that was before someone came along and shot it up with all the adrenaline that could be found in every hospital in the state. It came close to being as fast as a bullet with the addition of the sinuous movements of a cat on speed.

Nik threw himself backward in time for its talons to miss tearing off his face by the width of a hair. "Advice, Caliban, that would've been appreciated before the fashion discussion on footwear. Cal, I know it is a challenging task to simultaneously appear as if you don't care what you wear yet your clothes all have to possess the look of 'obtained from a maximum security prison's Dumpster designated for the street clothing of deranged murderers,' but try shooting more of the coyotes or you'll be wearing pink Hello Kitty sweatshirts for the rest of your life."

Cal was already firing three more shots at one coyote, but that didn't stop him from wincing at the threat. Pink wasn't as useful as black for hiding bloodstains. He winced again when the coyote he'd been aiming for suddenly was elsewhere, every bullet missing it by a large and nasty margin. The coyote, unimpressed and predator down to its unnatural bones, snapped frothing jaws at Cal and attacked again.

"*Bad* goddamn dogs," Cal swore before firing six more rounds, hitting the coyote this time and two more out of the six that he had been targeting. That sounds like crappy shooting. It wasn't. The coyotes ran and weaved with a

speed just shy of not being able to see them move at all.
Hitting half of what you aimed at was an accomplishment
when by the time you pulled the trigger, and no matter
how fast you did, they were long gone. Cal wasn't aiming
at the coyotes. He was aiming several feet from them in
his best calculation of where they would be when the bullet left his gun.

He was leading his target as hunters did with fleeing
animals. Hunters had it easier, as deer don't move too
quickly for anything but an afterimage to be seen. Deer
also tended to run in a straight line, allowing the lead to
be established, locked in and moving with the deer. The
coyotes didn't know what a straight line was and if they
did, they were too smart to use it. Each was a wild cork-
screw of motion all over the loft, making prediction close
to impossible and proving Cal a damn good shot. I'd remembered being the same at eighteen, when I'd been
him. Good to know the memory was true and not conceit.

Not that I'd give our ego that boost. "Where'd you get
those fifteen-year-old piece of shit guns? ACME?"

"Funny, shithead. Real funny. Wile E . . . fuck!" Two
more coyotes rushed him, one from his front right side
and one from the back left. "Shitshitshit." He threw one
leg over the other side of the couch, now straddling it to
make the attacks from either side rather than in front of
and behind him. Firing again with five shots, he nailed
the one coming at him from behind the couch. He missed
the one coming from the front of it.

As he was taking his shots, I was dodging the strike of
a snake, shooting one thirty-pound spider that had been
fifteen feet away when it had crouched and jumped to fly
through the air at a height high enough to hit me directly
in the face—fuck no on that offer, thanks—and stomp-
ing on the bulbous body the size of a basketball of another spider to spray mucous green fluid up several
inches past my knee. None of that stopped me from raising my other hand to fire half the clip at the coyote Cal
had missed and was now in midleap with teeth that were
inches from ripping out Cal's throat. Half of my clip hit

it in the hindquarters, spinning it one hundred and eighty degrees around where the other half of the fired rounds ended up as aimed—in its head.

I reloaded with a speed I hadn't shown with the knife play at the bar. Knives were good, but guns were my true love. Cal didn't thank me as that wasn't in his nature. Mine either. That hadn't changed, if most everything else had.

He did say ruefully, "*Old Yeller* made me cry when I was five. Scarred me for life. But now"—he tucked one gun under his arm, then dumped the empty clip on the other, replacing it with quick efficiency, not quick enough, but he'd get there—"I think I'm over it."

He did a quick visual check on Nik, knowing precisely where to look. You kept track of your brother in a fight. It didn't matter how overrun you were or if you were gutted and bleeding, you didn't lose him. The mountain lion was standing tall on its back legs, blocking Niko's katana with both upper paws. God, we'd faced—or I had—these things before, but not one this fast or deadly. I'd done the same check as Cal, if more quickly, and had lifted my now loaded guns, firing both. I'd put a bullet in each of the big cat's eyes. It wouldn't kill it, but it would give it something to think about. This one thought about swaying as sand poured in thick streams from now empty eye sockets before falling back down to all fours.

That's when Niko took its head.

Cal had just gotten his guns loaded and half lifted. He knew exactly what would've happened to his brother if I hadn't been there with years more experience. "Practice, you said?" he murmured, eyes fixed on Nik who was ankle deep in sand as it rushed out of the open throat. The eyes had been streams. The neck was a river. The body had collapsed and was slowly being buried.

Nik lightly kicked the head several feet away, with its jaws opening and closing but slower every time. "Is it dead?"

"Yeah." I did a quick scan of the apartment to see if we'd missed any creepy-crawlies.

Ah.

Look at that.

I see you.

I did see, and the sight inspired a thought. Congrats for me.

"It's dead," I confirmed, holstering my Eagle, but holding on to my Sig. "They're like the last person at a party. They're out the door, but slow as shit to get that way."

Cal dropped down to slouch onto the cushions with legs sprawled out in front of him as far as they could comfortably stretch. "You do this insanity all the time? On purpose. Fuck no. I'll stick with being a bartender."

His eyes were a little wild. I got it. More than that, I understood it. He'd had the foundation of his world shaken when that foundation had already been worn away over the years to the unreliability of spring ice on a thawing pond. He'd fought a monster half a minute after discovering that monster *existed*. It wasn't one equal to the Auphe levels of malignancy, but the skinwalker was considerably closer to their level than any Wolf or vampire, the only other supernatural creatures he'd known of until today.

"That went better than I thought it would," I said unconcernedly, because if anything pissed off Niko as my brother past and future, it was casual dismissal of danger to myself. The same would go for this Nik regarding his brother and make for a needed distraction. I groaned at the spreading sand that continued to spread. "Anyone see my jacket?" I kicked through the sand stained with blood, tasty and pulp-free arachnid juice, snake cuts, avoiding the multiple bodies.

"This, by the way"—I waved an arm around the skinwalker aboveground graveyard—"is your hint that you need to start hauling ass out to Jersey to buy Costco family-sized crates of heavy-duty garbage bags. You know what, go wild. Get a membership while you're there and as many twenty gallon jugs of bleach as you can fit in your car. Fortune favors the family-sized."

Normally Niko was the first one to take good advice, but not this time. "Better?" He wasn't coated in dust and blood by themselves, he was painted head to toe in disbelief. It showed that much more when he couldn't stop repeating himself repeating me. Being stuck in a mental loop was a sight seldom seen in my brother whatever his age: preteen, teen, adult.

"Yep, better." I cut him some slack. Your first skin-walker will leave you twitchy and jumping at shadows for days. "The next time will be, okay, not easier, but you'll be prepared. That's something."

"That went better?" Niko wasn't listening to me or he wasn't hearing me, one of the two. He didn't show much care about finding my jacket either. He stood, his shirt shredded, the claw marks on his chest livid and raw, but fortunately not actively bleeding. What had once been a braid had been torn into a loose tangled mess hanging everywhere in a way that made him look like an unsuccessfully homicidal Rapunzel, one that was popping steroid pills or had inexplicable high levels of testosterone. His hand was wrapped tight around the grip of his katana as if it were the only thing left between him and the abyss.

He looked at me—as much as he could do anything visually related in my direction, considering his condition. His head had turned toward me, making the looking assumption sound, although I saw at best mostly hair with the cold glitter of one eye visible through the strands. "This went better than you thought it would?"

My Nik would've been calmer. This was one more reminder out of too goddamn many that this wasn't my Nik. This was a younger one and he'd not seen or faced anything like a skin-walker until now. He had known they were a truth and not a mythological fairy tale, which was one more shock on top of a time-traveling brother. This Nik had his reasons not to be all that calm. "Are you insane?" he demanded, short and snappish. That was good. Anger was one way to get him out of a rare mental rut.

Using one hand to push the hair back out of his face, he twisted it tightly enough it wouldn't dare unravel when he flipped it over his shoulder to fall down his back. "Mentally unstable?" he accused. "A fucking suicidal idiot? Why didn't you tell us to run?"

"Let me stab him in the face, Nik. I think that'd even things up." Cal's offer rang with sincerity and an unblinking stare dark with the pure potential for violence. That was typical me at all ages.

"Kids. So cute with the attempted assault and murder," I said with mock nostalgia. "They grow up too fast. Be sure Niko frames your first mug shot."

Cal, it went without saying, was no surprise. Nik cursing however, I'd heard it, but not when he was twenty. It had been years and years later that I'd driven him to that. "You can't run from a skin-walker," I explained. "They never lose your trail. And, hate to break the news, but this one wasn't the toughest we've faced by far," I went on. "Our first skin-walker before was on a barge in the middle of the Hudson and its outer layer was a bear." Grizzly of course. You could not get a break when it came to skin-walkers. "And out of that came the mountain lion, then the coyotes, the—"

There was the flicker again, there and gone, under the edge of the couch.

I see you. Yes, I do.

Raising his hand, the one without the katana, Niko cut me off. "This was a walk in the park. A piece of cake. Fine. I'll take your word for it."

"And the barge was on fire," I added to help him flesh out the mental image. Pure evil, yes, but I could use all the diversion I could get. "Before it started sinking."

"Fine," he repeated with more emphasis than was strictly necessary. "Enough. I believe you." He was about to say something else, but he didn't get the chance.

There was something left. Something the two of them had missed. I hadn't. Years on the job had taught me the distinction between looking over a postbattle area in general and looking over a postbattle area if you planned on actually *surviving*. I hadn't given any warning when I'd seen the corpse-white eyes under the shadowed edge of the couch. I knew what waited there and I knew it wouldn't wait long. I was right.

It didn't wait long. It didn't wait at all. The rattler lunged out of the shadows, streaking from beneath the couch, kept going, and buried its fangs into Cal's extended leg.

The last snake had seen his opportunity and taken it. Just as I'd seen and taken mine.

8

The fangs made it through Cal's jeans and beat-up combat boots, and into flesh. Cal's eyes rolling back as he slumped sideways into instantaneous oblivion was a dead giveaway that the rattler had gotten past skin and into meat to inject a load of venom. A third of the toxic delivery system, I guessed, was imbedded, but no more. Why didn't it get any deeper than that? It was dead, and death slows you down. I had kept out my Sig Sauer for a reason. The bullet I'd put through its head was not a comfort to Niko, who was throwing himself at the couch. He couldn't know if the poison sacs were intact and still pumping venom. Odds were, slug or not, they probably were.

Dropping his katana carelessly, he hurled himself toward Cal. He was halfway to the couch and then right there in less than a quarter of a heartbeat as he reached to pull the shattered remains of the snake's head out of his brother's leg. Desperation gives you speed that can sometimes equal or surpass the supernatural kind.

I knew as I grabbed his hand with a stomach churning scant fraction of time to spare. Holding it in a vise of a grip, I felt bones shift as I laid my gun on the floor. "No,

Niko. Don't." With one hand freed up, I used it to pry the pulped spade shaped head loose, careful to follow the path of the curved fangs through Cal's leg muscle as I did. Clenching his hand with the same force, I told him, "Don't touch his leg, his jeans, his boot, nothing. If he drools, don't touch that. No bodily fluids." They were as contaminated as Cal's blood now. "Not until I wipe him off. The venom can kill a human if they're bitten. I don't know what it'll do if you get it on your skin." At those words, Nik's hand twisted with violent strength in mine, his face tainted with a hint of gray. "Human," I stressed. "But not Auphe. Not Grendels. I've been bitten before. It'll knock him out for about four or five hours. That's it. I swear. He won't even have a headache when he wakes up."

"He's only half Grendel. Auphe. Call them what you want, he's still only half," he argued.

"Nik, I'm him. I know this *shit* because I've lived this *shit*." I had been bitten before, once five times in one fight. It'd been two days before I woke up, but I did wake up. One bite was nothing. Cal would live, and he'd get in a nice nap. That was more than I could say for me. "Chances are, a full Auphe wouldn't feel a thing. It'd walk it off while eating the rattler as a snack. Like I said, I've been bitten before. Half is enough."

I released him cautiously, ready to seize his hand again if he made a move toward Cal's leg. "Can you get me some soap and water, towels, alcohol, a bandage, and some tape?"

He wanted to be the one who fixed up Cal, but he knew I was more familiar with this poisonous bite, if I'd been unconscious through them all or not. He knew my Nik would've told me what to do for the sake of the knowledge alone. He would do the same. "Yes." That was short and succinct. More than usual for him. That wasn't a good sign for me. There were occasions he hoarded words as a dragon hoarded gold—but with better security. Occasions such as his brother being injured. But I thought it was more than worry or tension.

His face was entirely neutral, his emotions hidden deep enough to be unfathomable, but I suspected something was going on behind that cover. He stood from his crouch, avoiding his brother's leg, but moving close enough to curl a hand around the side of his neck, bared as his head tilted to the side. "Cal, are you . . ." In there? With us? His eyes were now shut and his chest rose and fell in the slow rhythm of sleep or unconsciousness. Nik hesitated on finishing his question as the answer was clearly a big fat no.

"Hey, Cal." I slapped his other leg lightly. "You coherent? Alert? Remotely conscious? No? I didn't think so. Enjoy the nap. You know how we love them." Again, I was offering assistance that Niko didn't welcome, if his slit-eyed glare was anything to go by.

"Niko," I urged, "he's out and will be out for hours. I need the supplies if you want to shave a few hours off that, all right?"

He rested his forehead for a moment against the top of Cal's head, dark blond hair mixing with black. "I'll be back in a minute, little brother." He didn't glance my way again as he vaulted over the back of the couch and headed for the bathroom and our first-aid kit.

I'd never thought about it, thinking of all the times I'd been out for the count, if my Niko had talked to me. Now I knew he must have. I didn't know if he'd thought on some level I heard him or it had made him feel that he was doing everything he could to pull me back. He'd been like that. Doing everything possible wasn't enough. He'd done everything possible and more.

I felt my throat and chest tighten and knew it was time to do something useful and stop thinking before I crawled, like that snake, to hide under the couch, and stay there until I died. I reached for one of the knives I kept in my boot. My jacket was where I kept the majority of them, but it remained MIA under a sand dune somewhere. There was a silver lining. The sand cascading out of the dead mountain lion was now barely a trickle. We had a beach but we wouldn't suffocate, which was a concern if it had kept on channeling the Sahara in here.

When Niko returned, it was with all I'd asked for and more. There was a tub, not a container or jar, but a tub of antibiotic cream. It's funny the things you forget. These were the days before we'd known precisely how much having half Auphe roaming around in my blood made me less susceptible to getting sick or to being affected by infections, poisons, toxin, venoms. You name it. I wasn't immune by any stretch of the imagination, but I would likely survive and recover in hours from what would kill a human instantly.

I'd already pulled off Cal's boot and sock, and used my knife to cut off part of his jeans at midcalf. Dark crimson venom was seeping from four puncture wounds a few inches above his ankle. I was using both hands to squeeze his leg with enough force to expel more of the poison mixed with blood to run down his bare foot.

Setting the medical supplies beside me including several pairs of surgical gloves, Niko returned to behind the couch. He placed two fingers on Cal's neck to check his pulse, counted, moved it down to his upper chest to do the same for his respiratory rates, lifted an eyelid to test his pupillary response, and circled back around to crouch beside me. He was near enough to see everything I did closely but not crowding enough to accidentally encounter any of the few random small puddles of venom being soaked up by the sand. I opened my mouth, but he beat me to it with brittle sarcasm. "Yes, do not touch the venom. I'm aware. I'm a delicate human." I snorted at the thought of Niko and delicate in the same sentence. I didn't comment though. If his bruised pride kept him from keeling over from just looking at that evil shit wrong, that worked for me. Speaking of work, I got down to it.

I'd done enough first aid over the years that my hands worked automatically as I pulled on a pair of the gloves and scrubbed away the excess poison with the bowl of warm water and soap, wiped down the wounds with alcohol, dried it all, and applied the antibiotic cream to satisfy Niko for all that it was the same as a placebo for your average half Auphe. Next I wrapped the bandage one-two-three times around the leg before taping it securely. Taking off the blood-marred gloves, I let them fall in my mentally designated hazardous area. Taking two of the three leftover clean towels, I used one to cover up the foot-and-a-half-wide area that was host to splattered spots and streaks of venom until that could be cleaned up. I soaked a small part of the second towel in the alcohol to use on Cal's face. Cupping his chin firmly, I tilted his listing head upright. I didn't see anything, no drool—not that that would be caused by the snake bite. It was how we rolled when we slept, that's all. If the pillow wasn't completely soaked when we woke up, we hadn't slept long enough.

This was different. I didn't care if there was an Atlantic Ocean of saliva, I cared what color it was. This was something we'd, or Niko rather, had learned to look for after one fight with a skin-walker. I hadn't learned anything until later since I was flat on my face after being bitten. The venom of one bastard of a snake had been directly injected into a vein in my left arm with a lucky strike a surgeon couldn't have hit at that distance in the next to no light. Of course being venous blood, it was headed back to my heart and lungs for the usual recycle, and it was carrying the venom with it, which then was sent back out through my entire body via my arteries. That time I'd gone down, unlike Retro Teen's Goth Cousin Cal, I'd drooled dark pink foaming saliva.

Nik had been smart enough to notice and to not touch it. When I'd finally woken up, I was no worse off than with previous bites, other than probably becoming temporarily venomous myself, until it either flushed its way out of my system or aggressive Auphe cells gobbled it up like apple pie. The problem had been and still was that we didn't know if it could pass through a human's skin or what would happen if it did.

I had known one thing. We weren't using Niko as a guinea pig to find out. He'd suggested—the rare *you'll do as I say, little brother* suggestion—that solution over my usual extra-large pineapple-and-spam Hawaiian pizza I treated myself to after a post-snake-poison nap. I'd had an opinion about his little planned science experiment. It had been a strong enough opinion I'd actually put down my piece of pizza, gone to the sparring area for his favorite katana and had thrown it out of the window, across the street, and directly into the open Dumpster of Titsy VonTrapp's Jizzy Lube sex supply shop. Expired gallons of lube had to be hell to get off the metal blade of a sword. I'd counted that was a win in my communication skills Niko had always been hounding me about until two seconds later when my brother had me wearing my pizza instead of eating it. The place had smelled of spam and expired strawberry lube for days.

That wouldn't happen to this Cal or Niko, not if I didn't get my ass in gear.

Despite the lack of excess saliva, I wiped the entire bottom half of his face thoroughly with the alcohol drenched towel, rolled and tied it in a tight knot to toss on my growing pile of medical waste, and then opened his mouth with both hands, used the one to keep it open and stuck two fingers inside until I could've felt his tonsils if we'd been born with any.

"What are you doing? And why aren't you wearing gloves while you do it?" The edge in the demand was sharper than a few of my knives. He had snapped out of his crouch and was on the verge of choking me out. It was a bracing of the shoulders and set to his jaw I'd witnessed often enough when he was facing someone else that by the age of thirteen I recognized it as quickly. As, at the same age, I could also *do* it to someone else. Nik had been a good teacher then. Patient. He wasn't patient now.

"No choking me out." I tried to sound patient myself, but too tired to be a threat was the best I could do. "I'm almost done. And the venom when mixed in saliva makes both twice as slippery. Slides right off gloves back into the mouth. So you told me. Or will tell me."

I removed my fingers. They were covered in saliva, but it was clear, not a pink tinge to be seen. "I think to get a sample of the yummy poison-flavored spit from my mouth you ended up using a turkey baster you borrowed from our lesbian neighbors. The pregnant ones. You told me you boiled it first, but I'm pretty sure you were lying."

Pouring the rest of the alcohol liberally over my hands, I took the last towel and dried them roughly enough to both dry and take a thin layer of cells off . . . just in case. When I was done, I let it fall on the pile of others, the cherry on top of the biohazard sundae. "And we're done. He's clean. If he accidentally spits, vomits, or pisses on you, you won't die."

"You said you didn't know what would happen if the venom touched human skin. I assume you do know what happens when it touches your skin."

"It stings some. I can hardly feel it. But that I can feel it at all makes it a big risk to think it might be harmless to you. Don't worry. You're still the king. Love child of Chuck Norris and Bruce Lee. You could kill me with a hangnail before I could spit any rattler poison on you."

I started to place my hands on Cal's shoulders. Niko shook his head and nudged me aside before arranging Cal's slumped, limp body to curl up flat on the couch. His head ended up on the armrest as a pillow, and his legs bent at the knees in a very loose imitation of the fetal position at the other end. As Nik ran his hand over the still tightly bound black hair unlike the tangled mass that hung around my face, I felt a weird twist in my stomach . . . as if Cal weren't who I'd once been, but another brother, one like Nik if much younger than either of us. Or maybe it was that he didn't know all I now knew. The lack of knowledge had him coming off as naive next to me. No, that wasn't quite it. Neither of us had been naive a day in our lives. He wasn't innocent either—he knew that whether he wanted to or not. It made him seem younger than I remembered feeling at eighteen.

We don't ever remember exactly right, every detail, none of us.

"You're quite efficient at that," Niko remarked. "The first aid."

Damn straight I was. It had taken me less time with Cal than to microwave a corn dog. "It's what I told Cal with the knife. Practice. And that was all you, Mussolini. Born to be a fascist teacher no matter the subject." The word subject tasted of blood from a bitten tongue. It tended to happen, that flavor, when you were hit in the face.

That's what Niko had done. He'd punched me solidly and with not one sign of regret. "You knew it was there, the snake," he accused, his fury hot instead of his usual colder than an upstate winter. "You saw it and you knew. Yet you didn't tell us. You let it bite him on purpose."

He waited for my denial, anger growing if the tighter clenching of his fist was anything to go by. But I wasn't going to lie. I had kept quiet although I'd seen the serpent. I hadn't *let* it bite Cal, but I hoped it would. I thought the likelihood was high that's what would happen. And I had my reasons for it. "You were always so damn smart." I spat blood onto the thin layer of sand that had made it this far. "It's annoying as hell sometimes."

"Why? Why did you do it? He's you. Not figuratively but factually. It's the same as if you did it to yourself. Tell me why you let this happen." Angry and suspicious, that was a Niko no one wanted to go up against.

"I didn't plan it. I didn't know one had escaped until I saw its beady eyes under the couch when Cal flopped his careless ass on it. I don't speak rattler, and I'm not some sort of psychic snake whisperer. I didn't tell it to bite Cal. It was luck." I defied. It sounded true because it was true. "I got lucky, pure and simple. That and I'm bright enough not to sit on furniture that slithery, scuttling creatures can hide under before we'd checked that the battle area was clear. But you're right. I spotted it and I didn't warn Cal. I saw a break and I took it. And I'm not one damn bit sorry."

The second punch I dodged. As I did, there came a nearly simultaneous knock at the door. Fuck me. Would this day never end?

Keeping a wary eye on a Niko who was as furious as he'd been with the first punch, I turned, slogged to the door through knee-high sand, flipped the one lock the skin-walker had slammed into place and opened it. From the hall there was a strong drift of air that pushed its way inside. It carried with it the signature of dank water, rot, and old blood scent. All of which I'd encountered before.

I didn't bother to bite back the snarl vibrating up through my throat. It had been the longest, worst day of my life and I wasn't in the mood.

Covered liberally with coyote blood, shredded pieces of their intestines, and whatever green goop had sprayed explosively out of giant spiders when you put several large caliber rounds in their beach-ball-sized bodies, I faced the *rusalka*, the lamia, and the wendigo that I'd scented before we'd stepped into the building. I seriously considered killing them, but that was a change not yet necessary and one that would spread the word among the supernatural community. That we'd killed the skin-walker would make ripples of gossip enough. Adding more wouldn't be a good thing.

I leaned against the door jamb and kept growling. I had every right.

They were rude.

Not one of them had a fruit basket to thank us for taking care of the skin-walker, which would've craved a midnight snack sooner or later. If one of his people wasn't conveniently and immediately available, *paien* disappear much more easily than humans with friends and family. He'd have started with them first, although they probably weren't bright enough to know it. There aren't many true stories about skin-walkers as there aren't more than a handful of species with ferocious enough fighters to live through the encounter. These three, predatory breeds or not, weren't anywhere close to the type of *paien* capable of facing a skin-walker. The *yee naaldlooshii* weren't at the top of the food chain, but they were past the halfway mark. These three couldn't see the bottom of a skin-walker's feet, he was that much higher than they were.

They were gazing past me at an apartment littered with body parts and walls that had the equivalent of a new paint job donated by Carrie's prom committee.

Their own colors weren't any sort of improvement over what was on the walls. There were eyes of stagnant green rivers paired with the dark tangled red hair of a week-old drowning victim, a gaze of a starless empty sky of no color at all but difficult to see through the floor-length cloak of the lamia's own black hair, and then there was the decomposing cataract gray-white marbles, no hair but the distinct smell of Rogaine, as the three of them looked their fill, then shifted their attention from Niko and Cal's home back to what both coated a good deal of me and was soaked into large swathes of my clothes. It also dripped off of me like a slow, unnaturally thick rain. What's more was the fact that with my added years—Auphe maturity come finally—they, like the skin-walker, could sniff out that Auphe in me. That should've had them running until they hit New Jersey. It should not have them knocking at the door. But then again they were idiotic enough to live in a building with a skin-walker. Maybe they'd thought he had killed us and were going to interrupt his meal he'd made of us by trying to snipe our better apartment from beneath our cold, dead rent deposit. They had fingers crossed to snag the place with the killer view, the one they were hoping we'd died for. They were idiotic enough to do just that.

Some days it made me wonder why I bothered to carry a gun at all. I could easily beat them to death with my TV remote.

"Did you send your RSVPs?" I drawled, leaning toward them. All three muttered inhuman consonants under their breath as they looked away, sniffed again, and took a step back. "I didn't think so." I cocked my head slightly. "But, hey, the more the merrier. We love making new friends."

I gave them the crazed, warped chasm of a grin I'd held in all day, more and more difficult with each hour to do; the same one I'd learned when I ran with the Auphe and played their games as gleefully as they did. It felt as if it split my face in half, and, hell, maybe it did. "I'd think about it though. Think hard." Then I let my eyes bleed Auphe red. Niko was behind me and couldn't see, so why not? The combination of the grin, the eau de Auphe, and the eyes made me the farthest thing from a poster child for moderation when it came to maiming, mutilation, and murder.

"Done thinking?" I took a step out into the hall toward them to equal the one they'd taken back away from me.

"Now tell me . . . is this a party you *really* want to crash?"

It wasn't.

No surprise there on my part. They were gone as fast as if they hadn't existed at all. "That's what I thought," I grumbled with savage bite. As I felt my eyes turn back to the human gray, the color this Niko was familiar with, I stepped back into the apartment, closed the door, and returned to the situation at hand.

"We need to talk," I said. My foot hit a lump under the sand. I bent down and dug out my jacket along with my favorite knives tucked in the lining. "You and I, Niko, we need to have a long, serious as fuck talk. It's one that Cal can't hear and can't know. Not now. If . . . *when* we fix things, you can tell him if you want. Just not now."

I checked to make certain he was as soundly out of it as he should be. He was. "That's why when I saw the snake I let it do what snakes do. I needed Cal down and out for this. I hadn't thought of how to do it, didn't know I'd need to do it until today. And then, like a hundred-dollar bill on the sidewalk, there it was. The snake." Shaking the sand off my jacket, I slid another glance at him . . . him, me . . . this was one thing we were identical in. Eight extra years—hell, twenty years would make no difference. In this, we would be the same. That would never change.

"Our talk, it's one Cal couldn't be a part of without going off the rails, getting himself killed, or both." It was the truth. I knew as it had happened to me today, just hours ago.

"And like I told you, with the bite I knew he'd be okay. That goes for anything else I might do. I hurt him and I hurt myself." I bent over and pulled up the bottom of one leg of my jeans while pushing down the soft leather of a worn combat boot. Where the snake bite was on Cal's leg, fresh and new, there were faded white scars in the same place on mine. Four indentations of whiter than white dense tissue. "I didn't have that until fifteen minutes ago. Trust me, a little bite like this? I've had . . . he'll have worse. We're both your brother, Nik. You can trust me with him as much as my Niko trusted me with myself."

"If I didn't know you are my brother or who he'll be someday, I wouldn't have punched you for the snake. I would have killed you. If I didn't feel it as solid as the ground under my feet that you are who you say, you'd be dead," he bit off. It was a verbal bite but as sharp as any the dead snakes around us once had. "Do anything similar to this again and you'll wish you were. I can't kill you, but I can and will make you exceedingly sorry. As my brother, I'm certain you'd forgive me." I felt the slice on that one. It drew blood, if mentally instead of physically. If I'd thought Niko's edge had been any less cutting when we were babes in the woods, I was wrong.

"As for trusting you with him as your brother trusts you with yourself . . ." He didn't show any relief. The opposite if I had to label it. "I'm not a fool now and I doubt I'm one in the years to come." Resignation was seeping in to replace the anger that trickled out with the relaxation, finger by finger, of his fist. Snake sin aside, he'd said it: He knew I was his brother, or enough of him that he couldn't aim his rage at me for much longer.

"I cannot trust you with him at all," he finished. "As my brother, which means you as well, are both inherently suicidal."

I shrugged. "You don't really mean that, but funny you should say it." At eighteen I'd been reckless, had everything to lose, which had me playing the game all in or all out, but I wouldn't have run as long and fast as I had from the Auphe if I hadn't wanted to live. Now I was wild, careless, running as fast as possible as I was finally the one doing the chasing, taking any and all risks with my life and having a helluva time doing it. What's the point of having a life if you're not going to live it to the last crazy second? From the outside or to those who didn't know us, Cal's desperation to survive and my eagerness to live anything and everything once I *had* survived, it might've looked like we were suicidal. But that wasn't the case, not for Cal. And not for me.

Or it hadn't been.

I tossed my jacket across the chair after fishing a piece of paper clumsily folded several times from the pocket. Once more, I trudged through the sand across the apartment to boost up and sit on the end of the creaky rectangular-shaped kitchen table. It wobbled, but eventually stabilized to hold my weight as I sat cross-legged just as I'd seen Niko do a thousand times while doing yoga. "Whenever you're ready," I announced.

"It's story time."

"As in a 'Once upon a time' story?" Niko had taken the position opposite me at the other end of the table. As agile and lightly as he moved, I didn't have to see him to feel the faint shiver beneath me. I was surprised the Dumpster scrounged piece of flimsy furniture managed to hold both our weight.

Once upon a time . . . a few hours ago and eight years technically yet to come. Turn the page and read the next two words that waited.

The End.

Two lines. It was a quick read. Who didn't like that?

Fuck.

Giving in to the stabbing aches and complaint of every muscle in me, I slumped forward, letting my face rest in my hands, covered by my palms. The mess of thick hair I'd gotten from Sophia fell around my face to turn the weakly lit apartment into a place of complete shadow without a hint of light. Hiding me from the world. That was nothing but a good thing with what I felt rising inside.

Once upon a time.

I made a sound. I didn't think there was a word for it. It wasn't a laugh, not unless one could be a broken jumble of crazed choking and a strangled rasp that came from fighting back every molecule of air in my lungs wanting to escape in a frenzy of rage, hate, and despair. But letting out that kind of obvious clawing desperation might make Nik uncomfortable knowing I was neck deep in a mental breakdown, possibly panic the living shit out of him. I didn't want that. Nope. I wanted, I *needed* him in top form if any of us, here or there, were going to survive. I needed him at his best. Someone had to be, and I had no difficulty accepting straight up that I was so far from my best that I couldn't find it with a GPS tracker and a bloodhound.

So I held it back, all of it, behind gritted teeth, a locked jaw, and humorless barbwire tangle of my lips. I was lucky Niko couldn't see my face. He wouldn't believe that was a smile. No one in their right mind would. Swallowing thickly, I gave a shot at clearing my throat back to a voice more like my own.

"Once upon a time." It came out hoarse, but not insane. I'd take that.

Keeping my face concealed by my hair, I rubbed at eyes that burned from the fire, the heat, pain, exhaustion, and fear. It was a fear deep and dark enough to smother any but the smallest scrap of hope. I couldn't stop from admitting the last to myself, if not to this Niko or this Cal. I could lie to them, but about what had happened to my Nik, I couldn't lie to myself. As much as I wanted to.

"No," I finally answered him. I gave one last banishing swipe across my face. "It's not really that kind of story."

I straightened, sitting up to dig in the pocket of my jeans for a tie to pull my hair back into the ponytail I'd lost somewhere on the walk from the bar. If Nik had to hear this fairy tale that the Grimm brothers had nothing close to in competition, I should have to look him in the face when I told it.

"You never asked me, you know," I said, calm now. Detached. I had to be if I had a chance of pulling off any of this. "Why did I come back? Why not you instead? You're smarter. Quicker. Better at hand to hand or with any kind of blade. As good with guns as me too, as much as it kills me to admit it. And tactics, you memorized Sun Tzu's *Art of War* before you were in junior high. My Nik and you together, what couldn't you do?"

Not much. But there was one thing neither Nikos could do, but I could—as a last resort. That's why I'd been batter up. But this Nik didn't know about my Auphe gift for gating, traveling, and how it could be used as an escape or a weapon if worse came to worst and our backs were against the wall. As he didn't have any idea about that and wouldn't for a while, added to his massively overprotective complex when it came to brothers, one he'd never lose no matter how many years went back and forth, I'd been surprised he hadn't asked.

Why me. Why not him?

"I wondered," he admitted. "With the same temperament and methods, I would've found myself easier to work alongside." He raised a judgmental eyebrow and added, "To not punch in the face." He was untangling his hair from its twist and braiding it. It didn't mean he wasn't giving his all, listening to and analyzing every word, syllable, letter. It was just Niko, an action so automatic for most of his life, that half the time he was surprised to find a braid instead of a loose fall of hair at the end of our strategy and planning sessions for taking down the next monster payday.

"I am twenty-eight in your time. Ancient. I'm shocked you didn't say I'd fallen in the bathtub and broken a hip," he stated with a humor unseen but with the mildly punishing taste of hot pepper to the words. And it was something I would say . . . in different circumstances. Fingers moving faster, he asked, "Why then? Why not me? I would've argued for it, I know. I wouldn't have been easy to convince I wasn't the better choice. You are devious however. You've conned people since you were four. I'm a more difficult target, yet you've tricked me more than once to get your way, although your way was usually about helping me without letting me know it up front."

He finished off his braid with a loud snap of the black elastic. He was frowning now and the humor was replaced with disapproval. "Did you fool me? Him? When it is Cal's life on the line, my Cal, and your Niko would've been better suited, did you con him because you have come so far in skill and knowledge, I must admit, that you thought it would be simple. Did you think it would take you five minutes and the rest would be some sort of time travel joyride?"

I hadn't thought things could be any worse than what I'd seen, how it had gone. I was wrong. If that was what Niko thought of me, this Niko, then he could save Cal on his own. If they died and I consequently never was, I wouldn't be crying over it, you could bet your ass. Nik ... mine ... would never ... he would *never* fucking think that. He would never—but that was a goddamn given. He would never do anything at all again. He was gone, and I was an idiot for not going with him.

I should've thrown Robin's letter in the gutter and moved along with the bullet in the brain.

"*No,*" I spat, rage intense enough my vision blurred. My short nails dug into my palms until the comforting warmth of blood streaked my skin, cupped and hidden by my curled fingers. "Con my brother for the Mardi Gras that is saving that rude, careless, know-it-all, *thankless* piece of shit on the couch? What a fucking deal! Do you think I'd do that to my brother? Con him into his own coffin? Would your Cal do that to you? Do you think it's any different for us now? That when one of us is kicked off this rock of a planet that the other won't be far behind? That if I screwed up due to my ego and desire for a *vacation*, that my brother wouldn't be on my heels into the grave—if you survived long enough to even be him? To be there eight years from when you saw two Cals die?"

It was a stupid question. Nik wasn't there now. It was senseless and stupid. This Niko who'd once been my Niko didn't trust me, and that was one of the few things in my life that could break me. Which is why this was utterly pointless. I was already broken. Worse than a past Niko not trusting me was that my Nik was dead. And none of this trust bullshit mattered. It *couldn't* matter. This Niko was equally as dead. The explosion had been triggered. He was unknowingly biding his time, waiting eight years for the tsunami of flames to roll over him.

Unless Robin's letter was right.

It could be changed.

"Stop. Caliban, *stop*. I shouldn't have said it. You're right. My Cal wouldn't do that to me and no Cal he'll become would do it either. I know no amount of time would change him that much. I'm sorry for being fool enough to want to hear you say the truth aloud when I already knew what the truth was. I wanted reassurance of what I already accepted as fact. It was stupid and weak." He was prying open my hands and wiping off the blood with a ragged kitchen towel. "Buddha"—he let out an uneasy breath—"how did you do this with no nails to speak of?"

Motivation, I thought dully. The rage was gone as fast as it'd come. As angry as I'd been at this Niko, I was more angry with mine. How much fury I'd hidden away I hadn't realized. It was useless and would do nothing but hold me back. It was also unfair. Niko wouldn't have been angry with me if our positions had been reversed. But the resentment, raw and acidic, bubbled relentlessly under my skin. I couldn't stop it.

"Why you then? What happened?" He ripped the towel lengthwise, wrapped and knotted a strip around each of my hands.

He meant, what happened that I had come instead of him. But that wasn't the "what happened?" that I answered. The question I answered was bigger, the "What happened to you, them, the world? You acted considerably more in control and substantially less psychotic at Talley's bar. What happened?"

"What happened, Nik?" I was calmer, but not near as rational as I wished I was. The sanity I'd shown at the bar was a mask I'd worn a few times in my life. To make the people around me more comfortable and sometimes less likely to shoot or stab me in the face. I'd known one day I'd wear it out. One day it would break.

The words of a long gone childhood came back. "What happened for real and for true?"

It'd been a long time since I'd said that. We can have a Christmas tree this year? For real and for true? We can have a turkey for Thanksgiving? For real and for true? I was four years old when I'd stopped asking for promises my brother ultimately couldn't keep as much as he tried. Except for one. He wouldn't leave me. Not ever. It was the one promise I hadn't let go, the one I knew he wouldn't break.

I'd learned about reality, poverty, alcoholism, too and, oh yeah, crazy nightmare monsters before I learned to read. But I had Niko's promise and it made the rest of it, monsters included, bearable.

For real and for true.

"You lied to me. I guess that makes you the one with the con, huh?" It was said matter-of-fact and came from a face as blank as I could make it. Another mask to replace the shattered one. Under it, I could feel the cracked shards of what had once been me, burnt and blackened as the glass buried in the debris of a building baked to coals. What I would've seen if I'd hung around long enough.

"That's what happened, Nik.

"You lied to me.

"You left me.

"You died."

Then I told him how.

9

I'd forgotten the pizzas.

It was the second time I'd thought that, stupid everyday words I'd never forget, but that was where this nightmare had begun. I had to tell it in order. I needed Niko to know some of it, not all, but part of the story of my world's personal end. It was necessary that he knew saving Cal wasn't enough. If we did take out the Vigil assassin and I disappeared home to my time, Nik would have eight years of annual anonymous warning letters to send to Ishiah, his future lover Promise, and a year and a half before he warned Goodfellow personally with the promise not to tell him anything more or ask him anything else. Change for the better could be difficult, but I knew the universe was bastard enough to make change for the worse easy as it came. We had to save the others, but that wasn't enough. While doing that, Niko had to try to not alter anything else. Hopefully, as I wasn't going to tell him anything else about my past/his future, it would work. His discipline was unbreakable as I'd known, but his and his Cal's future was full of shit horrifying enough to tempt that discipline—if solely for his brother's sake and not his.

That's why I began there, with the pizzas, even if it was déjà vu for me.

That's how it had started.

For goddamned real and for goddamned true.

I'd forgotten the pizzas for the celebration/good-bye/come back soon/hope you don't get sucked into a wormhole by accident party and gated out of the bar a block to the usual place. There was a time months ago I'd thought I wouldn't be able to gate again. When the ability had slowly returned, I was relieved. I'd missed it. Not having it back with me long enough to take it for granted, I used it frequently. It felt good, like the stretch of a recovering muscle.

I left out the gating portion of the story and told the younger Niko instead that I'd exited the alley door. He and Cal not only didn't need to know, they couldn't know about that biological roller-coaster ride given to me by Auphe genes. If they did, saving the world from being remade by the Auphe in another year or so likely wouldn't happen. I didn't care about that now, but if I could stop The Ninth Circle massacre, get them back, my people, it was possible I'd care again.

What-ifs are the deadliest of all weapons.

That wasn't a thought I needed now if I wanted to be capable of telling this to the end.

I'd waved to my Nik and mouthed the word pizza in the bar's deafening noise. Opening a circular ring of killer-storm gray and the velvety black-purple of the bruises around a hanged man's neck, I had stepped through to appear at the pizza truck. The guy working it hadn't blinked. He wasn't any more human than I was, and he'd seen the show before. I came here weekly if not more often. It was the best pizza for the supernatural crowd with some special toppings that humans wouldn't recognize or if they did, like living, moving tentacles, would have them running for their lives. For a hefty tip I'd leave my spot behind the bar and run down to pick up a pizza. I didn't take a curious look under the lid after the first time when a squirming tentacle had poked me in the eye. Some things are better left a mystery.

The *balaur* that worked it was my size with only three reptilian heads—probably a teen to be that small and to have several scales bubbling up and oozing around each set of slit-pupiled eyes. He'd crouched under the cover of his extra large hooded raincoat to hide his hydralike nature and held out a scaled hand for the money. I had paid, and, as it was our pizza, tipped extra—hell, even I had some sympathy for an adolescent lizard with a bad case of zits selling pizza. Teen snakes needed a social life the same as any other kid. That was my humanitarian— okay, herpetarian—thought for the month. I could be an asshole the rest of the time.

I'd had two boxes of pizza in my hands, warm and smelling strongly enough of garlic, cheese, tomato, sausage, and pepperoni to make my stomach growl, when I heard metal crunch and scream. Car wreck. Happened all the time in the city, but not on a nonhuman *paien* street where humans subconsciously sensed not to trespass with an instinct left over from the days of living in caves. No car should've been there. The sound of it had come from the direction of Ishiah's place. Jerking my head around, I'd seen the panel truck half embedded in the bar where I worked, smashed into the front wall of The Ninth Circle, obliterating the door but blocking the space where it had been. Limited by the cramped street, it hadn't been able to build up the speed to go all the way through the brick. I'd had a quick flash of dark amusement at what this drunk driver would find when he fell out of the car. Wolves, lamias, revenants . . . all blood drinking and flesh eating, and worse than any DWI.

That had been when the flash had come, and it hadn't been a mental one this time. No humor in it either, none at all. The Ninth Circle had erupted in an eye-searing blast as bright and horrifyingly unfathomable as if the sun had plunged from the sky to crash on top of it. I'd thought numbly as the boxes slid and fell from my hands that we were all on fire. It was night but we were on fire. The entire world was on fire.

It wasn't.

That had been shock and despair clawing my brain to shreds. The fire had grown while a backwash of incredible heat and a concussive wave knocked me almost flat. So much fire; Hell couldn't have claimed it all. It hadn't been a simple explosion like C4 would've done. No, it would have had to been something like ANFO, a fertilizer bomb, to do that type of damage. It would've been loaded in packed metal barrels in the back of the truck and that truck would end up targeting the Circle. A fraction of a second after it hit had come the massive fireball, instantaneously incinerating the bar and everyone inside it. Burning with the kind of rage, flame, and heat I hadn't seen a single time in my life.

Not that I had determined all that at the time. That had come after my jump to the past when I was killing a murderous junkie and delivering warnings before chasing down the younger me. That's when I'd figured out the truck and the diesel fertilizer bomb as C4 wouldn't have done the trick, the fact that the truck had hit the building less than a second after I gated out to get the pizza I'd forgotten. That the bomb had been meant for me, that the truck had hit the place moments after I had walked inside because the driver, a Vigil bastard, had no idea I'd gated two blocks away to be the most unwilling audience to exist. But when it had happened, when there was a tower of fire, asphalt under my hands, I'd had only one thought.

I'd thought, Niko is dead.

My brother is dead.

My brother who had been the first and only one to hold me the moment I was born. My brother who had saved my life too many times to count. My brother who'd saved my sanity as many times.

My brother who had sworn not to leave me in this life without him.

My only family was dead.

He wasn't alone.

Goodfellow, my single friend, gone. Dead and no more.

My brother, my friend, my boss, the regular customers—the few that didn't fear me . . .

Gone.

"Then what did you do?" Niko asked, eight years younger but as curious about every damn thing as he'd been to the day he was murdered. Today. He'd been murdered today. It seemed like minutes ago and decades both. Neither hurt any less.

I shifted and felt the table rock under us. Past his shoulder I could see part of the enormous arch of window. The lights on the buildings outside were the only stars we saw in the city. I'd seen real stars too many times to be impressed, but something caught my attention. An impossibly large black hand passed between the apartment window and all the fake stars. What the hell could that . . . it roiled and separated, one bird, black—a crow, hitting the window with a thump. Nothing more than a flock of birds had me seeing horror story nightmares. No, thanks. I'd seen enough of that for the day.

Looking back down at the stupid scraps of towel looped around my hands. All for a little torn meat and a spoonful of blood. We'd be lucky not to see a river of the latter before we killed the Lazarus assassin.

"Caliban?" he prodded.

Then what had I done, he wanted to know. That was not anything that this Niko needed to hear. My brother, younger and older, but either way I'd protect him from the truth. When did the truth help anyone? Never. I lifted my eyes back to the distant lights and hummed lazily as if the question was too unimportant to answer. I let the answer spin, a tornado wind, through my mind, but I didn't say it aloud.

I'd thought, while watching the fire, that I couldn't deal with losing my brother, losing my friend.

I couldn't survive any of this.

I couldn't handle knowing Robin was gone.

He'd been over a million years old, but was charcoal now thanks to me.

And the last of the enemy had burned with them. The two who'd been left. I hadn't seen anyone running from the truck that carried the explosives. They'd burned as everyone in the bar had. I had been left with nothing. No target for vengeance. I'd once thought I'd tear the world down if Nik died. I thought I'd go insane with grief, that there'd be nothing but madness to spill out on every-thing and everyone. But there wasn't. I thought I'd go Auphe, but that option had been stolen from me. I hadn't thought it mattered though. If I'd been able to keep that rising genetic flood in me, I'd known I wouldn't do any-thing differently. Apparently even an Auphe could be broken if you tried hard enough. I'd had no will left to burn down the world anymore. Had no reason to take one more breath.

Pointless.

Everything.

Fucking pointless.

They'd been fuzzy, those thoughts, as they'd circled through my mind, faster and faster, pulling me down into an inescapable whirlpool that didn't drown with despair but tore and ripped everything from me with teeth and a devouring maw that left me completely hollow. Left me with one choice. It hadn't been until I'd felt the com-forting cool touch of metal under my chin and realized vaguely that the muzzle of the Desert Eagle was pressed there with my finger on the trigger, that the thoughts had become more clear.

It had only made my finger tighten.

That was when the pizza guy, whom I'd forgotten with a totality when the bar exploded that I was numbly sur-prised it hadn't wiped him from existence altogether, had hissed at me. There had been two names and several other words to get my attention. The first name had been mine. "Caliban." I'd barely recognized it as my own. My finger's tension on the metal increased. My name meant nothing now. But then had come the second name added to mine and the words of a dead puck following them both had snared my attention and snared it thoroughly. "Goodfellow." All the words spoken by three different tongues in three different mouths but precisely at the same time. "He left this for you." All three heads had stopped whipping about and all came to rest against one another to stare at me as one long multifingered hand extended toward me. I'd had to lower the gun to take and rip at the green-and-gold envelope that had dropped through the air into my lap. What was inside read short and to the point.

> *If the Vigil is more intelligent and wily than I would guess them to be—unlikely, but a true trickster never rules out anything, including the luck of idiots—this is for you. If they pulled off a coup de main and one of you brothers survive, I know you will be planning to follow the other into oblivion as you egoegoistikíistikí gioi tou skýles aways have and always will. Don't. Not this time. Do not exceed the idiocy of the Vigil. If there is a trap and you are the one left, Niko, you already know what to do as you possess a brain. If you survive, Cal, you couldn't find that oblivion you seek with a map, a llama, and a Sherpa. You've proven it in the past. Niko, Cal, neither of you are cowards. Suicidally codependent, but not cowards. If one of you is left, you stay. You stay and you fix this. I know that you can. Of course if we all die in some Vigil mousetrap, the pizza balaur is eating our food and enjoying nude perfection while he does so. A fitting end to my long life—porn and pizza? No, it is not. Whoever is left, and I refuse to believe no one would survive, you get up, put down your gun or katana and do what has to be done. Addendum: If nothing happens, balaur, do not eat our pizzas. I'll be out for them any moment.*

He'd been right, Robin, as he'd always claimed he was. We'd been planning to stop a catastrophe before it had to be fixed. I could still do that, little that I cared about it any longer, but I could do much more. I could undo this catastrophe, a larger catastrophe, before the fact. Robin had said it. That meant it was possible.

Failure, that was the only impossible.

"Caliban?" Niko flicked my forehead. The sting was

familiar—a hundred times so. "Are you catatonic?" he demanded, trying for impatience, but I heard the worry. "Come back and tell me what happened."

I stopped humming and let the lights blur away behind eyes dry and vision smeared from the lack of blinking. "What happened?" I repeated his question. "Robin happened.

"The pizza guy gave me an envelope from Goodfellow." I scraped my thumbnail, the edge lined brown with dried blood, against the plastic top of the table. "Don't, whatever you do, go looking for Robin. Don't even try to find his address or where he works, thinking it's harmless because you won't actually contact him. Don't do any of that. Forget all the geek babble about timelines and worlds being wiped out. If you meet Goodfellow before you should, the entire universe will implode. And that's if you're lucky. You'll meet him when you're meant to. Mess around with that . . ." I shook my head, almost capable of a smile at the thought of it. My brain couldn't begin to hold the smallest fraction of lies, trickery, chaos, and cataclysms that could happen. "Lovecraft couldn't come up with the kind of nightmare you'd unleash—but if he did there'd be massive amounts of pornography added to his work.

"So promise me, Niko," I insisted. "And that means not telling Cal anything, as we like trouble. Disasters, Acts of Malevolent Gods, any of that just screams adult only amusement park to us. We'd break in a day. Two days at most before we tried sniffing him out. Promise me you won't tell and you won't look for him yourself." I tacked on a bitter addition no Niko deserved, especially not this one, but I was exhausted and it slipped out. "And make it a promise you keep this time."

He reached over to move my hand back to my knee. There was a fresh drop of blood on the table's surface where my nail had dug into the plastic extra deep. "I promise." He was collected and cooperative with no offense at receiving a heaping helping of bitter blame he didn't deserve. Take a Niko anywhere in a thousand points in history, in a million alternate dimensions, give him a fucked-up brother as a present with shiny bow and all, and he becomes an instant physical and emotional guardian. There wasn't anything he wouldn't do to keep that brother safe. And all of it was unconditional.

If I'd shown my true fucked-up colors sooner, he wouldn't have punched me. Hindsight, she is a bitch and a half.

"The *balaur* didn't know you, but he helped you—rather, helped this Robin Goodfellow to help you. That's encouraging for our future. It's a probable sign that Goodfellow did receive your warnings. Also the *balaur* assisting is encouraging for interspecies cooperation," Niko pointed out.

Fuck me, he was so innocent. I'd never thought that in my life, but he was. Now, in any case.

"Not necessarily. Goodfellow is the oldest trickster alive." I knew Niko would've already recognized the name, the version that had been made over into something the same and different both by Shakespeare. "He wouldn't have needed messages from the past. He assumed the Vigil might not put all their grenades in one basket. If he was going to kill someone, he wouldn't depend on one trap or one weapon. While he thinks no one is as smart as him, his plans always include the possibility that there's a small chance they could be. That's why he never loses . . . never lost."

No, it took me to make that happen.

"There's a good chance he planted notes for weeks near every place we hung out. As for cooperation?" I laughed. It was split between mourning and mockery. "Robin paid him. The bastard even came out and *ate* our pizzas while I read the note. You and Robin were dead. I had a gun in my—" I cut myself off. Taking in a deep breath, I went on as if I'd said nothing. "Nothing is free, Niko. Not back when we were kids, not here and now, not in the days to come." The laugh hit me as hard as a kick in the gut and I leaned back with the force of it.

A hand rested on my shoulder carefully, easing me forward a few inches. This Niko didn't know yet. Didn't know that falling off a table would be funny, that falling

off the roof of a twenty story building wouldn't kill me,
wouldn't even hurt me, not unless I was unconscious before I fell.

Or if I was awake and wanted it enough.

But there was no time for pity parties now.

"Goodfellow sounds as impressively sly as the Bard
painted him when it comes to planning and prediction.
May I see the letter?" he requested, treating me with the
same careful caution you would a bomb. I didn't blame
him. I was a bomb. He knew only about the emotional
type that topped my list. I had other skills, I'd kept to
myself, that made me as physically explosive as the Vigil's bomb had been.

"Not much in it. It's mainly a 'talk you or me down
from the ledge' note. Everything can be changed like we
were planning before. Blah blah blah." I handed him the
letter. "There's no actual useful information like where
the shithead Lazarus is or will be, which means he didn't
know." Although if I had changed him dying in the explosion with my own messages he might know now, but
that didn't do me any good, what with "now" being eight
years away.

"Sorry about the nude photo," I added. "He printed it
on the paper. Hell, it might be on all his stationery for all
I know." I smirked with petty vengeance and reversed
my opinion. "You know what? I'm not sorry. I've had
seven more years of that pornographic perv to put up
with. No reason you can't start your suffering along with
me right now."

He thought he was ready, but his jaw dropped slightly
before his mouth snapped shut. "Do tell me he manipu-
lated the photo."

"Unfortunately, so goddamn unfortunately, and accidentally, important to know, I can tell you I saw the real
deal and nope, the bastard did not." I grimaced. "My
masculinity took a hit that day, crawled under the bed,
and is probably still there."

"And he's always"—he waved a hand at the full-color
photo-enhanced computer printed letter—"in a sharing
mood?"

"He is. He was. He will be." I was pure determination on the last.

"You can save him . . . and me. You have the time now," he pointed out, his hand remaining on my shoulder. It hadn't changed in the weirdness of who had once been my big brother now being six years younger than me, but at the same time he felt less a shadow of Nik and more a part of my brother. Only a part, but solid and real.

"I know, don't think I didn't start making new plans the second I arrived here. I don't have to be a trickster to have thought of that first thing." The world might be destroyed as a consequence, but I couldn't do everything. "Yeah, thanks to the Vigil and their two plans is better than one, I have the time to try to save my Nik and Goodfellow."

They had Operation Lazarus, but that hadn't been enough for them. They'd had one more plan—either to make certain I went down before I went back after Lazarus or maybe Lazarus wasn't as reliable as they hoped. Either way, they'd given me a second chance they'd be kicking themselves over if they weren't dead. By fang or by fire, in my time, every Vigil member was dead or had fled the city. Personally, I was hoping for the dead option.

I gave Niko a tight-lipped smile as another black blotch of a crow thumped against the window. NYC is friendly to rats and pigeons, but not much else. "Robin isn't the only one who can send letters, e-mails, leave voice mails. I've drowned him in them."

That's where I'd gone after arriving, hijacking the cab before eventually making my way to Talleywhacker's bar and Cal. I'd been spreading the word . . . written and using the drug dealer's phone. "Besides, every time travel movie I've seen is a how-to guide to fixing this kind of crap." Not that movies took the *paien* version of physics and all the other science they and I didn't have a hope of comprehending into consideration. Bottom line: It was a crapshoot.

Movies. Life should be so easy. And although the one movie was made before I was born, I'd really wished the

Kyntalash was a DeLorean. Near certain failure and death should have made the ride more entertaining.

"I didn't stop with Goodfellow either. The guy who will be my boss at the bar, the one that . . ." I could see the ball of fire, two, three, four stories high. How high had it gone and how far had it spread? I hadn't stayed to see. I couldn't have and kept the gun away from my head or my finger off the trigger. I'd left that subdivision of fiery hell as soon as I could stagger away.

"Anyway, my future boss, I left him a shitload of messages too." As well as Niko's future lady friend. Promise had given me a vampire flash of fangs when I'd referred to her once as Nik's "girlfriend," saying she was not a thirteen-year-old waiting for a boy to notice she'd grown breasts over the summer. "When that day comes again, no one will be there. The place will be empty."

Not that I could know things wouldn't change and the eddy and flow of time wouldn't turn into a vicious riptide that would have the Vigil striking at us earlier, somewhere else . . . which is why I was banking on Goodfellow predicting their possible behavior in that note he'd left. Between his talent for out-thinking anyone else's plan and my messages to him now that gave him eight years of planning time, we had a chance to save us all.

I couldn't know or have absolute faith, but I couldn't think the worst either. Simply by sitting here on this ledge breathing, I was changing a thousand tiny events and who knew what that would lead to?

"We only have to kill this assassin then and everything is taken care of."

"The assassin that the Vigil injected with several kinds of supernatural DNA in a serious case of hypocrisy. The assassin we have no idea what he looks like or what he can do, if he's remotely human still? No problem." That I did mean. I'd fought against monsters no one had defeated before. I'd fought Auphe and with Niko, Robin, and ironically the Vigil's help, had wiped them out. I could do this in my sleep. If I ever slept again.

Niko slid down from the table and opened the refrigerator. "Tell me more about the assassin and the Vigil. What is our situation?"

"Operation Lazarus. The project is meant to raise the order from the dead." I hopped off the table myself and fell into an equally flimsy kitchen chair. "As you can guess, original on names they are not. Calling themselves the Vigil in the first place probably gave that away. If you have a burning desire to call the assassin anything other than dead meat, call him Lazarus if you want, if you have time before I rip his goddamn head from his body."

"Why didn't the Vigil, a large organization from the sounds of it, not kill you in your own time? It seems far simpler than ancient technology and time travel." There was rattling from inside the fridge as Niko pushed around his tofu heaven.

"They tried, trust me, enough times I lost count," I said. "But when you have a friend who knows everyone and everything, not to mention has a few extra million in change under his couch cushions, he could hire better assassins than all the ones they sent after me. He could, if he wanted, decide an entire organization had been playing God too long to a pagan crowd, which meant no Hosannas were being sung in the Vigil's name. They had one crime and one punishment—be revealed for what you are and you die for it. Robin decided, and all the *paien* backed him up, it was time for the humans who thought they could keep us in check to go." Niko didn't miss it, he wouldn't, but he didn't say anything when I included myself with the nonhuman *paien*. "One way or the other. They either left the city or they died. Lazarus is the only one left, whatever kind of lab-created killing machine he is. Robin's contacts were never able to find that out."

"You said the Vigil didn't know this address."

"No." I glanced over at Cal. He was soundly out. He should be for several more hours. "But you can't stay here forever. And you can't be looking over your shoulder forever for Lazarus when you are already doing that with the Auphe." He wasn't going to like it, but I didn't see another way. "We're going to have to use Cal to chum the water.

Have him back at the bar. Not inside it. That pathetic-sized closet is a kill box, if ever there was one. But if Cal walks around the area, Lazarus will spot him. We let him follow us to something more private and with more room to work. Lots of room, as we don't know what he is or can do after the Vigil juiced him up. Then"—I shaped two fingers into a gun and let the "hammer" fall—"done."

"You want to use my brother as bait?" Niko reappeared with a Styrofoam container. "You referred to him as 'chum'?"

"Everything I say about him, I'm saying about myself. And you know it's the only way. I'd act as bait myself and let you lock him in a bank vault somewhere if I thought it would work. The Vigil wasn't that sloppy though. They would have made certain Lazarus could recognize the younger me from the older me. I wish it had been less than eight years and we had a better hope of passing for each other. I'd be happy as hell to help you stuff him in that vault. I have years of fighting experience on Cal." And I brought gating to the party with me, if worse came to worst. "If despite that, and Lazarus kills me anyway, your Cal won't stop existing. You'll have another shot at the asshole. But if Cal is killed, poof. Like a magic show, I'm gone. I never even was. This version of me won't have happened. You'll go from two Cals to none. I'd say if that happens that you could get Lazarus and take his *Kyntalash*"—I tapped mine through the long sleeve of my T-shirt—"go back an hour or so and warn us, giving us then two Nikos and two Cals at one time." I wasn't immune to a shudder at that thought. "But it'd be a lie. The moment Cal dies, Lazarus will be gone right along with me. If Cal doesn't live at least several years longer, enough to break the Vigil's top rule, there will be no reason for the Vigil to try to kill him, to make an assassin, and Lazarus, like me, will never be."

If that happened, it would be Niko's turn by the metaphorical pizza place, his own weapon aimed at himself. We both knew it. There was no need to say it.

"Then we'll endeavor to keep that from occurring." Niko opened the container. "You aren't looking well.

You're paler than normal, which means you're all but transparent. You haven't eaten since you've been here, I know you wouldn't consider it or remember food is a requirement for life after . . ." That halted him in his verbal tracks as he searched for words for my day that he thought I could bear to hear. He must have decided there weren't any and let it go. "Cal has some leftover lechon asado from his, both of yours I suppose, favorite food truck, favorite this month at least. You should finish it for him. It'll be five less miles I'll make him run."

Lechon asado. Slow roasted pork.

The back of my throat was instantly burning with bile. I swallowed, coughed against it, and fought not to breathe through my nose. It didn't make a difference. The smell of the meat was unavoidable and everywhere. If Niko thought I had looked bad before, he was going to have more to worry about when I vomited on the floor. Sliding the chair away from the table as far as I could get before it stopped, trapped by the deeper sand. Hand over my nose and mouth, I rasped, "I can say for sure I doubt I'll ever eat grilled or roasted meat again." Or be around any cooking meat—shit, eat meat of any kind at all. "It's your dream come true, Nik. I'm now a vegetarian."

The implication of it was instant. I'd been there, a block away while my brother and my friend burned. He knew my scenting abilities were equal to Cal's if not grown sharper with age. He could guess what it had been like for me. Dumping the box of leftovers in the sink, he covered it with three-fourths of a bottle of dish soap and turned the water on full. When it was as thoroughly neutralized as anyone could make it, he carried the dripping box to the bathroom and flushed the leftovers. He tore the box to pieces and flushed them as well. He had to have since he came back empty-handed. He didn't say word one about it. He knew, as he knew with the other Cal, it wouldn't improve anything about the situation. God, it was weird as hell all what he knew about me, considering how much I'd changed in almost a decade. Or thought I'd changed.

"I'm guessing tofu or yogurt is out of the question too." He was right. Food of any sort wasn't in the cards for me tonight. He did open the refrigerator again to give me four of the smaller bottles of Gatorade. "At least try to get these down. Collapsing from dehydration severely affects your aim," he said dryly before taking in the condition of the apartment. "I'll clean up here. I'll get you clean clothes and you can shower, then sleep. Take Cal's bed. You deserve it. As that garbage dump is your lifelong signature, I would be surprised if it's not the same at twenty-six."

I didn't deny the truth of that, but I shook my head. "You shower, leave me some clothes for when I do, and go to bed. Take Cal with you. You trust me mostly, but with that Cal"—I nodded toward the couch—"you don't trust anyone but yourself." And if Niko thought I looked bad, he needed a mirror. He'd had a series of shocks today with finding out his brother was the target of an assassin, the same brother but older came back from the future to save him, plus he'd fought his first skin-walker, which would freak the hell out of anyone who did that and lived. Lastly, he'd found out he was dead, which made me a suicide hotline's wet dream. That banking on the fact it was possible to stop my brother from dying was the sole reason I stood here alive now. He'd lived two years now with that scenario with both him and Cal alternating in starring roles in the back of his mind. He couldn't know how I felt, but he could imagine a hazy shape of it.

"Go," I reiterated. "I'll sleep on the couch just in case your neighbors show up and try to break in to drink our blood or other bodily fluids you don't want to know about. In the morning, Cal will be up and all three of us can clean up this petting zoo meets slasher movie."

He hesitated, but he knew his limitations. He knew when he should listen to them and when he couldn't afford it. Nodding, he went to the couch, bent down, and slung Cal over his shoulder in a fireman's carry.

"You can't tell him, remember. About the Vigil, the assassin, sure—but not about Goodfellow and not about my Nik. You're different but you're also the same. If he finds out about my Nik, he will lose his shit. It won't matter that it's eight years from now or that we might be able to stop it. He will still lose his shit all over the damn place because he'll have your gravestone in his head, a gravestone with the year you die. That you leave him. Then he'll do the only thing he can, be all over you like glitter and glue in a preschool art class. He won't leave your side for a second, so get used to pissing with an audience for a while. All that is going to make him worse than useless against Lazarus. He'll be like a live grenade someone tripped and dropped inside a tank full of soldiers. Bouncing back and forth, a potential messy death for everyone in the vicinity. Basically he'll be as insane as I am right now, both of us trying to save our brothers any way we can."

Niko tried to meet my eyes, but couldn't. I didn't blame him. He knew what was behind them now. "I forgive you for the snake. I'll tell Cal we simply missed it and he won't kill you over breakfast." He did raise his gaze enough to look at me. "Thank you. And stay with us, please, as long as you can."

Stay with us. Stay *alive* as long as you can bear it. What to say to that?

As it turned out, nothing. He'd taken the pressure of replying off me by turning and hoisting Cal to Niko's own, much cleaner, bedroom. If something made it past me, then they had Niko to face before they had a prayer of making it to Cal.

I waited until the shower went on and off and Niko's bedroom door closed. Taking my own shower, I didn't care that the water was cold. It hadn't been warm once the entire time we'd lived here. Scrubbing my skin free of blood, venom, spider juice, the scent of fertilizer and chemicals, of smoke and burned flesh, it was fine. If there hadn't been water, I'd have used the scouring pads we had for our one pot. Removing a layer of skin would've been good as well. After drying off and dressing in Niko's sparring sweats, I went back to the scene of crime, sneered at it, and then searched the kitchen for garbage bags. I found one small box with thin white bags two and a half feet tall. I tore a jagged hole in one by pulling it out of the box with too much enthusiasm. "You've got to be kidding me," I muttered. "How the hell did we survive without Costco?"

10

It was about 5:30 a.m. when Niko woke up. His normal wake-up time, but he'd gone to bed earlier by hours than usual last night. Skin-walkers did take it out of you. He was dragging a Cal with eyes three-fourths of the way shut. Shoving him into the bathroom, he said, "Shower. For a very long time. I put up with the dried coyote blood on you last night out of consideration for your fragile state in reaction to an overgrown garter snake, but my selfless and giving nature has its limits. Go and scrub until you do not smell like dead dog any longer." There was an incoherent snarl and the slam of the bathroom door. I sympathized. It was the same reaction I had to 5:30 a.m.

"What . . ." Niko had come up to and then gone past the couch, swiveling his head back and forth to cover every inch. "You were supposed to be sleeping. What did you do? No, that's obvious. Why did you do it? You said the three of us would clean up in the morning. And my Cal does not clean, making this highly suspicious behavior."

I snorted. "Your Cal has yet to live with the stench of leaving dead creepy-crawlies overnight to take care of the next day. The blood seeps between the tiles all night long and stays under there, stinking up the place more and more every day long after the bodies are gone. We learned our lesson the first time we had to rip up the entire floor and let it soak in bleach for a week before we could replace it with a new one. We like being lazy, he and I, but we like being able to breathe without choking or puking more."

Niko had gone from turning his head to pivoting his entire body. His eyebrows were raised so far that if you could sprain your forehead, he would've. "All the bodies, the blood, the venom, the —"

He had to be thinking about the thick slime that had sprayed out of the ruptured, punctured, and squashed spiders. "Ick," I supplied, slouching on the couch, my fingers rolling a long length between them, putting the finished product into a large Tupperware bowl old enough to qualify as an antique, and then starting on the next strip. "Just call it ick. You've used ichor enough times that the word is more repulsive than the actual gunk itself."

I don't think he heard me. "And the sand. Everything. It's gone." He finally ended up facing me. "How?"

"With what you guys keep in stock, it wasn't easy." I yawned, eyes gritty, muscles tight with the feeling you get when you're too tired to sleep. "But I remembered the *rusalka*, the lamia, and the wendigo. I've never figured out what *rusalka* get out of drowning people, but it does leave entire bodies to dispose of. The lamia" — I winced — "are a little like vampires, but they don't care about drinking blood. They care about drinking everything. You don't want to know how they do it. Don't ask. Point is it leaves bodies too, but they weigh less. They're like a juice box a snot-nosed little kid has drained dry. The wendigo eats everything but the bones. Disposal, you'd think, would be easier, but it's not. The bones spear through your average garbage bag like a knife through butter."

I shrugged and smirked wearily. "I just made like a friendly neighbor and borrowed all their heavy-duty extra-large family-sized boxes of Costco garbage bags." I was beginning to feel like an ad placement in my own life for those damned things. "Because this"—I glared as I snatched up one of his will-o'-the-wisp, tissue paper, tiny garbage bags off the cushion next to me and flipped it in his face—"does not get the job done. Thank fuck you had a few gallons of bleach around so I could scrub the floor once I got rid of the sand. You need to start shopping like a fanatically enthusiastic, wildly prolific serial killer. An 'I love my hobby, have multiple orgasms with each body I drag home, nightly cruising' serial killer. It's how you stay prepared for when assholes like the skin-walker come along."

He snapped the plastic away from his face, which wore a perplexed expression I didn't know he had in him. "What did you do with all the bagged bodies? What did you do with all the *sand*?"

"Bodies are in your Dumpster, which I then swapped with one down the street. Sand is in the hall. Without an industrial vacuum it takes weeks to get rid of sand. In the hall was good enough." I rolled up another strip and plunked it in the bowl. "Put industrial wet-dry vac on your Christmas list. I'm Mary frigging Poppins here to whip you two into shape. Aren't you lucky?"

Niko was beginning to focus more clearly as the shock of a Cal who cleaned, if for massacres only, began to sink in. He pointed at the bowl. "And that?"

"Snakeskin. I skinned them before I bagged them. Cal did say he wanted a pair of snakeskin boots when I made the offer." I didn't give a damn if he got the boots—unless he managed to hold on to them long enough they made it to me someday. Skin-walker boots. I'd impress even myself with those. More to the point, I didn't have anything else to do and sleep wasn't an option. Neither was eating.

Perplexed Niko was gone, replaced by unimpressed Niko. That was a Niko I was used to seeing every day. "You didn't sleep. Not at all."

"I'll sleep when I'm dead. Isn't that the saying?" A saying, prediction, an absolute truth if things didn't go my way. Rock, paper, scissors.

I had tried to sleep, against my better judgment. Sixty

seconds with my eyes closed was the equivalent of the longest IMAX movie made of the god-awful moment of my life. The flames were real enough I thought I could touch them. I'd tried. Then I opened my eyes and went with the theory that I had three days before sleep deprivation had me hallucinating. That was three days to put one in Lazarus's head. Time limits, I could deal with them easier than I could deal with sleeping.

"Hey, who stole my favorite jeans?" Cal stomped up, sheet around his hips as last night we'd run out of the six whole towels they owned, Niko and I using the last two with our showers. He was leaving a wide puddle on the floor I'd spent part of the night cleaning, but it was a clear puddle. Blood I'd wipe up. Clean water, that's where the laziness came in. It'd dry eventually on its own. Cal's soaked hair hung flattened around his face and dripping steadily.

"Your only clean pair? That'd be me. Niko's sweats were a complete loss with all the blood and guts I spent half the night in on my knees scrubbing like your combination babysitter and maid." I finished with the last strip of scaled skin, threw it in the bowl, and tossed the whole thing to Cal. He caught it one handed while losing half his grip on his sheet. "Here you go. Find yourself a boot maker. Oh, I borrowed a T-shirt too. I had a duffel bag with two changes of clothes and a shitload of weapons you'd give up sex for in a second—when you have it. I couldn't fit the flamethrower, but I had my varsity lineup in there."

None of it had done me any good, as it had been resting by Niko's feet for him to keep an eye on while I went for the pizzas. "Time travel didn't agree with them for some reason." I lied as easily as my heart beat—smooth and even. Not a single blip in my heart rate. Polygraphs are worthless when you're amoral and then some. "I came through, but no duffel bag. I'm lucky the trip included the clothes I was wearing and the weapons on me. Doing covert crap like walking down the sidewalk to a hole-in-the-wall bar while naked and it's not quite dark yet, that would be a pain in the ass."

I stood up and stretched, every bone in my back cracking audibly. "Wait. Where'd you get that shirt? Where did the shirt get *that*?" Niko had gone from perplexed, stunned, unimpressed, and was heading toward either embarrassed or disapproving. He'd used his entire weekly allotment of facial expressions in less than four minutes. A record if ever there was one.

"This?" I plucked at the medium gray T-shirt. "I borrowed it from Cal with the jeans." It was plain or had been. These were the days when my sarcasm was verbal. I hadn't branched out into visual to go with that for four or so years yet. Having none with me, I'd made my own. I searched around the drawer I vaguely remembered as the one drawer we'd used to hold all our pens, marker, notepads. Finding a red marker, I'd come up with my own snarky shirt, although it was a real place. It was a thriving franchise thanks to the Kin, the werewolf mafia. It read:

HUMPERS
Werewolf Strip Club
Full! Frontal! Fur!
Best *TAIL* in town!

I'd thought about trying for their trademark sexy wolf in the middle of it, but an artist I wasn't. "No," Niko denied firmly. "I am not leaving this apartment or standing anywhere near you if you wear that. You look like an unhinged interspecies pervert."

Cal was more interested than offended. "Werewolf strip club. Huh." He was less casual than he thought. "So is that a real pl—"

Niko clapped his hand over his mouth. "No. You are not starting down that path on my watch. You'd have fleas and be rabid within a week. You, Caliban, change the shirt."

"Okay, okay. Don't get your panties wedged up too high. You'll be sterile before Cal is rabid." I stripped off the shirt, turned it inside out, and put it back on. It now read:

Werewolves
Once you go furry,
You never have to worry.

I hadn't managed a wolf on the other side, but I did accomplish a mildly lopsided paw print on this one. "There. Happy now, grandma?"

"No. Disgusted and appalled, but I would *not* say happy."

I was thinking of an outrageous lie to make him worry about his own taste, something along the lines of the retro stage that would hit in two years that would have him cutting his hair into the longest mullet in the city, when there was a knock on the door. I gave up. He wouldn't have believed me.

There was only one reason Niko cut his hair.

"Yeah," I grumbled, "you two stay there. One half-naked sheet burrito flooding the floor and a seizure waiting to happen over my taste in shirts. Don't answer your own door." Not that I would have let them. If one of us had to die, I'd be the least damaging to all our lives. I reached for the Glock tucked in the back of the jeans I was wearing. We knew Lazarus wasn't aware of this address, but I'd rather be safe and alive than sorry and dead. At least if I did end up dead, I'd be buried in a hilarious T-shirt. Gun hidden behind me, I stayed to one side of the door in case anyone tried to shoot through it. After the second knock, I leaned over for a split second there-and-back look out of the peephole.

Wicked—and not wicked as in an impish, mischievous manner but more of the full-blown demonic kind—green eyes, brown hair halfway between curly and wavy, and a grin wide enough for ten car salesmen despite being just the one.

Oh, fuck me sideways. I should've caught his scent. Why hadn't I . . . The bleach I'd used to scrub the tile floor. It remained hanging in the air, a noxious fog that would block out any other smell for days. I slid over and rested my forehead against the door, holding back the impulse to bang it repeatedly. With the third cheerful knock—how could a knock be cheerful—I groaned, "Jesus Christ."

"Nope." The voice exceeded the cheer of the knock. And it was familiar. God, was it. "I dated his cousin though. Great set of yabbos."

"Damn," Cal commented, clutching at his sheet with one hand and balancing the bowl of snakeskin with the other. "I'm an atheist and I'm not sure I wanted to hear that."

I did bang my head against the door this time. I'd lived through hearing that line once before. Of all the things I could relive, hearing that again wasn't at the top of my list.

It wasn't who it was. Who it was had flashes of light darting across my sight. Shock led to low blood pressure, low blood pressure led to annoying yellow streaks, and wishing you had the luxury of keeling over to stare at the ceiling for a while. But I didn't and blinked them away instead. It was a shock all right, but the good kind, the best. If it wasn't for the fact that he was here a year too goddamn early. As he was the linchpin of us living through the next year, any mistakes at this point and you should go ahead, climb a mountain, sing "Kumbayah," and drink the Kool-Aid, because those nut jobs, for once, would be right.

"Stay here," I told Niko and Cal. "This is . . . complicated. Niko, tell your brother about how lazy shits who sit on their asses instead of sweeping the aftermath of a fight get bitten by poisonous giant snakes. And brief him on the Vigil/Lazarus crap while you're at it. I'm too tired to go over that again." Niko gave a minute nod to show he remembered what and what not to let Cal in on—nearly everything.

I yanked open the door just enough to slip through and keep the person in the hall hidden, stepped out, and slammed it shut behind me. Unlike Niko and Cal, he didn't look any younger. I could've gone back eighty years or eight hundred, he'd be the same. As a precaution, I started down the hall. It wouldn't matter if Niko caught a glimpse of him as he was one of the secrets Niko was currently keeping, but Cal didn't need to if we could avoid it. "You couldn't resist, could you? Not for *one* goddamned year?" I accused. "Never mind I told you to stay away until then or you could foul it all up."

"Your note said we have eight years before the world was deprived of me, the brilliance of its one true sun. There's clearly no hurry. And I never foul up, as you say, anything," he discounted smugly with an actual snap of the fingers. That was the same. I should suggest he get new annoying habits. That one was getting stale.

"I hate to tell you you're wrong, wait, no, I don't. You're *wrong*. It's not like what will happen in eight years is the first time we all almost die or *do* die," I snapped. "That's practically a yearly occurrence for us, like freaking Christmas. But we get through it or we would have if we kept everything the same. Yet you fucked that up in *nine* hours. What, did it feel like a year? Did you set your alarm wrong, one year to nine hours? Easy mistake, right? This will screw up so much future shit. Forget eight years. We'll be lucky to survive six months. In a year, we will be dead, as there's no avoiding that particular coming cluster fuck. We shouldn't have made it through the first time. This is all because of your"—impatience, curiosity, insatiable need to know everything as soon as puckishly possible—"because of you being you. We're dead . . . or worse."

"I think you exaggerate. And death? There are worse fates than death to you? Never mind. Boring topic, death," he dismissed. Death, my death, everyone's possible death. He was totally unconcerned. *Of course* he was.

"I heard enough of it during that threesome with Emily Dickinson and Edgar Allan Poe. On and on about funerals in brains. She wanted to dig a grave and have sex in a shiny new coffin. And then there was 'lost Lenore.' Angels crying. On and on. No one knew Eddie's Lenore was his pet rat. It died of old age, a *rat*, yet the man never stopped with the 'Night's Plutonian shore,' and the 'Nevermore. Nevermore. Nevermore.' And the weeping, such an incredible amount of weeping. We nearly drowned in that coffin. It put me off threesomes for a decade."

We hadn't swapped names yet, not officially, and he was starting with a sex story off the bat. I had to give that to him—he began as he meant to go on. Backward or forward, whichever direction you could go, Goodfellow would be the same. He matched my path down the hall, carrying a pair of shoes that knowing him were more expensive than a brand-new BMW with an imported on call 24/7 German mechanic who could relate to it at a cultural level that beat the effort of any American mechanic.

"I'd forgotten how much you let the pervert in you run wild and free in the beginning," I grimaced. "And let me tell you when I want to hear another story like that one." He thought I was honest and was raising eyebrows in sly challenge, while his brain eagerly tossed another filthy one on the assembly line to be delivered.

"Yes?"

"Never-fucking-more," I said flatly.

"Very well. On to the boring . . ." I began to turn around to head back to the apartment with the obvious intention of locking him out. The conversation was over. "Fine. Fine. Not boring. Perhaps more entertaining when punctuated with a few raunchy stories, but I can do without." I halted the turn and kept on in my original direction away from Niko and Cal's. With relief, Robin scuffled along heedless of the flying sand. "Then we do know each other or you think we do." That was complicated too. I could rip him a new one all day long. It wouldn't make him think twice of what he'd done. He wanted to know. Couldn't stand not knowing, and, being a trickster, he *would* know. No one could stop him, including me.

I should've been more careful about the note, but I needed him to take my warning seriously about his death eight years from now. He was a puck, the oldest puck. They assume you're lying as they're always lying themselves. That's why I'd left proof in a few names and a hook in the last name I'd used to sign the letter. I couldn't see any way that it could've led him here. It shouldn't have. I hadn't seen the risk, but if I had, I'd have done the same. I needed his one hundred percent belief to keep his horny ass from being wiped out by the Vigil's explosion.

"You aren't supposed to be here. I said so in the letter." I'd left it at his car lot. What would a puck and a trickster be but a used car salesman? "You *know* you're fucking up right now just being here because you were the one who told me that. To keep you away. You said, *'Change events enough, Caliban, and you won't fuck up impressively as normal. You'll fuck up spectacularly. The world, the universe, every dimension, you'll erase them all and then how will I get laid?'*"

I shoved his shoulder, not hard, but not particularly lightly either. "This is on you. I quoted you exactly in the letter"—except leaving out "Caliban"—"*I* listened to you. You didn't listen to yourself." I flopped down to sit on the sand. It had a taint of blood to it, but that was a smell I was used to.

He walked through the sand that was as high or a little higher than a few inches above our ankles until he caught up. He sat. I don't think it was as gingerly and careful of his suit as he'd planned on, the kind of suit too elite for people like me to be allowed to know the name of the tailor. He secured his ludicrously expensive shoes, the only kind he'd owned since I'd known him, on his lap away from the sand.

"I was curious, and I don't listen to myself all the time. How boring would that be?" he said, waving both arms to be sure I saw how boggling the concept was. "How many adventures would I have missed, destruction I wouldn't have wrought? The Tower of Babel would still be standing for one, and that was too hideous to bear. I could've been blinded by a structure so misshapen, such an eyesore, its epic hideousness has not been matched. The architect and builders should've been chopped up and fed to the pigs."

Switching subjects at a speed that used to cause motion sickness before I got used to it. "I didn't introduce myself, which could be awkward as I'm telling tales from my life that occurred hundreds or thousands of years ago. But as you addressed the envelope of your letter to Robin Goodfellow and not to Rob Fellows, a captivating and charming human car salesman but certainly no one whom mythological figures were based upon, you must know that already. Or think that you do."

He hesitated, absently sketching a few Greek letters sideways in the sand. "Your correspondence, on the highly exciting stationery that was the back of a flyer for Planned Parenthood said that we were friends." The last word was stated neutrally and with wary caution, but Robin, second trickster born, either couldn't hold back or had no idea the reality of how sad and fucking melancholy it was.

"I have people," he covered hurriedly, "and people to tell my people to talk to someone else's people. I have acquaintances, contacts, lovers, and potential victims of what will be spectacular cons if I get bored. But I don't have friends or I do, but they come and they go, in the blink of an eye. I never know when I'll see them again."

The letters he'd written in the sand spelled *Filous* in the Greek alphabet. Friends. He'd tried to teach me Greek, but I knew five words on a good day, to read and write. He'd taught me twenty or so of the filthiest curse words in the language. Those were for yelling, no reading or writing needed in learning those.

He was here and, year early or not, he wasn't leaving. It didn't matter what I told him. With Niko and me, he forgot that self-preservation was a puck's number one priority. I gave up.

Leaning forward, I scrawled a word beneath his. *Adélfia*. Brothers.

"No need. I know exactly who you are." My grin wasn't like his, unless you found predatory and wolfish to be charismatic. Fortunately, Robin did. He had that grin and worse in his repertoire. Ten thousand grins for ten thousand different types of cons.

"You think you do, do you?" He was doing his best to hide how shaken he was. I knew that as I knew him and had for a very long time. It was the hope. With what I was hoping to do and who I was hoping to bring back, I understood how painful and uncertain hope could be.

"Trickster Second, born of Hob, the Trickster First." I kept my grin and flicked sand at him. "You better sit down. I know green's your favorite color, but I don't think your skin gets included in that."

His eyes glazed, the blurred glazed stare falling to focus on something less confusing than me. Lifting up a handful of the grains of sand, he let them trickle between his fingers, back to where they came. He did keep them away from the flow of letters, painstaking in his effort to not disturb them. "Skin-walkers, a bargain compared to purchasing the sand." His voice was distant and stilted. But he was Robin Goodfellow, second trickster to walk the earth. He could recover quickly enough to make someone doubt the puck had been startled at all.

One breath, two, and the conceit and confidence was back full force. "If I'd known there was a beach party, I would've brought piña coladas." He brightened. How, I didn't know. He was already as bright as he could get without inflicting the permanent blindness you'd get from staring at the sun for hours.

"Ah! I've an idea. I invariably have ideas staggering enough in their brilliance that I'm surprised the earth doesn't confuse my mind with the sun and start rotating around my head." I tried to stop him but Goodfellow was faster with a phone than Doc Holliday with a gun. "Hercules. Raid the liquor supply in the limo. I want piña coladas, hurricanes, mojitos, sex on the beach. . . ." The puck raised an eyebrow as he looked me up and down. "Make that all the sex on the beach you *know* I can handle." He gave me a wink wicked enough that inside his apartment Cal's sheet had unraveled instantly until it was a pile of thread around his feet and he was naked as the day he was born with no idea how or why.

"Oh, and, Brutus, get the cabana boy outfit out of the trunk, you know the one I like, change out of your driver's uniform and into that before you get up here. I'm on the seventh floor. Bring a beach chair if we still have one after that incident last month. A beach towel if we don't. *Yes*, oiling your muscles is mandatory with that outfit whether there is sun or not, Adonis. You ask every time. Don't complain or I'll take away your unlimited employee gym membership." He turned off the phone and rolled his eyes. "What a whiny infant."

I couldn't resist. I made the effort. I had years of experience with Robin and his orgy-loving personality, but I couldn't keep the question to myself. "Hercules, Brutus, Adonis, you have no idea what the guy's name is, do you?"

I had years of experience, but Goodfellow didn't, not this time.

"I would be offended if it weren't the truth. But as he barely knows it himself, I can carry on under the heavy burden of massive guilt." His grin was brilliantly white and horny as hell. He'd denied that with every one of them he flashed, claiming they were magnetic and charismatic. He'd told me once, the fourth day we'd met, I thought, that horny was in the ass of the beholder, and had said it while his hand was *on* my ass.

The fourth day of what was supposed to have been the first time we'd met.

That had been the days of getting to know each other better through typical Alpha male butt sniffing, endless repetitions of my heterosexuality, and a face in the gutter drinking binge. We'd straightened things out—ironically enough, I thought—I'd bought him a beer and shoved him over onto Nik. Nik had been more polite and had put up with drunken, lustful, and predatory attempts at his virtue, which Robin had been certain he had locked in a chastity belt inside his pants. He'd waved a cocktail umbrella at him, slurring there was no lock he couldn't pick. Nik had in turn passed him on to a waitress with a rack large enough that Goodfellow had used it as a pillow and passed out on it.

Nik had been able to take care of himself. And good luck if he couldn't. As long as Robin had stopped with me, I'd been fine and less ... I admit ... terrified. And, after all, as the puck had noted, there were enough men, women, nymphs, Wolves, vampires to be had, although he'd made his way through the city once and would have to start issuing a repeat banging punch card, the prize being guest of honor at one of his orgies.

Yeah, I'd found out he had orgies—all the time. I'd told him he was that guy you heard about. He'd fuck a snake if he could get it to hold still. He hadn't been insulted. Hell, he'd been proud if anything, the arrogant bastard, and scoffed, "If a snake met me, it wouldn't hold still. It would be the one chasing *me* down."

I'd lived through the trauma of that once already. I was not repeating it. I didn't care how many years early he had shown up.

"Born of Hob," he murmured, audible but only if you had excellent hearing. "You do know me, then. I can't decide whether that's thrilling or dangerous. Hades warm and fiery cock, I like them both." He whipped up another wide grin. And, again, because I did know him, I knew it was his deceitful one like I knew he was defensive *and* offensive, wary, curious, ready to con me any way he could, hopeful it could be true. That I did know him. He was suspicious, he had to be. It was easier last time when I hadn't known anything about him at all. Ignorance he could trust. Knowledge, that was dangerous.

I'd seen him at his true work, not selling cars, on other people. Worse came to worst, he'd be tempted to get me in bed to see what information he could pry out of me, tempted to get me in bed simply to fuck me, tempted to kill me because better alive and horny than dead and never horny again, because hope his friend had returned? That hope was a splinter from a giant redwood that was delusion.

The thought of a seduction attempt was more horrifying than the one of a murder attempt by far. I groaned. "Look, I have lived this nightmare before. After massive suffering on my part, we called a cease-fire on your libido. You'll have to try your luck with the me who belongs in this time. He's young, wild, and barely legal. Put him in a kiddie harness, the leash in your hand and you'll be the happiest puck alive."

Under the bus I threw Cal Junior without a second thought. It was his turn to suffer now.

I rested my head back against the wall. "How'd you find me? I left an anonymous letter at your car dealership. Anonymous." Or anonymous in a way that couldn't lead to me. "No address. No fingerprints." Not that mine were on file. Only those who are caught are in the system and me? Caught? As if that would ever happen. I'd stolen the cabbie's gloves anyway. The house always wins unless you take precautions that it doesn't.

"You said I called you Caliban in a similar letter I left you." He was looking at me again, but this time not a leering up and down. He was taking in every feature. I knew him, but did he really know me? He hoped, but no puck ever relied on hope. "That's not how you signed the letter to me. Is Caliban your real name?"

"Sometimes," I answered, but didn't elaborate. "I also said I'd answer your questions after you answered mine. How'd you find me? It's important. If you can, someone else can. Someone we don't want to find us, not here."

"Recognition software," he sighed. "I have it all over the car lot and the building. It didn't ping on your face, but the software in the mail slot did flag your 'Robin Goodfellow' envelope. I have people in the city who know me, but they know when and when not to use that name. The system alarmed on my computer and I pulled up all the digital camera footage. I have the entire block covered in fact. I had your face, which went nowhere, but I had the license plate and the number of your cab. Some calls here and there. Money greasing palms, your driver was more than eager to give you up. He really didn't care for you. I went to where he dropped you off, called up a few minions, passed out some photos and fifteen minutes later I found you. I'd found *two* of you. But the note did talk about time travel and there was the proof . . . or could be. You could also be brothers."

He stretched his legs and yawned. "I left a handful of other minions, the kind that aren't noticeable to the human eye, around the bar." When I didn't blink about nonhumans working for him, he went on. "They followed you to this building and then this apartment, although normally they wouldn't have gone that far. Too risky even for them, but the skin-walker battle for the ages made it easier to find the floor and take a quick peek at which door was shaking enough to qualify as an earthquake. It was disappointingly easy."

I must not have had the most pleased expression on my face with the appeasing hand he held up. "Ah, ah, don't be touchy that you're not the James Bond you'd imagined. That was but the first part of my covert little operation. I didn't wait for the skin-walker escapade to be over, as depending on your skills, that could take all night or you could be dead in thirty seconds. I had no idea of your capabilities. And I was not ruining a brand-new Ralph Lauren Blue Label suit by running to join in. I've fought enough of them in my life and they are walking bags of every type of disgusting fluid you don't want to think about.

"Instead I went back to my penthouse, turned on my computer and accessed my database, which considering I own a satellite orbiting the planet for the storage alone, is quite extensive and I started running down your identities." He was sulking now.

I snorted. "That was the part that wasn't so easy, right, Sherlock?"

"It was very easy. I found hundreds." He started counting them off on his fingers and when he ran out, started on them over again. "Fake driver's licenses, fake social security cards, fake car registrations, fake car insurance, fake birth certificates, fake passports, fake pilot licenses, fake résumés with fake references and fake places of employment, two fake mortgages on houses that don't exist, fake library cards—Aristotle would be proud—fake bank accounts with no money in them as you are the cash and carry type. It wouldn't surprise me if you had a fake dog license and no dog to go with it. You have, or they have since you are eight years from home, seventy-five names between them. After all night of this, I came to one conclusion, no two. First, you deprived me of ten hours sleep or ten highly ranked escorts and no sleep. I'd have been happy with either. Second, and most important, I couldn't find an identity for you or the other two renting the apartment because you don't have and never have had identities."

He folded his arms and tilted his head to one side and then the other, adding up all the pieces and parts of me he'd taken in earlier. "No identity. Your black hair, your eyes—gray is rare but does pop up now and again among clans who appeared in Northern Greece six hundred years or so ago and the other clans they intermarried into, but your skin however, Snow White, doesn't fit. Rom, but only part Rom. Half, I believe. With skin that pale, almost inhumanly so, your other half would have to be part . . ." The words trailed away, but his mouth didn't shut as he stared, paler himself. It had taken him longer this time to recognize it in me, but time travel, anonymous notes, fake identities would distract anyone.

"No," he whispered.

I'd forgotten how afraid he'd been of the Auphe, of me, when our very first crossing of ways had involved a knife to his throat and threats. I, and Niko too, had been throwing those far and wide. Robin's fear of me had lasted seconds; he was good at sizing people up and I'd been nineteen, no idea what he was, and willing on the violence, but it was an obvious human type of violence. Goodfellow had decided I fell into that category: human more than Auphe. For those few seconds, though, he had been afraid.

"Relax." Sliding my hands behind my neck, I linked fingers to ease the strained muscle. "I'm not a murderous homicidal psychotic monster who lives to slaughter." I paused. "At least not unless it's necessary." The second hesitation was a shade longer. "Or some assholes really deserve it." I thought back and next told what wasn't technically a lie, as the Auphe genes weren't in control any longer. I was. "I definitely don't do it for fun." And I didn't, not *just* for fun. That wasn't to say I didn't enjoy it if it had to be done, such as putting down the skin-walker. Robin would know I was hedging, if it was about the past or not. You can't lie to a puck, not even by omission. "Not anymore."

There was perceptibly more white in Goodfellow's eyes.

"I'm making it worse, aren't I?" I asked ruefully.

"Yes. Stop. Please." With that he managed to finally close his mouth.

"Don't be a hypocrite. I know what 'born of Hob' means. I *met* Hob. He could hold his own with any Auphe, three at a time if he had to." More than that and he'd ended up in pieces—too bad for Hob. I'd shed a tear if ever I gave a shit.

"You met *Hob*?" His face was painted with revulsion and rejection. "Hob is dead. All puck know this. If by some unholy misfortune, he is alive and you met him, you would be dead. Whatever puck you spoke with lied, pretended to be him, took his name, fooled you."

"You were there. You knew him. I had no idea the first time who he was, what he was. I didn't know much more for part of the second time."

"No, it couldn't be." One last solid attempt at denial. "Hob, the true Hob, is *dead*."

"He is now." My smirk was the arc of a reaper's scythe with the shine and deadly edge of razor wire. That was a fond recollection. Not what Hob had done to make me kill him. The punishment, however—the one of the "worse than deaths" Robin didn't believe in and then a death I'd label unmatchable that had followed.

"He really did piss me off. All told, about twenty-five minutes of his combined face-to-face presence over three occasions and that managed it, no problem. It's what he did behind the scenes that earned him that extra"—I searched for the words—"time-out."

Thrown through a gate I'd made to the hell that had been the Auphe's home away from home, he'd have been dismembered and killed quickly if the Auphe were feeling generous. Too bad that the Auphe hadn't known the meaning of the word, they genuinely hadn't. They had been born for mayhem and murder. The emotions that went with that had been all they'd possessed. No less, no more—much like Hob himself ironically enough.

Dying slowly, inch by inch, was the best Hob could've hoped for—if the Auphe were already full and sleepy.

But I was bare minutes past Robin showing real fear of Auphe, of me being one. He'd managed to cover it up when distracted by the Hob subject change. Hiding it, I knew, didn't mean it was gone. I also knew, gone or not, that I didn't want to see it again by being a shade too descriptive on my guess at how the end of the mighty fucking Hob had gone down.

"A time-out," I repeated, able to keep the details to myself but not the satisfaction. It came through loud and clear in the vicious but peculiarly fond edge to my words and tone. Sounding for all the world as if I was nostalgic for a particularly painful cut I'd given myself while trying to shave with one of my knives. "An extremely permanent one." I drew more Greek letters, then the more familiar transliteration in the soft, shifting surface — the last words I knew how to write. *Chytheí stagóna aímatos tou adelfoú mou.*

"Spill a drop of my brother's blood," the puck read aloud for me. He said the rest along with it as well, although I hadn't learned to write those words yet. "And death will be the only mercy and miracle for which you will beg," he finished, not bothering to trace it into the sand. "You do know me. You know more of me than you should, but you are who you say. Friend and brother." The light behind his eyes went out and his smile vanished. "But you are Auphe. Half or no, Auphe is Auphe."

"The First Murderers to walk the earth," I admitted. Why pretend everyone wasn't aware of it and used to be hatefully hostile and gleefully thrilled to tell me, ten, twenty times a night at work? I cured them of that happy hobby of theirs with a resourcefulness and rapidity that left them with no idea it was *their* tongue I'd torn out and dropped in their glass of vodka. Until they tried to drink it ... or talk. The pink cocktail umbrellas I used to speared the bloody flesh was a tasteful touch, or so went my explanation to the boss.

"And Hob, the Trickster First, was the original of the second murderers to walk the earth, following in the Auphe's bloody footprints. You were the Trickster Second, now the Trickster ..." I shrugged and through my shirt scratched one of the coyote bites from last night's fight. I let him mentally fill in that blank himself on what he had been.

"It took me five years and a healer who was excited

as hell to have a second guinea pig to try out his shiny new genetic manipulation. Between the two, I got on the wagon." I flipped an invisible chip into the air. If the movement and the words weren't as serious as they should be, somewhat snarky, so what? I'd lived through it all, which was impossible. If my living was impossible, I wasn't going to ruin it being ungrateful enough to haul around ten tons of guilt. I was going to enjoy every day I shouldn't be that lucky to have. No one should be that lucky. That type of luck didn't exist, but here I was.

Or here I was if I was able to get my Niko and my Goodfellow back. If not, I'd give up that impossible life. I didn't want it.

"I'm not really Auphe"—but there'd been times I'd forgotten that—"but, say that I am, if there was a twelve step Auphe program, Auphe Anonymous, I'd have kicked its ass," I added.

Goodfellow's wide-eyed stare turned into narrowed suspicious slits. "If there were a twelve step program, how many chips would you have?"

Did chips come in halves?

"First you tell me how long it took *you* to get on the wagon," I drawled.

To be born of Hob meant Goodfellow would've *been* Hob. He would look the same—all pucks did—had the same personality, same memories, same murderous inclinations. That was how reproduction worked for pucks. They were a duplicate in all ways to the one who made them. It was years, fifty to a hundred at the very least, Goodfellow had said, before you felt the urge to separate from your maker, travel on your own, have your own experiences, see the world through slowly changing eyes, fight battles, choose not to fight them, make memories that are yours, no one else's, before the combination of it—every new day lived, every new sight seen—finally caused you to develop into a new person with a new personality and thoughts born of you, not Hob.

"How long?" I repeated, too smug for my own good.

Goodfellow was saved by the bell. If the bell was the ringtone of Robin's phone. It was an old song, a year or two before I was born song, but filthy enough any teen-age boy would be invested enough to find it. *"Me so horny, me so horny, me so horny. Me love you long time."* It cut off there, which was a good thing as that was the least offensive part. The puck grumbled and glanced down at the phone.

"You're the biggest perv in existence," I said, trying for judgmental and failing miserably.

"But you're a nun, knowing the lyrics of a song older than you are? Unless you age as slowly as an Auphe. No, the other you does look younger. Eight years to an Auphe isn't measurable as a unit of time, it's too small for their life span."

He frowned down at the phone in his hand. "That son of a bitch. Conan quit *via* text, the coward. He claims I'm too demanding. Me? The slander is unspeakable. And 'That it was unbearable, my sexual harassment'—which he misspelled, leaving the second s out of ass. How harassed can you be if you can't even spell ass? I swear, you cannot get good steroid popping cabana beasts these days."

"Did you harass him?" Like I didn't know the answer to that.

"Of course I did. I clearly didn't hire him for his spelling skills." He sighed. "And I've been blacklisted at all the employment and modeling agencies. Life is cruel."

"No big deal. In eight years when you're dead you won't have to worry anymore," I reminded him, making an attempt—A for effort, D for execution—to hide my momentary spike of resentment at how lightly he was taking this.

"Your life is a colossal whirlpool of melodrama, sucking in any proton of optimism or neutron of hope and devouring them." His exasperation was clear. We would do it. We would save them including himself. He was confident, doubt-free.

He hadn't been the one to watch, powerless. He hadn't frozen, unable to run into the flames and drag them out as they weren't dying. They had been dead since the first flare of light. He hadn't been confused by the dissonance of the oddly pleasant, almost sweet aroma of grilling meat while *knowing* that you weren't a kid in the white trash version of the suburbs. That it wasn't a distant neighbor's backyard barbecue on their six square inches of scrub grass. It was people burning, your family, your friend, burning. And that sweet-to-sickening odor became a sense memory you couldn't wipe away, part of you for the rest of your life.

It was debatable if I'd be around long enough for that to be a problem.

"Have faith in me. Have I or will I, should I say, ever failed you? An unmatched and illustrious reputation such as mine doesn't come about when you leave a bread crumb trail of failures behind you. I'm known for a multitude of sins, but none of them were the sin of failure."

"The dying was a damned big one," I said with a sour bite as I made it up and on my feet mainly by sliding up the wall.

"Which, thanks to you and the assistance, I'm certain, of my own genius, we have every likelihood of stopping that. You may have already in the first hour you arrived yesterday and left your letter to me. I know where not to be, where you, your brother and everyone else cannot be. I'll make it so. If it were more simple an undertaking, I'd hire an intern trickster to do it. Ishiah, however?" he questioned skeptically. "That pompous, hypocritical, mindless mouthpiece to the condemnations of heaven? That useless feather duster, squawking repent, repent, repent from whatever henhouse he squats in? I care if he's fricasseed or not in the days to come? Mind-boggling."

He stood and brushed the sand off his pants. "I will be your optimism, your hope, your faith." His hand squeezed on my shoulder, friend to friend. Brother to brother. "Bask in it. If doubt surfaces in you, tell me and I'll drown it without mercy as I find gloom and doom ruins my mood." Cal was going to be a life lesson for him then.

Shoes held up and safe, he took charge. "Since Apollo isn't bringing us any, we will have to go to the alcohol. Enormous amounts of alcohol. We're both going to need it. As a rose-colored glasses outlook is clearly not a facet

of the otherwise flawlessly glittering diamond of your
personality. You have a long tale to tell including how
you know parts of me and of my life I've not told anyone. Not to those I would have wished to tell. Friends
and brothers who were born and died in eras that
wouldn't allow them to understand. I told nothing to no
one. Not ever. I want to know why I did tell now, in those
eight years. And it'll be easier to hear if every word isn't
dripping with the tormented brooding reminiscent of
Heathcliff fresh from the moors. Therefore, you combined with alcohol to spare me."

"Little harsh on Heathcliff, aren't you? You have
something against cats? Or comics?"

He almost bought it, then said, shoulders slumping
with relief, "Sarcasm and a complete disregard for cul-
ture. You can be redeemed. We'll work on it. For now, if
I have to allow events to unfold as they're meant to, I
need to know what they are. Tricksters, pucks foremost,
aren't as bound to ourselves as most creatures are. Our
behaviors aren't patterns or if they are, we frequently
unravel them to weave different, more entertaining ones.
Our outlooks aren't as set. Reality's grasp on us is looser
than it is on others.

"Humans, unknowingly put in the same situation three
times over will make the same decision each of those
three times," he continued. "Pucks, on the other and more
superior hand, have a spark of chaos in us as all tricksters
do. Put me in the same situation three times and I could
react the same, I could make three entirely different deci-
sions, I could make nine—three each time just to tangle
everything up for my own amusement and not necessarily
know why. Whether I do or I don't, leaving me in the dark
cannot turn out well."

The door to the apartment opened and Niko and Cal
both leaned out for a look, then stepped out for a better
one. Niko had his katana. Cal had his Desert Eagle and
in spite of a half hour gone, remained half-naked in the
sheet. "What are you two doing?" Niko asked. "And who
is that?" As I had mentioned a few details about Goodfellow to him and mythology didn't always get it all

wrong, he had to have a good guess. Robin did have certain things in common with the descriptions of Pan, puck, and the one who he'd either taken the name or was the source of it. He refused to say.

Goodfellow glanced from Cal in his sheet then to me and back to Cal. The moan he gave was pitiful. "So many *Hustler* pornographic twin fantasies and so little time." Cal, showing exceptional sense, promptly disappeared without a word back into the apartment. Robin moved on to Niko. "We're off for some privacy that Caliban might tell me how not to undo all our lives and the universe with it in less than a week."

"Stay here and I mean it." I was the older brother now. It was my turn to give a few for-your-own-good orders. "This ass could find us, but it was hard enough for him that no one else could. I'll be back in a few hours."

Robin had noticed as I'd talked. "You," he said to Niko, ". . . you remind me of a young Achilles." Instead of making the lewd comment that should've been tattooed on his lips to save him from constantly repeating it, his attention was back on me again. "The name, the one you signed to the note you left, was it real? Was it?"

"Once." It was the smallest quirk of my lips, but it was as real as the name had been.

"Tell me again," he demanded, the desperation hidden enough that it wouldn't be heard by anyone who didn't know him and know him like they'd know themselves or a brother. "Let me hear it instead of only reading it."

I took two steps toward him, stopped at his side, close enough to his ear that he would hear it, but Niko wouldn't. When I said it, Goodfellow stood frozen for a moment, and then apparently said the hell with his suit and tackled me in the sand. "*Gamou. Finally*, you son of a bitch.

"Finally."

11

"Patroclus," he marveled. "You were Patroclus and you remember. What of the blonde in the hall? The one who looks enough like Achilles to nearly be his twin?"

"That's a weird one," I replied, rocking the table back and forth on its two uneven legs. As the others had three or all uneven, it was the best table at Talley's place. It was closed and empty this early in the morning, but closed meant nothing to me and empty was just a perk.

"Weird at it gets," I echoed. I remembered being vaguely disturbed by it months after finding out. "About four hundred years ago—wild guess, no one kept a history—our clan, the Vayash Clan, was traveling through Northern Greece. You know it's forbidden to dirty yourself with a *gadje*, an outsider, Rom is for Rom. But shit happens and one of the ancestors of Niko's father got knocked up by a Greek blacksmith who claimed he was a descendant of Achilles, which, fair, Achilles got around the villages and whorehouses. Not quite like you and I did, but he was no virgin. It could've been true."

"I would say to take it with the same grain of salt you would take mine, but it would be my natural competition speaking." He spun a finger in a get-on-with-it motion.

Pucks are fond of stories, and one that involves them? I was waiting for him to stick his hand down my throat and pull it out through my vocal cords to hurry it up.

"Secluded enough," I said wryly, but obeyed while salting my beer, "that the younger ones forgot or never knew there was a world outside and the elderly, the geezers with both feet and an elbow in the grave thought the gods had struck them down, but even they didn't remember the names of the gods. What they did know was growing turnips and sheering sheep. It was all they wanted or needed to know, except for Achilles. They knew the whole story from his birth to his . . . to Troy. They said they were of his blood. Three thousand years later and they remembered him and bragged about him while they'd forgotten the gods, the names of the gods, the world itself, that could make a person believe they were his blood. The Clan wouldn't have cared if it was true or not, but they'd cared enough when it came to what they could get out of it. A descendant of Achilles would come in handy. The Vayash had been all over Greece by then. A baby of Achilles could bring in the silver. They could show off the kid for a fee." I took a deep swallow of the beer, which thanks to Auphe partial immunity to poisons meant it did very little for me.

"Then four hundred years of some Clan inbreeding when no other Clans to marry into were around, and nowadays you occasionally see dark blond hair and gray eyes among the Vayash. They're known by it. Instant signature." I tried three more swallows, then simply chugged it as the next part was a little too convenient to have happened like that. It made you see the shadows of puppet strings. I'd had Auphe chasing me throughout my life to turn me into a puppet. Imagination or something beyond us; didn't know, didn't care, I was ignoring it.

"Which means Achilles"—I refilled my glass from the pitcher—"was reincarnated into his own descendant, and isn't that strangely coincidental, but you knew that too. Or guessed. We had told you about the Achilles bullshit legend our Clan told and you knew Niko had *been* Achilles, the real thing. You didn't tell us then or years later when the reincarnation reveal had jumped out to slap us in the face with the force of a yearlong frozen giant turkey leg. Not that I minded. I don't care how many years go by, three thousand or not, it's bizarrely incestuous to me. I don't want to think about it."

"Patroclus, as you said, scattered his seed about with even more enthusiasm than Achilles and they did have a fondness for sisters." He spread his arms. The abracadabra was implied. "Your blood could easily have ended up in the same family that—" I was one more of his words away from throwing a full glass of beer in his face. The growling and twitch of my hand was a sign readable to anyone. You didn't have to be a trickster.

"Yes, it is the first time it's happened that I know of, the first with you two. Why it did, if there exists a why at all, I don't know. Perhaps Achilles felt he had unfinished business. If we're meant to know, we will, but I'm hoping for coincidence. It is highly underrated and I am quite the fan of it. If it's part of a plan, it's beyond my sight and as nothing is beyond my sight, I'd rather not contemplate meandering down that mental path." His hands returned to his glass, a thumb rubbing idly at a smudge.

"But I agree on a change of subject," he said briskly. "It's difficult though. Those handful of years harbored many of the very best and the very worst memories of my entire life. Of a million years and more, these meant the most. For good and for bad. I try not to think of Troy. I start with all the good memories of that life, thinking I can stop at any point I wish, but I never can and am dragged to the end of them. It's Troy. She will not let me go, the *bitch*. I hear the sand gritting beneath my sandals, the blood I wear that covers twice the amount of skin that my armor, tunic, and greaves do, the funeral pyres burning and blackening the bodies of my friend and brothers, the flames scorching my face, the smoke—"

I was gone. In the bathroom puking up nothing but beer and bile. Thanks to not giving in to Niko, no food though. It made the puke session shorter and cleaner, if puke can be clean. It splattered less, let's go with that. I straightened, flushed, and went to the sink. Snatching a few rough brown paper towels from the slow, creaking, and groaning dispenser, I twisted a knob and scrubbed my face in pale orange water. After tossing the wadded paper on the floor, bent my head to get my lips below the faucet, got a mouthful of the rusty water and rinsed thoroughly. I spit and did it again. The entire time, I thought of nothing. I put it on autopilot, which I'd gotten pretty damn skilled at with my earlier life, let my body do the work and my brain switch off.

Back at the table, my ass halfway down on the seat of the chair, and I took the driver's seat again. Robin knew what he'd done, what he'd said. It had been in the letter I left him. How he had died, how everyone had died, in an explosion. The way the flames cooked everyone inside the bar as it ate the building itself, in all probability going on to burn down the whole block, and I'd escaped because I'd been at the end of that block.

He turned his glass around, one way then the other. Robin didn't often have to work up to saying something, but once in a blue moon, he did. This is what it looked like. Fidgeting of any type. Fiddling with anything in his hands or he could reach to pull into his hands. It was the only time he did. If there was nothing to latch onto, he squirmed and twitched. Not the puck suave he displayed as the majority of his body language. Whatever he was gathering up the guts to say, I didn't want to hear.

"Do you know wolves can smell a hundred to a thousand times more than a human?" I asked. Somehow my beer had spilled, I didn't remember how, but it had been wiped up with the now-soaking bar towel and my glass filled to the brim again.

I shook my head when he opened his mouth to answer. "But a dog can smell around ten thousand to a hundred thousand times more than a human. A wolf chasing prey so it doesn't starve. A dog tracking down a bowl of Alpo, you'd think it'd be the other way around. It's not fair, but, hell, is anything ever fair?" This time I took a small taste of the beer to see if it was going to stay down. It did.

"I don't know how much better an Auphe's sense of

smell is than a dog or a wolf, but I know it's better than
a human's. How much of it I inherited with the rest of the
prize package, I don't know either. I do know mine's better than or equal to some Wolves." Werewolves had so
much inbreeding I didn't think they knew what was average for them.

"Which means while I sat on the sidewalk with the
muzzle of my gun pressed under my chin and my finger
having pulled the trigger halfway home, I didn't smell
what you did at Troy. I didn't smell roasting meat. Not
that it wouldn't suck, I get *that*. Your friend, your brother
dead and you staying at the pyre until it was done. I don't
know if I could've done that. Fuck, I know I couldn't
because I didn't. But at least you knew they were already
dead when they burned." I was rolling my glass between
both palms a lot like Goodfellow, but faster, less controlled. "You knew we were dead for at least a day to
clean us up, put us in our best clothes that still smelled of
perfume from the whorehouses, laying us out with coins
on our eyes so those who knew us could pay their
respects—I'll bet that attendance wasn't especially large
for mine."

"You'd be wrong," he said, but quietly enough I could
ignore it and I did.

"Then you build the pyre and light us up, but you
knew." I lifted the glass and slammed it back down hard.
It didn't shatter. I didn't expect that. Instead I threw it at
the wall behind Goodfellow. It shattered then, a cascade
of glass, the blade-edged tears of the mad. "You knew
they were dead. They'd been dead for a day, two days, at
least."

I inhaled, held it, exhaled. Meditation breathing. My
brother had poured every gallon of actual dairy milk
down the sink and smugly handed me soy milk for my
Captain Crunch cereal until I broke down and tried it.
I'd hated that it had occasionally worked. I was calmer
now, self-disciplined like Nik would want me to be.

"I smelled cooking vampire—charcoal and old blood,
charred peri with their light bones and feathers flammable enough that I don't think they burned. I think they

incinerated instantly. Disappeared like a magic trick. Abracadabra," I echoed him flatly. "I smelled Wolves, fur, wildness, gamey flesh a crisp on the bones. The frying blubber of *vodyanoi*. There were more *paien*, but here it is, none of them smelled the same. None of them smelled like roast pig or barbecue or any of that utter shit. For every scent I caught, I knew who or what was burning.

"Of everyone in there, there was only one human and only one puck. I could smell you both." I rubbed a finger across the table until a splinter stabbed it, leaving a small drop of blood. "You smelled like grass, the trees, wild honey, blackberry juice crushed into wine, bucks chasing does, the smell of ever that surrounds you. Not forever. There's no such thing. Everything ends. But the ever of stars. They die, but live too long for us to see it. It was how you always were to me, your scent.

"Over that was charcoal, carbon, ash, all still burning when I thought there was nothing left to burn, nothing other than a layer, no thicker than a hair, of charbroiled flesh." I smeared the blood on his glass I stole, emptying it in one long swallow.

He was smart, Robin, had been all the times I'd known him. He didn't have to be smart to not ask what Niko had smelled of. Conscious or breathing and anyone would be smart enough to make that decision.

"Then there was the second explosion. The real one. The first was pure destruction, but the second was fucking Armageddon."

I flattened both hands on the table, looking at the scars around my wrists. I looked at the other ones that rippled across the backs of my hands. I looked at the black bronze ring on my right middle finger. You were given one by your Clan when you turned thirteen and became a man. The Vayash hadn't given it to me. They kept tabs on Sophia, they knew what I was. My true family had presented it to me, way past thirteen, not that it made a difference to me. I knew I hadn't been a man at thirteen. Sometimes I wondered if I was one now.

"I thought with the first blast that everyone was dead. They had to be. There were some tough sons of bitches in there, gargoyles—didn't see them often. But the first explosion—I thought I'd never seen anything like it . . . nothing could've survived. I knew Niko was dead. I knew you were dead. Then there was the second one and you couldn't see the end of it. It soared up to the sky and kept going. And I thought"—I couldn't raise my eyes yet, using my left hand to circle the ring around my finger— "why a second one? Did they have that much of a hard-on for killing me they wanted even my ashes to burn? Or did they think some might have lived through the first explosion?

"That's when it hit: Guess what, Caliban, you might've fucked up. They might've been alive and you didn't try to get them out. You sat there, in shock like a goddamn pussy, ready to reach for your gun to blow out your brains—like you have any—and they could've been alive waiting for help. Waiting for *you*."

An olive-toned hand landed on the tangle of mine, one twisting the ring and one clenching tight to keep it from being pulled off. "You know that's a lie, *adelfós*. They were gone. If one of them had exhaled a single breath, you would've caught that scent. Neither did. They died as some holier-than-thou militia cult assholes, sons of pox-ridden whores, aimed for you and by stupid, horrible luck, they missed and took everyone else instead. I know you think it wasn't good fortune—that it was the most evil of ill-fortune and you wanted then, more than you wanted anything, to have been there with them. To have died with them. Do you think I haven't thought that times uncountable? To have passed on with you and your brother? In one night I drank three entire vineyards wondering why I am always left behind. Ah . . . and five whorehouses. It was an exhausting night, but one without an answer. Several STIs as it turned out, but no answers."

Goodfellow had considered the same? I knew pucks were the most isolated and lonely among the *paien*. I knew he missed us, but we did come back. Did that make such a difference though? A hundred years without your friends and brothers is hell; a thousand years, I couldn't comprehend.

He would've died with us if he'd had the choice? Robin who wasn't human. Not in his most single part. He was a puck.

And reincarnation was not for pucks.

Where he went after death, if anywhere, I had no idea, but I didn't think it was a place we'd see him again. Nik, I would find. I wouldn't know our history and neither would he. It would be brand-new, a clean slate and I didn't like that. But it was what it was. That I wouldn't know Robin again, wouldn't know who he was, wouldn't realize he had been there with us, a constant presence, wouldn't realize he wasn't any longer . . .

I wouldn't remember he died. I wouldn't remember he'd *existed*.

They were both coming back. If the letters and the warnings didn't do it, I would burn the world and keep burning until someone somewhere made it right.

Goodfellow's hand gripped mine with enough strength to have the bones ache. "But you weren't with them and you didn't die. The second best you'll try is to make your life a daily living hell as that's what you think you deserve. You *don't*." He was raving on, not bothering to pause and indulge in that breathing crap Nik had forced me to learn. "They're gone, but if you can manage to stop punishing yourself over it, you can bring them back. And I still say there is every possibility you already *have*. One letter to me. One to the pigeon. One to some vitamin-popping former blood-drinking ancient VILF. There isn't a possibility, probability, or prospect that among the three that we would all be unsuccessful.

"I, personally, am infallible, we know that. Ishiah is unbearable with his judging and lecturing, but he is an efficient tactician and fighter. I don't know of this Promise who could not conceivably be good enough for Niko, whom I cannot wait to meet and see how much Achilles shows in him this young. Twenty. Unimaginable." I hadn't decided if it had been a pep talk or a bitching out, but it was winding down.

"Trust me, Pee Wee Patroclus is where you're going to run into trouble." I lifted my head, pulled my hands free to slap him lightly across one cheek, a little cheered at the thought. "Cal is going to ruin your life and drive you to therapy without trying."

"The true Patroclus was entertaining. He could keep up with *me*," he said, eyebrows drawn together in confusion. "Every drunken fun-loving bastard in Greece loved him. If there was a party he was there or he was throwing it or he was burning it down. Every wine house, whorehouse, orgy, gambling house—they all knew him. He was the first human to make me work to earn my reputation in whoring, drinking, and cheating." He folded his arms with rejection or disappointment either at what he believed a lie or wished it were. Whichever, he'd find out soon enough.

"One thing. Two," I corrected. I took off my rite of manhood ring that Niko had given me, pried a hand away from Robin's chest, and put it in his palm. His fingers automatically closed around it. "If I don't make it home. If we save Cal, but Lazarus takes me down, give this to Nik in eight years. I don't know if he'll remember our life or some new version made from this one. I don't know what will happen with this one either, two paths, two become one, physics can suck it. If I do die and you do get lucky, kick my dead body in the river or throw me in a Dumpster before these two see me. Tell them when Lazarus died, I went back home as soon as his heart stopped. If you could do that, you'd be my fucking hero—for the hundredth or so time. Otherwise those eight years are going to be miserable as they get for this Niko, knowing I might die in a little less than a decade, but am here, younger and so fucking emo, beside him now. Or I might not. Either way, he'd be in hell, not knowing what will happen."

"It won't come to that, but if it did, I will. But you know what he'll do when I give the ring to him instead of giving him his brother."

"What we always do," I sighed. "You've been there, every life, every death."

If a thousand lifetimes hadn't changed that, nothing would. "Second, this"—I pointed two fingers back and forth between us with a grim edge to the motion—"talking about what happened. What I saw. What I smelled, what I thought, and what I almost did," I said matter-of-fact as life and death. "We don't talk about it again. Ever. Not now. Not in eight years if we fix it all and we're celebrating, everything is wine and goddamn roses, you don't say a word to anyone. Not to Niko, not to Ishiah and, first and foremost, not to me. It's a memory I don't want and I won't keep." It wasn't one I could carry and function. I had to bury it deep, deeper than all the festive, bloody Auphe ones.

He frowned. "That's a good deal to carry and not be able to share the burden. It could break you. You're certain? Never again? Not at least once more to assure myself that while everyone else is safe and home, you're not home and broken?"

As if I hadn't been broken before.

"What'd your coffin fuck-buddy Poe say again?" I asked. "Oh, right. That's it." It was the perfect answer. If Poe hadn't been underground, I'd have thanked him for it.

"Never-fucking-more."

He wasn't happy about it, but he'd keep his word, puck or not. "I so swear it, then." He didn't put on the ring, aware of the insult that would be. To wear what my only blood family had given me to prove our connection. No matter how it wasn't complete humanity Nik and I shared on a biological level, it counted.

He took a breath, tucked the ring away safe and tucked everything said before that to a place inside where he wouldn't have to think on it for a long time. All of us were beyond skilled at that. "Let's talk about something less gloom and doom. All our past lives. You remember them? Why is baby Patroclus lover of all that is emo, and wasn't that the trend seven or so years ago? The Pharaoh's Divine Face-Painter, he doesn't wear eyeliner, does he?" If his face could produce a more appalled contortion, I couldn't picture it. "If you ever wore eyeliner and ironic T-shirts, Lazarus can get in line. I'll do it as a mercy killing myself," he continued, coming half across the table for a look at the shirt I'd taken a magic marker to for a saying of my own. "*Once you go furry, you never*—ha! That's acceptable, not ironic, and often quite true. I approve of the saying if not the hideously cheap shirt it's written on." He sat back, but remained eager enough to all but vibrate off the chair. "Do you remember when I was pretending to be the High Priest of Ra and Niko, you, me, and three camels hid in the Temple of Isis with a barrel of unfermented honey wine—"

"Nope." I reached for the pitcher of beer to top off Goodfellow's glass that was now my glass as he huffed and went to fetch another. "If you don't start, you won't get in the habit of it. The only reason I remember this go-round is thanks to the Auphe having racial memory. This Cal doesn't remember anything and won't for seven and a half years. Believe me, waking up part of that racial memory crap early would be epically bad. As in the type of bad that we might as well finish our beers, break the glasses, and slit out throats right here. If he digs up anything from ye olden days now, it won't be reincarnated good times like when we rustled Genghis Khan's harem."

Goodfellow laughed hard enough to bend over, the new glass in his hand wobbling wildly, but not lost. Collapsing in his chair, he laughed on, wheezing. "No food, no shelter, three heroes, and five horses for three thousand women. Never have so many women hated so few men with so much passion and so very many dainty, jeweled daggers."

Daggers they had no problem using on us. Dainty or not, they were needle-pointed metal capable of puncturing any internal organ they were aimed at. I don't think you can call yourself a hero if you abandon three thousand women in the middle of nowhere as you ride for your life. Or when you sell the jewels from the same daggers you slid out of your flesh as each of us had been successfully if not fatally stabbed two to four times each.

Goodfellow had run across us in all our different lives. He'd also partied with Buddha. He'd caught on even before Buddha though. We didn't look the same, except once, but our personalities were similar if exaggerated with the past, being more lawless some times and more ruthless all times.

Robin was over a million years old. Unbelievable when first heard, but true. Pucks were the only ones who could live so long and there weren't many of them. A million years of life, when everyone dies, so many you couldn't begin to remember all you'd lost, that makes for a loneliness I couldn't comprehend.

It was inevitable that when he found two people who kept living and dying then appearing again over and over and crossing his path in each of their new lives, he latched onto us. Goodfellow believed in the three of us, whatever bizarre fate was at work, he'd told me months ago when I'd asked. He had known and remembered us with each of our new lives, but we hadn't. We forgot him with each death and rebirth. Clean slate. He hated that. He lost us, waited, and then had us again, but not entirely. You can't have someone who doesn't know you—all of you.

He had us as friends and brothers-in-arms, but he'd had only part of us. But in this life, where we wouldn't burn him at the stake for blasphemy, the modern era of believe what you want, he knew Niko the Buddhist would accept it as true. I was an atheist and didn't believe in anything about death other than you were worm food. End of story, my story. But Niko, as ever, had been right. We died and lived again. Or, I suspected, Niko died, dragged my dead ass out of peaceful nonexistence into less peaceful reincarnation. Sometimes as brothers, sometimes as cousins, blood brothers, brothers-in-arms, but always together.

Robin had been dropping hints for over a year, eventually throwing a little hypnosis in for a different reason involving saving my life from another half Auphe, Grimm, who was older, smarter, quicker, a better fighter, and a better gater. He'd been fully functional in all the Auphe ways for too many years longer than I had. I couldn't hope to win against him.

But Robin could. There was no guarantee in a one-to-one fight, not with the gating, but in a *con*, the puck could defeat anyone alive. But that had depended on me not trying to take on Grimm myself. A little hypnosis, a few key words, and, in the worst of situations when I was already bleeding out, I would gate away from Grimm instead of toward him as I normally would have. Fuck the blood. I'd take his ass to hell with me.

Goodfellow hadn't approved of plans he considered suicidal, but I considered standard. In this case, he made certain I couldn't use any of them.

That's when the puck and his hypnosis had brought down that enlightenment he'd wanted by bringing my Auphe racial memory online. That had then let me use it for human memories despite humans not having the ability for racial memory—the Auphe in me was inextricably intertwined in each of my genes. I could use what the Auphe had twisted in every part of me *for* every part of me. Human or Auphe.

And then Robin had us, not the puzzle parts to a whole he alone could see, but all of us. I recalled it all, slowly and bit by bit, but it had picked up faster and faster. Nik hadn't remembered like I did, but he believed. That was enough. For the first time, he could say, "Do you remember . . ." whenever he wanted. Robin could relive all of our lives with us, or the less painful ones, and I could add the humiliating bits he left out. He was happy, *euphoric*, too goddamn so for me to bring up what he'd missed.

It had to be hard as hell for him to give that up, whether he hadn't had it yet or not. Simply knowing it was coming, but he had to wait as he had waited the majority of his life. Could it hurt to have it sooner when he'd endured what had to feel like an eternity without it?

Fuck, yes, it could.

"Yeah, good times. Couldn't get enough of the stabbing by tiny harem women who knew ten times the foul language that I did," I repeated dryly. "Like I said that's not what Cal Junior will remember. Mini Me has a lot of control to learn and his memories will be those of some Auphe ancestor gnawing on the leg of a screaming Neanderthal, eating him alive. Starting, naturally, with the feet— always start with the feet—and working its way up."

Robin wrinkled his forehead. "Why?" he asked, eyes narrowing either with curiosity or an uneasy widening of his pupils. He seemed suspicious—the same reason he was alive today after a million-plus.

"Why the feet or why will he remember that instead of swinging from chandeliers and pissing on the bouncing, over-yeasted breasts and beehive tall wigs of the flailing, screaming members of the French court when we were kicked out of the Musketeers?" I didn't wait for him to choose, continuing on with playing teacher-knows-best.

"Let's start with the last as, believe it or not, it's less disturbing. For you. Both are actually." I snagged a bowl of petrified peanuts and pretzels from the next table. "Racial memories one oh two. Despite humans not having the capability wired into their brain, I could remember my past lives and that Niko and you were there, in and out of them all. And I did it by using the racial memory from the Auphe. I just said that about three minutes ago, didn't I?"

I picked up a peanut, studied it, then dropped it back in the bowl and pushed it away. It wasn't meat, but it was food. Nik's veggie pizza on the asphalt beside me didn't have the scent of meat, but if I hadn't forgotten it in its disgusting broccoli cheese glory, I wouldn't be here now. Peanuts? No, thanks.

"I did say it, we both know that." I tipped my head, wondering as I'd had since then—did he really miss it or was it everyone's old friend, denial? "Here's the thing, and I don't know how you didn't catch this, the racial memory I was born with? The *Auphe* racial memory? It was meant for their race and their memories. For each and every one of the sons of bitches, from first to last. It's not all sword fights, whores, and stealing wagons of the Queen's French wine. Just as he and I are not all human."

"Graváta glóssa mou kai mou fainontai tyflí gia tin ilithiótita tha káno." He rested his forehead on the table. "No. I wouldn't have missed the meaning of that. I was being a selfish bastard who thought of himself and no one else."

"You think I'm surprised? You're a puck. I know that, I know what you are." I stretched and ruffled his hair, as he'd done to me when I'd been nineteen or so. "I don't care if I have more Auphe flashbacks when I can have the human ones too. I can remember being human, and, right now I can't help but think as a race they are on the puny and pathetic side, but I have the memories of a thousand other lives that tell me that's not true. I can remember being like Niko, being able to think like him and act like him because I am like him. I'm not a born sociopathic predator." I slapped the back of his head briskly. "It's worth it. I don't care who you did it for. To me, it's worth it. And if it wasn't, you wouldn't take it back anyway."

He raised his head. "You do know pucks." This smile was less car salesman and more stiff, but he'd come around. Pucks did—without fail. "So . . . the other part, the first equally disturbing part?"

"Racial memory one oh one. Eat up." I nudged the peanut bowl closer to him. "Feet. Why start with the feet when eating a Neanderthal? This was my first true Auphe racial memory by the way, and not just a flashback of being tortured in Tumulus in this life for two years."

"Two years at their endless lack of mercy? No. It can't be." His face was back down on the table. " 'The beasts, which you saw, once were, now are not, and yet will come up out of the Abyss.' "

"Is Ishiah reading you Bible verses as bedtime stories before you fuck like rabbits? Never mind. You don't know yet. Forget about Tumulus"—the Auphe hell I'd not completely forget but could now cope with— "you'll have years and years to worry about that later. Now back to the feet." Vengeance is mine and I was enjoying every minute of it.

"Feet? I'm not certain I wish to hear this." He was back up again, shaking his head with complete conviction, and reaching frantically for his beer.

I glanced at the small window in the door of the bar. There was nothing. The reason we were at Talley's drinking at 6:30 a.m. was in hopes Lazarus would show up. He knew Cal worked here, if that's all he knew. It'd be nice if we had more to go on than he would have marks on his skin, face, hands, arms—some sort of medium- to large-sized blemishes. They didn't know what color or what medium to large meant to the Vigil's science geeks. I was hoping he wasn't close to appearing human, that the *paien* DNA had mutated his ass but good. He'd be easier to track down as that than your average human in millions of them.

"It's educational," I insisted. One more small push and the bowl was all but in Robin's lap with his hand automatically dropping in it. It wasn't for my comfort, getting the distance between it and me, but to get a little revenge for all the relentlessly sneaky and wickedly sly tricks Goodfellow had played on me. I waited until he tossed back a handful of the snacks.

"You and Hob no doubt ate a few of the tough, gristly as hell too, guys yourself, but grilled them with mushrooms and tasty, tasty herbs as there were no chefs to do it for you then." I swung my feet up to rest on the table, drumming my fingers along the blunt toe of one leather-clad boot before saying casually, "You start at the feet because whoever you're eating lives longer, especially if you avoid the femoral arteries. There's way too many gushers up top"—I circled a hand around my head in demonstration—"in the temple, neck, the arms. They go quick. Start at the bottom and they live three times as long, which is three times the screaming. The Auphe liked the screaming with their food. It was like A.1. Sauce."

Half the nuts he spit across the table and half he choked on. I waited until he was able to finally swallow those. "That is . . . Why would you tell me that?"

"Revenge," I answered promptly. "And it wasn't me," I clarified, not offended. All right, not too offended, but exasperated—and he had asked. "It wasn't me. It was some douche Auphe ancestor.

"It's not like I've been around long enough to have been personally snacking on raw Neanderthal. I'm twenty-six and I was human, nothing but, in all my other lives. But that is the gift of Auphe racial memory. Little movie trailers like that every few months. I have eight years of hard-goddamned-won control. I've lived through enough shit to be able to handle that kind of memory, tell myself it might feel like mine, but it's *not* mine," I emphasized.

"But Cal doesn't have a year"—I went on to warn—"much less eight. If his racial Disney World ride kicks in too soon, he'll lose himself. He'll *be* that Auphe. It'll be *your* feet he starts on." A threat or a promise, both were true. "No pushing at the memory thing. It's just seven and a half more years and then we'll know, all of us." I hoped. "I swear it on Ajax's Clydesdale-sized balls."

"They were impressive. Difficult to believe the man could walk carrying the equivalent of a bowling ball between his legs." He exhaled. "Very well. No pushing. Go on then, tell me all that I must allow to happen."

The door slammed open to admit the rush of the Wolf I'd put a knife through yesterday and two of his furry friends, hoodied up and hidden from human eyes, ready to put a booted paw up my ass and claw off my face. I wouldn't have guessed he had the balls. "Holy shit," I groaned. "How stupid are you?" I pulled out two of my guns I hadn't wanted Cal to see yesterday if he couldn't smell the metal and oil on them. Failing a test makes the lesson stick more than if you'd passed.

I laid them on the table. "But bullets aren't that fun and I like my fun. With guns it's over too quick." I looked at the other two Wolves. "He didn't tell you, did he? Who I am? What I am? Too bad." I felt my eyes shift Auphe red.

"I'll tell you the same as I told him yesterday. No guns. How about we play a different kind of game? My kind of game. My claws and teeth to your claws and teeth. My gates to gobble you up and spit you out as bloody fur and bone paste on the other side. Sound fair?" I had gone for my glove from its concealed slit in the jacket lining and slipped it on under the table. Lifting my hand, I tapped six-inch-long matte black metal claws on the wood surface. "Sound *fun* now?"

Yesterday, the one had pissed himself. This time all

three did. The door slammed harder behind them than when they'd come in. The Three Pooches—Hairy, Curly, and Best of Show. "Idiots," I complained. "They were why spay and neuter programs exist."

"Can you do that? All of that?"

I, for a fleeting moment, wished I was thirteen again. Then I wouldn't feel humiliated if I rolled my no longer red eyes at him as I took off the glove and holstered the guns. "Now? No. The eyes are good for making assholes piss themselves. That's it. The teeth and claws—I had them once for about a week. They're gone for good." He was waiting for the other one, not budging. "Yeah, I can gate. Couldn't always, then could, then couldn't, then it made me—" I had the glove in my hand. I tucked it away.

"Look, we're going to cover this, all of this, and it's going to take fucking forever. I haven't slept since, shit, long enough I don't have the focus to do the math. Haven't eaten since yesterday's breakfast bowl of Lucky Charms, my brother is dead, my best friend is dead. You're both *dead*. Do you get that? And I am *alone* like I've never been in a thousand goddamn lives. I'd say I'm halfway to insane, but I'm already there, *already fucking there*, and I have been since I watched them die. Watched you die." I took a breath to help clear it away, everything, so I could get this all out and move on to finding Lazarus.

"You're in the right. I apologize." He was humble as Robin never was or had been.

"Are you being less pushy than usual because you feel sorry for me?" I questioned, cynical in the face of behavior unnaturally polite for a puck. "Or are you trying to stay on the good side of my insanity?"

"Do I have to choose?" With a winning smile, he refilled my glass. "Tell your tale. I'll hold all questions until the end."

"Asshole," I grumbled. "You are going to be so damn sorry you didn't listen to yourself in that letter. Remember, no matter what you hear you can't change anything. This is more than our lives. Once it was the lives of everyone on the fucking planet. If you do something, thinking that you're helping us when it's something that needs to happen, no matter how it looks at the time, you'll . . ."

Words weren't enough to describe what could happen. Instead I put my hands together fingertip to fingertip and spread them out in a visual explosion. "Boom."

He was good-humored again, unable to stay serious or, worse, take this seriously for a full minute. "Calm yourself, Caliban. I'm certain you exaggerate. Stop channeling the wailing despair of your Shakespearean namesake. You said in the letter we became acquainted when you were nineteen. One more year—the smallest amount of time. How much could I alter? How much damage could I honestly do in a single additional year?"

My imagination failed me.

It was my turn to let my head fall onto the table, forehead hitting wood with an audible thunk louder than Goodfellow had come near. "We are so fucked," I said flatly.

"Yes, yes. Fate of the world. Isn't it always?" he said, dismissing the warnings with little enough thought that it would've been equally insulting to just go on, treat me like a nervous puppy, and pat me on the head. That humility of his hadn't lasted long. I wasn't surprised. He'd lived a long time, longer than man. He'd lived alongside a thousand Cals and the crazy shit we'd gotten up to. He'd thought he'd seen it all, everything of the world, everything in all the versions of me—he'd thought he'd seen the worst in this version with Tumulus and memories of prehistoric Auphe roiling around in my subconscious.

He was wrong.

He hadn't seen a half-Auphe Cal. He hadn't seen what a half-Auphe Cal could do, *would* do. He hadn't seen that same half-Auphe Cal possessed by something even Auphe could pay but never command. He hadn't fought the entire Auphe nation when it was bent on wiping out the human race. And he had never seen anything fucking close to what happened when you combined it all.

And that had been the fucking easy part.

"From your letter I assume we're under some time

constraints. That this Vigil assassin will be showing up
sooner rather than later."

"He was supposed to arrive last night late or early
today from what my Goodfellow's contacts were able to
find out from a few of the last Vigil left. He flew some
specialists in from Greece, said they were gifted when it
came to being persuasive." Asking pretty please using
methods I didn't try to guess. I knew how persuasive
Robin and I both could be when the situation called for
it. Given a desperate situation, I crossed lines like a kid
jumping rope, and I don't think Robin had a line. For him
to call in a team he considered more expert than him, I
didn't try to guess what methods they had used. It wasn't
by asking pretty please.

"That had to be Nemesis, the Inescapable, the goddess of Revenge. She punishes crimes against the gods,
particularly hubris, and there is nothing more prideful
than mere humans thinking they could set rules for what
few gods remain among the *paien*. And I wouldn't have
left out Alecto and Tisiphone." The names rolled off his
tongue with fond nostalgia, but Goodfellow was nostalgic about everyone, whether it was the memory of the
sex or the memory of putting a sword through their guts.

"Two of the three Furies. The Implacable and Vengeance. Megaera wouldn't have come. She despises me.
Sleep with three sisters and there's always one that ends
up in the hell-hath-no-fury frame of mind. But considering she's the divine personification of Jealousy, I should've
seen that coming. That and the poison in my ambrosia, the
dagger aimed at my back. Pathetic attempts for the Fury
of Jealousy." He winced. "Until the pack of hellhounds
she set on me. I hadn't known Cerberus had sired a litter
of puppies. They would've been cute if not for being the
size of elephants and determined to tear me to bite-size
dog treats. You know how wickedly sharp puppy teeth are
whether they're a half inch or six feet long."

"You lay down with the dogs of Hades, you get up
with hell-spawned STIs." I had no sympathy.

"But enough of my endless sexual adventures through

history." Breezy as if it had been his idea all along. Two packets of honey appeared and he put both in his beer. I didn't ask. I'd seen it before. It was typically after he talked about the Mount Olympus days.

"It's been hundreds of years since our last escapades." He pushed his chair closer to the table to prop an elbow and rest his chin in one hand. Eyes gleaming the same as when he pulled off one of his unbelievably impossible cons, face animated and eager. He couldn't wait. You'd think he'd forgotten at least half our previous lives. They'd been bloody battles, sickness, slavery, and worse a helluva lot more often than they were orgies and stealing harems.

"Tell me of these exhilarating eight years to come before this Lazarus shows up and swats you like a fly while you're telling me what a bad boy I've been," he demanded. "I have an on-call dominatrix for that. So stop dragging your feet, *skata*, and *tell* me."

So much for cushioning the blow. All it got me was impatiently pissy demands. Tell him. Tell him.

And I did. No more warnings, no more preparation. I told him everything he'd asked to hear and more than he in reality wanted to know. I single-handedly did what no one else had. I killed a puck's curiosity. I'd seen three-week-old roadkill as a kid that wasn't this dead.

It was temporary, I hoped.

Or was hoping when three hours later I was punched in the face for a second time in as many days.

"Is there not one life, in all the thousands, is there not *one* single life where you couldn't be a married, fat, happy pig farmer who dies at the age of ninety-eight sitting in a rocker with his great-great-granddaughter on his lap?" He shook out his hand with a pained expression. "Fate of the world, I said. I've always known the truth was a worthless bitch."

He'd hit me with more force than Niko, who had confusing family feelings about me holding him back. There was the same taste of blood, but there was the warmth of blood trickling then running from my nose over my upper lip then lower and onto my chin to end up splattering my stolen shirt. I'd spent most of my life lying to outsiders, *gadje*, because this is what the truth would get you.

Dropping my feet from the table to the floor with a heavy thud, I grinned at him with blood-covered teeth, eyes I felt shining a brighter, glowing red, and became the third echo of those words, "'Fate of the world. Isn't it always?' I gave you what you wanted and you took my blood as thanks. Not very nice when it was you who asked for it. The bad boy wanting a story. '*Tellll* me a story.'"

Licking a thick swipe of salt and copper from my upper lip, I swallowed it, and kept grinning. "And now I taste your lack of gratitude. Maybe I should've told it in Auphe. Hours of hearing that will make your ears bleed. I've seen it. From all the screaming I don't think people liked it, but I could be wrong. We should see. We *should*." I leaned across the table towards him. "Let's do it for *science*. Let's do it for the *children*. Let's do it for *love*, for *money*, for the greater *good*, for our *country*. Let's do it 'because everything I do I do for *you*.'"

Angling back to the point he had to grab the chair to keep from falling backward, he produced the fakest smile I'd seen him wear yet, and took a second towel, holding it by the corner, the one he'd brought to the table with his new glass. He held it out to me while touching the smallest amount of that corner he possible could to keep the most distance between us. "This, I suspect, would be the insanity, then."

"Everyone needs a hobby," I drew a smiley face with sharp teeth out of my blood that had splattered on the table. "And the past day and a half have been an equal bitch and a half. Insanity is the least in my bag of tricks."

"It is quite impressive in its depth and scope, I must admit. It's equally impressive in your ability to conceal that depth and scope." He swallowed. "Could you, perhaps, as an incredibly generous personal favor to me repayable in any currency you like, conceal it again?"

I took the towel and told him the equivalent of "fuck off" in Auphe. While he winced at the sound, I wadded up the cloth and held it to my nose.

"Ah . . . ice. Let me get you some ice for my tragically

mistaken, unforgivable—pardon, *nearly* but not entirely unforgivable—act of violence." He hurried behind the bar and brought back another towel wrapped and tied around ice and a second wet towel to wipe off the blood.

Giving him a glare, I watched as he put both on the table in front of me as cautiously if they were grenades, but, me, I was a nuke. Our life, this one, had put the fear of choose-your-god into him. Horrified him beyond anything he could have imagined, all thanks to some Auphe sticking his dick in my whore of a mother. Of all the things that sliced at me, that was what cut the deepest. That she'd agreed to it. Taken gold for it. That when she made me, she made an experiment, *not* a baby, that it had been *consensual*.

None of it had been Robin's fault. He'd saved the three of us and helped wipe out the Auphe and I knew he'd been afraid then. We all had been. But he'd done it, fear be damned. The true bravery of being afraid but kicking your fear in the nut sack and standing up to it. It couldn't help that there was less to distract him now than before, no Auphe chasing me home, kidnapping me, the Unmaking of the World, a Niko, intense and on the same suicidal edge as I was here, or Goodfellow would've punched me within a week of meeting me the first time around.

And he was dead. My Robin was dead and that was on me. He died because he'd been my friend, my brother-in-arms. He'd died as he'd been unlucky enough to simply *know* me. A punch in the nose didn't beat that, did it? I pushed the Auphe from my eyes, dropped the blood-soaked ball of terry cloth to the table and picked up the wet towel.

"All right," I sighed, and used my other hand, empty as it was, to make a wiping motion from my forehead to my chin but inches away from my face—the imitation of putting on a mask. "Happy? I'm sane again. And I didn't go Auphe. I told you what Rafferty did. He healed me. The Auphe genes are there but they can't spread like before." I scrubbed at my face, the towel coming away red. "But before Rafferty, yeah, I could go Auphe. I did go Auphe

several times. That was what it will be like. I won't be that
way again, but that doesn't mean I don't remember. Or
that I don't use the memories to end fights before they
start when they're not enough of a challenge to be worth
my time."

He didn't strike me as convinced as he was standing
behind his chair with one eye on the door. "You pissed
me off, okay? You were a patronizing asshole. I warned
you and you ignored me. I told you what you thought
you wanted to hear, the truth, and you probably broke
my nose. You think I had a choice in my sperm donor?
My sell-it-with-a-smile mother? That I wanted to be
born this way?" I flipped over the towel and wiped again.

"You were a dick, you made me mad, and I wanted to
pay you back. Oh, and I'm insane, but not how I used to be.
Not Auphe insane. I just put on a show. I won't go Auphe
again either, that's true, but Cal? Cal will be going all
the Auphe that will have you shitting yourself and more.
That's my past, but it's his future. Your future too if you
stick around as you did last time." I added, "I can't believe
it. You lived through it, lived through everything, and,
here's the bitch of it, I eventually get cured and *then* you
die." After a few more sweeps, my face felt clean. I ignored the ice and used beer to swish around my mouth
and clean my teeth.

"I didn't think of it until now, but you could leave the
city. Stay away from them. The human race will be wiped
out and the Auphe will rule but they'd leave the *paien*
alive or they wouldn't have a food source, but you're a
survivor. You could make it through." He wouldn't see us
again. If there were no humans, we couldn't be reborn.
But having to choose between us and living this life as
I'd laid it out for him, I wouldn't blame him for saying a
thousand go-rounds with us was enough. Later, gator.
See ya, wouldn't wanna be ya.

"You called the Wolves idiots. Don't be one yourself,"
he ordered sharply. "And use the ice for your nose. I did
break it, and it's a picture Da Vinci would absolutely refuse to paint."

I was reaching for it with another insult on the tip of my tongue when he sucked in a breath. "Gods, there he is. There is Lazarus."

Jerking my face toward the small window in the door, I saw a pale smear. I couldn't make out any features, but I could see dark marks scattered on the almost white in contrast skin beneath. They looked larger than medium to me, but this was as good as it was going to get. This was Lazarus, although how Robin recognized him, I didn't know. "What? Holy shit, it is. How do you know?" Questions aside, I was on my feet and running. We'd had a demonstration that Robin wasn't right one hundred percent of the time, but after eight years now and too many years in past lives to count, I'd put him in the mid-nineties. Right too often to overlook.

"I know all *paien* races that exist. He was too quick to see, but I could feel him in the manner I feel very few, very strong races of *paien,* a claw scraping featherlight across the surface of my mind. He felt like none of them, but that I could feel him at all means he's powerful and he's nothing remotely human inside with what the Vigil did to him, not anymore. I couldn't guess what he's become."

"Then we'll find out. Classify his ass as we assassinate it. Ready?" I called over my shoulder as I yanked open the door and was out.

Goodfellow, who'd witnessed a thousand of my lives with not one ending peacefully, was right on my heels.

12

We ended up in the sewers.

If I got laid for every time a firefight, sword fight, or both ended up with me there in the unholy muck, my dick would've fallen off from overuse.

With Goodfellow leading the way, we ran eight or ten blocks. He didn't lose that prickle at the base of his brain. He said as we ran that it wasn't a solid, concrete awareness he had of those other *paien* races, the few of which were or had been before trickster races one and all, which made sense. Like to like. His link wasn't the same as the one I'd had with the Auphe, an inescapable sense of their presence depending solely on distance. The puck's was vague, a ghost of a tickle, which sounded easy to lose, but he didn't. Twice he stopped, at first we hadn't gone a block. "*Gamou*, it's gone. I've lost it. He's gone."

"Fast bastard." Damn it. He'd been here, right here, within reach of a hand or a bullet. This all could've been over. It could've been—

Robin had cut off my mental whining and bitching before I could get any further. "No, there it is. I have him again." There were about five more blocks of racing down the sidewalk, on the edge of the street, when we knocked down entire piles of people on their way to work. That's when we came to another halt, Goodfellow hitting every curse word in the Greek language as he spun around, trying to catch a wisp of what was iffy on qualifying for the definition of a wisp to begin with. And then he had a face-to-face lock. A phantom touch of an imaginary feather was how he described it later. The cursing ended abruptly when the puck said, "There he is yet again." There was a speculative note to the statement, but I didn't let it keep me from following him as he sprinted across the street, dodging and sliding agilely over moving car hoods as he went. As much as I wanted Lazarus dead, I wasn't about to let Goodfellow lose me.

"He's coming back when he loses us, letting you pick up his trail again." I vaulted over a baby stroller carrying a Pomeranian with a rhinestone-studded collar, and bright purple painted toenails. I didn't judge. For all I knew it was a cuter baby than I'd been.

"A trap, then. It's not a particularly clever one, but a trap nonetheless." Going by Robin's wide smile and laugh, he was reaping the adrenaline rush himself.

"It's always a trap, Caligula." My feet pounded the pavement behind him. "Did you forget my biography already?"

"Let me enjoy myself for a few hours before I'm forced to dive into knowing every step and action I'm required to take during the next eight years, which is a torture and a hell for a trickster. We live to be surprised. It's a rare treat as we most often see it coming. If our lives were a movie, we'd want a twist ending every hour of the day." He body slammed a hug slab of beef who'd parked his truck on the sidewalk to unload frozen hunks of meat at a restaurant. Beef had caught sight of us coming and, while giving off the look of a small-brained, massively muscled explosion of steroid psychosis waiting for an excuse to beat someone, *anyone*, to a pulp, it turned out he was a Good Samaritan . . . who was an explosion of steroid psychosis, as the Bible didn't say word one about steroids, and was waiting for an excuse to beat someone to a pulp.

"Stop running people down, assholes," he spat. "Act like decent human beings before I rip off one of your legs and beat you both to shithead pudding." He was already swinging a fist the size of my head, but it was slow and weighted down with muscle that was good for taking down people who didn't know how to fight . . . or dodge. It could be a slow dodge at that—sliding to one side while texting your friends about dinner plans later that night. Possibly he normally stuck with blind assholes, who rudely smacked people with their walking stick.

Robin wasn't blind, and he didn't stop running. In fact he avoided the hovering fist of doom, kicked the guy in the crotch, hit him in the throat with the stiff, callused edge of his hand, and kept running over the top of him as he fell, a less than mighty redwood. "Your concern is noted, Samson. We thank you for your input. And drop off your résumé. I have an opening for a massively muscled, tiny brained combination driver and cabana boy. You'd be perfect," echoed behind him as he kept going.

I ran around him as he was wheezing for air from the throat strike and was doing it through the vomiting that came with a brutally vicious punt to the balls. I'd had my fill of swimming in bodily fluids last night. If I could, I'd avoid it today. "Samson?" I caught up with Goodfellow. "I'd have gone with Paul Bunyan."

"Yes, but you also called me Caligula, showing how untrained your assessment of a person's psyche is. I knew Caligula. I tried to warn him horses weren't the—"

"Monogamous type. I know. I know," I grimaced. "You've said. I just didn't think then to ask if you knew that because the horse was cheating on him with you."

"You're half Auphe with the propensity on occasion to treat me as a buffet, starting with my expensive pedicure, putting an entirely new spin on foot fetish, but you give as good as you take, same as ever." He elbowed a Catholic priest in the ribs to shove him out of his path. "That was for the Spanish Inquisition. They never expect them, you know."

I did know, but around five years from now he, Niko, and I would have a Monty Python marathon. It wasn't a surprise, by any standard, but it was one thing I hadn't told him as it was too small to matter. I'd left out that and those like it that couldn't make a difference. Mainly due to a lack of time, but, too, because I did know how pucks loved their surprises and the next eight years were going to be either dull or a misery when it came to the notable events. I had to leave him something.

"I'm not half Auphe or I'd have given in and the world would now be dominated by the Auphe. And I'm not half human or I'd be dead twenty times over." I saw what was ahead of us. It couldn't be more of a trap if he'd painted the word on a sign and taped it up with a giant bunch of floating party balloons.

"Then what are you?" Goodfellow was slowing down.

"A lion." I bared my teeth, but it was friendly, one predator showing respect to another.

We'd run two miles in about fifteen minutes, which wasn't my best time by any means, but it was fair considering how many obstacles we'd had to go around—buildings—and how many we'd pushed through or gone over—people. The buildings weren't bad. The people were, depending on their size, the same as running over stacks of inflatable mattresses. Wobbly and unstable.

Coming to a halt, we stood in front of one of Canal Street's subway entrances. "Niko once calculated that seventy-three percent of traps occur in either subway tunnels or sewers. Given a choice, I'll take subway tunnels every time." I started down the stairs, ignoring the people pushing past me as I paused to glance back at Robin. Knowing it was a trap and walking into it were two different things altogether. And it'd been hundreds of years since our last lives together. He'd gotten a little lazy. "Coming? Now is when it starts to really get good. Think carnival without the creepy flesh-eating clowns."

He came down the steps behind me. "Seen many of those, have you?"

"Shot a lot of those," I corrected, taking the steps faster.

"Not all of them are children-eating monsters like the bodachs. Some are human."

"And still creepy and probably still eat children. Shoot all clowns is a PSA to live by." When we made it through the rush and onto the platform, I flicked Robin's ear. "Come on, Lassie. Which way did he go, girl? Is he twisting off Timmy's head even as we speak to use in his bowling league? Kind of soft, not much speed, lots of gutter balls, but it's aesthetics over efficiency for some."

"I'm shocked you know the word 'aesthetics' and are capable of using it correctly. And please do rein in your rampant enthusiasm when we close in on Lazarus. We know nothing about his abilities, the quantity or quality of them, or the predatory traits unique to him." He headed to the left. "Call me Lassie again and what I did to Samson's testicles will be gentle loving care compared to what I do to yours." He hadn't gone more than a few feet when he slowed to a fast walk. "A thought occurs. Let me check before I lose my signal." Punching in a number, he raised the phone to his ear. There was time for one ring, if that, before he was saying two words, "The Vigil."

He listened for three seconds, then disconnected. "Strangely enough, the Vigil has uprooted its entire organization and every single member is fleeing the city starting an hour ago. Planes, trains, cars, splitting up and stampeding in every direction. I think Lazarus gave them a little warning when he appeared in case I felt like doing what I'd done before."

Hiring the Lupa to kill every Vigil member who didn't have the sense to run. The new version of the werewolf mafia, the Lupa were all female under the leadership of their alpha, my ex-fiend with benefits, Delilah. They'd started, at Robin's direction and receipt of a massive fee, with the Vigil assassins who'd been sent after me. They dealt with them with their usual ruthless efficiency. Then every Vigil member was given a gun and made an assassin. Untrained, cheated on their salary—had to be—they'd lasted a lot less longer against the Lupa. When it came to the Vigil in NYC now, *my* now, there were none.

"See? We know some of his traits. Responsibility and respect to the organization that turned him into lab rat. He's a Boy Scout."

We were wrong, we found out after it was all over. Lazarus hadn't warned them. I'd forgotten or just didn't think about how the Vigil had a psychic or two. They weren't the more talented of their kind, but they had enough ability to see something headed straight for the city. Something cataclysmic enough to be one thing alone.

An act of god.

If I knew more about one subject than Goodfellow, it was the subway.

That would be because he refused to take it, took a car service, had his own limo, his own personal sports car, his BMW when flash wasn't what he needed for a particular con, and enough money to afford to park a fleet more of them if he wanted. He once had tried to Febreze me when I showed up at his penthouse after being stuck in a three-hour-long stall, saying I stank from marinating among the plebeian, which he helpfully broke down into urine, cheap perfume, cheap cologne, cheap soap, body odor from lack of those last three, polyester, rayon, sweaty feet, Minoxidil, deodorant made in China that both failed spectacularly and was infused with mercury, and Aqua Net that hovered around me in a cloud intensely and thick to the point that I must have sat on the lap of a New Jersey reality star hopeful.

We kept following Robin's sense of Lazarus for a few minutes before I realized it. "I know where he's going."

I had to remember that he'd lived in the city, he was a member of the Vigil who'd volunteered to be that lab rat as their last hope. Watching over the *paien* to see if they were staying under human radar meant knowing the city as well as the *paien* themselves did, including the home of the lowest of the low—the revenants—who used abandoned subway tunnels and sewers to get around the city, to stash the leftovers from whatever homeless victim they'd snatched, to sleep. It was all-purpose. The Vigil would know that and they'd know the both of them inside and out.

"Where? Hell? If so, we are there." He had a hand over his nose and mouth. "I believe I recognize this stench as the Morning Star's major weapon in the angelic Rebellion."

"Yeah, you're a delicate princess." I moved past him. There was a hidden cover made of heavy metal plate in the floor under a pile of junk in a long unused, by humans, maintenance storage closet. Below that was another maintenance tunnel, again, abandoned by humans, but an interstate to revenant and other *paien*, that weren't as disgusting but they weren't qualified to be handing out perfume samples at Macy's either.

"The Eighteenth Street subway station. It's been shut down since, hell, I don't know. The nineteen-forties? Fifties? You would know the exact date and time to the second if you ever got on the subway." That was true. Whatever the puck used or could be of use to him, he knew everything about, down to the last detail. The subway had no possibility of making his list.

"It's vulgar in smell, appearance, and the commonality of its populace. How can you bear it?"

"Because I'm not a snob," I replied. "And you've been sharing your opinion on the subway for years and years. Enough that I hear it now when you're not even around. You're off getting your feathered freak-on with Ishiah and I'm working the bar when out of nowhere I hear your bitching that if I think that mass transit that involves slithering under the surface world and through the dirt like a worm, then I should shower before funkifying your penthouse. It's like a song I can't get out of my head, except it's not my imagination. I hear your rich asshole voice smugly bouncing around inside my skull. I think it's growing into a parasite, growing big enough to eat my brain."

"I do not want to talk about that pigeon and when you return home, you are to obtain immediate monogamy deprogramming for me. Use a Taser to take me down if you must. There will be oaths on that in blood before you leave. And, for your edification, I cannot be a snob when I legitimately *am* better than everyone else."

"Uh-huh, sure, your Loftiness," I said absently, watching for the coming train. Once it passed us in an angry rumble, I grabbed Robin's arm and ran, pulling him behind me. "Go!" It was far enough down the tunnel that you had to be quick before the next train came and that one was considerably closer to the tunnel wall or the tunnel was closer to it. Either way, it was easier to get sucked up, pulled along, then thrown under it. None of those had struck me as worth risking.

We'd reached the door, but hadn't yet touched it when I heard the next train. "Great. Imminent death. What's new?" I had gone for one of my knives, the bowie with the thick, straight nine-inch blade that was my weapon and pry bar of choice. I wedged it between the door and its frame, and leaned on the handle with all my weight. The door groaned, the grinding sound of rust against concrete, and popped open. Shoving Robin ahead of me, I yanked the door shut behind me, and had out my flashlight, small but bright. Ten seconds later we were climbing down the metal rungs of a ladder. It beat the door out on rust. The ladder itself was purposely made of rust and the dull gleam of irregular metal patches was its sign of deterioration.

There had once been lights in the maintenance tunnel, but they'd gone dark, dying a quiet death who knew how long ago. There were rats too, but they were alive, plump, and healthy. Revenants were ravenous eaters, which made them sloppy eaters. Half a mouthful of their meal went flying with every bite. In the empty tunnels like these and in the sewers, the rats followed them or waited for them while they were out hunting. It was a good life for a rat.

It was good for us, too.

Full rats were slow and happy rats. They let you be. Hungry rats were desperate and bold, starving hyenas on a smaller scale. I'd spent a fair share of my life sleeping or squatting in houses and mold-infested two-room apartments where you could hear the rats in the walls, too many to count sometimes. When I was four I'd asked Nik if we could catch one and keep it as a pet. No? Why not? They weren't as ugly as the Chihuahua that belonged to my babysitter across the hall. Nik had said they were dirty and carried fleas, lice, and disease. That hadn't sounded any different from the Chihuahua, but I'd listened to my brother. Not that he was always right, although he was. Four years old and I'd known that.

I'd listened because he was the only one who listened to me.

Doing what he told me hadn't kept me from being bitten three or four times on my leg, but I hadn't minded. I'd *understood*. At four I'd known I was a rat myself, but I hadn't been half as good at going after food as they were. They'd taught me a lesson: If you can't find what you need for a growling stomach, you go and you *take* it. It'd been a lesson worth learning and worth the blood. I'd been asleep on our mattress on the floor while Nik took a shower for school in the morning. Sophia wasn't there. She wasn't there a lot at night and when she was, I wished she wasn't. She hadn't been there during the day much either, but it hadn't mattered. Whether she was or not, Nik had taken me over to Mrs. Sheckenstein, who watched me while he was gone.

It hadn't mattered she'd smelled of a bathtub full of lavender flea market perfume and a full diaper or that she'd get irate at her TV talk shows and smack the screen with her walker. She'd fed me lunch, *every* school day, which had been as close as meeting a real live Santa Claus, flying reindeer and all, to my four-year-old self. And she'd taught me to play Monopoly and Clue and Texas hold 'em. She'd been a great old lady, who cackled each time I'd swept home a pot of Peanut Butter M&M's, told me I had a gift at bluffing like nobody's business. I'd known that once she'd explained bluffing was lying for fun. I'd lied that young for survival not fun, but it'd been nice to hear someone other than Nik tell me I was smart and good at something.

When I had been bitten, Nik had come out of the shower to find me awake in my Batman shorts and a once red, now faded pink Flash T-shirt from Goodwill. I'd been sitting up, the blanket the two rats had crawled under tossed aside, and had been very cautiously placing my carefully hoarded seven M&M's in front of the gaunt pair crouched by me. I'd been four, but I hadn't been stupid. I'd had blood running down one leg where they'd tried to take a few bites out of me. If they were that hungry, they'd gnaw off the tips of my fingers if I let them.

Nik's face. It hadn't worn that expression before that I could remember, not at four. It was gray under the dark olive, mouth open, not widely, but as if he had been in the middle of saying something and forgotten what it was. Now I knew he'd been horrified and guilt-stricken to come out and see rats had tried to eat his little brother. But at four, horror and guilt and the flu looked the same.

His eyes unable to leave the blood and bites, he'd reached for the baseball bat he left propped against the wall. He'd hit robbers breaking through windows and Sophia's "dates" with it several times by the time he was eight. They'd deserved it, but the rats hadn't.

"No! Don't. They're hungry, Nik. They didn't bite me because they're mean. Just hungry." Niko and I had both known what that was like, but my brother had always given me a third of his food until I had turned eight myself and was skilled enough to steal at least the makings of one big meal or steal someone's food at a fast-food place when they left it on the table to go to the soda machine with their cup. It'd been enough to split on the days at the end of the week when Nik's paycheck had refused to stretch that far. I'd not been as smart as my brother, as polite or human—the human wasn't my fault—with classmates or teachers and other authority figures, but I'd had my own talents. I'd been able to lie, steal, blackmail, and commit arson (only the once) like a motherfucker by the third grade.

It was something that Niko hadn't had it in him to do. He would try before he'd let me go without, but his morals would strangle and trip him up. Or, I'd told him, let me do what I'm good at, being sneaky. When you try and they catch you, and they will, they'll drag you off to foster care or a group home, and I'll be alone with Sophia. If I'm alone with Sophia, stealing won't be a problem as I won't eat.

I'd been eight then, but when I'd made promises to

my brother, he'd known they were real. I wouldn't eat if the cops or the social workers took him. I wouldn't eat until I saw him again and as poor a shoplifter as his conscience made him, that might've been too long. He'd given in. There was nothing else he could do.

When I was four, though, hunger had been more familiar. "You share with me when I'm hungry," I'd said. "I should share with the rats."

Nik had bitten his bottom lip until it was as bloody as my leg, but had let me finish feeding the rest of the M&M's to the rodents before wrapping them up quickly in the blanket and shaking them out of the window, lucky we lived on the first floor, to be on their wild way . . . right back inside our walls, but we'd been young then. Not quite as smart as rats. Nik had cleaned my leg with peroxide, curiously upset to a four-year-old me who'd reassured him it hardly hurt. And the sight of blood hadn't bothered me . . . ever, I guessed, as far back as I could remember. Blood was blood. Why would that disturb anyone? Except Niko's blood. That disturbed me to the point of taking the baseball bat myself and making who'd caused my brother to bleed to bleed three times as much themselves.

In the end I'd had my leg wrapped, and a brother who'd sat on the mattress with me while I promptly fell back asleep while he stayed awake all night, watching for rats. The next day had been a "field trip" to the free clinic for a tetanus shot that had hurt like a bitch. The four bites Mickey and Minnie had given me combined hadn't been as painful as that.

To this day, I didn't hold a grudge at the memory. I *had* understood hunger and I could tolerate anything, rats included, over a Chihuahua. I didn't bother to look down when several ran over my feet to flow into the darkness ahead of us. "You don't have a problem with rats, I take it? In your future business, which I fear is spent entirely underground surrounded by disgusting smells, that if you did have such a phobia that you'd have to become accustomed."

In the spill of the flashlight's glow I glanced over at

Robin's comment and laughed with not a shred of humor to show for it. "I told you about the future and the Auphe. My past you'll have to get from Cal Junior. I left something for your curiosity. I know pucks and I know you—how insane it would drive you to not have anything left to find out, dig up. So never bitch I didn't give you anything. But, just this once, no, I don't have a problem with rats. Having a few take a couple of mouthfuls out of my leg when I was a kid is probably one of my happier memories."

I didn't ask about Goodfellow and rats. As old as he was, he would've caught and eaten rat at some point in prehistory and counted it a choice morsel fit for a king.

The maintenance tunnel was about a third of a mile long before we stood in a much larger area with crumbled pillars. Although these weren't marble, I still thought it had to be a duplicate of the abandoned platform above us. Why they had a half-finished duplicate down here, I had no idea. There were also piles of trash, heaps of bones, and graffiti on one cracked wall in what I suspected wasn't brown paint, but dried blood, and in a language and alphabet I didn't recognize. It curved and looped in a manner unfamiliar enough that it made my brain think about aching, then decide it wasn't worth it. I gestured toward it. "'For a good time, call Shub-Niggurath'?"

"With her thousand young, I think she's had a good time and then some. 'Azathoth thinks he was here but being the blind, idiot god, who knows?'"

"If you knew Lovecraft, tell me he was insane. I think I'd feel better about tentacles specifically and the universe in general."

"He was not"—his smile was sly and devious, the perfect reflection of his personality—"at least he was not until he mentioned to his substitute geometry teacher in high school how he wished to be a writer and that teacher told him a few stories."

"You are Satan, aren't you? The fucking devil," I groaned. "I knew it all along."

"How was I to know about the evolutionary unviable streak of mental illness that ran in his family? I did, if nothing else, support him in his hatred of geometry, Euclidean or non. *That* is the devil's tongue; mine is simply hypnotically convincing, eloquent, provocative, seductive, and occasionally indecent." He was shining around the spare flashlight I'd given him. Bright as it was, it couldn't begin to penetrate the nearest alcoves. Everything past that was a starless night. "It was only three days. I was undercover. There was a wood nymph on the grounds, beautiful, with the softest bed of pale green flowering moss shading her—" I kicked him in the ankle while using my light to get a look in the other direction.

Hissing in pain, he emphasized, "It was blooming for me, tiny star-shaped jasmine with a come-hither fragrance leading to a silken passage toward—" The second saving of my own personal sanity was a light rap of my flashlight to the back of his head to cut him off.

"Do you write romance novels for great-great-grandmothers? For nuns?" I was weaving, the exhaustion of the fight with the skin-walker, the sleepless night . . . the crushing inability to turn and see my brother. And I was having a repeat of the spotty vision.

"It is the poetry of erotic temptation, you heathen."

"But talk about a guy or guys that you've screwed, or when you did before Ishiah stamped monogamous on your forehead while slapping a chastity Speedo on you, and I'm tortured with 'huge cock,' 'dick that could go all night and I'm talking an Alaskan three-month night,' 'an ass almost half as fuckworthy as mine,' 'hung like Seabiscuit on Viagra,' and 'dick holster'—that was new to me. Thanks for that. Where's the 'throbbing manhood radiating incredible heat, wrapped in silken skin and a passion that needed no words to breach my heavenly gates'?" Mrs. Sheckenstein read a lot of trashy romance novels out loud, very out loud as she was half deaf, so I wouldn't be bored in between the poker games and her TV shows.

I narrowed my eyes. There were more streaks I couldn't blink away. They were dark now, not yellow. And they were coming toward us, sinuous and slinking as they moved.

"That is the foulest of foul. Heinous enough to drain

one of the will to live and so hideous to the ear that if you do, you'd pray to be struck deaf and blind. There is something profoundly wrong with you. And if you say monogamous once more"—he gagged twice when he said the word—"once and only once, I will take my sword and—"

I slapped my hand over his mouth. This Robin wasn't as familiar with me as mine had been after a few years. He was . . . he had . . . fuck, *had*, been easier to interrupt. Mine had learned to keep talking over me and if my hand had come near his face to casually attempt to stab it with an antique New Orleans gambler's push dagger, the two-inch blade perfectly concealed in the palm of his hand. I'd wanted one, love at first sight, but he'd refused to tell me where he bought or stole it, the bastard. As he would've been a gambler in New Orleans a couple of hundred years ago, he'd likely bought it then and there.

"Yeah, take your sword," I said quietly. "Now."

Was that the scrape then quick scuttle of claws? I unholstered the Desert Eagle and shifted the light over to two pillars on the right. Nothing. Next to me Goodfellow had his sword out and it was one of his longer ones in spite of the shorter—helluva lot shorter—pricey suit jacket he was wearing with no addition of a long coat over it. "*Where* do you keep it?" I kept my voice low, but didn't bother hiding the exasperation. "I've asked you before and you won't tell me. Where the hell do you fit that in just a suit?"

"Have you ever seen me nude in this not quite utopian future?"

"Unfortunately. By accident." I made sure the emphasis was audible if the words only just were as I swung the light to the left.

"Then why aren't you asking me where I keep my cock instead? The difference between it and the sword is negligible. In fact, the length of the sword may be somewhat less." He examined it for comparison. I was relieved he didn't whip out what he was comparing it with to be positive.

The dark shuddered again. The light had touched them on this side, but if they'd been set a few inches farther back, it wouldn't have. It wasn't in the light themselves I saw them. I nearly did, but what had been a solid black shadow melted to a puddle of darkness in a blink of an eye and was gone. It was in the edges of the light, the faintest of dim glows, that I could make them out. Deep and velvety black—but without the depth or gleam of fur, there was a mass of them too entwined to separate and count. They were supple and boneless as weasels, if weasels were about six feet long, without any eyes that I could make out. I couldn't see teeth either but there was the snapping of jaws with a ringing echo that is heard when there is a full mouthful of needle pointed fangs gnashing together. I pointed the flashlight directly at them. These didn't melt—strength in numbers, always a bitch—but they did untangle their knot and writhe away from it.

Unfortunately that writhing was bringing them toward us.

They didn't seem to like the light. They'd hump and slither away from a direct, head-on beam, but they'd keep to the dying glow where it dimmed to one side or the other. Apart, I could guess each would weigh about eighty or ninety pounds, but as their movement said every pound was pure, agile, and, knowing my luck, fucking gymnastic muscle. But with the no fur, no eyes, no mouth or teeth that I could see although I definitely heard that much, they were bizarre shadows except shadows aren't that dense or solid that you could hear their teeth clashing and the scrape of nails against the cracked and crumbling floor.

"No idea what they are," I said grimly as I shot the one in the lead to see the bullet swallowed and hear the impact of it on a wall or pillar behind it. It'd passed through it as if nothing was there, but knew that wasn't true. "No idea and don't like them," I corrected.

I fanned the light back and forth to have them peeling off. It didn't stop them, but it slowed them some. Goodfellow had stepped away from me to get space to swing his sword. It was a lighter version of a broadsword, heavier despite that but with more reach than the Roman short sword and more weight and force than his rapier. While I wished I hadn't run that description through my head for a mental weapons checklist that was now labeled Goodfellow's cock checklist, it'd been a good choice of weapon. It was too bad that it did nothing at all for the puck as the blade passed completely through the shadow and the shadow laughed. It was similar in no fucking way to the sound of a real weasel, but it was goddamn creepy as hell, no doubt.

Robin swore and aimed his own light at it, shoving it right into its face. And I do mean "into." His hand vanished in the shadow that made up the creature. It squealed and backed away swiftly as ribbons of black began to pour from where the light had gone in. More swiftly than that, its entire narrow head fell apart. Turning into a rain of ebon, it fell to the floor, bubbled, and dissipated with the same consistency of mist. Its body began stretching and thinning as it began to grow a new head to replace the lost one.

I'd been counting and there were at least ten to fifteen of them. They were everywhere, then somewhere else. If one leaped into the darkened area our lights didn't reach to our left, it would slither out from an equally lightless patch to our right. We couldn't hurt them. Our weapons didn't work on them. We could injure them with the flashlights, but not in a permanent way if they were growing back their heads. If anything, it irritated them more than anything else from the chorus of high-pitched squeals that had risen from the others in sympathy for the one who'd lost, and, goddamn it, seconds later grown its entire head back.

"We should meander, I think," Robin suggested, holding up the hand that was gripping the flashlight he'd used to attempt brain surgery on our new friend. It was covered with blood. The skin of the back of it had been practically *flayed*. Long slices that had torn through every piece of skin that was available without completely skinning it altogether.

We couldn't hurt them, but they had no difficulty hurting us.

"Yeah, we should go." Regroup. Get out of this damn

dark tunnel up into the daylight and, if pushed, shoot anyone whose shadow seemed too big for them. "Go and drink more. I don't think we really tried hard enough with the drinking."

They were coming for us, joining again into one mass undulation. They were between us and the direction we'd exited the tunnel onto the platform, but I'd been down here a few times before. I knew there was another way out. Stairs to a boarded-up door behind a fake facade of a small brick shop from WWII. Or, quicker and safer with instant gratification, there was another option. "I can gate us out of here," I said as we backed away, pinning some in place and slowing other ones down. It kept them from leaping on us as a pack for as long as we could.

Goodfellow shook his head with enough force I wouldn't have been that surprised if it had snapped. "No. I'd rather be eaten. What I said before, about doubting there were things worse than death, I'd forgotten the exception. I would truly rather be dead. I mean that and as you pointed out, technically, I already am dead. I'm already lost. So respect my wishes. Do not do—that thing. Just don't."

"Why?" I frowned, puzzled. I did get that the vomiting wasn't much of a recommendation for gating, but it was less of a pain in the ass that certain agonizing death. And after a few trips, he'd gotten used to it and made it past the puking. He didn't stop turning green, but he had toughed it out. "I've gated you before around twenty times at least, and you didn't say anything. You didn't say anything the very first time, which would've been the occasion for speak now or forever hold your peace."

When had that been? If he was saying something about it now, he would've said something then. He was not a hold your peace type by any stretch of the imagination. What had . . . Ah. I had it.

"I remember. I didn't give you any warning as I didn't have any warning. A Babylonian sirrush tried to bite you in two, poisoned you, and, as I was dragging you away from it, it jumped us. It was fly or die time. There were no luxuries then, like thinking, when you were three-fourths dead on the floor and there were jaws about to snap around my head. Hey, you're the information broker of the, hell, world. Here's an interesting fact I picked up as I was half swallowed. The sirrush not only has tonsils, it has six of them." I caught an ambitious weasel wriggling behind a mound of rubble close to one wall and used the flashlight beam to slice through its body in front of its back legs and tail. That was a big chunk to regenerate. Hopefully it would take it longer.

Being thrown in the deep end without knowing prior to the push must have gotten him past this death-before-gating philosophy. He'd continued to survive gating if not to like it, but no one liked it—no one but the Auphe. He hadn't, though, said why or what had happened who knew how long ago to make him like that. He hadn't hinted that he was or had been like that. Sooner die than gate? That was a double scoop of profound phobia.

"I'm not three-fourths dead now and I am saying no gating. Leave me if you have to, but gate me and one day, years from now when you've forgotten this festive discussion, I'll break into your place and cut off your testicles." His face was set and unyielding as marble.

"You're serious? I've thought you were a crapshoot of borderline genius and borderline insane, but I didn't think you were an idiot," I snapped. "I'm not leaving you to die."

"I gather then you're not particularly fond of or attached to your balls. You unquestionably won't be attached to them if you go against my wishes." Damn, the weasels were on the move. He gave me a hard push. "Run!" He followed his own advice as we raced through across the platform, then jumped down and back into the tunnel in the opposite direction.

We raced as fast as we could force our legs to pump. Our lights bounced and scattered as we tripped or vaulted over rubble. I couldn't resist a glance over my shoulder as the scuttle of claws followed us. I couldn't tell how far back they were. I didn't have time to turn the light on them and keep running without falling on my face.

"The Vigil turned Lazarus, normal human asshole, into some sort of unkillable pack of shadow weasels? I get the unkillable part is a benefit, a bonus package for being their guinea pig, but it doesn't quite equal out to having to live as a pack of supernatural shadow weasels." I felt teeth bury themselves in the back of the top of my knee and rip all the way down to the bottom of my heel—combat boot and all, a switchblade through butter. Slick as you please. "Son of a bitch." I swiveled, impaled an inky neck with my flashlight and felt it vanish.

I hadn't stopped to face it. I'd struck while still turning and let the momentum carry me around back to where I started and worked on running faster. There's nothing like a little incentive and I had all I needed snapping at my heels.

"No. I saw him for a fraction—less than a fraction of a second actually. A fraction of a fraction. I couldn't make out any details except that he was human in shape. Perhaps these shadows are pure unadulterated stench brought to unholy life." Beside me, Goodfellow was keeping up easily. He was in good condition. Too good. He was arrogant as shit about his clothes, face, hair, but particularly his body. Yet I'd never seen him do anything resembling exercise.

He knew *paien* monsters, but he didn't chase after them. Why would he? He hadn't had a reason to until Niko and I had made a business out of it. He did the weekly orgy workout. That much sex could equal the ten miles I ran and the hours of sparring I'd both done daily, but I doubted it. If he could run like the Boston marathon was a stroll without regular exercise, what did it matter other than to hoard simmering resentment that he was an undeserving lucky bastard?

"Since we are going to die embarrassing deaths by shadow rodents—"

"Weasels aren't rodents," he corrected as automatically as Niko would have, but he tossed a handful of smug on top of that educational serving.

"Death by weasel isn't less humiliating than death by rodent. Trust me, the loser quotient is equal." I tripped on a wide crack hidden in the darkness, bounced off the wall, and kept running. If I'd learned one lesson in life that topped all others, it was if something already plans on eating you and is on your heels with a fork in one paw and a knife in the other—keep running. "I'll be taking it to my grave anyway. Tell me why this gate phobia? Auphe phobia I get. Everyone gets that. But phobia versus death? Gates separate from the Auphe part"—although they never were—"how'd that happen?

"And it would be my gate," I added, confident. Why wouldn't I be? I hadn't doubted myself in a while now. "Not an Auphe and its gate. You trust me with my own, don't you?"

There was a telltale silence, airless and still. It would be what you heard when you woke up in a coffin after being buried alive. The uncomfortable sound of a lonely and imminent death by suffocation. Robin's silence wasn't as uncomfortable as that, but it stung. He knew me, not yet this time around, but he'd known me a thousand other times, and I'd never turned against him. "You don't. You don't trust me. Niko doesn't trust me and he was my brother. I can't say 'is' my brother. My brother is eight years from now" and likely dead. "Either/or, this Niko *had* been my brother once and he doesn't trust me. Cal hates me." That I could live with. I wasn't too fond of the little shit myself. But this, this I couldn't deal with. Not on top of this Niko. They were shadows of what I'd lost, but shadows, sometimes, can let you fool yourself into pseudo-sanity long enough to remake your own world. "You think I'm Auphe," I said neutrally. "You think that because half of my blood is theirs that I'd, what? *Eat* you? Like the weasels?"

I turned and clenched my hands in my hair, banging my forehead on the sewer wall. "I should've thrown your letter in the gutter. I should've gone through with what I wanted, shot myself, followed my real brother the same as in every life. But the goddamn letter ruined everything." I laughed hard enough to taste the salt of a scored throat. "I didn't know there was anything *left* to ruin; I was as fucking wrong as it gets on that, wasn't I? I came back because you told me it could be done, and because I trusted you, I believed it. I gave up my ticket out of this nightmare since you own my trust. You and Nik and no one else. I gave it to Niko and you, every scrap I ever had. I should've thought. I should've *known* that I'd come back and you'd still be dead. You aren't Goodfellow. You aren't Robin. Niko isn't Nik. You're memories, not people, and memories can't give a damn about anyone. Can't trust anyone. Can't do shit for me."

"No, that's not how it is." He was trying to pull me away from the wall despite the fact that I was simply leaning against it now, forehead to cold concrete. He could talk all he wanted. I wasn't buying it. There were reasons not to like gates. There weren't any that included "sooner die" than gate. A gate was a tool, a gun, and a gun was nothing but a paperweight without a hand to aim it and a finger to pull the trigger. He thought I was the hand and I was aiming at him with lethal intent. There was no excuse to prefer dying over letting me get us the hell out of here.

"That's exactly how it is. You always trusted me before, but now I'm Auphe. Now I'm a monster, and you'd sooner die that trust me, you son of a bitch?" My Goodfellow hadn't been like that, not once, and that was before I had known shit about the whole thousand lives past. "Hell, are you even real? Is any of this real? Or is it memories and nothing else? You can't change memories or the future with them.

"If you are real, more than a shadow, then you know that in all those other lives, all through history, I never once betrayed you," I snapped. "Never. And, believe me, asshole, there were certain centuries when life was brutal as fucking hell, where everyone, including three-year-olds, were ruthlessly amoral enough to slit your throat to steal everything on you and yank out your teeth to make jewelry for the rich. And there was me in that god-awful life, who wasn't moral in the best of lives. I would've cheerfully beat the shit out of a nun for a slice of moldy cheese. And the price on your head was higher than I could *even* count. If ever there was a fucking occasion to not have faith in me, it would've been then, but you knew better."

I would have kicked the crap out of the nun, too, without thinking twice about it. When you're straddling the line between hunger and starvation, there's not much you won't do. With each life, the world changed, people changed, morals changed. "You do remember that life, right? What I did and didn't do when it came to you, despite the daily goddamn misery that was survival. But you don't trust me *now*?

"Half starving in the woods, no shelter, with a sociopathic madman who planned on hanging us all at once— one drop and seven broken necks. He and his men searching the forest every single day and night, knowing if he caught just one of us . . . one of us starving, sleepless luckless bastards who followed *you*, who believed in *you*"—Robin who'd be a better king than the one who deserted us and the one who was stealing and starving the country blind—"well, that one luckless bastard would tell them everything.

"But when they caught me"—we'd separated, the easier to lead those chasing us into circles—"when the edge of the hill collapsed and I fell"—fell forever—"landing on the rocks by the stream and breaking my leg"—I'd seen the snapped bone and a shard of it spearing through the meat of my calf and my threadbare trousers—"they were there, and I said nothing." I'd screamed when one had kicked my brutalized leg viciously, but screams weren't words. "When they'd tied my wrists, yanked them up over my head, knotted the rope around a horse's saddle, and dragged me back"—along the ground, aiming my leg at any good-sized rock or broken branch, laughing as I shredded my bottom lip to a bloody pulp when every step of the horse felt like it was tearing off that leg, piece by piece—"I said nothing."

There had been a castle five or six miles outside the forest, a small and blocky building, not the kind I'd picture now and the dungeon wasn't underground. It wasn't a dungeon at all. It didn't have a single chain. It was just a room with a window high by the ceiling, no bigger than one foot by one foot. No way to get out of that if you'd had two working legs, but you could see the sky. It was gray every day I was there. I thought it had been three days then five, but after the first day, I didn't know. It could've been a day, a month, or a year. I did know one thing.

I didn't see the sun again.

My leg had gone bad in hours. The cloth below my knees frayed to nothing and let the open wound and bone crust with dirt. It smelled so strongly of infection that some of those holding knives for cutting and knives heated until they glowed red hot and a heavy poker for shattering bones had gagged, staggering out. I'd laughed, lying tied stripped naked on a rough wooden table scrounged from the kitchen along with the rest of their makeshift torture devices. Wasn't that a sight? Torturers with weak stomachs. And I could laugh. The pain of my leg had gone past agony to a place I couldn't feel it anymore. I was cold, the cold that seeps into you and holds you down when you fall through the rotted pond ice in early spring. It was a cold that numbed you to anything, even to the pain of fiery blades that had me screaming after the first ten burns despite swearing I wouldn't give them that. I wouldn't give them anything: words, screams, *nothing*.

My laughing brought more sliced and seared flesh but I didn't feel it. The sheriff, a man who would've done his sworn duty for free when it included this, wasn't one to give up. He pulled out two fingernails before the blacksmith's tongs broke. He'd hurled it across the room. If he was trying to hit the wall, he was too angry to aim. It slammed into the forehead of one of his men, who swayed, a dent deeper than my thumb in his forehead, then fell to the floor. Deader than the doornail that had been hammered into the back of my left hand. If he hadn't been mad before, the sheriff was now, flecks of foam and the glassy sheen of insanity in his eyes.

He burned Robin's name on my chest. If I was that stupidly loyal to an enemy of the crown, I could wear my stupidity for the rest of my life. That joke was on him when he was the one who gave me the key out of that life. After that it had been a fog, heavy inside my chest. It had me coughing, but it passed. There was a morning mist that if you'd had a small cottage and a blanket or two, you could've lain on a pallet of straw and watched it through the window. I'd never had a home like that, but I could imagine it. The mist and sprinkle of rain that covered up any voices shouting to tell them now or they'd pour boiling water meant for their dinner broth on my arms until the skin peeled off in long pieces like the ribbons in a girl's hair. Screaming at me to breathe, you worthless son of a whore. Breathe and say where he was, where he would be, one word, tell them or I'd boil. I let the rain turn the shouts into whispers too far away to make out.

I didn't think they'd gone through with it. I knew they would have if they'd had the time, if I'd still been there. But I wasn't. The weight in my lungs was gone and the air was fresh with the smell of wet grass. Getting up, I'd wrapped the blanket around me. I left the cottage on two strong, whole legs, with skin whole and unmarked, no pain—none anywhere, and I walked into the mist. When I left the cottage that never was, I left the room that shouldn't have been.

I had moved on.

"They tied me to a table in some random room they decided would be the dungeon. They had to raid the kitchen for whatever they could find for the interrogation. The sheriff was purple he was that furious. He finally gets to torture someone with real information, something he wanted more than anything he'd wanted before and he had to depend on the Betty Crocker Line of Torture and Interrogation Devices." They had worked just as well. Humiliated as he'd been, I thought he'd gone the extra mile and made them work with greater efficiency.

I checked behind us again for the weasels. "I died on a fucking kitchen table waiting for John and . . . for Niko and you to come for me, but you didn't."

"Don't. Zeus, please don't say that." The appeal came

out with the same pained grunt as a kick in the gut would cause. "Don't *think* that."

"I'm an Auphe. Isn't that right? We think things you couldn't in your darkest nightmares." It was stated blandly and without emotion as there are occasions a lack of emotion inflicts a hurt sharper than the slice of the malicious ones. "I don't think even an Auphe could come up with slow torturous death by kitchen utensils though.

"I hope you didn't tell anyone the humiliating truth about that. Where I died." I went on to snort bitterly, "Those were the days no one sang heroic songs about that kind of shit." Tortured with heated spoons and dull knives, had several bones in both feet broken with a metal poker and that had been the first few hours. Necessity is the mother of invention and Betty Crocker was a bitch and a half.

"We found you," Robin talked over my last few regrets about no heroic songs for me with enough agitated denial to drown me out. "We *came* for you. We shouted at his men to tell him I waited for him outside, and they laughed. They didn't believe I'd risk certain death to save a peasant boy who followed me with the others. I was a would-be king and they thought you were nothing. Kings don't give up their lives for common trash who were as wannabe as I was, but wannabe soldiers. They didn't believe and they didn't tell him. It took us two days to kill enough of them ringing the castle that the rest barricaded themselves inside. We surrounded the place with the straw we'd gathered and set it on fire. Cutting down a tree and using it as a battering ram to break through the door. We searched through the smoke and we"—his jaw worked—"we found you in a room on the second level. Two days and you were already cold. Colder than the room. Cold as the night before. *Two* days fighting and killing without stopping. Using anything as a weapon when our swords shattered and we ran out of arrows. Smashing men's heads in with stones. Pushing their heads under the water of the pond and drowning them. Our bare hands strangling the life from them. Anything we could make work. The morning of the second day we had fought our way close enough that you might hear us."

He looked behind us, too, but I didn't think it was for the weasels. "We shouted your name. We told you that we were coming for you. Screaming and swearing again and again at you from sunup to sunset when we finally broke through. We're here. Don't give up, Will. Don't give up. But we were shouting at ourselves. You were gone. You'd been gone since the end of the first day. You'd died in the night and you didn't hear us. Weren't there to hear us. You thought, Gods Above." He struggled and tried again, "You thought you were alone. You *weren't*. Even when you couldn't hear us, we were there. You were never alone."

"Huh. Only a day. Seemed longer," I said distantly. "Much longer."

Reluctantly, I did have to be honest. "I thought I was alone. But I didn't think it was because you and Niko wouldn't come for me. I thought it was because it was impossible for you to come. Impossible was all that would stop you two."

His running had slowed and I pushed him along with my shoulder. "Aren't you going to tell me what they did? What he did?" he asked, his shoulders braced as anything I said would be as equally physical as verbal a blow. Wasn't I going to punish me for losing me and not saving me in time?

"You said you found me"—he and Niko, because Niko would've been there, no stopping that—"said I was cold, dead since the night. So you saw me. Did you see your name burned into my chest? The sheriff did that personally, had his fingers crossed you wouldn't miss that. That was a present to himself."

Goodfellow nodded, his throat moving, but he didn't get out any words. I put them out there for him. "Then you know what they did. As long as you've been around, I know you saw everything those motherfuckers did to me. But here's what you don't know because I'm pretty damn sure that Niko went looking for whatever soldiers and sheriff's men he could find and fought them, ten men, twenty, fought and didn't stop until they finally killed him. And I'm just as sure after that you left. Maybe you buried us if you could get to our bodies, but you left. When we leave, you leave too." He'd told me that. When Niko and I died, he would put countries between him and our latest graves.

"So this is what you don't know. While they were doing all the rest including hammering a nail through one hand, during all that they went from asking where the other six of us were to just where you were—you who convinced us freezing and starving in the forest for years would somehow lead to a plan that put you on the throne. You with all that gold on your head and me with all the pain they said they would take away if I told them all the bolt holes where you hid, but I didn't care about the gold. And I didn't give you up. I *never* fucking gave you up." I twisted around, impaled the beam of light into another weasel's head, turned back and ran faster.

"I went through it all, with the last face I saw that of a man who hated you enough that he would've taken me apart piece by piece if I'd lived that long, and I didn't say a word about you. Not one. Hell, I tried to bite off my tongue so I couldn't say anything if my fever went higher and I became delirious. But I couldn't get through the damn thing. It's tougher than you'd think. Too tough from all the talking I did. I never did shut up in that life until then, the one time I made myself," I laughed, the same one from that room with the gray sky long from here. Then I sobered to tell the rest of it. "I was lucky though, three times over. They only nailed my right hand down."

"No." He saw it coming, but not exactly. He'd known all along, but Robin was the best liar born. That trumped having seen every kind of death there was and learning to recognize exactly how they had happened. "He sliced open your throat. I saw the cut. I covered it with my hand as if that would make it not disappear. Make it not true."

I kept going. The lies he told himself were his own to

come to terms with. "Lucky that I couldn't feel any pain by then. I lost some skin when I twisted my left wrist free from the rope knotted around it, but I didn't feel it. By that point I didn't feel much." The blood had actually helped by making my skin slick.

"No." It made sense if you could lie to anyone, you could lie to yourself as easily. Denial would be your best friend. "He killed you with his prize ruby pommeled *gamisou* dagger he flaunted in everyone's face and then he left it there on the floor. Threw it away because he was the sort of bastard who thought your blood on the blade made it trash."

Robin stumbled over a jumble of warped metal and concrete. I had no idea what it was, but I caught him as he fell face-first and kept him on his feet. He didn't notice it had happened, distracted, refusing to stop the fight between what he wanted to believe and what he'd realized was true from the first moment he'd seen my body. That was a lot of years of denial to overcome—if he could at all. "Isn't that how it was? He murdered you, didn't he?" he demanded or he tried. It fell flat. You don't need to demand when you already know the truth.

When I didn't answer, he almost fell again, the difference being there was nothing to fall over. "I murdered you. Not him. I did." The statement was a disjointed spill of fragmented syllables meant to be words but too broken to want to be.

"Same dramatic ass now as you were then. And I'm a fucking idiot. Was a fucking idiot, I mean." I smiled, cocky, warm, and sad. It was the smile I'd had over five hundred years ago for two people, no others. "I thought you'd be proud. The skinny little bastard with a dead mother, no father who'd claim me. The kid in rags who begged and stole food, fought dogs for the scraps their owners threw out for them. The boy who, when the assholes were angry at their wives or drunk and pissed at the whole damn world, was kicked instead of those dogs. But you said I was more, that I was strong inside, and my body would catch up. You told me I was as good as anyone and better than most, fuck what the hypocrites in the village said. You took me in and beat half to death any man who laughed at the thought of me fighting for you.

"I proved you right. I grew and I fought for you. I died for you and I wasn't sorry." Not through the pain, not through the blood. I'd never been sorry. "I was as proud of what I did as I thought you'd be." But that wasn't the end of the story that wasn't merely a story. There was nothing merely about it.

This . . . this was the end.

"The sheriff wouldn't let his favorite dagger be ruined heated in a fire. That dagger was at his belt and when you're burning letters into someone's chest, you have to be close. Close enough I hardly had to reach but a few inches." Close enough to save Robin from what I might say when the fever did reel me under and I wouldn't know where I was or who was who. But too close to get my hand between him and my chest, to slide between my ribs into my heart.

I slit my throat instead. It wasn't as quick a way to die. But it felt oddly familiar . . . oddly right. That it was how I should die with the warm rush of my own blood filling up my lungs.

"I'd seen people die of fevers like mine," I explained, "and they thought the people caring for them were their dead wives, their brothers gone fighting in the Crusade, and they would say anything. Their wife they loved could be trusted. Their missed brothers, they wouldn't whisper a word of what he told them. I had minutes before that was me." It hadn't been a risk. It had been a truth absolute in minutes or less as the room swam and rippled, colors I couldn't name bloomed and painted the walls. "Those bastards couldn't have broken me, couldn't have defeated me. You'd taught me that. My own body, though, it could have. I couldn't let that happen."

The dagger had fallen from my hand and numb fingers. I'd wished I'd had the strength to cut a second throat, the one of the son of a bitch above me. His mouth a gaping snarl of a wolf, he was screaming. I'd heard it, a little, but it had faded fast.

Robin wouldn't be surprised, I'd thought hazily as I drifted down a river bright as poppies, the same color as my name. He'd raise a mug of ale in my name, mourn and bury his grief in any willing woman he could find, and he'd be proud. Skinny bastard kid that I'd been when he first met me, but he'd seen something in me, he'd said. At my core I was strong. My skinny legs and arms would grow, but I was already strong. From the moment he looked *into* me and not *at* me, the village bastard, he'd known what he'd earned with a few words. He'd known I'd die for him, as I'd die for John, as they would die for me. They hadn't come for me, but that only meant they couldn't. If there were any possible way, they would have.

Sometimes you have to face death alone.

It was worth it when I hadn't had to face life like that.

"I never gave you up," I said quietly, one foot still in the past, the part of me that had followed Robin since I was seven, filthy and starved, who had *worshipped* him as larger-than-life starting then and not stopped, who had died for him and would do it again. "I didn't betray you once in all the lives we've lived, but most of all, not in that one."

Then I snapped back to the present and recalled how pissed I was and why.

"I would've beat a nun for a slice of cheese with one helluva crop of penicillin growing on it, and I was a hero." Vigilante, but hero according to the idiots who'd have turned on us in a heartbeat if they'd been literate enough to *read* the price on the wanted posters. "But throw a little Auphe blood in me and I can't be trusted with a gate. Throw a little Auphe blood *and* a gate in me and I *am* an Auphe. Can't have one without the other. I can't be just part. I can't be something different made new from a combination of their Auphe and human DNA. I'm the monster terrifying enough that you'd rather be weasel chow than take a ride with me."

Reflecting on it, I thought the nun thing, when I'd been a human of dubious breeding but a human without denial, was equal to a great deal of shit the Auphe had gotten up to. But I hadn't been doubted then. Wasn't that a bitter pill?

"My Robin believed in me," I said, grim and far past tired of the subject. "Three days after we met this time around, to save my brother, I threw him as a distraction at a goddamn troll, at fucking *Abbagor*." Abbagor, who all three of us had taken on and still lost against. In hindsight that was no surprise, considering Abbagor had been number two badass monster in the city. He fought Auphe as a freaking substitute for his weekly *book club*.

"He believed in me even after that because he knew exactly why I did it. The Auphe in me didn't matter to him. When a year is less than a minute to you, you shouldn't be this different, but you are. You're not him. None of you are. This Niko is not my brother, this Cal is not me, and you're not my friend. My Robin is dead." I shook my head, done with the entire mess. "Fuck it. You're some random puck, and I don't need your trust."

"Caliban, no." His mouth twisted and I smelled the desperation on him before it turned into the adrenaline spike of anger. "No. That isn't how it is. It's not about trust or belief. It's not about what flows in your veins. It's about me," he insisted. "I should've told you, as humiliating as it is. Hob certainly never let me forget. I'm sorry I was a fool to try to hide it." He sucked in several breaths as we ran. "You have to listen. You will *listen*. It's about what you've been saying. About being the Second Trickster and walking the earth when only Hob and the Auphe did. Thirty seconds is all I need. Please, give me that much."

I was considering telling him that, no, I didn't have to, but, Jesus, it was Goodfellow or that's what I'd thought when I'd heard his stupid line and seen his conman grin all over again, and he'd never before, not *my* Goodfellow, entertained the thought of turning his back on me at my most Auphe. He'd been jumpy a time or two, but anything edible in the area had been jumpy at those times. I hadn't held that against him.

We were tearing down the maintenance tunnel as our

dodging either became worse or the tunnel began to become more crowded with rubble. This Robin and my Robin and a thousand Robins before, weren't they one and the same? I'd never betrayed him, but he'd never betrayed me either. I couldn't begin to wrap my mind around any of the three of us being capable of stabbing the other in the back. And why would he not trust me now when he had and would years from now in the days that I lost control as often as our satellite lost its signal?

He wasn't a shadow. Robin was incapable of being anything but real. Nothing else in this world came close to the unbreakable solidity of him. Any more real and the sun would revolve around him and the smug conceit of *that* would never end.

Maybe he was telling the truth. It wasn't me. Maybe it was something else. Maybe he did have a reason I hadn't had the chance to find out the first time around Hell's merry-go-round.

Before I could tell him, fine, I would listen, but it'd better be extremely fucking good, we ran into what had to be a pocket of abruptly humid air, but it felt similar to hitting a giant floating bubble of swamp water. It had to be the boglike odor thickly tainting the air that had it crawling down my airway as I coughed. It couldn't be clogging my lungs. I couldn't drown from humidity. Ah, hell, but I could asphyxiate from methane gas. I tried to choke back another cough and then a series of them.

A hand gripped my elbow to support and pull me along although I hadn't realized I'd slowed any. And within a split second that hand was gone. It didn't drop from my hand; it was torn away. I staggered to a halt, taking in two scenes almost simultaneously: the approaching weasels dancing at the far reaches of my light and the hole in the concrete at my feet. Round and edged in metal, it was covered, or had been, by too many rags, rotting boards, dead rat carcasses for Robin to see it. But not enough to keep me from smelling whatever was below, which had done us exactly no damn good at all.

It seemed a little coincidental those things should drift into a pile precisely in that particular location, a manhole that had lost its metal cover. They were smart. I'd say smarter than your average weasel, but I didn't know how smart a not-too-bright weasel was, let alone your average ones.

Right now, pondering the intelligence level of a shadow weasel's brain wasn't at the top of my list. However, throwing myself down the hole after Goodfellow was. Not that I went down as fast and catastrophically as he must have. I saw the embedded ladder and flung myself onto it. I hit every third rung on the way down. The force of each one jarred me from heels to teeth, and I nearly fell more than once. One hand held my gun, the flashlight tucked in my jeans with light pointing up to hold back the shadows, leaving only one free for gripping. Luckily it wasn't far. Twenty feet and I was at the bottom. There was no standing water in this long forgotten sewer line, but plenty of thick, clinging mud. And lying in that mud was Robin.

On his side with face half buried in the mud, he was moving, but they were slow, uncoordinated movements. He was either stunned or half-dead. Either choice wasn't too fucking great. I get one Goodfellow killed and then make it a two-fer. *"Shit."* I bent over, and slid my arms under his to pull him bodily to his feet. Holding him up, I gave him a good, hard shake. It wasn't precisely First Aid protocol and if he'd broken his neck, I pretty much would've finished him right then and there. But that would've been a quicker and more pleasant way to go than what was getting ready to descend on our heads. "Robin, we have to run. *Now.* They're right behind me." I didn't give him a chance to respond. Stepping to his side, I grabbed his arm, slung it over my shoulders and took off. For the first few seconds he was about as helpful as a sack of potatoes, but following that, he began to move his legs and feet. Sort of. But, hell, I would take what I could get. As for our talk, it would have to wait.

"What ..." He spat a mouthful of mud and tried again, a little less thickly this time. "What happened?"

"You, Lord Style and Agility, fell down a manhole," I grunted, trying for a faster pace. "And lost your sword

and your flashlight." The mud sucked at my feet with the
tenacity of quicksand. It wasn't methane gas though or
we'd be dead by now. It did smell enough to put every
sewer in the city combined with every swamp in the Ev-
erglades to shame. I struggled to breathe without puking
knowing sooner or later with this kind of stink my nose
would quit working for a few hours. There. That was
something to look forward to. Who said I had no optimism? "I think the weasels covered it up with a bunch of
crap, which makes them smarter than us. Correction,
smarter than *you*, as you fell and I used the ladder."

It was dark down there, the only light coming from
my flashlight and some funky-ass lichen creeping along
the walls. And I do mean creeping . . . literally. But it was
a slow and sluggish movement and I'd seen it in areas
before if the sewers had been abandoned by humans a
long, long time. It was some sort of *paien* sewer shrub-
bery and harmless, but it would eat a dead body although
that too would take a long, long time.

That was when I heard it, the tap of claws and the
smooth slide as if oil was pouring down the metal. It was
the weasels coming down the ladder.

"Okay," I prompted when I didn't receive a snipe back
for mocking his intelligence, which worried me. "Are you
positive you don't want me to gate us where the shadows
won't eat us?" I gave him one more chance. "Feet first,
remember? Like the Neanderthals. No fucking fun."

His chin had dropped to rest on his chest and his curly
hair, now matted and dreadlocked with mud, fell over his
face. "What happened?" he repeated in a mumble. "*Poú
eímai?* Where am I? Are the . . . Where was I . . . Ah . . .
the gladiator quarters? Lie they in this"—he vomited
down his and my front both. Undeterred, he coughed,
wiped his mouth on the shoulder of my jacket and finished—"direction?"

If I got home and there was not a Mardi Gras fucking
Resurrection Parade waiting for me with beads and bare
breasts and my brother, *everyone* was dying. I was shooting everyone. If you were already dead and buried

twenty years ago, I was digging you up and shooting you
just to make sure.

Okay.

I'll need truckloads of bullets and two hundred shov-
els. Make a note.

Moving on.

Goodfellow was out of the picture ... at least mentally. That meant as tempting as it was to gate, it was also
out of the picture. Ordinarily, if he'd been poisoned,
choked out, broken his legs, anything not related to his
brain, I would've gated us out and screw the "I'd rather
die." He could've punched me again if he'd wanted since
he'd still be alive to do it and cry about his phobia and
reasons later. Head wounds, though, they were tricky.
Once Robin had been gated involuntarily his first time
with me, which is what not sharing your phobias gets
you, and the times after that, he'd been able to mentally
brace himself for it. With every gate, however, whether it
was Robin or Niko or both, they came out the other side
sick as dogs. Eventually the fetal position moaning and
projectile vomiting had stopped after repeated exposure,
but the sickness didn't go away. They just adjusted to it.
Everyone, everything, every creature out there hated
gating and they all ended up temporarily sick.

Worse than that, as Goodfellow could puke all day
and it'd be worth it to get away from these nightmares
sniffing at our heels, was the brain. When I'd first begun
to gate, it wasn't easy. I'd had skull-splitting headaches,
nosebleeds, and if I pushed hard enough, I'd bleed from
my nose, ears, and eyes. It hadn't happened to Nik and
Robin during gating, but that's when I was young and I
was the one doing all the lifting, light or heavy. I was the
plane, they were only the passengers. Nonetheless it'd
made me think then what I was thinking now—gating
didn't make for a healthy brain if you were a prepubes-
cent Auphe. I was fine with it now. I'd hit Auphe puberty,
was full grown with the physical capability to gate with
no effort or side effects. But if you were a human or a
puck who already had a head injury, if you were bleeding

inside your brain before I took you through a gate, I had
no idea if it would make things worse or not effect anything at all.

Snatching a look as I aimed the light over my shoulder, I discovered to no real surprise that shadows and
weasels move faster in mud than I do. Put the two together and we were out of luck. And in the confines of
what was basically a stone death trap, their snapping
jaws and what had started up as they came down the
ladder as manic, crazed low whispering was ten times
louder, ten times more terrifying. We were about fifteen
seconds, maximum, from being eaten alive.

Out of the corner of my eye I saw a shadowed recess.
It was either a doorway, an alcove for the exhibition of
sewer art by some exciting new artist who was big in the
1940s, or a cruel hoax. I didn't have time to weigh the
odds of each. Carrying Goodfellow along, I lunged
through the archway. And for once, luck wasn't something I made myself. The doorway actually was a doorway and as we passed through I saw an iron door resting
against the lichen covered wall. Easing the puck down as
quickly as I could without actually dropping him, I shoved
my gun away, held the end of a dysentery covered flashlight in my mouth and used both hands to push the heavy
piece of metal through the mud to close with a muted
clang. I barely made it. Immediately something hit the
other side with brutal force. There was a lock, a dead
bolt, which I shot, but it was wood and while it had once
been thick and sturdy, years of dank, humid air couldn't
have been good for it.

Crouching down beside Robin, I peered into his eyes.
"You in there, Caesar? Looking for those gladiators or
ready to come back to the real world? I hope so, because
we've really got to haul ass."

"Caesar," he echoed, rubbing a slow hand across his
muddy face. "He was boring. Always off putting it to
Cleo while claiming he was overseeing the training of
camels for the Roman cavalry. But you recall that. One
of them bit you in the ass . . . no. That was Keos. You're . . .
they took you, William . . . they *took* you."

"Will," I corrected absently, from a time when I had been Will with the only surname given a bastard village boy. Bastards received one surname, all of us. Bastards had whores or adultresses as mothers. Women painted in red. Scarlet. "Will Scarlet," I muttered, then let it go. That life was over. "Not anymore. It's Caliban. I'm Caliban."

"Caliban . . . with the horrible beer." He looked at the mud on his hand, obviously confused by it. "Where am I? Have I asked that before? Where . . ." And he was gone, wiping the mud from his hand onto my jeans. His pants? No. That'd be insane.

The important thing was he still seemed partially out of it. There was a bloody scrape on his forehead, evidence he'd hit his head on the way down. I could use the flashlight to see if his pupils were even or not, but that wouldn't necessarily mean his brain wasn't bruised, concussed, or anything else that might have it leaking out his ears if I gated us away.

He was talking and moving, more or less. Given ten or fifteen minutes, he might improve. "Come on, Goodfellow. Up. We have to go before the weasels break down the door."

"I'm not up in the penthouse?" he asked absently as he continued to wipe again at his face with scrupulous care. "Take the elevator. No stairs. My head aches."

"No, we're not in your penthouse and like you've ever taken those sky-high stairs once," I said with a healthy dose of desperation. "We're in a sub sewer being chased by weasels made of shadows and I think they missed their breakfast. We need to find a way out. For that you need to help me get you up. Do you get that? Do you understand? We need to move or be eaten by shadow weasels."

He screwed his eyes shut and his mouth twisted in a pained grimace, but it was a thoughtful grimace. I had faith. He was thinking about getting up, how simple standing was, especially when someone else was doing ninety percent of the work. "Shadow weasels. The tunnel. The sewer." Opening his eyes, he looked at the door. "My sword went through them. Your bullets too. If metal can go through them"—the whispering outside the door sounded now more like maniacal laughter—"can't they go through metal?"

Wasn't that a thought, shiny and crammed full of logic?

"Mother*fucker*. You putrid, evil bastards." They were playing with us. For food or for fun, it didn't matter.

A mass of narrow pointed black heads passed through for a look at the prey of their little game. They slithered back and forth away from the narrow beam of light. Between the laughter and whispers I thought I heard words here and there. *"Light . . . dim . . . nothing to fear . . . shine of moonless night."*

Great. I loved it when they talked. Unkillable and untouchable weren't inconveniently ghastly enough. Let's raise the bar and have them spit sinister whispers at you for shits and giggles.

Robin was trying doggedly to get his feet under him—getting *on* them wasn't going to happen. I lifted him up, slinging his arm around my shoulder and my other around his waist. I kept the flashlight balanced by his shoulder and had put my Desert Eagle in its holster. It was useless anyway. I was able to accomplish it before the weasels came through the door completely, although they had crept halfway by now. I'd raised Goodfellow upright too fast while his feet were too unsteady to hold him, and was again bathing in another waterfall of vomit, but I'd rather bathe in vomit than be eaten alive to avoid it.

"Bite . . . eat . . . take . . . bite . . . eat . . . take."

"That's elementary and middle school all over again. Biters everywhere you went." I dragged the puck away from the door. I could keep backing us up while keeping them in sight and exposed to a flashlight they were less impressed with all the time. Or I could turn and run. If I lifted Goodfellow over my shoulder in a fireman's carry, I'd make better time than half hauling, half carrying him, but the few moments it'd take to get him and his uncontrolled, limp limbs up off the ground and on my shoulder would take longer. We'd have good odds of being torn to pieces before I could begin to run.

"They hurt you? When you were . . . a child?" The

weasels he'd forgotten, but he was outrage incarnate over schoolyard bullying.

Shadow weasels were one thing, but there hadn't been a day of my life I couldn't protect myself from another kid like me. Why? For the plain reason that there were *no* other kids like me.

"Priorities, Goodfellow," I said. "If we don't die, you should look into how you rank those." Ruefully, I went on to admit, "And actually I was the biter, but they brought it on themselves. I'd been small for my age, but I'm a lion. Lions—small, medium, or large—fuck with us and we will kick your ass. Or bite off your ear. Depends on our mood."

I decided keeping the weasels in sight would get us killed, but it would allow us a few minutes more to think about what a horrible death it would be. Now or in minutes. We'd die the same way—no better or worse there. I'd take the minutes. I'd learned a long time ago, minutes you thought were useless could save your life. The weasels were sliding slower behind us, not as anxious to attack with the light in their faces. Technically, they didn't have faces—wedge-shaped light-sucking heads. They didn't fear the light, not quite, but they didn't like it either. That meant even more minutes.

If we were going to die, hell yes, I'd fight for those minutes, every one of them.

I swiped the beam of light to the side and stopped a stealthier than the rest weasel in its tracks as half its jaw vanished. Behind it had been another that leaped at us over its injured buddy. Smacking it across the chest, I stopped it before it reached Goodfellow. Its front two legs became a memory. But our minutes were counting down and no matter what I did to a weasel, it was whole again before it fell farther than halfway down the pack. Keeping us both backing away from the flowing river of shadows, I came close to losing Robin.

"Ah . . . *skata*." Robin's brief surge of energy had in reality done more harm than good. His legs gave out under him, and I barely kept him from falling with a grip tight enough to crack a rib or two if he was unlucky. His eyes closed. "Head aches . . . *gamisou*, it hurts. Tired. Too tired for . . . all this. This? What is this? Don't . . . care. Sleep. Bed. Home. I want . . . home."

Him and me both.

The two of us weary, wanting home, but his home and mine were years apart. The weasels were too close to run now. If it runs, you chase it. If you chase it you kill it. If you kill it, you eat it. Auphe taught me that and lions on TV taught me that. I preferred the lions, but the end lesson was the same. "We are fucked now, you know that?"

He shook his head and immediately hung his head, a groan imprisoned behind clenched teeth. Pain and nausea, that sounded like a concussion. I didn't have to watch those gory medical soap operas to make that guess. "No . . . we would've been fucked . . . if we'd found the gladiators." He had cleared some, but he was back neck deep in confusion again.

"Can we forget the gladiators? As a favor?" The smell of mud, slime, supernatural lichen on the walls, brackish water pooling on top of the thicker, denser mud, it remained in the air. But there was a new scent. It reminded me of a storm, of the ozone lining the clouds with vicious threat. But warped to something more dangerous, sending an electric tingle down my spine with the same feeling you had when you were eight, lived in a trailer, heard the tornado siren, and stepped outside to see the green sky with a mile wide Wrath of God headed straight toward you.

I shifted us both around, Robin and me, keeping the light on the weasels to stall them, leaving none to see what was behind us. There was nothing I could make out in the dark, thick enough to breathe like air. That was it. I was gating and hoping Goodfellow's brains didn't ooze out his ears and he coped with his phobia.

Then came what I couldn't see. A short, rough laugh— more intelligent than that of the weasels, but more sane? I had a feeling. When predator faces predator, you can scent the rabid on them. It . . . he . . . didn't sound insane, but the best of us don't, do we? "Goats for sacrifice. Mutts for stew." His words were as rough and amused as his laugh. "Bow your head before your better. Kneel as my pets rip bite after bite from your bodies. Your flesh, your blood, it would please me."

"How about a flashlight up your ass instead? Maybe you're a shadow too. Nothing goddamned more than that," I said coldly. He hadn't been in the truck that had destroyed the bar, or he'd have burned with the others inside. I'd watched. The truck had been driven and precisely aimed. I'd seen no one get out of the flaming heap, no one run away. No, he hadn't been there. That had been a job for a regular assassin or two, not a waste of a genetically altered monster/human hybrid. He had been Vigil once. As fierce a hold as they'd had over their members, remained Vigil.

Behind the voice lightning flared, sizzled, and struck twenty or more areas of the sewer wall. And it didn't stop. They kept going, the multinumbered electric arms of an Indian goddess of death. That was bad. If I was hit by one or more of those baleful arms, gating wouldn't be a subject of conversation for a while. Enough electricity shorted out my ability to gate for a good long time.

The weasels didn't strike me as that ominous now. Unkillable. So what? It was just a word. On reflection, I wasn't positive it was a word.

The lightning was blindingly bright, enough so that now it was lighter than we needed or wanted. Vision swimming with white and blue, blinded to the point I couldn't see the glimmer of my flashlight, or Lazarus. I saw the outline of a storm-shadowed figure at most. The black figure of a man, tall and broad, but I couldn't make out anything else buried in the dark—until his arms both lifted. There was something in each one. It swung, against the blue-white corona of lightning, the same shaded black—narrow, almost serpentine—and they moved. Or he moved them.

Didn't care, didn't know, didn't want to know. I was done.

Goodfellow had felt a *paien* he'd not felt before in his life. I'd seen Frankenstein on TV and I knew a puzzle piece monster when I saw one. Human shaped with inhuman powers and control of pets formed from the dark that had herded us to this spot. The Vigil and genetic engineering had done possibly more than they'd expected. Lazarus could be worse than any *paien* the Vigil had put down.

"They are for you." The lightning doubled and I was completely blind, but not before I witnessed the swinging movement, the twisting and coiling, as whatever they were came nearer, extended by the eddy and flow that were the outlines of fists. Our clothes crackled with visible static.

I could almost taste his breath beyond the ozone and sewer reek. Almost. But I felt it. It was cold, colder than the ice of a zero degree day frozen in a strangling hand around the metal pole of a street sign. He was there. He could touch us. He could also electrocute us, have his weasels eat us, and do something god-awful with whatever the fuck was writhing in his unseeable hands.

"They are the takers of your last breath.

"As I am the taker of your lives.

"The receiver of your souls."

I felt the brush of something coarse against my face. Coarse then silken, but moving in the independent S-pattern of a snake or a serpent. Slithering toward my throat. Where else would it go? Taker of my last breath?

All right.

Now I was done.

That whole cope with Robin's phobia of gates, hope his brain isn't injured enough to pour out of his ears when I did gate us? Those issues? Nope. Did not give a shit. Fuck his phobia, and right now his explanation could wait. He might rather die or be eaten. Too bad for him only the fully conscious and oriented people got to make that decision.

"If you have the brainpower to waste on gladiator fantasies, then you have brains to spare to survive a gate." He had tumbled back into half-consciousness and it was a risk, but Lazarus wasn't a risk. He was a sure thing and that sure thing was death.

Sometimes you have to roll the dice.

When it came to getaways and gates, lightning was

pulling up the rear. I was faster, but not only that—nothing passed into my gate that I didn't want there. I built it around us, no time for dramatic walking through. We were there, we were shining with purples, cyanotic blues, black, and the several shades of corpse gray. It was an odd, strangely colored light, but it shone. Not in the manner most would want to see or be able to see, but it was my sun and my moon and it got me the hell out of Dodge. It was the adrenaline life or death feel of a skydiver's rush as he plummeted through the air into a desert of glass and stone and the bones of a dead race you'd destroyed before they destroyed you. It was the sensation of your feet hitting the red sand, the burn of acid wind, the yellow sky that watched you from above. I never did go there after my last escape, not in reality, as it was the hell that had eaten half my soul. But for two years it had been home, complete with torture to make me believe it was home. It hadn't been, wouldn't ever be. But some feelings the Auphe shove into your brain, you couldn't get out. This was what I thought of briefly when I gated. The feeling of coming home.

I wondered why it didn't feel that way to anyone else. Going home.

13

I had gated in front of the door to the wendigo's basement abattoir, although it took a few minutes for the lightning glare that spread in a white blindness across my vision to clear enough to see I'd put us precisely where I'd meant. I was familiar with that location thanks to my pursuit of makeshift body bags—I did need to make a note to kill it when I had a spare moment. Good neighbor or not with the sharing of supplies, he was eating people. Couldn't really let that go.

The location was convenient. It was somewhere close to the apartment, but nowhere Cal or Niko would accidentally see me if they were so anxious to die they'd ignored my advice and left their place to poke around for the Vigil assassin on their own. They'd been uncooperative enough to come strolling out in the hall to take a look at Goodfellow after I'd told them, told Niko—the responsible of us two—to stay inside or risk all of us dying thanks to some insignificant change. And it would be long before eight more years, knowing our luck. If I could stop Lazarus and get back home without Cal and Niko seeing me travel as Auphe alone did, that would be the only souvenir I'd need. *"I traveled in time, kicked as-*

sassin ass, and didn't give my toddler self a psychotic break." Slap it on a mug and I was good to go.

If Cal did see it, that would be a spiraling mess of every self-aimed negative emotion in the book, a confirmation of the monster he suspected he was. It'd be an emo-explosion none of us had the time for. At eighteen everything is about you. I don't have the right car. I don't have the right clothes. I don't have the right friends. I'm a monster. I'm an abomination. I'm going to start eating people.

How Niko had resisted smothering me in my sleep for this particular chunk of years, I had no idea.

I had outgrown it, that was something to remember.

When the gate disappeared, leaving us here, Robin was no longer half-conscious. He was down and out. I'd gone from carrying most of his weight to all of it. He'd been talking before the traveling. That made me think this wasn't a very positive sign. I was giving him a few minutes to come around before I put him down on the floor. If I had caused more damage, if he lost part of the brilliance, ego, and sly intelligence that made Robin Robin, that was something I couldn't fix. It would be worse than if I'd left him to die.

One more thing I couldn't live with. I'd add it to the list.

"Goodfellow," I urged, "wake up. Gladiators wait for no man or puck."

Nothing.

"Robin, Hercules says Zeus is your father and your mother was a donkey. The cock you're so proud of is a donkey dick. That your sexual partners are literally sucking donkey dick."

There was drool pooling over my collarbone, but that wasn't the response I wanted. Drool is not as communicative as, say, words. Neither was the sewer slime, mud, blood, and a gallon of vomit we were both wearing. Robin did like a big breakfast. I exhaled and whipped out the big guns. "Do you remember this one? I don't. Likely because Nik gave me a crack to the skull that makes yours a fucking fairy kiss. Do you remember how you got his ass so drunk in Rome that when he passed out, you hauled him to a tattooist and had MY LUST FOR PHILOSOPHY IS TEN TIMES MY SEXUAL DESIRE FOR MEN, WOMEN, OR THE STALLIONS OF CALIGULA'S STABLE inked on his ass? He wasn't that interested in philosophy that time around either, hated it, making the insult worse. But you never cared about building the better mousetrap, only the more offensive insult."

There was a questioning mumble and the chin resting on my shoulder moved, shifting his head with it. He was trying to get a less blurry look at me. After a blow to the head like that, you're always half out of it in the beginning when you came around with no idea where you were, how you'd gotten there, or what had happened. That had been what happened in the sewer. I had no idea if the gate had knocked him back out or if whatever phobia he had was that bad. Considering the other time, he'd puked but not lost consciousness, I was going with the gate knocked him out. Being gate-sick on top of a concussion would do it. That he had shown and was again showing signs of waking up was reassuring. The sound I'd heard when he'd hit the concrete could easily have been the fracturing of a skull. Showing some signs of consciousness this soon for the second time was a relief.

I felt the nibble of lips and teeth on my ear and the mumble went from curious to enthusiastic.

That was *not* a relief.

I sighed and tightened my grip on his wrist, keeping his arm in place over my shoulder. "Less with the molesting and more with the walking. Try moving your feet. We have eight flights to climb, Goodfellow, and I am too worn-out to carry your ass." He did move his feet, but not in a manner that facilitated walking. They were limp and aimless enough to snag on each step. How unlikely was it that he wouldn't miss getting caught on at least one? That was a puck for you; defying all odds.

The mouth moved from my ear to my neck and the teeth became more involved. "Jesus fucking Christ. Goodfellow, *wake* up and get off of me. I am not above hitting an injured, barely conscious man. Normally I think of it as a bargain. Half the work's already done for me. I will seriously beat you like a rug and brag about it afterward." I kept progressing up the stairs, picking up the pace and putting in more effort and less care about bruised ankles. If I broke one, then I'd contemplate feeling remorse. I didn't think I would feel it, but I'd mull it over—if I wasn't too busy. If I broke both of them, I would give it some thought. I'd decide it was blaming the victim, me, and dismiss the remorse midthought, that was a given on my part. Know thyself, right? But thought would've been involved. What more could anyone want than that?

"Safeword . . . fanny pack. Wait. That was . . . last year. Now is . . . Velcro . . . means . . . hell . . . no."

"My safeword is a kick in your face and I'm about to use it." The warning was clipped, grimly serious, and completely useless.

"Toybox . . ."

"I don't want to know." God, I couldn't think of anything I less wanted to know.

Less talk was fine by him and he was back on my throat, attached firmly enough for it to be his biological purpose in life—remora to my shark. He may have hit his head harder than I thought. He may have fractured his skull, have a bleed in his brain. It was possible he could have brain damage. He'd *better* have brain damage.

I lifted my hand from its grip on a fistful of his shirt and suit jacket, trying to push his head back with no luck other than nearly dropping him. One hand wasn't going to do it. Two hands and a crowbar didn't inspire faith in me either. It might take the Jaws of Life. I wrapped my arm back around his waist again.

The thump thump of his feet trailing along the stairs behind us hadn't caused any complaints. I didn't think I could go faster carrying all of his weight. Getting up each flight alone would've been a shock, being weary enough to have double vision. But somehow I was making it and if I didn't actually lose one of his feet entirely to bounce down to the landing below, I'd give faster a shot.

I think Moses, did the guy not know east from west using—I don't know—the freaking sun, led his people across the desert in less time than it took me to get the both of us up the stairs to the seventh floor using every ounce of energy left in me. It was ten minutes in reality, but it felt like the biblical forty years. Robin hit full consciousness between floors five and six and got his feet steady under him between six and seven. I hadn't wondered how many bruises a puck could leave on your throat while half-conscious. It hadn't been an issue, hadn't imagined it would be an issue, might have gone ahead and said, fuck it; sorry, Nik, and shot myself at the pizza cart if I'd *known* it would be an issue.

When I was finally at the door and pounding at it furiously while picturing it as Robin's face, he snatched a quick glance at me, looked away quickly as I jerked my head toward him, spearing him with a glare heated enough to melt his face with a swiftness and wrath that the Ark of the Covenant couldn't begin to match. "It . . . it's not—"

"It? *It?*" I started kicking the door in addition to beating my fist bloody against it.

"Um . . . ah . . . if we're going for unnecessarily strict accuracy, I meant 'they.' They aren't that noticeable." He attempted to pacify my rage. My full justifiable edging toward homicidal rage. "With enough distance, no one will see them."

"Distance? As in the distance from *space*? I've been attacked by a nest of giant demonic hazardous waste–marinated mutant lamprey eels that did less damage than you," I hissed. "And they were a hundred times easier to pry off. If I hadn't thought you were already brain-damaged from the fall in the sewer, I would've dragged you up the stairs by your ankles and let your head bounce off every single fucking step."

"I was not at all aware, I promise you. I was confused. Head injuries are well-known for causing that, I'm sure you know. Safe and consensual have ever been my watchwords. My humble apologies." He swayed, steadied himself against the wall, and gave me all the sincerity a puck could deliver.

As little as that was, thanks to the evolutionary development of their rapaciously scheming species, I didn't feel very forgiving. "I was going to switch you to a fireman's carry, over my shoulder, but I didn't want your pit-bull jaws locked on to my ass doing to it what you did to my neck."

The fact that he was picturing that precisely as I'd put the mental image out there like the idiot I was had my next blow at the door, which swung open abruptly, close to taking Cal's head off. "Motherf—" He ducked and fell backward, managing to miss the broken nose Robin had also given me hours ago. A pace behind him, Niko braced him and kept him upright. "Jesus." He put a hand over his nose and mouth the same as Goodfellow had in the tunnels. "You guys stink worse than a sewer."

"No. We stink exactly like a sewer as that's where we've been." I pushed past him.

"What the hell? What happened? Your leg is a mess. My favorite jeans that you stole like an asshole are fucked. You're giving me the cash to buy me another pair." Cal, what a humanitarian—one quality that hadn't changed in the long stretch between us. He had homed in on the blood-soaked jeans I was wearing first. I wish he'd stayed fixed on them, but that wasn't my life. He'd moved on to my neck. "That is nasty. Did something try to strangle you? Something with suckers you see on a tentacle? That giant octopus in the weird *Twenty Thousand Leagues Under the Sea* movie. How are you even able to breathe?"

Niko, unfortunately, was a little more observant and a great deal more intelligent. He tipped his head once, then twice for views at different angles. I said something to him that I hadn't before at any age. Until this incident, I couldn't have conceived of saying it, but desperate times call for desperate measures. I couldn't pretend this was an exhaustion-induced hallucination if I had to hear another word on the subject—from anyone. I shoved a finger in his face, near enough he could've bitten it off if he was more like his brother, both versions. "Niko, *shut* it."

His visual examination continued to take in the rest of me with a more sympathetic adding up of blatantly visible injuries, the blood I was tracking with one foot as it had run down my leg, into my combat boot, over-flowed, and was leaving a crimson tread pattern behind. "Consider it most thoroughly shut," he agreed mildly.

"If Goodfellow falls over, leave him in the hall for the wendigo to eat." I went straight for the bathroom and locked the door behind me.

By the time I made it out of the tub equipped with shower head, taking both a bath and shower, I felt as filthy as when I'd first stepped in. I looked clean though. It was the dirt and shadows in my mind I couldn't wash away. After brushing my teeth with Cal's toothbrush, which made it mine, I bagged my clothes, stained in everyhing you wouldn't want in your hemisphere, much less on you. I then dug into the tiny cabinet over the toilet. The first-aid kit was back but it was as woefully under stocked as last night. I yelled through the door, "Niko, where's your stitches, needles, lidocaine. You know, the shit that keeps us alive?"

His answer, patient and quiet from the other side, didn't improve my mood. "We don't have stitches or li-docaine. I do have a needle from a kit I use to repair my sparring padding."

Shit. If nothing else, that was a big enough needle. And the man flossed as a second religion. It'd have to do. "Needle," I demanded, then added, "please." It wasn't his fault that while their lives were in daily danger from the Auphe that they hadn't been wounded severely and of-ten enough to play Martha Stewart and stitch up each other or themselves.

Moments later there was a knock and I unlocked the door with a freshly washed towel around my waist, did a careful Goodfellow check, and took three different-sized needles from Niko. "Thanks."

He frowned, taking in the briskly bleeding cut, after a good while too, from the back of my knee to my heel. "What are you going to stitch it with? How are you go-ing to stitch it without intensive contortionist training?"

"Dental floss. Glad you use the unflavored kind. The

mint burns like a bitch." I sat on the lid of the toilet and started threading the middle-sized needle. "And awkwardly, but not as awkwardly as if you offered, ended up with my leg hiked up on the edge of the tub and my junk in your face."

The impatient look down his long nose was the same it would be in every year to come. "As if I have not seen your 'junk' since you were born. But if you've become that shy, you can lie on my bed with your towel and both of us will be spared the sight."

It would simplify things some. Stitches from the angle I'd be coming at them with wouldn't be neat or as effective, not that mine were that neat in spite of long experience. Niko's would be neat, tight, but slow. That was the downside of lack of a considerable amount of wounds and the stitching that went with them. The lack of lidocaine sucked as well. The cut was in the muscle of my calf. When your brother makes you run ten miles a day, you don't have extra flesh on your calves—only muscle, which was harder to get a needle through and, like mint dental floss, hurt like a bitch.

I shrugged, gathered the supplies including another towel, alcohol and a light bandage so it wouldn't scrape against whatever pants I was able to steal later. "First time?" I knew it was. He'd bandaged me several times before, but stitches hadn't been needed. He nodded just as I was grabbing the bathroom garbage can. "You might need this."

"Why? I have one in my room. I can toss the leftover supplies in there before bagging them for the Dumpster." I followed his blond braid to his bedroom. I'd have tugged it if I had an extra hand.

"This isn't for leftovers," I said blandly. "Not the kind you're thinking of."

I limped into the main room wearing another pair of Niko's sweats. Cal looked past me. "Where's Nik?" The sound of flushing and water running from the bathroom was muffled but audible.

"Taking a short time-out. Be thankful. The first time he stitches you up, he'll have the vomiting out of his system." It wasn't that he had a problem with blood or a natural queasiness when it came to medical procedures. It was simply impossible to prepare for—sliding a needle through your brother's skin and flesh, mainly as it didn't actually slide. Flesh and skin are tougher than that. The first doesn't give and the second stretches past where you would imagine it could. On occasion you have to punch the needle through and as long as my cut was, that had added up to over fifty stitches easy. That's more spearing than you'd counted on through the meat of your brother's leg.

Who had been your brother.

Heading for the chair, the only chair, I dropped carefully in it. Niko's idea of pain killers was over the counter herbal crumbled leaves in a bottle that had the SAGE label peeled off and replaced with ORGANIC HERBAL PAIN RELIEF . . . SUCKER. The sucker was implied, but I knew it was there, because the pain relief I was receiving was good for seasoning a Thanksgiving turkey and accomplishing nothing else.

Robin was already showered, hand bandaged, scrape on his forehead cleaned and covered with a Band-Aid, hair shampooed with, hell, *product* in it. He had a faint floral odor around him and was wearing nothing but a rich ruby red sheet—a silk sheet. He sat on the couch, eyes closed, head resting on the back cushion and hands folded across his stomach. Looking far more comfortable and pain-free than before, he'd apparently also gotten much stronger medication than I had from the same location as the soap, shampoo, and sheet.

There was one bathroom in this apartment, and I knew bathing in the kitchen sink limb by limb wasn't in the realm of possibility for him, but he was clean and bandaged before me. My stitches had taken longer, but I could see the bathroom from Niko's room. He hadn't been in there. The floral smell from a woman's shampoo and soap and freaking product; the silk sheet in the color of passion for women and patriotism for older Russians.

"You went over to the *rusalka*'s," I accused. "She cleaned and bandaged you up, fixed your *hair*, you vain son of a bitch, and gave you a sheet to wear? A goddamn sheet? How many people's dead drowned bodies did she have over there?"

"You're terribly quick to condemn," he tsked. "She keeps her apartment immaculate, no dead bodies at all. She's pleasant, attractive, and if we don't all die, I, as thanks, plan on escorting her for dinner and an all-night festival of orgasms—also to return her sheet. And why not a sheet? It's of excellent import, comfortable, and I couldn't fit in any of her clothes. I wasn't about to wear any to be found in this . . . abode. Ah, I nearly forgot. She said to remind you that you owe her two cases of Costco heavy-duty garbage bags."

"I have never tried so hard to not kill a handful of people in my life." I paid no attention to the damp hair sticking to my face. "And for it to be people I know. People I sincerely give a shit about." I narrowed my eyes. "*Gave* a shit about rather. It's unbelievable. Someone give me a knife. I want to stab something. *Anything.*"

"You can't kill me." Mini Me was getting snarky and smug again. "Kill me, if you're capable of it, and you'll disappear. Eight years dead. So suck it."

"It's hysterical how you think that a) I can't kill you with the TV remote if I wanted and b) that nonexistence right now would remotely be enough to stop me," I said darkly.

"You're worst than identical twins as neither of you are the good one." Niko was out of the bathroom and examining the image on the couch. His face, wet from the splashing we'd heard from the bathroom, was blank as Niko's tended to be when there were too many vexing emotions swirling around and he was choosing one to focus all his exasperation on. Disbelief. Disgust. Appalled. Shocked. Had enough of this day—time to put my katana to good use. "Goodfellow, you are wearing a sheet. No, I apologize for the misinformation. You are draped with a sheet, meaning your naked genitals and ass are kissing

cousins, so to speak, with our couch cushions. Guests do
not put portions of their anatomy where they don't belong."

The puck opened his eyes. "If I paid any attention to
that rule, then I would never get laid," he drawled. "In
further refutation to that decree, Niko, was it? This piece
of what you refer to as furniture is pleather or similar
and that should not be put near the locations of portions
of an innocent guest's anatomy as it could cause chemical dye burns, and the peeling off of skin scalded by its
faux hoggahyde upholstery—at least I hoped it was fake.
If a hog like that had existed, I didn't want to know about
it. Then there is the once hearty will to live that is currently being siphoned from me down to between the
cushions where Morlocks doubtless dwell. I await your
apology, provided I am not drained to a husk by this
monument to incredibly bad taste before hearing it."

I thought about throwing something at him, but there
was nothing within reach and I was not getting up. Wait.
There was a sock stuffed behind me. I could feel the soft
wadded shape. I snatched it up and nailed the puck in
the face. From his choking and the watering of his eyes,
it was one of Cal Junior's epically ripe ones. It was the
first genuine grins the two of us had exchanged, at someone else's expense or not.

"Leave Niko alone. Of all of us, he's the single exception to the soulless bastards banner we all fly," I said.
Whether his trust came and went. It had better stay from
now on or I'd do this job with Robin, if his excuse—
when given—was good enough, or I'd do it alone. I
wasn't fighting shadows by the sides of shadows.

I dug around subtly for another discarded sock as I
introduced them. "This is Rob Fellows to humans. Robin
Goodfellow, puck, Pan, trickster of tricksters to *paien*.
Those are the so-called monsters if you've forgotten. I
left him a message to pass on to my Niko if I don't make
it back." The letter part was true—not what was in it—
but a letter did exist, and this Niko knew the real reason
for the letter. He knew that Goodfellow was a puck, an
acquaintance—I hadn't been willing to get into how he

was more or why his death, if a disease, would be as terminal to me as my Nik's. He knew to not approach him early. To wait a year like it was meant to be and not take chances by doing otherwise. Niko would've followed that to the letter. He wasn't fond of the smallest or safest of gambles.

It was Goodfellow that had not met a rule he wouldn't tie in a thousand knots, a gamble he wouldn't take, or advice he wouldn't ignore. "He was supposed to wait a year like Niko to let the natural order of things fall into place. But he's a know-it-all dick who doesn't listen to anyone but himself, and that's how it is." I shrugged. "The long and the short of it is there's nothing we can do about it now. If there's damage, it's already done. You can't get rid of him now that he knows. He's more tenacious than the world's worst venereal disease."

I waved a hand at the puck. "So, here you go. Have a friend for nine years instead of eight. You're welcome."

Niko asked, eyebrows arched and bemused. "You're *giving* him to us as a present? A friend? Like a cat would gift its owner with a dead mouse on their pillow?"

"Trust me. This will be less irritating than when he stalked us originally, especially as he stalks from about three feet away," I promised, hand in fake vow to a fake God. It could be less irritating. It wasn't impossible.

Cal was standing behind the couch, glaring down at the cheerful gaze that looked back up at him. "I don't want a friend. We don't need a friend." We've never had a friend. We've never trusted anyone. They went unsaid, but meant basically the same as Cal's words. We don't know how to trust anyone but each other.

That's what I'd thought when I was young and naive, such as . . . last night when Niko had dropped the first bomb.

"Are you certain he's not Lazarus? He could be some sort of shape-shifter like a Wolf, but more skilled." Look at Niko. He'd gone from nothing but vamps, Wolves, and Auphe to skin-walkers, *rusalka*, lamia, wendigo, and now was willing to believe in shape-shifters.

"Yeah, no. We ran into Lazarus in the sewers and if

there's anything out there more badass than him, we should murder-suicide pact it right now." I slid a glance at Cal where he was lurking behind the couch and recognized in his eyes what I saw often enough in mine. "Cal, don't stab Robin. Believe it or not, in the future you'll need him."

"How'd he know you were here? Here as in our fucking address here? He'd have to know or how'd he come here showing his face a year early?" he demanded suspiciously, of me or Goodfellow or both was the question. I guessed both.

"After I left him the letter for my Nik, he did what he does. Figured it out." There was a spasm that passed over Cal's face at the mention of the letter. Leaving one for his Nik if he died, this Cal knew how that would end. "He ignored the instructions to not change things. He ignored the warning about bringing the world down around us and all. I shouldn't have been surprised he decided to come early."

"Coming early is a disaster in certain vital situations," Goodfellow agreed slyly, "but this is not that situation."

"But you didn't tell him where to find us. You didn't want him here early; you wouldn't have given him our address." Niko backed a few steps away from the couch. "How did he find us? 'Figured it out' is not explanation enough considering we've spent our entire lives avoiding people and . . . things." Auphe was what he didn't want to bring up. "We, and it is no exaggeration, excel at it."

"We do. For humans. He's a puck. A trickster. A *born* trickster, evolved or created to do this and nothing but this. He could find anyone if he tried. Remember that stupid *Where's Waldo* book when I was a kid? You never see those anymore. Probably because Goodfellow found Waldo and sold him into sexual slavery," I grumbled. "There were cameras, recognition software programmed to detect his real written name. Who does that? Then from that and the cameras he was able to get the cab I was in on tape, bribe the cabbie to find out where he dropped me off, and had minions sweep a ten block radius from that point with my picture from the tape.

"He was Tommy Lee Jones. There was a hard-target search of every gas station, residence, town house, coffeehouse, teahouse, clubhouse, penthouse, courthouse, schoolhouse, firehouse, warehouse, whorehouse—"

"I think we have it," Niko responded wryly. "He is good at what he does."

I jumped in before Goodfellow could talk about how excellently not good he was and of all the many, varied, often sexually illegal in every state with a single voting Republican activities he was excellent at in addition to the innate trickster capabilities in him. "From there on, it wasn't difficult. He or one of his minions followed us here."

"And we didn't notice?" Cal questioned. Con artists didn't care for it when someone was more talented than you and when we were one person, Cal and I had conned our way across cities, states, and the entire country for that matter. "How likely is that?" He was shifting his weight again. That was another sign I knew well from the mirror.

"Damn likely if it's Robin. Hell, for all I know, his minion is a giant hyperintelligent cockroach with my picture taped to its back. Nothing we'd be looking for offhand. And I see that little stabbing boogie you're doing. Do not stab him. I'm not kidding. He saves your life some day. From eight years on the other side now seeing what I used to be I don't know *why* he did, but he did. If you want to live, don't stab him."

"Or shoot me. That's equally as annoying as being stabbed. Of course neither is one quarter as irritating as your complaining. The conniving I'd approve of if you, the younger you"—Goodfellow nodded back toward Cal—"weren't somewhat of an amateur at it. If you were properly trained, you'd have caught on to Caliban's little tricks by now."

"Amateur?" Cal was all but frothing with rage. If he were a dog, anyone would've put him down for rabies with a clear conscience. "I've been conning people since I was four."

"I didn't say *rank* amateur." The puck's voice was

placidly soothing, but there was a wicked glitter in his eyes. A fox winking from a depthless forest. Tricksters did love to poke and prod at people's vulnerabilities, and Cal had an uncountable number of buttons waiting to be pushed. I had too until I'd decided I didn't like multiple areas of exposure. I didn't care for having a buffet of weaknesses open to greedy hands. I'd unplugged the whole system, burned down the restaurant. It had resulted in fewer opportunities for my customary level of violence, but you can't have everything.

"*Four. I was four.* Lying, stealing, conning, arson by the age of seven. *Seven.*"

"And I'll bet you were adorable." He rearranged the sheet he was wrapped in to make everyone but him even more uncomfortable and spread his arms along the back of the couch causing the cloth to ride up farther. That *rusalka* needed to invest in a larger bed for the larger sheets required. "I've been conning since I was born, not that *Homo erectus* was that taxing to fool or had anything I wanted to con out of them. Pointed sticks, sharp-edged rocks. Sharp-edged rocks tied to pointed sticks. Nothing I'd care to put on my shelf. And, Athena's wit and wisdom, they were boring." He yawned.

"I couldn't force myself to do it for sheer practice. They spoke about four words and grunted a great deal, granted they made those four words work for them. Sex. Hungry. Stranger. Kill and eat the stranger for he is different from our kind, which causes fear among our community—dibs on his liver. I take it back," he commented. "They did a lot with that fourth word. It was the rest that wasn't that impressive." He opened and closed the fingers of his bandaged hand. You didn't want any wound to stiffen up, but especially not a hand wound when you're ambidextrous in the use of weapons of many kinds, which we all were. "Speaking of hungry, while liver doesn't sound appetizing, I did skip breakfast." Lie. I'd been covered in his breakfast before my shower. "Could someone feed the guest?"

Cal didn't know what to do with the first part. We should've studied the evolution of man more when we were kids. He'd have known if Robin was lying then. I

knew he wasn't lying about the million years and I didn't
care about the home life or nutrition of *Homo erectus*.
Niko, however, was interested. Goodfellow, sooner or
later, would be drained dry of all the knowledge he'd let
Niko pry out of him. Cal, seeing what I did, gave up on
that one. He knew the unstoppable thirst for learning his
brother had. He made a quick subject change before
Niko could get started and went straight to the second
portion of Robin's rebuttal.

"He's treating us like the sole reason we exist as more
than amoebae"—he had to get his shot back on the *Homo
erectus* name-dropping—"is to scrub his toilet. He's ordering us around like he's the richest asshole in the city and
we're the kind of human lapdog that follows him around
hoping for his greasy used Armani-clothing crumbs. If he
wants food, there's a fridge with one shelf of food, health
food, which is all we have since Nik threw out my leftovers. You, dick, can get your junk off our couch, which
you're *defiling*, and make yourself a carrot juice, yogurt,
tofu parfait for all I care."

Goodfellow shuddered. I think he'd have rather eaten
one of the rats from the sewer. Raw. I didn't blame him.
"You are too kind, but I'll pass. My appetite has miracu-
lously vanished. And, for future reference, I *am* the richest asshole in the city. That's what my tricks gave me."

"Richest man in the city? Then why aren't you ordering all of us lunch and a new couch on the side?" Cal was
on the canvas and the referee was counting him out.
From the creasing of his forehead, his headache must've
been hugely painful. He gave up and washed his hands
of the puck for the moment. Goodfellow could drive a
person to that with impressive skill and speed.

"That's an excellent idea. My phone was destroyed in
a wading pool of sewage the likes of which I've not
smelled in my long life. Caliban apparently knows all the
places in New York that no one wants to see or experience. He has an aptitude unparalleled. I've not seen its
equal. Could I borrow yours?" He directed the question
to Niko with a pornographically predatory smile that
this Nik was destined to see for years. He did the smart

thing, tossing it to him while staying out of reach. He also
ignored the sexually charged smile to mouth "no meat"
at Robin and tilt his head to indicate me. I exhaled, too
tired to want to do this over again.

"What tricks? He said I should've noticed your 'little
tricks'? *What* tricks?" Cal pressed, from me now, circling
the couch and past it to where I slumped opposite in the
chair to get directly in my face. "How does he know I'm
complaining, conniving, and like to shoot things? And he
does know, doesn't he, because he said don't shoot. He
didn't say anything about the stabbing part . . . Wait, how
the fuck do you even know I was going to knife him in
the kidney?" Cal demanded, face tight with irritation
and mistrust. I could easily picture the matte black KA-
BAR combat knife in the hand hidden behind his back.
"You weren't even watching. You want to tell me before
I put it in your kidney instead?"

It was official. Goodfellow had pushed one too many
buttons.

"You know you're trying to intimidate yourself, don't
you? We aren't intimidated by much of anyone, you and
I, are we? I know *I'm* not by my diaper-wearing younger
self, yeah, not happening." Stretching out my legs, I
crossed my ankles that were covered, half my feet as
well, in another pair of Niko's too long sweatpants. This
time travel crap was hell on clothes. Lazarus and his
shadow weasels. "Forget the tricks. They're harmless or
you'd have noticed by now. Picking up on the complaining and conniving is thanks to him spending the first part
of the morning drinking beer while I scared off three
wolves who wanted to rob Talley's place. I complained,
connived, and threatened to shoot them." I hadn't threatened to shoot. I'd threatened worse, but I'd displayed
enough guns to show they were more than a hobby.

"Drinking at six something in the morning?" Niko
asked, tone both skeptical and disapproving at once. If
you hadn't grown up with him, it could be confusing. He
wasn't skeptical about six a.m. beer. He was skeptical
that availability of alcohol was why I'd chosen Talley's.
He'd guessed—no, he *knew* I'd gone there to purposely

draw out Lazarus and he did not approve of me doing it without him. Cal was his to protect and maybe I was too, if in a strangely skewed manner. I'd thought Lazarus would show up searching for Cal and I would get a look at him. See what he was. I hadn't thought he'd try to lure me into a trap and kill me. It was pointless for Lazarus to kill me now, only killing Cal would reset it all. It was useless, killing me, but the Vigil was having no problem holding a grudge beyond the grave.

"Talley's? Is *that* what happened to my keys?" Cal wasn't hiding the knife any longer. He was using the blade to tap an annoyed and annoying rhythm on the arm of my chair.

Robin murmured, "That would be one of the little tricks." He went straight into Chinese on the phone, putting in an order for, the longer he went on, what sounded like a lot of food. I didn't speak Chinese so I had no idea what kind of food, but that it was food was all I needed to know. I waved my hand at him, a "none for me, thanks" total dismissal. He disregarded it and me entirely.

Cal growled, "You thieving asshole."

"You were just telling Robin you'd steal anything not nailed down. Where'd that pride go? And we've both been stealing since we were four. You do get we were the same exact person, from your point of view, until yesterday? I've explained it. Niko probably explained it again this morning when I was gone. We're not the same person now, but from birth until yesterday of this year, *same fucking person,*" I groaned. I knew I hadn't been this bad and while I had hated myself for a while, that had been a mental tangle of self-loathing from what the Auphe had done to me, what I had done for the Auphe. I hadn't hated myself simply to be petty and spiteful. "Should I say it slower? Every insult you throw at me for something we both did and still do is like kicking *yourself* in the balls." I blinked. "I finally get what everyone was always saying."

The tapping of the blade picked up its pace.

"People told me I was a dick, went out of my way to be a dick, would climb a mountain to find a hermit at peace

with the world and be a dick just to fuck it up for him. I
don't get peace, no one gets peace. They were right." I'd
known they were right. I was a dick, it came naturally, why
fight it? But I was somewhat stunned at seeing in a living
mirror the depths of my dickery. Unfathomable depths
where my insults, attitude problems all swam down so far
they should be albino, blind, with glowing tentacles, and
weird enough to have Jacques Cousteau gleefully crawling out of his coffin to examine them.

"Huh. You don't get life revelations that profound
very often." I examined it thoroughly, three Mississippis
at minimum. One Mississippi, two Mississippi, three—
fine, two at minimum. Three would be excessive and un-
necessary. I'd come to a conclusion. "All right. I'm over
it. We were born dicks. We're good at it. Best of the best.
Keep up the good work. Refusing to exercise our gift
would be spitting in the eye of God."

"You don't believe in God." Niko wasn't letting it
slide, leaving them behind while taking on Lazarus, but
he was more relaxed and amused, less disapproving.

My lips twitched. "Dick, remember?"

Goodfellow was tossing Niko's phone back to him
while simultaneously giving me a dubious sidelong glance.
"There are some life choices I'm suddenly questioning."

"That shows a firm grasp on reality," I said. "Be proud."
The nonstop tapping of the knife finally made its way to
my last pluckable nerve. It was strung taut as piano wire,
piano wire I could wrap around Cal's neck for a little quiet
time. I took it from him the same as I'd taken the other in
the bar. Same in that the result was identical. I took his toy.
He was more prepared, counting on it. I wasn't any slower
though and he wasn't any faster despite his anticipation.
He did wrap a hand around mine, trying to pry my fingers
off the grip. It helped him, but not enough. His other hand
had disappeared behind him again. Yesterday I would've
guessed, but yesterday had been decades ago or that's how
it felt. Today I was too damn tired to speculate or care what
weapon he had squirreled away.

Exasperated, I tightened my grip until my knuckles
were bone white. I'd added muscle and Nik had taught

me how to use it more effectively in those eight years. The knife was going nowhere unless I wanted it to. But none of us were getting anywhere either. We needed to talk about Lazarus.

It was time to settle out of court.

Under my breath for only Cal to hear, I said, "If you pull out from behind your back a gun, a knife, or an empty cardboard toilet paper tube, I'm going to hurt you. I'd actually, considering my mood, which is not fucking good, like to cut off one of your toes. No empty threat like at the bar. I will cut it off and regret it not one iota. One of the smaller ones I wouldn't miss. It'd keep you out of my face for a while and wouldn't hurt me at all. Eight years and time heals all wounds they say. But Niko wouldn't like it. He'd stop me. Then we'd likely all three kill one another making this Lazarus shit fucking moot. So back off, stop screwing with me, I'll stop baiting you, and we'll catch an assassin. The sooner we do, the sooner I'm gone. I know we both want that."

He hesitated, then dropped his hand to his side. It was empty. No weapon in sight. "I'm not sharing my brother," he responded, his voice as quiet as mine had been. "Not with you, I don't care if I will *be* you someday. That day isn't today. And I'm not sharing him for one day, much less eight damned years with some horny, conceited, rich asshole. He's mine. He's the only family I have, the only person I trust. If anyone knows that, you should. The puck has to go. If he won't on his own, I'll make him."

I'd be gone soon, one way or another. He'd be fine there. But when it came to Robin? Robin had to go? And Cal, my toddler-self thought he could *make* him? The same Robin I'd tried to kill, for a good cause, on the second day we'd met, when on the first day I'd threatened to have Nik slit his throat in the office of his car lot? And he turned back up on the third day with a "bad start with you trying to murder me, it *was* a good cause, but you can ask next time, still forgive and forget, let's go drinking"? I turned borderline hysterical laughter into a fit of coughing, rubbing my throat as if the "strangulation" was responsible. I'd laughed in my life before, not often, but I had. I had never laughed at anything approaching that level of hilarity. When I saw my Nik again, and I would, I couldn't wait to tell him that one.

Recovering, slowly, but shoving it back down, I advised solemnly, "For a con man and trickster, he's a reasonable guy." Add "least" before reasonable and "in the history of time" after guy and it was the truth and nothing but the truth. "Talk to him. He'll understand you needing space for family and family only. I would give him the year to save your life, but after that? Free as a bird. And he's rich. He can travel anywhere, buy anything, has all those orgies. He'll forget about the two of you in an hour, maybe two. It'll work out."

Or he'd buy people-sized plastic hamster balls and seal Niko and Cal in them—for their own protection, of course, and his own entertainment as they wouldn't fit back out his penthouse door once drugged and trapped in the balls constructed around them as they slept.

"Pax?" Goodfellow asked as he swiveled on the couch to recline, being nonchalant enough with his sheet placement that Cal went from wanting to put a knife in some sensitive part of me to wanting to put it in any part of the puck *except* the most sensitive part.

"Pax," I confirmed. "Now cover up, you pervert, before Cal throws over the couch, traps you under it, and starts stabbing you through it."

Niko hadn't interfered with the hushed conversation between Cal and me. I hoped he would've interfered some if Cal had gone through with bringing another weapon to the game, but as Cal hadn't, it was over and done. "Now that peace is upon the land," he said dryly, "care to finish?"

"Why not? I stole Cal's keys. I know that lock. I remember it. It was halfway to impossible to open the door with a key. Ever try to pick a lock that old or that rusted? That's halfway *past* impossible. It's easier to kick in the door, but I didn't think the boss would be too happy about that.

"Wolves showed up to rob the place"—more or less. "We scared them off. The rest of the morning was like I told you. We avoided being eaten by Lazarus's minion weasels of death. How he had enough time to scoop up evil worker bees to do his bidding, I've no idea. What would you pay a shadow weasel? But—" I let my eyes unfocus as I thought on all the monsters, *true* monsters, we'd faced. They'd all had one thing in common. "The down and dirty, narcissistically lethal, 'My name is Legion' shits do love their minions though." I shrugged and kept my smirk to myself. "We saw Lazarus himself in the sewer with the weasels, but just an outline. It was too dark."

"Do not forget the light show," Robin reminded me. "I was not all there, to be certain, but that made an impression I didn't need much consciousness to hold on to. From behind him, a continuous halo of lightning as large as the sewer would fit. They weren't strikes. Not one of them stopped the entire time we attempted not to soil our pants." He narrowed his eyes as if recalling only now how we had escaped. There was one way and one way only. "I told you not—"

"No," I cut him off before I gave him a matching necklace of bruises, but I'd be using my hands or a garrote. Niko was bound to have one around here somewhere. "Those are two things that I do not want to talk about yet. I'm, what do they call it? Processing. I'm processing and pissed. You'll have to wait and you'd be fucking wise to get over thinking you have any right to give me crap about any of it. They are also two things you know, but Niko and Cal don't. It stays that way. You follow your script, don't start making up what you think are improvements on the fly or . . ." I cupped my hands and then spread my fingers in the shape of a large ball then spread them wide, the same as I had earlier.

He held up an imperious hand. "Yes, I have it. Boom." While the gesture was pure arrogance, the face behind it was apologetic, deeply so, the likes of which I'd not seen Robin show often. "I can wait, and I know how little right I do have, believe it or not, but I swear it had nothing to do with you."

"Loving the cryptic shit less and less," Cal growled.

"But getting hit in the face with more and more of it. If you can't tell, stop hinting around like gossiping old women."

"I have to agree with Cal. It is annoying. And why did you take Goodfellow with you and not us if you were waiting for Lazarus, to see if he'd show up? You could've told him whatever it was you can't tell us." Niko's inquisitive nature had taken a blow there. "You could've gone someplace other than Talley's bar, and when you were done, called us. Three or four, whatever it would've been, against one is improved odds over what you faced. That is something we not only can know, but need to know."

"Two birds with one stone?" I shrugged in apology as Niko deserved one, but I wasn't that sorry. "To try to keep you both safe until I knew what Lazarus even is?" We didn't yet either, other than he was bad-fucking-news and deserving of an MVP trophy for Monstrously Vicious Prodigy for doing the Vigil proud, hopefully to be posthumously given. "Plus I've seen Goodfellow fight for almost a decade now and he could take all three of us with his sheet alone." Take away my gating abilities and that would be true. "But I fucked up and we lost Lazarus and his subcontractors. Next time it's all four of us. It'll be a field trip." If the bus was idling down the highway to Hell.

"With the sheet? It's not a lie?" Niko gave the puck a reevaluating look over for signs of his fighting skills. Goodfellow enjoyed it for other reasons. After all the time I'd known him, I didn't need to see his grin to know.

"You trust him to be your backup? You trust him as much as Niko?" Cal questioned. "I don't trust anyone but Niko. When did I get soft?"

Short truce.

I slid down in the chair, half an inch away from being too low to call it a slouch, and closed my eyes. If they were crimson now, that wasn't Auphe. It was the weight of fatigue crushing me to the point that it made breathing itself a challenge equal to having eight hundred pounds sitting on my chest. "Goodfellow is conceited, arrogant, more sarcastic than we are and we hate that competition; is a more skilled swordsman than Niko who won't admit it but also hates competition. He knows everyone, knows at least something about everything, has been everywhere and loves to rub it in your face even as he's using it to help you. He never stops talking—never goddamn ever—is cocky, which wouldn't be that bad if he hadn't earned the right to be more cocky than he actually is. He tells ridiculous stories of ancient Roman orgies he attended that are obvious lies, then proves they're true, *throws* orgies to this damn day but tells *you* Niko's been asking to see his antique weapon collection—bring him and the popcorn. His penthouse door has an automatic electronic lock with an algorithmic code that changes hourly, meaning once you realize it is an orgy, no weapon-collection viewing, you panic and you *should* panic because you can't get out." That was a PTSD-level recollection that had my eyes opening instantly as I let the full-on body shudder go on as long as it wanted.

"He lies, steals, and cons and, thanks to being a born trickster, expects a Hallmark congratulations card from you despite the fact you were the one he lied to, stole from, and conned. He's horny twenty-four hours a day and would hump a ficus plant if it said yes, will one day have a camera planted in the locker room at Niko's dojo, give the tape to Michelangelo—*the* Michelangelo as he's alive, some type of vampire, and owed Goodfellow a favor. It ends up—that joke will never stop being funny—*ends* up as a marble sculpture of Niko's ass displayed on a pedestal in the penthouse foyer and Niko will never notice whose ass it is, much less that it's his. Worst of all, eventually, when you accidentally see Robin naked, he will remind you every fucking day how you're the Vienna to his Polish sausage."

I picked at a bleach spot on the leg of Niko's sparring sweats. "But he's loyal. He won't fail you. He'll risk dying for you," which he had when he'd come for me in the castle. It wasn't his fault he'd been too late. "And that's something considering how long he's lived. If it came down to it, he *would* die for you and no one in our lives, no one outside Nik and I did that or had done that. He had to teach us how to trust outside the two of us because we had no idea. We'd never learned. No one ever taught us. It wasn't easy either. I'd have given up on us a hundred times in the first week. Hell, I never would've tried at all."

"But you did." Goodfellow tossed a pillow to me and pointed to my sliced and diced leg. I slid it carefully under it. It helped. Morphine would've helped more, but it helped. He smiled, sincere and a little sly with a touch of we both know something no one else knows. "If you hadn't tried, in eight years you'd eventually have gotten a lucky shot and tossed me in the Dumpster behind Goodwill"—it was his turn to shudder—"to be able to kick me in the balls even after death."

Cal crouched down to say something in quiet privacy to me. Anyone else would know what he was saying and thinking. Everything I'd said about Robin, how he was more like us than you'd imagine, his absolute determination to watch out for us, do anything he could to keep us alive, who would trust us and teach us to trust as no one else had bothered. That he'd die for us. Cal would be a little dubious that he couldn't see something in Goodfellow, something that wasn't friendship or trust now, but a seed had been planted and someday a possibility could be born. . . .

Anyone could see that. Anyone would know Cal would know this was a chance he'd never had with anyone but his brother. Anyone would know he'd want it for his brother even more than for himself. Anyone could sense the hope.

Anyone else would be wrong.

Except me. I knew exactly what he was going to say.

"You couldn't see me when I was behind the couch. Seriously, how'd you know I was going to stab him?" he asked, quizzical and a little sly himself. It was important knowledge to gather. One day soon he might want to stab me. He'd need to be prepared, and luck does not favor the fucked.

"It's what I would've done."

I snorted after I said it, but back then? Back in the now at eighteen? I would've tried like hell. Then Robin would've kicked my ass. And the next day he would've shown up and said the same as before.

"Forgive and forget."

14

The Chinese food was delivered in an hour and a half.

Inventively.

I wasn't asleep and I wasn't awake. Drifting without reflection, a large chunk of brain was shut down producing nothing, and the rest was aware of the syrupy, surreal quality of the air. I had a vague wisp of amusement wind in and out of my brain at the thinnest streamer of a thought. I wasn't hallucinating yet, but when I did, how would I know? Lightning . . . shadows that were weasels or were they weasels that were shadows. I followed the trailing end of that. What came first? The chicken or the egg? The weasels or the shadows? Did it matter? They were shadows now, ones that hadn't feared the beams of our flashlights, losing only parts of themselves to grow more, but they hadn't liked the flashlight glows either. They had to be painful, but they hadn't shown any pain, hadn't screamed or cried out. I knew they could have because they were laughing it the fuck up toward the end of our frolic in the sewer.

The beam of light hadn't hurt them.

It had disintegrated a piece of them if you were close enough to ram it into their muzzles or heads. Black mist flying out and vanishing as their new head began to extend from the long length of the body, making it leaner, but whole. Reforming using shadow from its own body. The shadow was destroyed by the light. It didn't scatter then join back together, reattach to the whole or make a new weasel. It wasn't making anything new. It was using what was left.

It had to build from what was left, but what if there was nothing left?

"We need flash bangs." I jerked up out of my slouch, my leg and pillow falling off the footrest of the recliner. "Now. Today. Shitloads of them."

"Yes." Robin sat up as suddenly as I had and pointed at me.

"Caliban, if you don't sleep, I will choke you out. I don't want to, but it would be for your own good." Niko was picking up the pillow with one hand and wrapping the other around my foot to put both back in place. He had a case of the guilts that Robin had noticed that a guest and Niko's Once and Future Brother, rolled into one, had been lying with his weight directly on half a leg's worth of stitches that were holding together a painful and deep cut.

"No, he is"—Robin paused—"then again, yes, it's true that rest, any rest, would do him well. But unfortunately now is not the time." His finger remained pointing in my direction and he snapped his fingers. "Flashbangs. That is brilliant, in more than one way." He grinned. "I saw, but I did not *see*."

Cal was lying spread-eagle on the kitchen table, flipping a butterfly knife up in the air. It would rotate the necessary amount of times to land back in his hands closed and concealing the blade. "I can't decide whether that cryptic crap makes me want to stab you for being too dramatic to inflict on the world or you're dick enough to sound like a fortune cookie while I'm starving to death and our Chinese food is late."

There was an enormous thud in the hall outside the door. It kept us from hearing Goodfellow's response although safe to say it would've gone along the lines of "sit

on my lap, cookie, and I'll show you what enough dick
is," which would have had Cal attempting to stab him in
the eye, Niko disarming his brother while stepping on
Robin's sheet and accidentally stripping him naked—
which would have resulted in harm to everyone's eyes.
That was the closest thing to running a day care center
from the bowels of hell that I could imagine. And I
wanted the least amount to do with it that I could. I was
up as quickly as I could move and headed for the door,
but Niko beat me there.

He did the automatic peephole check and dodge. "It's
dark," he said. "The hall lights are out."

"They couldn't have followed us." That was an absolute. They couldn't have followed us from the sewers. The
gates were mine, no one could hitch a ride when I built
them around me or who I was taking with me. If I opened
it as a door to walk through, they could try to follow, but
all that would get them was cut into two pieces when I
closed it as they were halfway between one side and the
other.

Goodfellow had the sheet tied in a neat and secure
toga. If he had to run, tripping on a silk sheet while escaping weasels isn't the worst obit. It wasn't even bad. In
our underground world, it was the equivalent of slipped
in the shower and broke his neck, but that didn't mean
Robin didn't already have his ending written: died by
orgy, this sex god the likes of which the world has witnessed but once and never shall again took one hundred
grateful souls with him. All expired from an excess of
sexual pleasure their bodies could not withstand but
their souls could not live without. Praise he who was Pan.
In lieu of flowers, have wild, uninhibited sex in the streets
while condoms fall in a rain of color, glitter, and different
flavors as you scream his name in one last prayer.

That was an image I didn't want in my brain again.
"We need lights. The brightest you have."

Cal vaulted off the table and followed Niko back to
their bedrooms to dig through supplies. "How did you
guys get away from Lazarus again?" Cal, out of sight in
his room, called back. "There was the running through

the sewers, offshoots, grates, places too small for him to follow you—big guy—but the weasels should've been small enough to follow you anywhere. And you said as shadows they just went through shit, walls and doors, like they weren't there."

"I have a concussion, and I was not conscious most of the time." Slick and prompt, Goodfellow had had that one on tap, waiting to pull it out if backed into a corner.

I elbowed him hard, thought about taking a look myself, but if the hall was dark, I wasn't going to see anything more than Niko had. "Let's see," I started. "I was trying to use the flashlight to keep the weasels back and at the same time to see where we were going and not end up face-first in a pile of concrete rubble. Decide whether the weasels were whispering and laughing or I was dying from methane gas on the floor of the sewer and that was what I got at the end. No meadows or bright lights calling my name. I got carnivorous shadow weasels laughing at me. I was also carrying Robin who kept asking where the naked gladiators were when he wasn't spraying enough vomit on me that he could double as a fire hose in emergencies. Then there was the lightning, a big son of a bitch who wanted to sacrifice Goodfellow as a goat and eat me as mutt stew."

True enough as it went.

"We ran some more, found a ladder up to a grate, got back in a subway tunnel, up, out and caught a cab." I knew one of them was going to ask and added it before they could. "No, the cabbie wasn't happy with the sewer and vomit stink, so I threw him out and stole the cab." Which was what I'd done the day before, and not that unlikely with my general behavior. The rest was weak, but the only way we could've actually escaped would be if Lazarus let us go. Which, thinking about it, wouldn't be the first time that had happened to me.

"Or we got out because he let us. The nastier and meaner they are the more they like to play games. It wouldn't be the first, hell, second or third time it's happened. The more powerful they are, the bigger the asshole they are. It's an unwritten rule. However it happened,

I know we weren't followed. It's a sunny day. They wouldn't have come out into full sunlight. The flashlights did some damage. Not much, but enough to know the sun would do a helluva lot more."

"It's not sunny any longer." Niko was back and going through the trunks we had for sparring equipment. He had two flashlights already, but regular ones. The one he dug out of the trunk was high-powered and big enough to use to beat Godzilla to death. Rain was beating against the window as I looked over.

"Well, shit." It was pithy and summed things up nicely.

"The shadows, they were whispering, laughing?" Robin asked. I shrugged and held out a hand to make a so-so gesture with it. I'd thought they were, but at that point I thought we were dead, no way around it, too. I wasn't committing on talking weasels in the face of that. But . . .

"I think so."

"Hmm. I know of a few creatures that they could be. If nothing else, it narrows it down. As for following us, I have a guess. It would be a better one had my skull not been all but crushed and I hadn't been weak from hunger thanks to poor hosts—"

"Your food is in the hall, prick. The dark hall that is probably also full of hundreds of weasel monsters with millions of teeth," Cal yelled as clothes came flying out of his room. He was searching under the bed then. "Have the fuck at it. Eat up. Tip 'em an arm or one of your feet if they brought extra fortune cookies."

Goodfellow folded his arms, as comfortable in his toga as he'd been in his late departed suit. "You are extremely lucky I find you tolerable now. That it takes you eight years to become so is not the best of news."

"Eight? Nah. I hit tolerable in five or six easy." I didn't pay attention to his huff while I pressed my ear to the door. Nothing. That was a positive note. No whispering or laughing or the crack of lightning. "How did they follow us? You were about to say before the Boy Wonder pissed you off."

"Five ... you'd best be lying." He scowled, but returned to the subject more appropriate to keeping our asses uneaten and unfried. "If his shadow weasels come aboveground around dusk, at night or during rainstorms, let us say, they would have all the shadows they needed to hide in. It's possible they could talk to other shadows. Ordinary everyday shadows. Nothing *paien* or supernatural. Many of those type of ephemeral creatures we faced, the kind that can take the shape of shadow weasels, can use ordinary shadows. With all the shadows in the city come night, all passing information back and forth to one another, they could've found us here easily. Niko and Cal have been here for a few months now, yes? The shadows who live here know them."

"Shadows are alive?" Cal came out of his bedroom with a flashlight in one hand and two rusty batteries in the other. "Come *on*. We can't afford cable. There goes my personal private party time. The highlight of my day." He held out the batteries to Niko, who regarded them and his brother with the pleased expression of someone who had received a lemon juice enema. "We're lucky to have a single bulb in our bathroom," Cal groaned on. "No way it's not crawling with Peeping Tom shadows."

Niko tossed the antique batteries over his shoulder to land in the trunk. "You must feel so used," he commented, not with a lack of sympathy, but a perfect vacuum of it.

"Check the kitchen for batteries," he continued, "ones on which you have *not* spilled entire liters of Mountain Dew."

"What about the shadows, the normal ones, not the talking ones?" I pushed the puck for the story he hadn't had a chance to finish. "I know that hasn't come up any time down the road. I'm with Cal Junior on this one. Shadows perving on you in your own bathroom. That's creepy as hell." I caught the judgment Niko had tossed at Cal, but was now aiming in my direction.

"Really, Nik?" I pushed my slowly drying hair behind my ears and lifted one eyebrow that was an iden-

tical mockery of his disapproving one. It had been one
of my latest ways to tease him that didn't cross the line
from amusing him to earning a five-hour sparring marathon. It'd taken me months to get right—it was a challenge when you couldn't stand to look in a mirror for
years.

"Admit it. Whether you're getting laid on the regular
or not, every guy is still going to want to Jack a little Jill
once in a while. Are you going to try to tell me you never
polish the katana on occasion?" I asked. "You think in
twenty-eight years you haven't forgotten to lock the
bathroom or your bedroom door at least once? That you
might be smacking and jacking it with your personal lu-
bricant. Organic, I know. You left it out one day, blessed
by Tibetan monks too. The body is a temple thing."

I slid a hand between Robin's arm and chest to act as
a crutch, holding him up as he started to glide down the
wall toward the floor. He seemed content to go, but I
kept him up anyway. "What was it?" I was trying to remember. Bs. Lots of Bs. "Butter . . . no. Buddha? Yes.
That's it. Buddha's Butterful Bliss. And gluten-free; I almost accidentally mistook it for a pudding cup. I had a
spoon halfway in it before I caught on. You should keep
it in your bedside drawer. For my sake."

Niko's eyebrow had frozen. It couldn't decide to go
down to join the other one or have the other one go up
to join it. "But, for future reference, I'm sorry I didn't
knock," I apologized. "I'd never have guessed you went
all out nude for your extracurricular activities."

Down Goodfellow went again. My stitches were killing me and I let him go. His eyes were lifted up to Niko
as if he were a messenger of God surrounded by a halo
of light. "I am the most happy I have ever been," he said,
sounding as if he'd reached his tailor-made nirvana.

"One more word that is not about killing monsters in
the hall and I'll kill the two of you instead." Eyebrows
under control, in a tight V of pure rage, Niko ordered,
"Now everyone get a flashlight and a weapon." Unspo-
ken was "so that I can beat you to death with them." I

didn't think he meant it. We all, Niko included, have bad moods and bad days.

"We're moving out in less than a minute," he finished, swinging his flashlight with a contemplative look at the floor. Measuring the distance between me and him— maybe he did mean it.

He switched his glance to Goodfellow. "Goodfellow, you may borrow one of my swords, which will be returned without a single fingerprint that indicates it has been fondled in any manner. You will also tell us about the shadows and if they can give away our location to the others and how long it takes? Hours, days, months?" he ordered. "Caliban will keep his mouth shut completely or I'll use my new stitching skills, the remaining dental floss, and sew it shut myself. Cal, if you laugh even once, I will have Goodfellow remove his sheet and force you to observe what he is trying very hard not to conceal beneath it.

"Now *go*."

I was a lion, but if he'd had a whip right then, I'd have hidden in the corner of my circus cage. Goodfellow kept his attention on Niko's hands, wishing, I think, that he *did* have a whip. Cal was under the onslaught of more emotions than he'd experienced at one time. I knew at eighteen I hadn't. But we did as we were told, despite that.

We went.

By the time I had a flashlight in one hand and a gun in the other, and another pair of Cal's boots, Goodfellow had picked out a sword. He'd gone in another direction in footwear, a pair of sandals to go with the toga theme, deadly serious that none of the Walmart, Goodwill, Salvation Army clothing in here was contaminating his body. In addition, he was halfway through the normal, ordinary, bathroom-lurking shadow explanation.

". . . so, no, they aren't alive. Think of them as clay, less solid of course, but as impressionable a texture. The ones that appear in the same place every day, if the same people pass by, the same events happen, slowly that seeps into them. It can be read, not as a language, but like a picture book—images can be seen. Intense emotions can be felt. That is, if you're a creature that is made of and lives in shadows. If they found us, that's how."

"Fascinating as fuck," Cal offered, face blank with boredom. "Can we kill something now?"

"For once I agree with Tiny Tim," I said, jacking a bullet in the chamber.

We all did, as armed with weapons for Lazarus and lights for the weasels, we rushed the door. Niko and I both opened it together, keeping Cal behind us. He didn't like it, but he was the target. We swung the lights up and down the hall, in every corner and the depth of other door jambs. There were no weasels. No Lazarus.

There was, however, our Chinese food.

And a deliveryman that no tip in the world could help.

He'd been hanged.

Big deal, right? I'd seen a hundred worse ways to die. Inflicted a few myself. But this was different.

He was hanging still, suspended on the wall, his feet dangling two feet above the sand-covered floor. It would've been less disturbing if there had been a rope holding him up. There wasn't. The indention pressed deeply in the flesh of his neck and slanted at an upward angle added to his broken neck: He'd definitely been hanged, not strangled. He also had burn marks around his wrists and ankles, blackened and charred. Lazarus's lightning, but not done here or we'd have heard it. The burns were wider than I'd have thought for lightning, three and a half to four inches, and in a perfectly circular band. His eyes were burnt too. There was no reason for that other than to torture the poor bastard. It wasn't as if he'd lived long enough to be a witness, to tell us anything about Lazarus if he'd seen him.

It wasn't as if he'd lived to hear Lazarus or the weasels, whichever had put him here, leave. That hadn't been an option, whether there had or hadn't been a reason to kill him. It took one face-to-face encounter with Lazarus to come to that conclusion. He had a hard-on for death. He'd want to watch it come. Through his own eyes or through whatever functioned as the eyes of his shadows. We'd seen that Lazarus wasn't separating and shaping the whole of himself into a pack of weasels. He was apart from them, a being independent. It didn't mean he couldn't mentally be inside of his nasty pets. It wouldn't be that unusual for a *paien,* and that's what he was now, with that amount of raw power to be able to do that.

"How the hell is he just . . . hanging up there like that?" Cal backed away from the smell of burnt flesh. I knew the feeling and had backed away faster, ignoring the piles of food and sand I was stepping in and gagging as I went. "And that's not our normal delivery guy. I mean, there's Chinese food everywhere, but he's not him."

"What gave it away? The thirty pound weight difference? The six inch height difference? The extra twenty years in age? Your eye for the smallest of minutiae approaches supernatural levels."

"No, Cyrano, you smartass," Cal snorted. "Bruj has FUCK YOU, BAT-GWAI tattooed down his arm."

"White devil, I do appreciate an accurate tattoo," Robin drawled. "Did he have it done with you specifically in mind?"

Cal shrugged, but admitted without a grudging snarl or any sign of shame, "He said he did. He didn't have it until he'd delivered here a few months. Told me no one was a shittier tipper than me."

"What did you tip," Robin asked, "that caused him an annoyance with you of such profound levels that he'd mark his skin for life thanks to you and only you?"

"Tip?" Cal snorted. "I don't tip. No one tips me at work. I'm just paying it forward."

"He was clearly not a delivery person of any sort, ours or anyone else's, not with what he's wearing." Niko was examining him at a range that would capture any and all details . . . and soak up the odor of barbecued meat with the effectiveness of a sponge. I took another step back. "He was a security guard."

He reached for a brass name tag and unpinned it from

the uniform. "Zachary Adams, from that ship docked at Pier Seventeen as a museum. The one Colonel DePry had built, the largest pleasure yacht at the time. Suspiciously too big with too many men needed to sail it. Naming it *The Nomad*, he took one cruise around the harbor and then the ship was gone. Sold, he said, to some rich duke in England more willing to pay enough men to sail and maintain it. A lie and all were well aware of the fact. While slavery was illegal in New York then, other places and people were lining up to buy slave ships."

Another look was aimed at the burns and I turned my back on it. The body, the three of them. I'd listen and that would have to count as adequate for the job. "They are the size of shackles," Niko confirmed. "There's a faint tracery of burns trailing around his arms that are link-shaped. Chains. It's why this ship is famous. One trip, its last as a slave ship, the prisoners rebelled, took over, forced the slavers to sail to the nearest port, and *The Nomad* ended up where it had started. There was a trial, not that one was needed, and the prisoners were freed, given the ship, and a crew to sail them home. They renamed her *Never Wander, Never Roam, Ever Free, Ever Home.* The South Street Seaport Museum had an exhibition quoting some people from the day saying that was a poem and a bad one at that, not the name of a ship. Considering very few of the freed slaves spoke more than a word or two of English, I don't think they did that badly. Regardless, once they were home, they sent the ship back with the crew. They never wanted to see another ship to their dying day. The crew brought her back to New York, simply called her *Ever* and eventually the museum bought her."

"Sad story. Happy ending. Humanity at its worst and best. Now I'm getting the fuck out of here." I couldn't handle the seared stench any longer. "As an arrow pointing 'I am here. Come and face me,' it gets the job done. Lazarus wants us on the ship. Tonight, late, we go." I was going as I spoke, flashlight showing the way, moving down the hall and halfway to gone. "We need flash bangs, other supplies, the kind you two don't have yet. Haven't needed." I was at the door to the stairs and ready to head down. "My supplier doesn't know me yet. She'd shoot me if I asked to buy a firecracker from her. We'll have to hit up the Kin or see if Robin has contacts with the good stuff."

"Where are you going? Now, I mean. Where are you going?" Niko called after me as I started down the stairs.

"Don't know and, as long as it's not here in this hall or your place"—because of course we'd left the door open behind us and the smell would be in there now—"don't care."

And I didn't.

Didn't fucking care at all.

15

Robin, toga and all, followed me while Niko and Cal packed up more weapons. He'd suggested we could stay at his place until he talked to several somewhat illegal people about several excessively illegal things. I hadn't believed that ludicrous a statement came out of his mouth. "They know your place, the shadow included. *Everyone* in the city knows your place," I snorted. "Orgy central. The weasels don't have to know your face like they know Cal's and mine. They need one glimpse they held on to from the sewers and every nonsupernatural shadow will point them straight to your penthouse." I shook my head and limped on. "*Nuns* teaching Catholic school know and have been to your place."

"And most who visit lost their virginity there, I can assure you."

Maybe that's why he had died in fire and flames, burned at a functional substitute for a stake.

As it turned out, Goodfellow had no problem hailing a cab in a silk sheet toga when, fully dressed, I couldn't get but a few to admit I existed and those few veered into the next lane over to get farther away from me. "What is it? Do I have 666 stamped on my forehead?" I demanded, getting in the backseat of the taxi with him. The driver, who hadn't glanced once at Robin's toga, raised his eyes to the rearview mirror for a look when he heard me bitching. The inside of the cab was instantaneously drowned in the cologne of an entire ocean of fear sweat. "I haven't had this much of a problem until I came here," I complained. Here being 2005.

"I surmise, and this is but the wildest of assumptions based on no evidence whatsoever, that it's your face. Keep in mind the wildest of assumptions and no evidence portions and take it with a grain, no, an entire shaker of salt."

"What the hell . . ." I gave up and slammed back against the seat, folding my arms. "It's in mind. I've taken an amount of salt so damn large it would kill me if I had a heart condition. Now tell me."

Robin gave an address to the cabbie whose hands I could see shaking on the steering wheel. "One problem, the smallest you could imagine, infinitesimal really," he offered with his widest car salesman smile. "Odor? Damp? Dead fish in the glove compartment? Ridiculous, hand to God, this car was never submerged in the Hudson."

"But it could conceivably, in the craziest of worlds, have something to do with the fact . . . did I say infinitesimal?" I growled and I put a heavy hit of Auphe in it. He sighed, "Your neck appears as if you were strangled, hanged, strangled again, and then suspended headfirst into a vat of a few thousand leeches."

"You son of a—"

"But I wasn't lying"—he kept on. Why not? He had only his own personal strangulation to lose—"when I said that was the smallest consideration if a consideration at all. The main reason is your face."

"My face? What's wrong with my face?" I pressed.

"It would be most accurately described, by people that don't know you or will know you, judgmental people who assess others by purely unimportant physical attributes such as skin color, weight . . ." By now I had unfolded my arms, made a fist and was pulling it back to let it fly. "Fine. Try to spare a person's feelings," he huffed. "No good deed goes unpunished." He shifted in my direction to face me and poked a finger in the center of my forehead. "It's this. What you're doing with your face. The best label would be," he paused, then gave a decisive nod.

"Murder face."

I wasn't counting the reasons, good ones, that I deserved to be suicidal, resigned, and insane, but I'd thought I was hiding it from Niko and especially from Cal. I didn't try with Robin. I had been doing the best twenty-one some odd years of conning and lying had taught me. With everything I was attempting to do and to not do, I wouldn't have been surprised if an emotion had slipped through my mask a few times, the resignation, the despair, but this made no sense. "I don't have a—"

"Murder face. Yes, you do. You could go with madness face—it's appropriate, but murder face is slightly more accurate. It says that you are on your way to murder someone or you have murdered someone or you desperately want to and will murder someone as soon as that someone hurries up and looks at you in the most minute of wrong manners. Murder face," he rattled off without hesitation or any other indication of doubt in his appraisal.

The cab stopped at a building on a corner and Goodfellow paid the cabbie. As with his sword, having no wallet on him, dressed as he was in a sheet, I didn't know where he'd been keeping that Black Amex card and wad of cash, and I wasn't curious about it in the least. If he'd tried to tell me, I either would've run or shot myself. I was finding on an hourly basis more and more reasons to go with the inevitable and shooting myself.

Starting down the sidewalk, he continued as if he hadn't stopped. "It's a billboard that screams 'I have a day pass from the Hospital for the Homicidally Insane, and I earned it by dismembering everyone else in my group therapy session,' 'Death row is my summer home,' 'I hunt to prevent overpopulation—ever notice how incredibly overpopulated the world is?', 'Charles Manson has a restraining order against me,' 'I have the mind of a genius, the heart of a poet, and the liver of an alcoholic—they're in the three jars on my shelf,' 'Mary had a little lamb, eating a baby sheep is wrong, Mary was tasty though,' 'The Apocalypse came, saw I was already here, and left screaming.'"

We had rounded the building at the corner and walked on three more blocks. Robin came to a halt in front of a black marble building, not that tall, but it gave the impression it was expensive to the point that there was no sense in making it taller as no one was left in the world who was rich enough to afford another floor. He nodded at the doorman, a tall, thin man with dark skin, perfectly round inhuman yellow eyes, and what could be the tips of white hair or tiny feathers showing beneath his uniform cap. He, despite the title, did not open the door. Goodfellow moved to an array of security crap the likes of which I'd not seen. There were retinal scans, fingerprint scans, a hair for DNA analysis, and fifty or sixty different codes to be entered.

The door opened by itself and the doorman said, "Congratulations on the escape of a grisly death and the devouring of your soul, Mr. Goodfellow."

"Thank you. Your manners in the face of disappointment are impeccable as always, Mr. Kikiyaon." There wasn't any humor there. The puck was uncommonly polite and, of course, tipped him. Cal should take a lesson. I should take a lesson. I did tip now, but no one would call me a good tipper without swallowing their tongue. "I have two other guests coming. Male. One with a blond braid and one that looks like this one's younger brother. Please do not eat the soul of that one. I will understand the temptation, trust me when I say more understanding I could not be, but they are both my guests. I will make it up to you. Ah, before I go." He tipped him again. "Consider this to be from the one with the black hair. We would all die waiting a vast infinity of years until the universe fell dark and all life perished before he would do it himself. And, quite frankly, I don't think you would care for how his soul tasted."

He gave the doorman a shallow bow that was returned with a bare tilt of the head and then we were inside, the doors shutting silently behind us. "Before you ask, he's an African soul cannibal. They are excellent in the field of security. Now"—he ignored the elevators like anyone who didn't want to be trapped in one like a roach in a roach motel, and headed for a door that led to the stairs—"should I go on?"

"No," I said grimly. A "murder face" was going to be harder to hide than other emotions if I was walking around in broad daylight unaware I was wearing one.

"It will pass," he said, his voice echoing in the stairwell as solemnly as if we stood in a church. Not that the oldest pagan alive would care about church etiquette, but it reminded me of that. "You've only been wearing it since we escaped Lazarus and it's also been off and on, when Niko and your emo clone weren't watching. You said Lazarus wasn't there at the explosion, but he is Vigil. I do think the same as you. He is as responsible for what happened to Niko and to me."

I asked what had been gnawing at me since the explosion. And repeatedly since. I'd had the thought about Niko and me being together again, a little different, a lot the same, in our next reincarnation, and how it bothered me to lose any memories of any lives I'd spent with him, but I'd be human next time. No more Auphe racial memory, and lose them I would. We would be family and together as always though . . . but not Robin.

Pucks don't reincarnate. If they did Goodfellow would've told us by now.

"What happens to pucks when they die?" I didn't look at him when I asked. I, fuck, I just couldn't.

A warm hand gripped my shoulder. "That is a tale for another time."

"You don't know, do you?"

"Another time," he reiterated firmly.

He didn't know. For Robin any story he could tell was for now; waiting was not in his vocabulary when it came to bragging and stories and tall tales. If we didn't save him, he was gone. There might be puck heavens. He'd mentioned being on Mount Olympus, the Elysium Fields,

Valhalla, all heavens in their own right. Didn't that mean he could go there when he died? Or did he have to be alive and have living gods or goddesses themselves open the door and invite him to the party? When he died was he just no more? Niko and I, we'd never see him again, but a Goodfellow that was no more—that fucked up my life, all my lives to come, fucked up my world.

"Okay. Yeah, okay." I wiped painfully dry eyes as I wouldn't let this shithole of a world *make* me cry. It could kiss my ass a thousand times over first. Straightening from where I'd begun to slump, I started to climb the endless stairs again.

Goodfellow's hand remained on my shoulder, keeping me from moving. "I do have a tale for now." He added, "And a need to breathe." He sat on the stair above us and pulled me down next to him. He clasped his hands in his lap, tight enough for his knuckles to whiten. His eyes stayed fixed on them. "There was—oh what there was—in the oldest of days and ages and times and beyond the dreams of gods that did not yet exist."

His lips curved but not in what I'd label nostalgia or amusement. "That's how stories first began. That was the birth of 'Once upon a time.'" He cleared his throat. "In those oldest of days and ages and times came the First to think, to have thoughts, not that they cared to use them. They preferred the killing and slaughtering of the animals that inhabited the land then. Or themselves. Either would do. A time after that was born the Second to think, to have thoughts, and he cared very much to use them. He also greatly enjoyed killing and slaughtering but not of his own kind, as he was the only one of his own kind. As he didn't know of the First, as the world was large, and their meeting unlikely, he made another Second. He thought it would be a toy and torturing and slaughtering it to be the best of entertainment. What he didn't know is that what he made was himself. Identical physically, mentally, even in his memories. They were the same and as willing murderers they wished to be. They were equally balanced, for when you are the same, how can you defeat each other? Disappointed, the first of the Second left the second of the Second, not to see him again for hundreds of thousands of years."

Glancing off to the side as if he saw something, he went on. "Second of the Second, same in his digust and disappointment as same as the same is the same, went in the opposite direction. Years passed. Too many to count, but eventually the second of the Second noticed he was changing. His thoughts, his ideas were different. He had new memories. His own and no one else's. That didn't make him less bloodthirsty. It took many more years, a race called humans, and other races called *paien* to develop to show him what rocks, trees, and prehistoric sloths could not. But that is not this story. This story is when he first noticed new thoughts, new ideas, new memories, but one thought didn't occur to him. If he had new memories, then there were more to be made. He couldn't rely on those of the first Second being all that made up the world. Not that it mattered, as the first of the Second had never known of the First. Had no memories of them. Didn't know they existed. And neither did I."

Unlocking his hands, he rubbed one over his face. "No one these days can say that. No one can say they didn't know of the Auphe, no one but me. Five of them came out of this madness, induced a rent in reality, sank claws in me before I could think to move, and dragged me through the gaping tear that screamed as if it were dying. I fell up and down, sideways. It turned me inside out and twisted every organ inside me. We came out hovering over a live volcano, and they dropped me before beginning their version of tag. They were not polite enough either to wait for me to stop vomiting from the 'trip,'" he said bitterly.

I knew I had to be paler than my usual blizzard white. I felt like vomiting myself. To know about the Auphe and have them take you or chase you or both, that was a horror few lived through. To have it happen and not know of their existence, to be dragged behind them through the bleeding, screaming ether as you were turned inside out. To not know what they wanted when everyone now knew it had been the worst death they could give you. No wonder he had a fucking phobia of gating. "How . . . Fuck, how'd you survive?"

He waved a hand, dismissing the question. "There was a ledge. I'm agile enough that the Cirque du Soleil come to me for lessons. I caught the edge of it. I ran. I fought. I made weapons. Mainly I ran like a swan with Zeus on her tail feathers." He shrugged. "I am me, after all. But all of that is nothing compared to the moral of the story." Leaning his shoulder against mine, he gave me a solemn promise, "It was never about trust. I have and will always trust you. I have and will always trust Niko. The sole reason I didn't tell you about the gates in years to come is that you managed to get me through one when I was poisoned and dying, as you said. And once it was done, it was done. I no doubt told myself I was beyond idiocy to sooner die than gate with someone I have trusted a thousand lives over. And I am sorry I didn't tell you in the sewer. I knew this life has been one of your worst, and I should've known that trust would be something beyond value to you, especially as you never had a reason to doubt it before in all our days and years and aeons.

"Now." He stood and held down a hand to pull me up, not that I needed it, but wasn't that always what he'd done? Whether I needed it or not? "We work on finding Lazarus, saving the three of us—the only worthy part of the world worth saving honestly—and getting you home."

"I miss my Goodfellow." God, there was an understatement, but . . . "I think I'm going to miss you too, conceited jackass that you are, because the same as the same is not the same. Eight years makes a difference, even in million-year-old pucks."

This grin was nothing but glee and cheer. "I'll mail you a Valentine's Day card every year to a PO Box then give you the number when we see each other again at the end of those eight years. Sparkly, tacky, pornographic, singing cards. It'll be a thing of beauty."

"Jackass," I repeated. "I take it back. I won't miss you at all." Plus, he would be there. He'd be home with Niko and all the others: Ishiah, Promise, Ham, Mama Boggle and the kids, Rafferty and Catcher.

Home. And I would make it there. For when we all survived, the Niko and Robin here and now and the Niko and Robin in the future, my misplaced present, rising from the flames like a true phoenix. Not the fake phoenix I'd imagined at the explosion, one that brought death, ended in death, and never rose again.

They'd rise, if they hadn't done so from the moment I'd dropped the letters off yesterday, and were already waiting for me.

Unlike the whiny slacker in the poem Robin's coffin-buddy-with-benefits had written, I wasn't sitting around hoping for someone to bring them back. I wasn't asking when they'd bring *themselves* back. I wasn't playing Twenty Questions with a goddamn bird instead of going out, kicking the universe in the balls until it gave them back. And when would I give up? Like that obnoxious bird said:

Nevermore.

16

Robin had a client. He was evasive on what he did for this client or who they were, which was weird as he loved bragging and name-dropping every opportunity he had. Whoever they were, they weren't using their penthouse for a few months—or years—and Robin set us up. In more ways than one. A temporary safe house, new clothes—the scorched odor from the security guard was on the ones I was wearing and I stripped them off while still on the stairs before entering the penthouse floor. I hadn't borrowed any of Niko's underwear, brotherly codependence only goes so far, which meant it was me, my holster, guns, knives, and birthday suit waiting for Robin to do the same. He did with alacrity. Naturally. I went rummaging around his client's penthouse that took up the entire floor for the clothes he'd promised would be waiting for us.

He'd lifted a phone from someone he passed to call his "people." He'd lost his in the sewer and, despite the alcohol wipe down mine had been given by Niko, Goodfellow would sooner steal one than touch mine, which hadn't been lost, but had bathed in sewage. Then again, my phone was also stolen, looted from the body of the junkie who'd tried to kill me and who I'd killed first and better. I couldn't claim the high ground on stolen phones. Robin had made a call minutes before we had caught the cab and arranged for clothes, toiletries, stocking the refrigerator, extra ammunition as it was mundane ammunition and easily available, and anything else his people might think of.

While I was hunting for the clothes, I'd let him make the call to Niko and Cal with directions to the penthouse and instructions to do the same with their clothes I'd insisted we do with ours. I could hear Cal bitching in the background as Robin talked to Niko. Nude conspiracies were mentioned. I told Goodfellow flatly that Cal could be naked for two minutes and live or wear the clothes he had on and die. And it wouldn't be Lazarus who did it. If he tried to come on this floor wearing those same funeral pyre stinking clothes, I'd shoot him myself before he made it off the top stair. Pass it on.

The bitching and complaining was dire, but they both did as they were told, bringing only their weapons and getting new clothes from Robin or from me from Robin as Niko had a condition of his own. He'd stand in the foyer directly off the stairs in front of the penthouse door all day and night nude if I didn't lock Goodfellow up until Niko was dressed. Niko was being as patient with Robin's quirks now as my Niko had been, but being patient did not mean he lacked self-preservation.

The clothes had been delivered before Goodfellow and I had made it there. His employees, people, *paien*, or hyperintelligent—and hyper*active* to be that quick—cockroaches, excelled at their job. It was all what I would've picked out for myself and was perfect for night work. The puck had gone so far as to bite the bullet and let us have our generic jeans, T-shirts, and leather, no Armani or Ralph Lauren. He'd remembered how I'd DIY'ed Cal's T-shirt and went the extra mile to have one either printed up personally for me or picked out with my personality in mind. No magic marker needed.

YOU HAVE TO TAKE THE BAD WITH THE GOOD.
I, MOTHERFUCKER, AM
THE BAD

Nice.

I was stretched out on the couch, as it was that or wait a few more minutes until my legs folded bonelessly under me. The one with the weasel slash was less painful as in no pain, none. There wasn't a twinge or an ache, nothing. I couldn't exactly *feel* that leg or the other one, but it was a fair trade. Robin's people, damn, I loved his people, loved their huge compassionate drug delivering cockroach hearts. They'd provided me with real pain meds. The bottle was labeled with a long complicated name that would mean something to a pharmacist, but not to me. Goodfellow told me it was Vicodin, gave me a bottle of water to chase two down, and told me if that didn't help there was a morphine pump in one of the closets somewhere. From the looks of the place, I believed him.

Every piece of furniture was upholstered in a material with a different animal pattern on it. Tiger stripes but purple against blue, cheetah spots that were forest green against a black that reflected colors like a raven's wing, and a bizarre chair that was covered in something similar to chameleon scales except chameleons didn't come that large or change color randomly. All fake with those colors except maybe the chair. That could be from a *paien* creature or an alien for all I knew.

"By the way, is this velvet?" I knew it wasn't fur. I ran my hand over the cushion beside me. It was—the thick plush velvet you saw in the high-class pornos—which meant it was equally tacky as hell, but cost considerably more. As in crazy-stupid-money that could feed the hungry of every single third world nation on the planet and have enough left over to buy Canada for the skiing. I'd heard the rich like to ski.

"Holy hell. Is your secret client Hugh Hefner? How many drugs was his decorator on? Although the velvet, I asked if this was velvet, didn't I? This velvet is the most comfortable thing I've laid on . . . except for Delilah's naked body. I miss her naked body." I mourned as I kept on petting the velvet like the dogs that ran before I could pat them, hating the Auphe in me so much. I cheered when the idea came to me and I asked. "Is it the *paien* version of Hugh Hefner?"

"No, that would be me, except I'm infinitely more attractive, far younger in appearance, and without need of erectile dysfunction medications." Goodfellow patted me on the head with the fond gaze you'd give a puppy who hadn't quite gotten down the walking part yet.

"You are damn good-looking. If I weren't straight and we didn't have this brotherly bond thing going, I'd screw you. No, wait, forgot. You have that weapon of mass destruction in your pants. Sorry, no matter my orientation, you'd have to keep Godzilla to yourself."

"What the fuck," Niko cursing again—unbelievable, "did you give him?" He had the puck by the arm with a grip that had to be painfully tight. I should share my drugs with him.

I held up the bottle in my other hand that wasn't fascinated by the velvet. "Vicodin. Want some," I asked the puck, "for your arm? Niko, want some for your mood? You're not this pissy that often. Well, more pissy than you think you are, like dirty dishes are the call to release the Four Horsemen. Jesus, let it go just once." I yawned. "But you're my brother and I love you. If I'd had to raise me, I'd be pissy, too. Actually if I'd had to raise me, I'd have sold me in the Walmart parking lot when I was a baby and still cute. Hadn't started biting ears off my classmates yet, which did not taste good. Cold and clammy and the ear wax was no fucking A.1. Sauce." I waved the bottle at Goodfellow. "Remember, start with the feet. The screaming is like A.1. Sau—"

Niko's hand clamped over my mouth and he let go of Robin to seize the bottle out of my grasp. He read the label and of course he recognized it as he'd probably gotten a pharmacy degree in two weeks, saving up the time by skipping bathroom breaks. Meditation had given him complete control over all bodily functions. "This is the generic name for Vicodin, but what did you *actually* put in the bottle?"

"Oh, that's nothing. MS Contin, oral morphine, and he took only two. The recommended dose," Goodfellow dismissed. "It was what was in the water. Thorazine, Ativan, an entire handful of Rohypnol, and ten or so doses of MDMA, ecstasy if you're not familiar, to make him happy. He deserves a little happy after the two days he's had."

"Won't that kill him? Really, fifty times over, kill him? Deader than dead? That seems over the top. If it seems over the top to me, when I want to slam his head against the wall over and over until Jimmy Hoffa or D. B. Cooper falls out of his ear, it has to be classified as excessive as fuck." Cal, who had to be worried if he thought I was dying, hid it well . . . and deep, incredibly deep, too deep I assumed as the concern hit rock bottom and bounced back straight into curiosity.

He snapped his fingers and for the first time showed some enthusiasm toward Goodfellow. "This is like that Russian guy. Were you hanging around Rasputin? Which one were you? The one who poisoned him, stabbed him, shot him, cut off his dick, or threw him in the river? Or did you do them all?"

"No one cut off his penis. I am beyond exhausted of hearing that rumor." Robin headed in toward what I vaguely remembered as being the direction of the kitchen. "His hygiene was far too lacking for anyone to entertain the idea of undoing his pants, much less touching what nested in the filth underneath. Dogs could smell him coming from miles away and would flee howling."

"He's going to die. We can't take him to the hospital. They'll know he's different. His blood work, he's only half human, who knows what the blood work will show. If they could save him, it would to be to dissect him later." Niko, every inch of visible skin a dirty gray except his lips, pressed to a bloodless white. His katana was slicing toward Goodfellow at an angle to separate his head from his shoulders. "You've killed him." Robin dodged beneath the blade. "Murdered him." This time he jumped back and flipped over the lizard chair. Niko went right over the top after him, spitting venomously, "When he swore you were his friend, that you were loyal." Look at that. Niko was trusting me more and more. I had to die to get there, but it was worth it. He swung the katana in from the side where it was promptly snared in a metallic bronze and silver zebra striped rug. Niko was thrown back over the chair landing facedown, the rug-wrapped sword kicked out of sight, the chair's cushion yanked free to drop on Niko's back, and Robin took a seat on it.

"Told you he was a good fighter," I said, unfazed by this or anything: the world, life, death. It would work itself out. "Try the morphine, Nik," I urged, enjoying the placid, floating sensation. "You'll feel no pain." I shook the bottle at him again before I realized I didn't have the bottle any longer. He'd taken it.

Cal, who I was beginning to think didn't much like me . . . the little prick, was pointing his Glock at Robin. "Get off of him. I know you're not going to hurt him, and I know Caliban isn't going to die. You said it yourself. You both had eight years to pull that off and neither of you did. But get off my brother or this crap will go on all night and I'm hungry. I couldn't save any of the Chinese."

Goodfellow grimaced. "Disgusting child." He stood, caught the cushion that Niko flung at him with ease, and held down a hand. "Caliban told you. I could kill all three of you with a sheet. Imagine the horrors I could inflict with a cushion." Niko ignored the hand and gained his feet without the assistance, not that he needed it. Robin sighed, "Pissy indeed. Caliban will be fine, but he has not been fine the past days, has he? He went through"—his eyes slid toward Cal, who'd lowered the gun—"some trauma, and time travel with the *Kyntalash* is not meant for humans or anyone with a single cell of *Homo sapiens* in them. It's extremely debilitating. He should've dropped after the first step he took into this time, dropped and stayed out for a day at minimum. Instead he's been fighting skin-walkers, shadow weasels, running like mad carrying my half-conscious self through sewers and up flights of stairs. He hasn't slept, that's easy to see as he appeared to have two black eyes before I broke his nose. Apologies again, Caliban. And from his reaction to my ordering of the Chinese food, he hasn't eaten. By the time we go to face Lazarus, Caliban might trip and kill *himself* falling down the stairs."

Niko was putting out fewer waves of rage, which I'd not realized you could see if you tried hard enough. They were purple. I'd have thought red. Every book says so. I saw red. My vision was red with rage. Nope. Purple. "And you decided to what? Put him in a coma?"

"Hardly. He told me the things I need to know about the coming eight years. He told me about having the Auphe resistance to poisons and venoms, how that's increased as he matures and with repeated exposure to a multitude of said poisons and venoms." He paused for a quick aside to Cal. "You, at this age and little exposure to poisons, I might have killed. So do not drink any bottled water you see in here to be on the safe side. Tap only, or sample the wide variety of juices, sodas, and ales of the world all in the refrigerator."

And he was back to Niko. "Also he's building up an inconvenient tolerance to various drugs, which is becoming a problem when he needs minor to moderate surgery. You have been forced to use more and more anesthesia to keep him under while you stitch him back together, but that's a problem for another time and another you."

Niko had been getting his color back. He lost it again instantly at that revelation. I was proud. My brother the black market illegal doctor. Robin was going strong yet. "He told me where the levels of his various tolerances are. I knew how much to use. I had no plans on killing him or inducing a coma, *skata*, distrustful bastards that you are. This is what is going to happen." He held up a finger. "*Prota*, we're going to feed him now that he's in such an amenable mood." He held up a second finger or it could be a fourth one. Things were becoming blurry. "*Defteros*, he'll sleep until we go for Lazarus. Four a.m. seems the best time for the least possible number of people at the Pier." Another finger went up. I didn't attempt to estimate which number that was. There were fingers everywhere now. He was an octopus there were that many. "*Trítos*, one of us will sit with him at all times while he sleeps. We can take shifts, however you like, but he will not be alone. Not for a bathroom break, not to get a snack from the kitchen thinking as you can still see him, what could go wrong? Not for a single second is he to be alone, and if you have but the smallest scrap of a soul, then while you sit with him, you will hold his hand. Are we clear, *sas agnoeí paidiá*?" Waiting for an answer wasn't part of his big plan. That would mean there was a chance they wouldn't do what they were told.

When Robin Goodfellow was pissed, everyone did as they were told.

He would've been a good king.

He let his hand fall and used both of them to comb efficiently through my hair. It had dried finally on the cab ride over. It was Sophia's hair, straight, but the thick weight of it made for a mess of stubborn twists and knots if I didn't brush it while it was still damp and pull it back into a tight prison of a ponytail to let it dry completely.

"I wasn't alone." In the room with the small patch of gray sky high on the wall.

He murmured at my ear, "No, Will, you were never alone. And, Caliban, you won't be alone either."

"I don't want to sleep." If I slept, I'd dream, and I couldn't see it again. Even under the foggy weight of the drugs, I didn't forget that. "I'll dream. Don't make me dream."

Niko's face had gained years and weary lines during the puck's speech. I understood that. It had been long. Very . . . extrem- . . . incredib- . . . just long. My brother but not my brother, not yet, knew why I wouldn't want to dream. I'd told him about the explosion and how they'd left me. All of them. It was a good reason for showing no confusion over Goodfellow's military style command of hand-holding. "You won't. If you start to, whoever's with you will wake you up. I promise, little brother." He wasn't mine and I wasn't his, but I had been once and he would be again.

Cal was the opposite. When he spoke, there were emotions everywhere, high and low, waves crashing on a beach. Confusion, irritation, anger, jealousy, stubborn bucking of authority, resentment knowing he was being kept in the dark about something everyone else knew, and it all kept building and building. It was amazing to watch. I'd never gotten to see them on me, especially not as many and all at once. They combined, hit fury at record speed, and poured over his face in a cascade of . . . "Ha!" I got it now. Robin had been right. I pointed at Cal and announced with wickedly gleeful recognition.

"Murder face."

I woke up screaming and I didn't stop.

Not for four or five minutes, maybe longer. The three of them were there, two were talking, mouths moving fast, but I couldn't hear them. I could hear only the explosion, the first blast, the devouring hunger of the flames, the second detonation, the howling of a tornado made of whirling fire, the sky falling. The third one's mouth was shut, but his eyes were too wide, pale skin paler yet. Shocky. That's what they'd say on some hospital show. He looked shocky. The first two came closer to me, one's hand reached out to grip mine so tightly that my fingers were the blanched blue-white of interrupted circulation, but the third one, he moved back. Moved away and crouched on the floor, his arms wrapped around his knees, his hands fisted, knuckles white.

I knew who they were. I knew their names. But just as I could see their mouths move and not hear the words, knowing their names didn't mean anything. I could see them spelled out in my mind, superimposed over the flames and smoke, but I couldn't read them. I couldn't say them. I couldn't remember the sound of the letters spilling out into the air. And I couldn't comprehend how I could see the three of them, the people with names no more use to me than hieroglyphs. How could I see them and the room around us when I was sitting in the street, surrounded by pizza boxes, watching my family burn? How could I see both at once?

Did I care how? No.

I didn't care. I didn't care. I didn't care.

Wedging myself in a corner of the couch, yanking

away from the touches, ripping my hand out of the one
that was squeezing bones to dust, I snatched up the cushion next to me, retreated farther into my space, and
pressed my face against the cloth. It didn't block out my
screams from the world, but it blocked out the world—
this one—from me. I let myself fall back into nothing but
the loss and the screaming.

Those I understood.

"Caliban."

Robin had one of his cars sent over and drove it himself, ditching it blocks away, destined to be towed. We
were making the rest of the way to the *Ever* docked at
Pier 17 on foot. I didn't think it mattered to Lazarus: On
foot or by car, he'd be well aware we were coming. It was
less trouble in that it made it easier to avoid security
guards such as the one hopefully not still hanging across
from Niko and Cal's apartment.

My stomach was uncomfortably full. It was a given
Niko and Goodfellow were too smart to overfeed me
after days without food, but by the same token, a small
amount of food would stretch a shrunken stomach. I
didn't remember what I'd eaten, it wouldn't have been
meat—I trusted them on that. I didn't remember eating
period, which meant I'd been too loopy and far gone to
do it myself, choosing instead to paint my face with it
and think I was making art. They had to have fed me,
spooned it into my mouth like I was a goddamn baby. I
closed my eyes and had a flash of someone making air-
plane noises. That fucking Cal. I didn't get how Niko and
Robin could trust me, now, all my life, when I couldn't
trust myself. Going by this Cal, this version of me, if my
arms were longer, I'd stab myself in the back. And I'd do
it with enough eager enthusiasm. I'd likely have balloons,
a cake, and a magician while I did it—make a real party
of it.

He hadn't been shining bright with enthusiasm during
the screaming. Wrapped up in a ball, trying hard not to
piss or shit himself, staring at me like I was his worst
nightmare. That would be because I was. He'd seen me

screaming loud and long enough to bring down the building on top of us, and he knew. Whatever had happened to
me to put me in a hell I couldn't scream my way out of, it
was going to happen to him. That was in his future and his
future wasn't looking pretty.

I hoped he *had* shit his pants, the spiteful little bastard.

"Caliban." It wasn't said with more insistence. If anything, it was said with more desperation.

I wasn't pissed at Robin or Niko about the, not
nightmares—that wasn't what they called them. The terrors, that's what they were. *Terrors.* It was worse when the
terrors were one in the same as your life. Robin and Niko,
it wasn't their fault. They'd have noticed the first tremor
or twitch and kept their word to wake me up. It hadn't
been their shift though, as they were catching some
needed sleep of their own for facing Lazarus. It had been
Cal's watch, and he had enough respect for his brother
and enough wariness of Robin's display of fighting skills
and icy command to sit with me as he'd been told. That
didn't mean he cared enough to watch me. A nightmare.
So what? He knew how bad nightmares could get from
months of them after escaping his two years with the Auphe. He'd lived through them. If I had one, I'd live through
it too.

Whatever he'd been staring at, the wall, the ceiling, his
own feet wondering if they were still growing and
whether his latest pair of combat boots had started to
feel cramped, I had no idea. He hadn't been keeping his
eyes on me though, as that tremor, that twitch went unnoticed and then the abyss gobbled me up, chewing at
me with teeth like serrated knives all the way down.
Yeah, what Cal had been watching instead of me, I had
no interest in asking him.

I did know he damn sure hadn't been holding my
hand. But I hadn't expected that. I'd just expected him to
watch. There was no question he didn't like me. I hadn't
known that he hated me miles more than he'd ever hated
himself.

Once I'd managed to climb out of the pit of nonono-

nonono, stop screaming in horrified denial, and recover enough to project the thinnest veneer of fake sanity, I'd regained the ability to talk ... some ... which is a good thing to have. I'd pushed Robin and Niko back and away with no real force, saying I needed to shower, which was true. I was soaked in sweat and stank of fear that human noses would be able to pick up. I reclaimed my hand from the puck's grip as no matter how many times I'd torn free of it, he kept coming back to snag it. He realized, hell, everyone in the room realized, I was panicked, confused, not remotely oriented, had no idea which of the whens I was in, which of the versions of who were with me, had no idea what was real and what wasn't, and smothering in terror that *all* of it was real.

As much effort they'd put into talking me out of it, it became clear that I'd have to crawl out myself. But Robin kept his promises when he made them to us. He told me I wouldn't be alone and if I couldn't hear or understand him to know that I wasn't, he'd shown me in the only way left. No matter how viciously hard I'd shoved at him, or clawed my hand from his, he was right back, his grip as solid and tight each time. Trying and hoping I would know he was there somewhere in the screams. Not alone. You're not alone. When I'd finally come back and was getting ready to head for the shower, I'd shaken my hand to regain the circulation and let one corner of my mouth quirk. "This was not a first date, Goodfellow, I don't care what you tell your friends." His smile at my effort was bigger than mine, but, beyond relieved, not any more genuine.

"Caliban, stop."

The shower was enormous with a water flow like Niagara Falls, but through that I heard the yelling that devolved into twice-the-volume, full-on drill-sergeant shouting, the kind of red-faced screaming that preceded many second-degree, fit-of-rage murders. I kept scrubbing off the sweat and fear. It was not my problem. It was kind of a pity Goodfellow couldn't kill him as I'd cease to be, pop like a soap bubble, and vanish into the neverwas. But if

he could've snapped Cal's neck with no consequences to
me, it still wouldn't have been my problem.

When I'd come out of the shower, wet hair jerked
back into an elastic tie at the base of my neck, I was
dressed in new less sweat drenched clothes, a new
Caliban-friendly shirt—THAT WHICH DOES NOT KILL ME
HAS MASSIVELY *FUCKED UP*. He'd had it made while I
slept as under the letters was a small cartoon weasel on
its back, with X's for eyes, a lolling tongue, and four feet
in the air to demonstrate how dead it was. It was a black
shirt with the letters and weasel, except for the deep red
X's and tongue, a dark gray. Personalized and good for
night work when you wore dark colors or you ended up
as a cartoon weasel.

Niko had this *look*, not on his face, but on all of him. It
was everywhere. In his expression, in the tense lines of his
body, in his eyes a shade empty and his eyes weren't that.
He could hide any emotion behind them when he had to,
but even then, they weren't empty. They were the lid to
Pandora's box and you could see the potential in them, if
not what it was the potential of that was inside them. He
wasn't hiding anything now. He wore his disappointment,
invisible chains wrapped around him, the weight of them
changing how he stood, how he moved, and what it did
do to his face did show as disappointment, but more, it
changed it to someone else's face. He had Niko's features,
complexion, eyes, but it wasn't the Niko I'd known every
day—until two days ago. He hadn't looked like this—
ever, not at the height of my seriously fucked-up Auphe
shit.

"Caliban, wait."

Robin was armed, I assumed—there was no nonmen-
tally scarring way to check, ready to go, and carved from
ice. He had his back turned to Cal and that I had seen
before. Not aimed at me or Niko, but at the puck's ene-
mies or those he didn't consider worthy enough to be an
enemy. As far as he was concerned, Cal didn't exist. That,
despite my opinion in the shower . . . that was *my* problem. Shit. It was another impossible thing no one could

imagine. Goodfellow was family and he would always choose Niko and me over anyone else. He wouldn't know how to consider differently. He would be mentally incapable of *thinking* that it was a choice. But when he was faced with two Cals, he could have a different thought. If one of us injured the other, then only one of us was his brother, since his brother wouldn't do anything to hurt Robin purposely. And hurting Robin's brother-in-blood was more of a wound than hurting Robin himself.

Cal would've been better off if he'd stabbed Robin in the kidneys as threatened. Instead he'd hurt me in a way that had me preferring a stabbing myself. It would've been less painful. If Robin could've killed him, if he'd been anyone but what he was, he would have. As he couldn't, he wrote him off. He wasn't his family, wasn't his. I was. Robin had a choice and he chose me. I didn't blame him. He didn't know this Cal yet, and while technically only knowing me for several hours, he knew me for thousands of years and I knew him the same. For the first time, I knew all the lives, all the Calibans and the same Robin they had known time after time. Thousands of years of every exciting, amazing, horrifying, crazy, stupid thing we'd done. Compare that to a few hours of knowing a sullen asshole kid who'd stabbed us both in the back. Had done the same to Niko, Robin's other family. It was a logic knot even a trickster could unknowingly tie in his own brain.

"Would you just wait, *damn it?"*

Cal had hurt us, the three of us, but it hadn't been purposely—or not purposely enough to be considered premeditated. He'd been careless, didn't give a shit about me, hated me, but . . . Niko would forgive him. Niko had no choice in that. What Cal had done, Niko would think . . . thought it was wrong. Dishonorable. Spiteful. Not simply amoral, but over the edge into something darker. It was something Sophia would've done and that had to hit the hardest, but Niko wouldn't have thought that if Cal had been that careless with someone else. A stranger. Someone we didn't know or trust. Pretty much anyone outside the circle of Niko-and-Cal. It was that

Cal had done it to someone who would be Niko's brother that had him looking at, then away from, him with disappointment and disbelief. In the end though, Cal was Niko's brother. I was only the potential of his brother. Cal had to come first. He'd forgive, he'd try harder to forget, but they'd be all right again. It might take a few days or a week, but Cal was Cal and Cal was his. There was nothing he couldn't forgive him.

But I'd be gone sooner or later and while that'd be better for Niko and Cal, what the fuck would happen with Robin? Without him, both of them would be dead in a year. If he stayed that long, to save them out of obligation, and then walked away . . . well, we'd be dead a few more times.

More than that though, Cal without Robin to teach him, yes, life was dead set on killing him personally, but all the more reason not to take it so seriously. Laugh. Have some fun. You're a virgin because you don't want to make more baby Auphe to eat the maternity ward nurses? I know this meadow nymph. She can have kids only by *pollination*. I'll set you up. You're a monster? Ha! You wish, Damien. Go down five blocks to the Goth club and emo it up with them. Whine about no one understanding how evil you are. Get that goat's head pentacle tattooed on your ass, stock up on eyeliner. You're a four-month-old puppy thinking his spiked collar makes him badder than all the big dogs who'd swallow you whole, spiked collar and all. Stop your moaning, a Spielberg Gremlin could kick your ass, and serve me some decent wine for a change.

"Caliban, you asshole, don't make me shoot you in the leg."

Niko had to think I wasn't a monster. He was my brother. But Robin, long before he'd ever told us about reincarnation, someone not my brother telling me that? Wanting to be a friend? Proving, and we'd made him prove it more times than anyone else would've tolerated, that we could trust him? Showing me life was dark, but sometimes the best parties happen when the lights go down. Getting me *laid*? Without Robin doing all that, being that friend, showing me shit I never wanted to see but had made me laugh it was so disgusting. Without Robin there would be no Caliban. No me. I don't know what I would've been, a self-fulfilling prophecy of the dark, the grim, the monstrous—someone with less humor and faith in me to fight the Auphe tendencies when they came. Turning his back on Cal was the same as doing what I had. Taking my gun and putting it to my head, but this time the trigger would be pulled, it would just be Robin who was doing it.

And he didn't know.

Fuck. Try to stop an assassin, resurrect your family, and you ended up in a goddamn soap opera.

We'd left Bridge and Broad Street and were now turning on Pearl. Then it would be Wall Street, South Street, and Lazarus. We'd kill his ass, with extreme prejudice, and finally I'd go home. I'd find out if my letters worked, if the ones Robin said he'd continue to send, had a service set up to continue to send if something happened to him, and of course his sly and sneaky self, better than any letter, if just one thing had worked. If I'd fixed it.

Or if I'd go back to the beginning. Stand by the rubble, blackened and cold by the time I returned, pay my respects. Put Niko's hand-sized statue of Buddha on the street in front of it, throw a handful of the tackiest brightest colored glitter speckled condoms on the burnt mountain of bricks, say see you soon and so long for good. Buy a slice of cheese pizza, no meat, eat it, and then put the Desert Eagle's muzzle back under my chin and blow out my brains.

It'd be one of the two.

Guess I'd see.

"*Stop*! Caliban, Jesus Christ, please, just fucking *stop*!"

A hand grabbed my arm and halted me in my tracks. He was lucky I'd heard him behind me, asking me to stop, and had been ignoring it. If I hadn't, I'd have put a knife in his gut. On edge didn't cover my emotional state right now. I glanced at his hand and he let go of me instantly. "What." I said it flatly. I didn't ask it. It wasn't a question as if there was an answer I didn't care about knowing.

"I'm sorry." He bent his head to carefully study the asphalt beneath our feet. We didn't say that too often, either of us. Cal's own ponytail was losing strands and sat a little lopsided on the nape of his neck. "I didn't know that would happen. I just thought . . . nightmares. We both had them. We both slept under hotel beds and had nightmares every night when we came back from"— he looked back up at me and swallowed—"that place. So I slacked off, what with hating you like the world's worst case of crotch rot. I sat with you, but I didn't watch you." He gripped the bottom of his leather jacket and straightened it or, as it was already straight, made it crooked. Now it matched the rest of his unbalanced look. Wrinkled T-shirt from repeated yanking of cloth by fisted hands. Jeans with a half-undone zipper. A streak of gun oil along his jaw.

Behind him by at least a block I could see Niko and Robin arguing. Niko for giving Cal a chance to make it right, and Robin for keeping him the hell away from me. I could take care of myself against almost anyone after the eight years I'd told him about and Goodfellow knew it. But I couldn't do anything to Cal without doing it to myself and he knew that too.

I'd learned to use sarcasm before I'd learned to use a knife. I could depend on doing verbal damage. I didn't need to physically hurt him.

"I didn't know that . . . whatever that was would . . . shit, I didn't know. And I am sorry and not because Niko . . . because my big brother is disappointed in me. Or because that puck you know is pissed enough that he would've already cut out my heart and shoved it down the garbage disposal if that wouldn't make you, alakazam . . . poof, disappear, never existed those eight years to be this you," he said. "I'm sorry as no one should have to go through that, whatever that was, besides terrifying as shit."

"That's a lie. *Mostly* a lie." I gave him a grim smile, the odd grimmer than grim as the corners of your mouth turn down, not up, but somehow it's still a smile. "You are sorry that you made Niko *ashamed* of you. Disap-

pointment falls pretty short of how he looks at you now."
Pull of the trigger and bull's-eye. He actually staggered
back a step. "You aren't sorry about Robin; that's true
since you know he can't do anything to you. Physically."
Cal didn't know Robin well enough to imagine the damage he could do with his words.

"For the rest of it, I liked the phrasing. No one should
have to go through that. Not that you, Caliban, shouldn't
have had to go through that. Lie by omission but a lie all
the same. What you meant was *you* shouldn't have to go
through that. Uncontrollable screaming, panic, horror,
insanity, that doesn't look that fun when you realize
they're making one in your size, that it's coming for you.
But you let it happen and now it will. It'll be rap, rap,
rapping at your chamber door. *That's* why you're sorry.
Now you know seriously bad shit is going to hit you in
eight years. Shit so horrific that it'll make those nightmares of two years in Auphe hell, for real and for true,
not that bad." He flinched, at the truth of that or at our
old childhood saying of for real and for true, or both.

"You'll get to relive that bad shit because a hateful,
spiteful bastard of your younger self lets you. And you
don't even know half of it. You saw the screaming and
mental breakdown, you have no idea what was under
that. What I felt. What I feel. You think it couldn't be
worse, what you saw, right? But it was. It still is. Now.
We're talking blah blah and I'm feeling it. I never stopped
feeling it. I just stopped screaming. You know what the
best part is?" I jammed a thumb into the lowest part of
his stomach right about the waist of his jeans where the
bladder's located. I didn't do it with enough force to hurt.
It was just sufficient pressure to remind him for a block
or two. "I pissed myself." I smiled, sharper . . . to cut.
"Have fun with that."

Robin and Niko, neither had said anything about it.
Cal had been too far from the couch and me to notice. I
hadn't pissed myself during the Tumulus dreams and I'd
been sixteen and feral. I was twenty-six and insane now
and, considering everything, I'd have been surprised if I

hadn't emptied my bladder, ruining a hellaciously tacky but expensive sofa in the bargain.

"Try telling me you're sorry when you're sorry for the right reason. If you ever are sorry. Hell, if you ever fucking know the reason." I started to walk away, then paused to add, "You and me, we're not the same and in some way, I don't know how, I don't think we ever were. I'm not a monster. I know that. But you? You are."

I left him frozen, his mouth open. I'd killed a junkie in self-defense, but I'd let him die slow, drop by crimson drop. He'd murdered kids. He deserved it. Some people would agree that he had death coming, but the slow part, that was torture and that was wrong. I thought it was punishment, well earned. I didn't feel an ounce of guilt over it. I was a predator. We didn't do guilt. But even I, twenty-six and not only a lion, but a man-eating one, wouldn't have done what Cal had. I wouldn't have hurt one of our own.

That's what monsters did.

17

Of course it took the rest of the walk to the *Ever* before it struck me that I was doing what I was afraid Robin was going to do: fucking this kid up. He and I had our monster issues off and on for a long time, but eventually outgrew them. Learned the truth of what we were and what we weren't. We weren't human, but we weren't monsters either. That's how it had gone.

How would it go when your future self, and who would know you better, tells you that you *are* a monster? It was safe to say it could possibly put a damper on outgrowing that fear or recognizing the truth if it bit you in the ass. I, future I, thinks I, present-day I, am a monster therefore I am one. I think therefore I am. *Puto me ergo monstrum monstrum.* Just as I'd been telling myself for two years now.

Cal wasn't the Cal I'd been at eighteen. But at eighteen I hadn't had future Cals popping in, telling my brother things he then wouldn't tell me. My brother who told me everything and always had, he was now listening to someone else over me. Then strange pucks are dumped on my couch, when I wouldn't have known pucks were real, and this other Cal is saying here's your new best friend. You've at least nine years to bond, party, and kill things together. Enjoy.

This asshole Cal, because it's not me—I wouldn't steal my younger self's brother, shake my life up and down like a snow globe, push people I didn't know or trust in my home—is saying, sorry if you have an opinion, don't care, and this is how it's going to be. And the one person I'd had in my life, the one and only person that cared if I lived or died, the one who was my mother, father, brother, and all I ever had, all I'd always known I ever would have, he was suddenly split between three people. Everyone knew something I didn't. And the one person who was the only person in my life was still the only person in my life, but I wasn't the only one in his, not anymore.

I wouldn't have behaved any better.

I might have behaved worse.

But that was thoughts for when shadow weasels weren't chasing us across the deck of the *Ever*.

We'd came across one security guard, choked him out, handcuffed, gagged, and hidden him in the trunk of his own car. They really needed two guards to get good coverage by the ship, but I presumed number two was the unfortunate son of a bitch who had been hanging in Niko and Cal's hall. Niko had informed me that, yes, he had removed the body. Had he lost the use of half his brain in the future that would make me think that of him now? Then came the great awkward moment when he realized he'd spoken before he thought, and that he'd lost *all* the use of his brain when he had *died* in a massive explosion in front of his brother's eyes.

The *Ever* had dock lines—that's what Goodfellow called them—securing her to the dock, but she also had a wide sweep of shallow wooden stairs built for tourists that led straight up to the deck. Handy. We didn't bother to sneak or hide. Weasels were already slithering up and down the far sides of the stairs, some curled up like sleepy cats. There should've been lights around, up high, keeping the ship fairly light whether it was night or not. They had gone dark. From the smell of ozone in the air, that had been a simple trick for our favorite assassin. I sighed. I

wanted it to be simple. I'd expected it to be. Inject three
to a hundred different *paien* DNA samples in a human
member of the Vigil and it could be impressive ... if you
gave him a decade or two to work with the mess roiling
around inside him. My Robin's contacts said at most he'd
had a week, the Vigil had been that desperate, the experiment never tested, no one had any idea what the results
would be. I'd been surprised their guinea pig hadn't
melted into a puddle of goo. Simple had been the game
plan ... before the explosion. Afterward nothing was simple, but I did expect Lazarus to go down quick and easy
and be the least of my problems.

The shadow weasels on their own, the slinky bastards,
had proved me wrong there. Then the lightning, and,
yeah, that didn't enter the category of simple or easy.
What Lazarus himself would be, I might have to unveil
my backup after all, gate the shithead into oblivion, and
hope Cal's mind didn't explode and he ended up on the
deck sucking his thumb or, better and better, he went
Auphe early.

The rough voice from the sewers abruptly split the air.
"Death waits for no one."

Grade A megalomaniacal psychopath. Those were
the ones that when you put them down and finally, finally, finally walked away, they'd have a chunk of your
flesh clamped in their dead jaws. "Is it always like this?"
Niko asked quietly. "A clichéd Old West gunslinger
shootout, where you face each other, trade insults, and
see who precisely is Doc Holliday and who is dead?"

"Only when they're bigger, badder, and crazier than
us and like to play with their food," I answered. "It's not
a good sign."

"Do not keep Death waiting." It boomed, a voice you
would hear across battlefields.

At that the weasels stopped playing and lazing and
came at us in the same pack style they'd used in the sewers. Goodfellow grin, sword out, "I've been looking forward to this, you sleazy evil *porni gious*." He ran up the
stairs with a bounce to his step that said he hadn't seen a
good fight in a long time. The sewer didn't count. We

hadn't been armed for our particular opponents. We'd
made some changes there.

We followed him, Niko also with a sword, Cal with his
Desert Eagle and me with mine. Isn't it cute when people dress *and* arm their identical toddlers the same? The
weasels were at our heels until we turned the high pow-
ered flashlights, nothing like we'd had in the sewer, on
them over our shoulders and they squealed. Some faded
back to a safer range and a few faded out of existence.
We kept running and aimed the lights away. They were
effective to a point, could even destroy a few weasels, but
not all of them. There were uncertain whispers behind
us, then a shrill razor-edged whistling, aggressive and
predatory. They weren't laughing now, not like before.
Now they were mad, which made it more surprising we'd
survived them in the tunnel and the sewer when we
hadn't known that they were merely playing then.

Dodging them, neither Cal nor I fired; we'd told them
how useless that was. The four of us were nearly to the
center of the ship when we gathered back-to-back in a
loose circle. We waited as the weasels surrounded us
from all sides, the whistling getting higher and higher in
pitch. Watching them until, shadows or not, we'd seen
their hindquarters bunch in preparation to leap on us, a
clan of hyenas rushing a wounded zebra calf to mound
and wash over it, vanishing its body from sight as they
tore it to pieces.

But they weren't hyenas and this wasn't Animal Planet.

"Now!" Goodfellow called. "Curtain is down! And the
lights are on!" We'd all dropped our weapons already and
put in the ear plugs. Now we put a hand in each pocket
we'd turned into goody bags, pulled two pins with each
hand and threw them out before throwing ourselves flat,
closing our eyes, and covering our ears. A second and a
half later someone bombed the *Ever*. With eyes closed,
face pressed to the deck, hands covering ears and ear
plugs, it was what I'd imagine being at ground zero would
be when someone dropped a nuclear bomb. Flash bangs.
Military grade light and noise stun grenades. They more
than lived up to their name. The light that crept through

the space between my face and the deck lit up my closed lids bright red. But the light itself, it was white, a pure intense white, nothing like flames and fire, nothing like a real explosion. I kept that repetition going in my mind. Not an explosion. Not the explosion. Not my explosion.

I didn't open my eyes until I felt a tap on my shoulder. Not my explosion. No one would be tapping me there. I cautiously opened my eyes, ears ringing despite our precautions and let Robin pull me to my feet. I did a quick turn and scan. There wasn't a single shadow weasel left. Every last one wiped out. That's what working with the proper tools did for you. Niko and Cal were up too and Cal was the least sullen and depressed I'd seen him in hours. He was grinning, not a huge one, but me grinning at that age was a miracle. "That was fucking *fantastic*," he declared/shouted to be heard over our temporary semi-deafness.

"Impressive, carrying the light of a storm in your hands to kill my pets. Pity for you I have more pets."

The figure stepped out of the shadows, a faint halo of lightning circling above him. It was enough to let us see without our flashlights and from what I knew, this bastard, who carried around an entire pet store as to not run out, could see in the dark.

This was him. This was the Vigil's last hope: Lazarus. He stood, still as a stone, as he stared at us—or at Cal rather. Killing me was too little and too fucking late for the Vigil, although he'd treated himself to a little entertainment by trying anyway. But that had been all it could be for an assassin, a distraction. He had a purpose and that, to an assassin, would always come first.

It was Cal who was the true target.

Over six and a half feet in height, six eight or six nine, I thought, and thickly muscled under his natural brown leather shirt and pants, medium-sized strangely familiar ivory tube shaped beads were scattered through his hair, grouping it all into at least fifty or sixty separate dangling long twists. It made it difficult to tell what color his hair was—brown, the darkest brown you could get without edging close to black. It was streaked with a deep rusty red, but the red didn't look . . . right. There was something about it. The whole mass of it fell past his shoulders, unseen in length, except for a few stray pieces that fell midway to the front between his chest and lower abdomen. It was matted enough to be dreadlocks. Not from the texture but from dried substance mixed in it—blood. From the smell, it was fresh, no more than two days old. That explained the red streaks. There were beads, too . . . or tubes, they had their own distinct odor, one I didn't recognize. I'd come across similar but nothing exactly the same. Some of them were whole, some cracked and twisted and the color was not old ivory, but fresh and dazzling white. Then I realized they weren't beads. They were bones. Finger bones carefully stripped of flesh and polished. The chalky tang, a different odor of death, told me the remnants of life that lingered in them were fresh, no more than two days dead. With Cal alive beside me, the blood and bone pointed to nothing but bad.

Random kill . . . for *bones*.

A purposeful kill to take what he needed to look this way. What way this was or why he chose it, it had to do with the blood of one of the *paien* injected in him. Its DNA changing him as my DNA had once changed me.

Holy shit. I was beginning to think the Vigil had gone further than they'd planned. This wasn't the assassin they'd wanted, one with a single goal. This wasn't an assassin. This was a murderer of anything and everything for no reason at all with several types of *paien* genes that had gone overboard and then some in doing their job in remaking him. They had given him abilities that could make him a killer without limitation. They had screwed up in the deadliest of manners. They, in wanting to put me down—remove what they thought I was from the world—had done the opposite and made something closer to what they'd labeled me.

Monster.

The Vigil had once rubber-stamped me a monster waiting to happen and then restamped me a monster scheduled for destruction. Yet at my very worst when I was twisted up into the mind and body of what the Au-

phe had half brainwashed me into being and let the
other half, their genes, do the rest, I had blood-soaked,
nightmare urges. I had cravings, for slaughter, murder,
hunting prey that could speak but it was their screams I
wanted. So many urges, so much blood to be had, so
many kills I wanted to make, but not one of them had
ever been for *fucking fashion*.

As he took a step toward us, I could see that his eyes
were a pale, pale blue; that if they'd been any lighter they
would've been white . . . until they spiderwebbed with
jagged veins red as blood. In the air around him was a
faint whisper. It came and grew until it was the sound of
men shouting, metal clashing against metal, and the call
of crows, the ones that circled the battlefields that had
been their banquets. They would wait for the fall of a
blood-covered fighter, then instantly plummet down,
perch on unmoving chests, and use their sharp beaks to
pluck hungrily at dead eyes. That's when they came. He
had said he had more pets.

Shadow crows flew out of his chest, through his skin
and shirt without touching either with the pointed beaks,
black claws, wings that were faintly outlined with the rip-
ple of feathers. They kept coming, a river of them with
no signs of stopping. Up they went, the new weasels, and
I raised my eyes to follow. Above us and the size of a
storm cloud, they wheeled, shades against the city's
light-polluted orange night sky. The circle of them was
wide and thick enough for thousands of the scavengers,
all waiting for that first single fall to descend and gorge.

"He appears to be a Viking," Niko said quietly, "if that
wasn't impossible as he's *paien* now, not human any longer. The sound effects and show above us, however, are
evidence he's both."

"How does pumping a guy full of monster blood get
you a Viking?" Cal asked, his Glock was already out and
pointed at Lazarus. "Could someone tell me that? You
know what, never mind. I don't give a shit. And don't
bother playing Kevin Costner any of you. I can save myself." He pulled the trigger and shot Lazarus several
times in the face. Like Nik had always taught us, in a fight

use every advantage. When you're fighting for your life there's no such thing as playing dirty, only playing to live.

But I beat him by pulling the trigger of the AR-15 I'd obtained, along with a few extra magazines tucked in my jacket. I sent four hundred rounds a minute toward Lazarus and I hoped I'd have a chance to rub it in Mini Me's face. If we got past him hating me, to where I could mock him a little without getting shot in the face myself. It could happen. If I came off as smug or conceited, it'd be all in good, wholesome fun.

Well . . . maybe.

Little bit.

But it didn't happen that way.

What did happen was so fast that at first I didn't know how I'd ended up on my ass. There'd been a blinding light, air choked again with ozone, the feel of being thrown. I rubbed at my eyes and staggered up to see a rain of liquid metal between Lazarus and us through the halos and streaks across my vision. Four hundred rounds were now a curtain of silver and copper falling to the ground. An unshot Lazarus rested a hand on the crackling white light that circled him after destroying every bullet Cal and I had fired . . . over four *hundred*. It was impossible, but impossible or not, Lazarus wrapped that eye-searing light around his arm and sent it back up to where it belonged—the sky. Wasn't that where lightning lived—the sky? I thought so.

It had been who knew how many bolts of lightning that had disarmed us. The asshole could control god-damn *lightning*, we were aware of that since this morning, but to melt four hundred bullets? Gotta love a challenge.

Blinking again, I could see there were dark marks, different shapes and sizes, scattered on every part of his skin that was visible, his face, his arms in the sleeveless leather shirt, his hands, and they were moving. They coalesced into tattoos. Pure black, they were either an arrow or a spear was my closest guess. Starkly primitive, it was made of two lines—a vertical one, then the second line that topped it. They were all pointing upward. If not for the peak of the second line giving it a sharp point aimed up at the sky, they almost could be Ts. A memory hit me. Runes. It was some kind of rune. Niko had studied them as he'd studied everything. I'd caught a glance over his shoulder a few years ago at a page of them in a book he was reading. They had looked close to this.

That's all I had the chance to think when Lazarus extended both hands. He shifted his focus from Cal to me. "You began this. You, Caliban, fired the first shot." I hadn't expected much talking from an assassin, but I hadn't expected the Vigil to screw up so profoundly with their Frankenstein creation and make a monster instead, one that could stand shoulder to shoulder with any Auphe. And if I didn't expect talking, I didn't expect the wide mocking grin, glacial as the hand of death in the cold stretch of it. He lifted both arms and the hands that had been empty now held nooses. Made of shadows naturally, but managing to show the coarse texture of a hangman's rope.

"But the first shot is nothing when I am the *war*."

Cal spat, the disgust blatant enough to fly through the air as heavy as a thrown rock, "You're as far from human as I am. You let those hypocrites do that to you? Take away who you were to make you into a monster like me, the thing you Vigil bastards hate?"

He took us all in now, his grin became more derisive. "The Vigil did not make me. I have always been. They guarded the human's ignorance. They took one of their own, trained in the ways of weapons and the coward's kill of assassination. They thought they had made an undefeatable soldier to fight for humans. But I am not a soldier. I am a *warrior*, the likes of which hasn't been seen here since the Blood Eagle flew, and I care nothing for humans. With their mayfly lives, they do not live long enough to be counted as more than toys made to die for my amusement. The Vigil did not make a savior. They did not make a twisted unnatural creature with powers it did not deserve. They did not make anything new, nothing with a mind or a spirit. Instead, they created a vessel.

"My vessel."

He lifted both arms above his head, hands wrapped with rope, the nooses raised high. I felt a sudden tightening around my throat. I touched my throat with fingers ready to rip away whatever was strangling me, but there was nothing—nothing but the nooses Lazarus still held. That wasn't impossible, but it was unfriendly as fuck. I was choking for breath as beside me Cal was doing the same.

"Do you not know me now? He who shares the title of The Hanged One. I bring Justice, but I *am* War."

He shouted it at the sky and I thought I felt the ground beneath me shake.

"I am War. I am War. *I AM WAR!*"

Oddly, for him, quiet until now, Goodfellow, who stood close behind us, gave a painfully hard yank on my hair that turned me around. He pulled me frantically into motion, and when he did, the pressure around my neck loosened before disappearing. He was also snapping at Niko and Cal to move their idiotic asses and run. When they hesitated, I emphasized his command while coughing out, "Options, Vanna says—hanging, eyes pecked out by crows, electrocuted, or run. Pick one!"

No one else had self-preservation skills close to a puck's who'd dodged the reaper for millions of years. I knew when to listen to him. I had full confidence in him—until I noticed we were running toward the other end of the ship. I didn't know the name—bow, aft, rudder, the "I'm the King of the World" spot, the shrimp buffet bulwark and open bilge bar. I knew nothing about boats, what to call any of it, and I didn't give a damn about guessing.

I *did* know we were racing toward the end away from the dock, the end beyond which was nothing but water.

He was cursing now and it wasn't his usual bitching about getting boggle blood on his Armani shirt. This was the kind of cursing he saved for the times he thought it was likely to be the other way around: What was trying to kill us would get *Robin's* blood on its nondesigner scales. "*Forpoutanas gie!* Tyr! He has the blood of *Tyr* in him. The tattoos. The nooses. The duplicity of his position

when he was Justice, when all who he judged were
judged guilty without exception, and he watched each
hanging with his dick in hand."

He spat in disgust and kept moving and talking. Pucks
excelled at doing both simultaneously. "The insatiable
thirst for blood, brutality, and vengeance he disguises as
victorious battles. The glory of wars that he rules honor-
able, declaring the other side to have twice the number
of warriors he leads when in reality they have less than
half. He lies his way to legend. His tongue tells nothing
but lies, not that such a fact makes him any kind of trickster. He tells his lies for no other reason than senseless
slaughter and any excuse for war. He says he is War. He
wishes he was Death, the butchering bastard."

I threw myself down at the scent of ozone and lightning streaked over my head. Then I was back up and
running again. It was a fair-sized boat? Ship? I was guessing, but the length to run from one end of the *Titanic* to
the other couldn't be this far.

"But how did they get his blood? He cannot be dead.
I would know. News of his death, the hypocritical, devious, genocidal *kolotripa*, would be more than a rumor. I'm
a trickster. It's my avocation to know all these things.
Yet, where would the Vigil get the blood? What have I
missed?" He hadn't let go of my arm when I'd hit the
floor, the deck, whatever, and was continuing to drag me,
which I hated to admit was faster than I could run. The
bastard was a fucking cheetah.

As I was a lion and not a cheetah, I wasn't surprised
when I stumbled, but used the chance to check that Niko
and Cal were behind us and keeping up. Robin ignored
my near fall and kept going, keeping me upright and taking me with him. "The lightning and shadow could be
dealt with. The lightning and a slave ship. It must be the
blood of an impundulu, a South African Lightning Bird—
the shade of what it was living within him. Fighting us on
this ship, it is nothing but a pretense at vengeance for
those long dead slaves as Tyr himself has slaves by the
dozens. The shadows . . . I still haven't pinpointed them
yet. Whatever they are, they and the impundulu, they are

shades within Tyr, not living but not dead. They're weaker, capable of being defeated, but the majority of him is Tyr. But with two hands now instead of only one and two nooses to go with them," he groaned. *"Gamisou!"*

He was more or less talking to himself, but I was long familiar with that. When we were someplace safe enough he could speak slower, use smaller words, and give us the unthinkably bizarre free of charge explanation, we'd get filled in then.

Without another word to me, he turned and pushed me with enough force I was actually off my feet as I was thrown to land hard—just as another bolt of lightning flew by exactly where I'd been while running. "Thanks." I staggered back up and started to run again.

"There has to be a way we can take him. And who is Tyr?" I asked, beginning to feel the burn in my chest, the need for oxygen, and we hadn't run far, nothing like the ten miles I was used to. I felt my throat tightening again and the air I was pulling in and exhaling was coming and going with a stark wheeze. The noose was back.

Goodfellow heard it, my increasing struggle for air, and didn't reply. Silent now as he kept the grim grip on my ponytail pulled over my shoulder from my back to the front to be used as a leash. I could see where he was headed and what he had in mind. We were going for the edge of the ship and he planned to pull us both over into the river. It might have worked, too, if the noose hadn't kept tightening. I clawed at my throat, but it was the same. Nothing was there. Nothing I could touch. I stumbled and asked one last time before I fell. "Robin ... who ... is ... Tyr?" I was on my knees then and my throat was closed completely. I couldn't get any air to pass, not the smallest gasp, not a fraction of a breath. I couldn't breathe. That didn't stop me from trying to get up, to get to the edge. I had to stand. I had to make it. Robin wouldn't leave me. I had to get the fuck up or when I died here, he'd die with me.

I tried, with everything in me, I tried.

I failed.

Barely on my knees now, I was wavering, about to fall

on my side. Robin was in front of me then, on his own
knees to face me. His hands were on my shoulders keeping me upright. I might not be able to breathe or speak,
but I could get across my point, last that it was. I put my
hand flat on the puck's chest and pushed him toward the
side, toward the river. I could hear Niko shouting that
Cal couldn't breathe, that he was blue. I was most likely
blue as well. His eyes held mine.

We were all fucked, but Niko, Cal, and I would come
back and live again, fifty years or a hundred. Goodfellow
wouldn't. If he ran for it, if he survived, we'd see him
again. If he died with us, we never would. Of course, *of
goddamn course*, he wouldn't do the smart thing, the
puck thing, the selfish thing. *"No,"* he snapped, looping
fingers around my wrist to keep me from pushing again.
"You died for me on a *gamisou* kitchen table tortured
with the medieval version of Ginsu knives in a pathetic
excuse for a castle. You did it because you wouldn't give
me up—you said it yourself. That is not who you are. You
would not and could not give me over to the mercy of a
sociopathic bastard that wanted me hanged for treason.
This is a different life, but I won't shame myself by doing
less by you. I am not giving you up to the exact same
kind of monster you faced for me."

That's when Robin answered my question about Tyr.
I wished he hadn't.

Then he hoisted me over his shoulder and ran for the
edge, jerking and dodging streaks and bolts of lightning
that were so thick in the air, I didn't know how we
weren't dead on the deck, hearts stopped. I saw Niko
through a distant haze. He had Cal over his shoulder and
was running all out toward the edge and then was over
it, both of them a distant splash. Robin avoided one
more streak of lightning so close that I smelled burning
hair. Then we, like Niko and Cal, were over and hitting
the water. I couldn't see much—black and yellow swirling across the world—and then I couldn't see anything. I
didn't hear the sound as we sank into the depths of the
water, but I felt the cold fist of it close around us. It faded
nearly instantly as did the agony of oxygen-starved lungs.

I was almost gone, but that didn't worry me. The time for worry was over. I was certain that was going to be my last thought. I didn't know if I was right or wrong. Did where you have the thought count? Who knew? I did know I'd stopped breathing minutes ago. I recognized the very last beat of my heart when I felt it.

I knew I wasn't in the river any longer and wouldn't be again.

That's how it was—always had been, always would be. It was time to go.

"It hasn't changed." Another thought, I'd give you that, but I didn't have it in the river. That was ancient history. Now I stood in a cottage and stared out the window at a meadow of dew and grass and mist, not a river in sight. There was a pile of fresh-smelling straw to one side, a blanket thrown carelessly on it that would be warm against a morning chill. Would it kill someone to update to central heating? Apparently. As everything here was as I remembered in as minute detail as if I'd seen it yesterday, rather the infinity of moments since I'd been here last. When I'd left the room with the small window of gray, sunless sky, I'd walked the red path this way, drifted atop the deep scarlet stream to a place beyond pain, but that had all been closer to forever ago than to yesterday.

Like before, next I would wrap myself in the blanket and walk out the door to someplace new.

This is how it goes.

I frowned and didn't reach for the blanket. That question, it could've been forever ago as well, I'd asked Robin ... What was it? I snagged at the ragged end of the memory and yanked hard. I'd asked him—I pulled harder yet and there it was. I'd demanded, "Who is Tyr?" And he'd answered me, eyes gone from green to black with a fury so fierce and a fear so profound I didn't think Robin even knew that consuming an emotion. I went to the cottage door and opened it.

This is how it goes here. You know that. It always has been, always will be.

"Tyr is a god."

A god, Robin had answered me. How could we fight a

god? I was dead anyway and standing in the doorway to what was beyond death. This death. It was time to go, but now it wasn't the cottage I remembered clearly. It was what I'd left behind to come here that was splashed in vivid colors of desperation behind my eyes. I wanted Robin to survive. I wanted Niko to do the same. He wasn't my Niko, but he would've been. And any Niko deserved to live. I wanted Cal to live and with me gone, went back to the way he'd been before I'd come in and stomped all over his life. I wanted him to be around to see Robin for the friend he was. I wanted them all to make it out of that river and walk away, but if they did, Tyr would still come after them. And Tyr was a god.

It is time to go.

No one could fight and win against a god. Not even the three of them. Not by themselves.

Not alone.

I hadn't been alone fighting for my life in the gray room.

I hadn't heard them, but they'd been there for me the entire time. They'd fought for me harder than I was able to fight for myself. On that first and last day in one, the day that had counted above all the rest, they had never left me alone.

It is time to go.

And I was not going to leave them alone either.

No one could defeat Tyr?

It is time to go.

Damn straight, it was time to go. I slammed the cottage door on that boring and bland painting of a Thomas Kinkade clichéd misty meadow. Then I turned back into the cottage, moving from where I'd come. There was a door other than the one that led to the wet green silver grass. This was a door that was supposed to open once then lock behind you. Fortunately for me, I'd been picking locks since I was five years old and I didn't care if they were solid or goddamn metaphysical. If I wanted that door open, then, by God, it would fucking open if only to let me prove Goodfellow wrong.

No one could defeat a god? What about the First who

were born before them? Ruled before them? Invented murder, death, and war before them?

No one could defeat a god?

Good. I didn't want to simply defeat him. I wanted him dead. Could someone kill a god when he was born of the First? Could he with all he'd learned from the First? Even if he wasn't quite a First himself, not entirely.

I grabbed for the handle of the door I didn't remember coming through.

No one could defeat a god.

We'd *fucking* see about that.

The second part of the story will continue
in the next Cal Leandros novel,
coming in winter 2016 from Roc.

ABOUT THE AUTHOR

Rob Thurman is the *New York Times* bestselling author of the Cal Leandros novels, including *Slashback* and *Doubletake*, the Trickster novels, including *The Grimrose Path* and *Trick of the Light*, the Korsak Brothers novels, including *Basilisk* and *Chimera*, and several stories in various anthologies.

For updates, teasers, music videos, deleted scenes, social networking (the time-suck of an author's life), and various other extras such as free music and computer wallpaper, visit the author online.

CONNECT ONLINE
——————
robthurman.net

ROB THURMAN

THE CAL LEANDROS NOVELS

"There are monsters among us. There always have been and there always will be. I've known that ever since I can remember, just like I've always known I was one... Well, half of one, anyway."

NIGHTLIFE
MOONSHINE
MADHOUSE
DEATHWISH
ROADKILL
BLACKOUT
DOUBLETAKE
SLASHBACK
DOWNFALL

Available wherever books are sold or at
penguin.com

facebook.com/AceRocBooks

ALSO AVAILABLE

SLASHBACK

A CAL LEANDROS NOVEL

by *New York Times* bestselling author
ROB THURMAN

Taking on bloodthirsty supernatural monsters is how Caliban and Niko Leandros make a living. But years ago, the brothers were almost victims of a (very) human serial killer.

Unfortunately for them, that particular depraved killer was working as apprentice to a creature far more malevolent—the legendary Spring-heeled Jack. He's just hit town. He hasn't forgotten what the Leandros brothers did to his murderous protégé. He hasn't forgotten what they owe him. And now they are going to pay…and pay…and pay….

"Thurman continues to deliver strong tales of dark urban fantasy."
—SF Revu

Available wherever books are sold or at
penguin.com

facebook.com/AceRocBooks

R0181

R0081